THE LANGUAGE OF EQUALS

உடனெடுத்தவர்களின் மொழி

THE LANGUAGE OF EQUALS

உடனெடுத்தவர்களின் மொழி

David Ackley

Rain and Breeze Books

MOSCOW, ID

David Ackley/Rain and Breeze Books, LLC
P.O. Box 9874
Moscow, ID 83843
www.rainandbreeze.com

Publisher's Note: This is a work of fiction. Any references to historical events, real people, or real places are used fictitiously. Other names, characters, places, and incidents are a product of the author's imagination and any resemblance of these to actual people, living or dead, businesses, companies, events, institutions or locales is purely coincidental. Locales and public names are sometimes used for atmospheric purposes.

Book Layout © 2014 BookDesignTemplates.com
Cover photo background top: istockphoto.com/ePhotocorp
Cover photo top: istockphoto.com/Oleh_Slobodeniuk
Cover photo background bottom: istockphoto.com/Nirian
Cover photo bottom: istockphoto.com/lellobot
Frontisepiece: Wikimedia Commons, public domain

The Language of Equals/ David Ackley. -- 1st ed.
Library of Congress Control Number: 2019914970
ISBN 978-1-950631-04-9 (Paperback)
ISBN 978-1-950631-05-6 (Ebook)

This book is dedicated to many friends in Madurai in appreciation of their generosity and kindness: Vidya, Sekar, Arun, Rohini, Rema, Raghu, Sujatha, Ranjani, Jasmine, Niranjana, Chitra, Rani, Muthu, Kartiga, and Solomon.

All my best work since then has been bound up in theirs, and it is obvious that my association with them was the decisive event of my life...to have collaborated with both Littlewood and Ramanujan on something like equal terms. G.H. Hardy

CHAPTER 1

1914

It's just like a heartbeat, thought Ramanujan as his attention turned to the constant mechanical pulsing of the huge steamship engine that was driving him further and further from home. He was sitting cross-legged on the steel floor, and the incessant thrumming vibrated upwards through his thighs and buttocks. Staring at the small shrine holding the goddess Lakshmi and a few miniature god figures that he'd set up in the corner of his metal cabin, he was again overcome with incredible homesickness. These sparse Indian items in his otherwise austere stateroom brought his thoughts back to the day he'd put his mother and his wife, Janaki, on the train in Madras. The two women had needed to return to their home village of Kumbakonam while he remained behind in the larger city. He'd hated to see them off, but it was necessary since he would be caught up in making preparations for his own upcoming departure. Two weeks later he'd boarded the steamship *Nevasa* to begin his journey to England.

"Please?" Janaki had begged at the Madras station while his mother was seeing to the train tickets.

Ramanujan had stared at her fourteen-year-old face with its beautiful, sad eyes and said, "We've discussed this many times, Janaki. It'll be difficult enough for me going on my own. How would such a young Indian woman ever cope in that foreign land?"

"But you must take me with you," she'd said, trying her best to sound as adult and as resolute as possible. "Who will cook for you? Feed you? Wash your clothes? Clean your room? You'll fade away to nothing without someone to care for you."

"I'd love to have you come, but don't you see? It'll take even more of my time to watch out for you and keep you safe. It's much better for a man to go alone into English society. We don't know enough of their ways for me to fit in well, let alone a young thing like you."

"What will become of me then?" she'd asked quietly as tears had begun to flow. "Your mother hates me."

"Now, now, she doesn't hate you. This is the way with all new wives in any household. She's just establishing her authority so that you both know the rules and your duties. You're settling in just fine, and I'm sure she values the help you give around the house."

"Then why does she never show it? She's always yelling at me."

"That's just her way. She's always been a little strong-minded. Besides, I can tell that my leaving has placed an incredible strain on her. It's not easy, suddenly having her eldest son travel so far away. Mr. Hardy has promised I'll have a stipend that I can send home every month to make sure you're all well taken care of, but still, she worries."

"Do you realize how long you're going to be away?" Her eyes had seemed to fill with renewed sorrow and some alarm. "Two years! Two whole years!"

Just then Komalatammal had come up to them with the tickets in hand and she'd found a small boy to struggle with the luggage.

"What's wrong, Ramanujan? You look worried," his mother had asked, now eyeing Janaki. "Janaki, you mustn't upset Ramanujan just as we're leaving. He has enough on his mind as it is. He needs to prepare for a momentous journey. Now, stop your fussing and help this lad with our bags."

Ramanujan had then set to the business of seeing his wife and mother settled into a spot in the crowded carriage, and all three were in tears as the train bearing the two women had left the station.

The sea was now a glassy gray-green, peaceful, and yet somehow still threatening with small swells undulating the surface. He'd watched the shoreline slowly disappear, leaving nothing but water and sky along a blank horizon as far as he looked in any direction he turned. On solid ground, Ramanujan knew that he could always locate water, even during the dry season; out here, however, he doubted whether he could ever find land again, no matter how far he might paddle. He struggled to appreciate the oceanic vistas that he'd never imagined, nor ever desired seeing, and tried to concentrate instead on things near at hand—the white deck, the numbered cabin doors, and the other passengers as they sat or strolled by. It helped him stay focused and away from a subtle but continuous sense of unease.

Like a building wave, his terror of the journey had crested on the first days of the voyage, but was now slowly subsiding. He could breathe evenly again and stay calm as long as he kept away from the railing. He thought back, somewhat abashedly, to the day he'd left Madras. "Don't look so worried," his friend Narayana had said, laying a hand on his shoulder. "You've prepared for this trip, and all of these dignitaries and friends have come to see you off. You'll be just fine. Remember, even the goddess, Namagiri Amman, has given her blessings." Some city officials, a judge, and the head of the university had arrived impressively by motor car, and the other well-wishers had straggled in by foot or horse cart. Ramanujan had bowed and responded to their kind words, but his thoughts during the brief speeches had kept returning to the two weeks prior and the tearful farewell with his mother and young new wife at the train station. The time between then and the speeches had been a blur of nervous preparation that had eventually winnowed away the excitement and left only a dull feeling of dread.

After the crowd had dispersed, he'd stood holding his meager baggage on the dusty shoreside beside Narayana, staring down the long plank dock with the *Nevasa* moored at the end. He'd then turned to his friend as tears had suddenly welled up in his eyes. "How can I possibly trust that rickety dock, let alone that steel boat?" he'd stuttered, trying unsuccessfully to keep his emotions at bay. "I sense that I'll never see my mother and wife again." Yet, somehow, he'd managed to make it aboard and had settled into the small metal-walled cabin.

That cabin had become a prison cell. The weather during the initial three days of the voyage had been rough, and Ramanujan had become convinced that the gods were intent on showing him the folly of his decision. He'd been violently ill as the cabin had perpetually pitched and rolled and he'd partially filled two buckets with the contents of his protesting stomach. Unsure of what to do with the pails, he'd left them both in a corner where they'd fouled the small cell's air. He knew that as a Brahmin he'd be defiled by touching them after he'd been sick, so there they'd sat for the duration of the storm. And during the battering the steamship had endured he'd been unable to contain his misgivings, weeping spasmodically at his churning thoughts. *I've done the unpardonable – travelling over the abode of the gods and disturbing them; betraying my religion; trading my love of my family for the love of mathematics. What was I thinking?* After a solid day of agony, sleep had finally given him a much-needed respite.

"Oooh, you really do need some help here!" exclaimed Charlie as he fanned the heavy portholed door back and forth to try and get some air into the cabin.

Ramanujan nodded, standing sheepishly off to the side, "I was a little sick after we left Madras."

"So I can tell," coughed Charlie. He took a deep breath, strode into the room and, grabbing the two buckets by their handles, carried them off, keeping them as far away from his body as he could stretch his arms.

"You poor sod," said Charlie when he'd returned.

"Thank you for…" began Ramanujan.

"No, no need to thank me. Every one of us Jack Tars has a job on this tub, and this is one o' mine," said Charlie. "First time on a ship then?" Ramanujan nodded in reply. "Well, you'll soon be right as rain, I reckon," he continued. "It takes a few days the first time out to get used to all of the pitchin' and swayin'. You're going to England?" Again, Ramanujan nodded. "All the way to London?"

"Yes," said Ramanujan. "I'm going to Cambridge, but this boat only goes as far as London. Some friends are supposed meet me there and then take me to Cambridge."

"Cambridge, eh? Oooh, that's fancy. Going to school there?"

"Yes, I'm going to meet with a mathematics professor— Mr. Hardy, and go over my equations."

"Go over your equations? You're going to learn you some maths there? That's a noble goal!"

"Not really, I'm going to show him some of my discoveries and I hope we'll collaborate on getting them published."

Charlie shook his head back and forth as if to clear it. "You mean to tell me that you not only know math, but you're going to put some into one of those journals? I thought your lot could barely read and write. How did you learn it?"

"I learned it mostly on my own. I love mathematics—I studied it and it just sort of comes to me now."

"Comes to you?" asked Charlie. "Money might come to you, or luck, but I can't see math coming to anyone. What kind of math? Like sums?"

Ramanujan nodded, "And more." He went over to his bed where he picked up a sheet of paper with a derivation he'd been working on and began to hand it to Charlie.

"Oh, my lord," said Charlie taking in the scribbles on the page as if they were an evil spell. "No, never mind, I don't think I want to know." He took a step back and looked Ramanujan up and down. "If you don't mind me askin', how can the likes of you ever afford a trip like this?"

"Oh, Mr. Hardy and the university are paying for it, and they're going to give me a monthly stipend to live..."

"Well, I never..." interrupted Charlie appraising the Indian once again. "You're something else there, Mr. Ramanujan. You really are," he said with a laugh. "Welcome aboard," and Charlie steered himself towards the aft of the ship shaking his head again and muttering something under his breath.

Ramanujan's feet were aching and needed to breathe, crowded into the unfamiliar shoes. He tugged again at his tight collar, finished his coffee, set the service aside, and then rose from his lounge chair to take a walk around the deck. The swells were minimal, but he felt as though he were being gently shoved from side to side by unseen shoulders in a crowd.

Perhaps Varuna and Mitra were each nudging him subtly out of a straight line as he walked forward. *The Lords of the Ocean and of Truth and Order must still be upset with me,* he thought, *to jostle me about like this.* It was a relief for many reasons to sit back down in the deck chair, but in his mind's eye he could see Varuna riding his sea-creature Makara just beneath the boat.

The humiliating hair-cut and loss of his long thick black locks, which he'd endured the week before boarding the ship, had been the critical juncture—the moment when he'd first become aware that not all of the changes that lay in store for him were going to be positive, and when he'd understood that things were going to be very different in so many ways from that point forward. His stiff collar and the requirement to wear constricting pants were the irritating concessions necessary to enter a foreign space, one that was evident from the moment he'd stepped onto the ship—a miniature version of the England yet to come, and one already so different from the India of home. This morning's coffee had been yet another reminder of the transition. The flavored water they served on board was insipidly weak compared to the dark beverage his mother produced from boiling the coffee grounds in milk; it was nearly the color of the tea most of his British shipmates were taking. And their brew was so different from the heavy tea made back home where the aromas of cardamom or ginger and other spices rose from a milky, sugary concoction. To him, it made matters worse that his coffee had been brewed by unknown, unclean hands—but he drank it anyway, trying to accustom himself to inevitable change.

. As he watched his fellow passengers on deck, something about them struck him as odd. Then he realized that everyone was spread out to whatever extent was necessary to preserve their large personal spaces, except when with someone very familiar to them. *If this is how it is, I may never be close to another human being again,* he thought. At home, jostling crowds and proximity were the norm. It was, after all, a very populace country. A train bench, for instance, was never too full and one more body could always squeeze in, no matter how small the space—although this always required a little additional room for his extra bulk. Among the men, it was comfortable to put one's palm on the neighboring hand, or an arm along someone's back in a close indifference. Merely mentioning where you were from or your caste made you fast friends with anyone sharing those connections. On this boat, however, the deck was dominated by British citizens—probably all of the same religion and most even from the same country—and yet they all behaved as someone might act with foreigners, or mere acquaintances at the very closest.

He suddenly broke from his observations when, unexpectedly, a girl sat down in the chair beside his and began to stare at him, or at least he thought she did. *She's obviously unpracticed at sizing people up*, he thought, since at home one could gaze uninhibitedly at someone until his curiosity was satisfied, however long it took. This girl's eyes drilled into him but in such quick flashes that he was initially not even sure if she noticed him. Whenever he turned his eyes towards her, she was looking at her shoes or at whatever she might have in her hands. He tried to make eye contact, eventually capturing a moment when her eyes didn't dart away, and he used this opportunity to give her a smile. She grinned in return, and it took several of these back-and-forths until he could finally nod and ask, "How are you?" She smiled shyly back, replying, "I'm fine," and then rose to quickly step over and join her parents at the rail, a dangerous area of the deck he hadn't yet dared to explore.

CHAPTER 2

His earliest memory was of being caked in sand and mud as a child. He remembered he had on nothing but a black cord tied around his belly, with a *peepal* leaf-shaped gold plate, thin as paper, covering his penis, and he had rolled around in the shallows of the Kaveri River to escape the heat. At that age, he was able to walk, but not swim, and so was naturally restricted by his parents to the small pools away from the main flow of the current. The water was refreshing but he would scramble out onto the stone steps or the nearby bank to both warm himself and to find relief from the eeriness of being so near the endlessly flowing and fathomless river as it passed by. He recalled sitting on the banks and peeling off the flakes of mud as they dried on him, the thinner bits hardening faster than the thick mud on his calves and feet.

This was the season when the Kaveri ran full and wasn't restricted to the narrow channels of drier periods. He remembered staring out at the river and perceiving it as an incomprehensible force, but still realizing that it had limits. He could easily make out the opposite bank even though, to him, it was very far away. And the water came from somewhere and ended somewhere. He was sure of it. It didn't cover the entire earth—him sitting at its edge was proof of that. He remembered, even then, being as interested in the limits defined by the banks that contained the flow as in the full extent of the great river itself.

The reason that this day had stuck in his mind was because the outing coincided with the evening Shaivite festival of Karthikai Deepam. His mother had packed snacks and sweets and also a small dinner of lemon rice as they were not to return home 'til after dark. Although this wasn't their family's festival, being Vaishnavites, they enjoyed the spectacle, nonetheless. As dusk descended and the light faded from the brilliant oranges of sunset, long-tailed parrots headed home to roost, noisily filling the skies above. Near where his parents had set out their small meal, families held *pooja* on the banks of the river and lit miniature clay oil lamps that they then floated off into the larger current as an offering to Karthikai. He and his parents were sitting on the banks at a curve of the river, when he saw a single lamp float by from upstream. Then came two lamps, then four, and what became an ever-increasing number of little lit bowls floating around the bend. As he watched, the shimmering candles were not tiny flames alone, but they brought the feeling of great things building from small beginnings.

....

CHAPTER 3

Suddenly the girl, whom he guessed to be around twelve years old, was back and plopped herself down on the deck chair next to him, unabashedly peppering him with questions about why his English was so good, what he ate, and where he was from. In short order, he came to know all about the string *kathputli* puppets her parents had bought her, the carved ivory set including a small fort with miniature soldiers and elephants, the snake she'd seen charmed out of a basket, the *sadhu* with a small trident stuck straight through his tongue with no blood, and the weird costumes and face paints used in the Kathakali performance she'd seen in Kerala. "Oh, by the way, my name is Amanda. Amanda North," she introduced herself, formally sticking out her hand.

Not completely sure of the custom, Ramanujan gently gripped the small hand and let Amanda move their arms up and down in a shake. "It is nice to meet you, Amanda. I'm Ramanujan. How do you do, and what brought you to India in the first place?"

"I'm fine," she smiled. "My parents brought me to visit my grandparents who're stationed in Bangalore. That was all right, visiting them and all, but the best part was exploring southern India by train. I love the palm trees and the rice paddies and the water buffaloes and..." She suddenly looked up. "Oh, Mummy and Daddy!" exclaimed Amanda as her parents strolled by. "This is Mr. Ramanujan," pointing at him, "and these are my parents, Lord and Lady North," pointing to them in turn.

"A great pleasure to meet you, Mr. Ramanujan," said Lord North, offering a hand in greeting. Ramanujan stood and his immediate response to the offered hand had been to press both of his palms together near his own heart, but then he quickly recovered and met the outstretched hand with his own. Again, unsure of the intricacies involved, Ramanujan allowed his hand to be fiercely gripped and pumped up and down.

"And a pleasure to meet you as well, Lord North," replied Ramanujan. "And Lady North," he bowed to her and she nodded in reply.

"How are you enjoying the voyage?" asked Lord North.

"I'm finding it much better now," said Ramanujan. "I was terribly ill the first few days. They call it seasickness."

"Oh, I know all about seasickness," said Lord North sympathetically. "You should have seen me on the trip over. But this time it hasn't been bad for me at all. You'll get used to it, old chap."

Ramanujan nodded hopefully. "My biggest regret is that while I was sick in my cabin, I missed seeing the remains of the bridge to Lanka," he said.

"I don't believe there is a bridge connecting India to Ceylon, and besides, we passed on the opposite side of the island from where one could see it if it did exist," said Lord North correcting him.

"Oh, there was a bridge," replied Ramanujan with certainty. "Lord Rama had built it from the small island of Rameswaram to Lanka in order to rescue his wife from the evil king Ravana. But Lanka had burned during the rescue, and perhaps the bridge did too. I had been to Rameswaram when I was younger with my family to visit the temple, however, there had been no opportunity for us to travel the several miles from town to the spot that was said to mark the beginning of the bridge."

"I'd never heard that," replied a slightly amused Lord North.

"Oh yes, even the poet Tirumangai Alvar mentions the killing of Ravana in a song of praise to Lord Rama. There is a temple dedicated to Lord Rama at Puḷḷampūtankuṭi, a few miles northeast of my home in Kumbakonam," and Ramanujan beat a rhythm with his hand and sang softly:

> The place of Māl who drove the enemy demons of Lanka
>   into the jungle and killed their chief,
> Who split the horse's mouth, destroyed the wrestlers,
>   and pushed over the maruta trees
> Is Puḷḷampūtankuṭi, vibrant with flowers in the fields
>   where, in cocoanut gardens, fruit fall
> Making the kayal fish jump and scaring away the herons.

"What does that mean? In English?" asked Amanda, and Ramanujan provided a translation as best he could, explaining that Mal was Rama as an avatar of Vishnu.

"A little confusing, but interesting, and very graphic, isn't it?" asked Lord North.

"Yes, Tirumangai has sung pictures of all of our famous temples," answered Ramanujan. "All with praises to Lord Vishnu."

"Well, I'm sorry we missed seeing the spot where that bridge was," said Lord North evenly.

The elder Norths had also been eager to speak with an actual Indian heading to England for the first time. They were keen to discover his expectations and to tell him about their own experiences on the sub-continent. In spite of his interest, Ramanujan's growing discomfort began to show, although this was due to the restrictions of his clothing and not because of any unease with the conversation; and so their discussion came to an end, but they separated warmly, regardless.

After those first three days of the journey spent sick in his cabin, he'd gratefully enjoyed the fourth day off of the steamship on solid ground in Colombo, Lanka's capital located partway up the island's southwestern coast. He'd initially brought enough familiar foods to eat in the peace of his cabin, but had ended up chucking the lot when they'd spoiled during his bout of seasickness. His only real meal since the start of the voyage had been in Colombo, and a Brahmin restaurant in the city had offered very good and familiar vegetarian fare cooked in the proper manner for his caste. He'd been ravenous then and had consumed more than he'd thought possible even though his normal eating habits were much more moderate.

Now, with growing hunger pangs as he hobbled past the dining area after his conversation with the Norths, he was suddenly hit by the aromas from cooked meat pouring out of the galley doors. These were odors he rarely encountered back home and yet he found them somehow not entirely unpleasant. Due to this heralded prominence of meat in the upcoming meal, however, he lamented that the ship had left in its wake one of his favorite comforts—the flavors of his mother's cooking.

He became slightly nervous at the thought that he'd soon join the rest of the passengers for a regular meal in the galley—this dinner was the first after leaving Colombo and was to be his first among his shipmates. He wondered what vegetarian dishes he might find and became worried about how he'd perform, having only begun using cutlery in the few weeks before the voyage. He also had misgivings about how the food would be prepared, and about eating with people outside his own caste—something he rarely, if ever, did.

Back in his cabin before the meal, he took a quick break from his tight-fitting clothing. Removing his shoes and freeing his feet was like breaking out of the hardened mud from his childhood memory. He spent some time massaging his cramped toes and thought of the varied footwear that Europeans used to hide their feet. He wondered at the purpose of shoes since they allowed absolutely no air circulation and they were utterly constricting. And, of course, they were made of cow leather which only added to his initial revulsion, since cows in India were sacred, and for a Brahmin such as himself to wear leather was unheard of. As a child, he'd been barefoot and then slowly adopted wooden sandals for special occasions—when he'd attended school or especially when he'd begun his clerking job. His thoughts drifted to the familiar.

Feet: padding along the cool stone floor of the temple; raising dust on the red clay streets; becoming hard as leather from continual contact with the earth. The bright red lines around the soles of the feet and the brilliant scarlet toenails of the *Bharata Natyam* dancers with anklets that jingled as their feet slapped out the intricate beat. The wide imprints with splayed toes left in the mud by farmers walking along the tops of the small dykes separating rice paddies. Feet holding raw cotton while the women dropped, spun, and redropped the spindles making thin strands of yarn. The sides of the bare feet of the cross-legged musicians tapping rhythm to a *raga*. Silver rings on the toes of his young wife proclaiming her marriage to him. Stooping as a child at bedtime to touch his mother's feet while she placed her hand on his head in blessing.

After a brief rest and once more aching for home, he became disconsolate when he had to squeeze into and retie his shoes. Each step to the galley brought utter pain but the splash of faces, smells, and sounds of chatter and the clatter of silverware upon entering the dining room made the agony retreat. He stood in the middle of the main aisle unsure of what to do or where to sit. A waiter noticed his confusion and said, "We have assigned seating for dinners, Mr....?"

"Ramanujan."

"Ah, yes, that would be..." said the waiter consulting a list, "table 18. Please follow me. You'll be joining the Steeles and the Jenkins."

He thanked the waiter when they arrived at his assigned table and was introduced to the two couples already seated there, Josh and Sara Jenkins, and Clive and Emily Steele. Ramanujan was inwardly happy that there was no handshaking involved. "Ah, finally, a nice roast beef is being served up tonight!" said Clive as Ramanujan took his seat to join them, "real English food that you can sink your teeth into."

"I could smell it from when it first went into the oven," replied Josh. "I haven't had any good beef since the voyage over here, and for us that was quite some time ago."

"The same with us," said Clive. "I wonder if they'll have mustard or horseradish to go along with?"

"I guess we'll find out," said Josh, "but as long as it's roast beef, I really don't care!" and they all laughed. Then Josh turned curiously to Ramanujan and asked, "I don't suppose you'll be having any? It's delicious."

"No, it's not something I would even think about eating," said Ramanujan, "but I suspect that you will enjoy your portions, based on what I have heard here already."

They were all eager to tell of their experiences in India and had many questions about the curious sights they'd witnessed. "Now, Mr. Ramanujan," began Josh. "I'm fascinated with the stories of the murderous Thuggees one hears about, and wondered if normal Indian citizens, such as yourself, live in constant fear for your lives? Those assassins sound a dreadful menace."

"I have only heard of the Thuggees through stories told by travelers, and no one I know personally has had any experience with them. In fact, no one's father or grandfather has had any contact with them either. I expect that the Thuggees can now be safely moved into the category of myth." This explanation received a nod of reply from Josh.

"I say, old boy, have you read Rudyard Kipling's *Kim*?" asked Clive, turning to Ramanujan.

'Old' and 'boy'? What does that mean? And he's addressing me? thought Ramanujan for an instant as he answered the question for the tenth time since boarding the vessel. "No," he replied, "but I hear it is a very good story," as dinner arrived.

Ramanujan had found the odors from the roast interesting and had not thought much about the meal that was being served to the others at the table. It was when Clive took up a knife and cut into the reddish meat that Ramanujan's insides revolted. He felt he was about to be sick and closed his eyes with his head bowed down while he tried to regain composure.

"Ah, before meal prayers eh, Mr. Ramanujan?" asked Josh lightly.

Ramanujan nodded, opened his eyes, and reached for his water glass, resolving to keep his eyes fixed solely on his own dish or the faces of the others, and ignore their plates as much as possible.

Since there were several fellow Indians traveling to England with similar dietary restrictions to his own, he was able to order a passable vegetarian plate. Surprisingly, he noticed that many of the British passengers were also eating the curries and rice, some even using their hands, which was something he dared not do in the present company. The western sensibilities dominating the British ship accounted for the spice mixtures used to make the *dal* and curry on his plate—all the Indian dishes were flavorful, but the recipes tasted odd to him and lacked the spicy heat of the meals served to him at home. As he tried to ignore the roast beef being shared among the Jenkins' and Steele's at his table, his perpetual small pang of homesickness grew to a sharp stabbing sensation in his abdomen.

He was trying to wrestle some curried peas onto his fork without using his hand to keep them in place when he happened to glance up. Sara Jenkins caught his eye and dropped her eyes to her own plate. She took the fork and mashed down on the peas so that they easily clung to the fork and then lifted them to her mouth with a smile. He nodded and raised his eyebrows as a gesture of thanks and soon had the technique mastered. But he was still conflicted about the meal. *Who prepared this dish?* he wondered. *How many non-Brahmin hands touched the food as it was prepared? Was the kitchen well cleaned? Did this food touch the meat?* And after a moment he decided that it didn't matter. Just sitting here with people outside his caste and eating at the same table, being served by an obvious non-Brahmin was enough that this meal was defiled—making him, in turn, impure. He sighed as he struggled again with the fork and the rice. *At least I'm not being required to share a dish with the others,* he thought. His family members were all Iyengar Brahmins and never ate food prepared by a member of any other caste. No Iyengar Brahmin ever did, and as an Iyengar he followed the cleansing rituals before and after meals, never ate with non-Brahmins, never shared food off the same plate with anyone, never ate meat, and never, never ate with his left hand.

The left hand was reserved for other purposes and was thus very impure. He'd shivered slightly as he'd watched nearly every diner grasp their fork with their left hand and use the knife in their right to help guide food onto the fork. He was extremely unfamiliar and uncomfortable with his left hand being guided towards his mouth except, perhaps, with an occasional cup of water. *Still,* he told himself, *even though I'm eating with my left hand, it's really only the fork touching the food and not my fingers.*

This dining experience was as uncomfortable as he suspected it would be, and he'd tried to mentally prepare himself for the reality of leaving his customary routines and entering the unknowns of British society. The sessions hastily arranged by his superiors in Madras to teach him proper dining etiquette, to clothe and groom him in the current fashion, and to brief him on English manners were, it was becoming clear, not the same as the efforts that would be required by himself to actually accomplish the integration.

As they were finishing the meal, Clive unwittingly added to Ramanujan's discomfort by asking, "India is so noisy and smelly—truly foul. How can a gentleman such as yourself endure it on a daily basis?" Ramanujan stared back at him blankly. "I mean all of the bells and shouting and chanting, on top of the incense and the unpleasant smells from the heat, they must drive one to distraction, don't you think? And the crowded conditions—some houses are just shacks really, aren't they? I don't know how those stationed there can stand it overly long."

Sara once again came to Ramanujan's rescue. "Clive, I believe it's a matter of habituation. These are all comforting signs of home to someone who lives there, just as the poor souls crammed into inner-city London wouldn't change it for the world. Right, Mr. Ramanujan?" He nodded and gave a quick smile of gratitude as they all rose from their seats at the meal's conclusion.

Shuffling back to his cabin he was morose, now realizing the permanence of his circumstance brought about by the single act of walking along the wooden dock and stepping onto the decks of the *Nevasa*. Standing at the open stateroom door, however, his thoughts were suddenly buoyed. Here on his bed was his notebook in which he'd recorded all his mathematical discoveries, and he was heading to England where he'd be welcomed by a like mind—someone who could appreciate his ideas and share his thoughts and enthusiasm for his equations. He immediately pried off his shoes, stripped off his pants and shirt, and wrapped a long, white *veshti* around his hips. After prayers, he ate the last of some of the sweets he'd brought from home that hadn't spoiled. Then he became lost in a theorem he'd begun to work on. At some point, he found himself dreaming of the theorem and lay down on the too-soft bed to an easy sleep.

A bell clanged to mark the time of the watch and Ramanujan lay on his bed momentarily disoriented. He'd been startled from sleep and his initial response had been to rise for his morning trip to the temple, but it was still the middle of the night. He was slowly becoming accustomed to the watch-bells, but as he tried for sleep again his ears echoed with a more familiar sound.

The temple bell would begin before sunrise, a clear, penetrating peal that would start with a slow rhythmic pace and then quicken to a double or quadruple-time for the last minute—calling all within earshot to morning prayers. He'd respond, the little puffs of dust rising up under his heavy feet as he made the short walk to the Sarangapani temple. His eyes would be on the red clay ground in the dull morning light and in his mind, as always, he would be singing the songs of Tirumangai Alvar. All the Alvar poets were good, but Periyalvar and Tirumangai were his favorites, and their works were constantly in the background of his waking hours, even here on the steamboat. Puḷḷampūtankuṭi temple was only a few miles away from his home, and Tirumangai had composed a set of verses praising its virtues which Ramanujan now sang to himself while he finally drifted off to sleep again.

The place where eternally abides the Trickster in the form
 of a dwarf brahmacarya
Who possesses the world, who is difficult to know,
 and who rules me,
Is Puḷḷampūtankuṭi where sing bees with spotted wings
And where drones hum on fragrant blossoms,
 while colorful peacocks perform their dance.

CHAPTER 4.

The open-ocean journey from the tip of India to the coasts of
Africa and the Middle East was finally becoming enjoyable to
him. He had, as one of the ship's officers had proudly pointed
out to him, 'gained his sea legs,' and the perpetual swaying of
the *Nevasa* no longer bothered him. He'd also gathered the
courage to go all the way to the railing, grasp it, and stare out
at the endlessly vast and unimaginably deep sea they sailed
upon. He'd begun to hope that he was travelling above the
dwelling place of the sea god unnoticed as the weather had
remained calm since leaving the sight of India's coast.

He'd always been one to enjoy a good conversation, and
the company of his fellow passengers was very agreeable.
"Hello, Amanda," greeted Ramanujan as she neared him on
the deck. "Have you eaten?"

Amanda gave a sharp laugh and asked, "Why do you always ask that? Of course, I've eaten! They won't let me go for
more than an hour without offering meals, snacks, tea, and so
forth. I swear I'm going to burst!"

"Well, I did not even realize I had," apologized Ramanujan
quietly. "As it is, in India we do have a problem with many
people who cannot find enough to eat, and so I guess inquir-
ing about eating has become a customary greeting. We had
a terrible famine a few years ago and so food is foremost in
people's thoughts even now."

Amanda had the grace and years to be able to imagine the impact of food scarcity in India and gently said, "Oh, I see."

In their short time on the ship, he'd become friends with Amanda. He learned that she was 13 years old or, 'nearly fourteen,' as she would proudly point out in nearly every new introduction to fellow passengers. During their conversations she'd learned of Ramanujan's love of mathematics, and now politely turned to this topic, as if it were expected of her.

"I must say, I've passed my exams in mathematics, but it's becoming something of a sticky wicket, um... more difficult for me each year," said Amanda. "They say that boys are much better at it and that it isn't suitable for girls anyway, so I guess it doesn't really matter."

Ramanujan came from a society where, although the families were ruled by the highest-ranking women, men were the only ones to undertake meaningful employment. The civil service system he came from was bereft of females except for the cleaners and cooks. He had, however, expected a different attitude from modern British society, since the British women he'd met seemed to be supremely independent to his Indian eyes.

"Well, I am not sure that is the case," he said kindly. "From what I have heard, English women are capable of anything, including mathematics."

"I just don't see how I could stay interested in such a dull subject," she sighed. "Most of the class just falls asleep as soon as the lectures start, and most juicy notes are passed during that period. Well, excepting that snoozing and passing notes may be the case in our history class, as well."

"Oh! But each and every number is interesting and important—not in the least bit dull!" exclaimed Ramanujan. "And you will learn how fascinating numbers can be and all the ways that they work together as you advance in your skills. Here, let me tell you something about these marvelous numbers," as he took a seat in a nearby chair and Amanda pulled one over to sit next to him. "Take the number, or lack of number, in zero. It symbolizes nothingness, and yet it is also the fountain from which all other numbers spring. It is the origin of all things, and yet it is empty. The number one is the opposite—it is everything. From nothingness comes the substance that comprises all things. It is the first number, and so does not really qualify as counting; it is either there or it is not there. It is all of existence—unity."

Amanda nodded thoughtfully and gazed out at the flat ocean horizon where sky met sea.

"Now, take the number two," Ramanujan continued. "Two is the source of opposites—if you have two, you have black and white, hot and cold, good and evil. It is the first prime number, since we are exempting the number one. Did you learn that a prime number is any number that is only divisible by itself and one?" he asked, and Amanda nodded as he continued, almost not stopping for the reply. "And it is the only even prime number because of that very definition— every other even number will be divisible by it. Three is the source of body, heart, and mind—the physical, the mental, and the spiritual. It is Brahma, Vishnu, and Shiva. It is the first odd number, and the first number to make a series of prime numbers—two and then three.

"Four is the first multiple of two prime numbers, and the first square of a prime number. It is also the first even number that is not prime. Five is the first odd number made up of two different prime numbers, two and three, but is not divisible by either of them. And we can go on, and on. Each number has its own personality and is actually very rare and special. Go ahead, pick a number and I will tell you what is unique about it."

Amanda grinned at the challenge and said, "OK, how about 27?"

"Twenty-seven is the first cube using an odd number, three. It is the first number ending in seven that is not prime. It is the only number that is equal to three times the sum of its two digits, 2 and 7. And, coincidently, it is a number that is the same as adding all of the integers from two to seven—$2+3+4+5+6+7 = 27$," said Ramanujan after closing his eyes and appearing to drift subtly away from the conversation.

Amanda was amazed. "OK, what about 5057?" she asked, on a whim.

"Oh, let us see," said Ramanujan. "It is the product of two primes, 13 and 389, and so can only be factored by those two numbers. Otherwise, it is not overly special.

"Now, one of those two factors—389, is somewhat more special," he continued. "Because it is one of the prime numbers for which the number you get reading it backwards, 983, is also a prime number."

Amanda gaped at him. "How can you possibly know that, especially so quickly?" she asked.

They watched some seagulls rise from the surface and take flight, the only visible living things before them.

"I find any aspect of numbers or how they fit together to be fascinating and so I pay special attention to each of them. Take prime numbers for instance. You can discount all even numbers, except the number two, from the list of primes, as well as any number that ends in a five or a zero except for the number five itself. So, we are left with only the numbers ending in one, three, seven, and nine, and yet the number of primes appears to be limitless. If we had a way of eliminating every third number after 3, every seventh number after seven, every eleventh number after eleven, and so on, then we would be left with only the prime numbers. However, that is an impossible task. You might think that prime numbers would diminish in frequency the further out in the series of integers we go, but that does not appear to be the case, at least not dramatically. There is so far no way to predict whether the next number in a series of integers will be a prime number, but it may be possible to get near to, but not exactly calculate, how many prime numbers will occur within a given number of integers in a series. Primes are just baffling. Which makes them even more intriguing," he added with a smile.

"So, you see, I have visited these numbers many times, both when awake and asleep. In my thoughts and dreams, I often see numbers in different ways. Sometimes I see them as different properties emanating out of the mouths of gods, especially my goddess Lakshmi of Namakkal. Even when I was a small boy, any number I worked with or any equation I encountered would stick in my mind, even the first hundreds of digits of the number pi. So, I would say that numbers have become a very real part of who I am, and so I do not consider them to be dull in the least."

"OK," said Amanda, impressed but still not entirely convinced. "To you, maybe."

Not all of the passengers were comfortable in the more formal clothing worn during the voyage, and Ramanujan noticed one well-tanned man in particular continually pulling at his collar and wiggling his feet. Within a week he'd switched to a long cotton kurta and sandals, as, over time, did several others. One or two of the women even began wearing saris in the heat.

He happened to enter into a conversation with the gentleman he'd noted earlier and introduced himself in the galley at lunchtime.

"Pleased to meet you, Mr. Ramanujan," said the man. "Cyril Fields here. Please, call me Cyril."

"All right then, Cyril, it will be," said Ramanujan. He noticed that Cyril was eating the same curried lentil dish that he'd just ordered.

Cyril took a bite of curry from his plate and then asked, "So, do you mind if I inquire about the purpose of your trip to England, Ramanujan?"

"No, not at all," he replied, "I am heading to Cambridge where I am to consult with a great mathematician who teaches there. We have corresponded, and he said he is very interested in meeting with me."

"Cambridge, eh? Who is this mathematician?"

"His name is Mr. Hardy, Mr. G.H. Hardy, and he has a lecture position at Trinity College."

"Ah, Hardy!" said Cyril. "Well, you can't do better than him. I've never met the man, but he's a colleague of my mathematics professor in Oxford. Elliott had nothing but praise for the man." Ramanujan's plate arrived and Cyril asked, "So why are you meeting with Mr. Hardy? Are you beginning studies in Cambridge?"

"No, as I say we will consult, or perhaps collaborate."

"I guess I don't understand," said Cyril.

"I have been consumed with mathematics since I was young," said Ramanujan, momentarily ignoring the dish set before him. "I have studied and followed lines of exploration until there was no one in Madras, or possibly all of India, who could help me with, or evaluate, my work. I sent letters and samples of some of my findings to several professors in England with no response, until finally Mr. Hardy answered my queries. He said that he saw enough in what I had sent him that he wants to meet with me and find out more about what I've discovered. The college is even paying for my voyage, and for my stay in Cambridge."

"Well, I must say, that is impressive, Ramanujan," said Cyril, pushing his empty plate away from him. "You must really have something to offer in order to capture Hardy's attention like that. What sort of work have you done?"

"Well, it may be hard to describe, but I can go and fetch my notebooks if you'd like to see them? They are proofs and formulae that I've developed on my own."

Cyril put his hands up, "Perhaps another time, but you must be ecstatic to be travelling to England to meet with Hardy and work with him."

Ramanujan finally noticed his plate and took a tentative bite, then looked up slowly at Cyril.

"Yes, I am excited, but also very nervous."

"Well, that's understandable—travelling to a foreign country and moving to new surroundings—all on top of meeting new people. Anyone would be nervous."

"Yes," said Ramanujan. "But I also wonder. What if I am not what they expect? What if I am not as I have represented myself?"

"Don't worry," said Cyril. "Someone like Hardy is smart enough to be able to tell the wheat from the chaff. I haven't seen your work but would bet it is something exceptional if it captured his attention."

"Yes, but it is still a concern, since we have never really met." He paused for a moment as if he had another question, but then switched topics. "By the way, I couldn't help but notice your change in clothes recently," continued Ramanujan, coming back to the original point of his curiosity. "I must say, I am envious. I don't think that my wearing a *veshti* would be well accepted by the others."

"Well, you're probably right there. And isn't that peculiar? You're required to strictly adhere to what's deemed proper in our society or be roundly criticized as being 'native', and yet

I can get away with wearing whatever I like, because I'm one of them—one of us. What an odd world."

"So how did you dress when you were in my country?" asked Ramanujan.

"Well, at first I was in khakis like the rest of the lot, but took to wearing the local styles which were much cooler and helped me not stand out as much. You see, I was a surveyor for three years for both new railway and telegraph lines. I'd usually be days and miles ahead of the rest of the crew, and it became easier for me to work through more remote areas if I fit in a little better and wasn't appearing like a soldier. Mind you, I was no Kim going in for disguises—I really was a surveyor."

"Kim?" asked Ramanujan. "I've often heard the title of this book, but have no idea what it is about."

And Cyril explained the novel by Rudyard Kipling.

After that conversation, Ramanujan began to note how much the British read. It wasn't common to see people pouring over books in Tamil Nadu, unless they were students. And even then, he had very few friends who read strictly for pleasure. Here were passengers engrossed by what they were reading at every turn. He began to notice titles, and discovered that *Kim*, *The Jungle Book*, and *The Moonstone* were all popular, since they dealt with India, but he also recognized *Pollyanna*, *The Lost World*, and *Death in Venice* as sought-after novels.

The small salon/library was not always available, especially when the men took it over in the evenings before and after dinner, and so a little storeroom off the main deck became a mini-library with piles of books and stacks of a magazine named *Union Jack*. Ramanujan had tried to begin reading *The Moonstone* but there was something about a fictional story concerning another person that failed to capture his interest, and he couldn't shake the feeling that reading it was a waste of his time. To his relief, Ramanujan discovered that when he'd bring his pencil and paper out to a deck chair and begin working through some formulae, no one took any notice.

CHAPTER 5.

He was vaguely aware of the scent of jasmine nosing at the edges of his consciousness.

"Ramanujan," came a soft voice, and he was suddenly wide awake. He sat up. The walls of his stateroom seemed to have drifted away and a white vapor infused the space. He became aware of a gigantic lotus flower floating towards him bearing a glowing figure—his goddess—Namagiri Amman. She was seated on the purple lotus in an iridescent sari, wearing a gold chain necklace and crown studded with brilliant gems. Two of her four hands held unfolded lotus blossoms and from the other two poured a stream of gold from each ornamented palm. He bowed his head forward and paid rapt attention.

With a radiant smile she reached down with her lower left hand and tugged delicately at one of the huge lotus petals which easily came loose. The flow of gold from the lower palms had ceased, and the left hand held the petal while the right produced a gem-studded stylus. She held the petal so that he could see as she wrote in red on the purple surface.

$$\varphi_0(q) = 1 + \sum_{0}^{\infty} q^{n^2} (1+q)(1+q^3) \cdots (1+q^{2n-1})$$

With the closing of the last parenthesis, Namagiri Amman withdrew into the mist and everything connected with the vision began to fade. He blinked as he sat on his bed in the small, gray-walled cabin staring towards the steel door. Recovering, he immediately rose and started scrambling around for his notebook, but not finding it, he quickly scribbled the equation on a wrinkled sheet of scrap paper. The summation was remarkably similar to a line of enquiry he'd pursued a few days before, but with a unique twist, and he spent the rest of the night until dawn exploring this intriguing variation. The pink light of dawn beckoned him out of the room and the scrap of paper became lost in the pile of his accumulated notes.

While he was standing at the railing as one of the first on deck, a morning haze hovering low over the water reminded Ramanujan of last night's vision and he was taken back to his many pilgrimages to the home of the goddess. He recalled his perpetual awe in seeing the gigantic rock into which was carved the inner sanctum of the temple at Namakkal. The smoothly worn bare rock, like many that peppered Tamil Nadu, rose 180 feet out of the flat plain surrounding it, and at the base of the steep western wall of the hill stood Narasimhaswami Temple with its adjacent shrine to the deity's consort, Namagiri Amman.

The first rays of the sun seemed to flood him with warmth and the thoughts of Namakkal made him feel as if his mother and his friend Narayana Iyer were standing with him at the railing viewing the scene. His most recent visit to the temple had been with Narayana and they had chanted, prayed, fasted, and slept outside the entrance to the temple for three days waiting for Namagiri Amman to give him some indication of her wishes for him regarding a journey to England. She'd finally appeared to him in a dream and graced him with her approval of the trip. A similar appearance of the goddess to his mother had made all of the family in agreement on the journey despite the costs that Ramanujan would suffer by leaving his caste and homeland behind.

On one other visit to the temple which particularly stood out in his mind, his mother, pregnant with his younger brother, had insisted on making the journey from the train station to the temple on foot as part of her devotion and dedication to Lakshmi. Rounding the hill along the southern flank, the mix of town dwellers and pilgrims had become weighted heavily towards pilgrims until they were in a crush of devotees anxious for entrance to the temple.

Passing through the gated portal and into the walled complex, they'd wrestled themselves away from the main throng which was streaming towards the columned entrance to the carved Narasimha Temple and had walked the short distance to the smaller free-standing temple of Narasimha's consort Lakshmi, or known at this temple as the Goddess of Namagiri, their goddess Namagiri Amman.

He pictured it: his mother was exhausted from the trek, and they shuffled to the side of the Namagiri Amman temple where a large banyan tree offered shade. A square white-washed stone stoop was built around the base of the tree and his mother rested against it. Strung around the trunk of the enormous banyan were looped hundreds of long strings, each of which was bound with a small saffron-colored cloth packet given in offering—one of them may even have been tied around the tree by his mother on a previous visit. Also hanging from the lower branches were many miniature cradles, some bearing a likeness of the baby Krishna nestled in them. Next to the tree was a small raised and covered platform containing several stone-carved images of the snake deities—*Nagas*—two intertwined serpent bodies depicted with single or multiple colored and garlanded heads sometimes bearing the image of a snake, sometimes that of a human face. The packets and cradles adorning the banyan tree were prayers to these deities for fertility and blessings for a new child. His mother said a long and fervent prayer in thanks for the blessing she had received, and for the blessings necessary for this potential new life within her to continue.

At the other end of the slate platform were also several women sitting cross-legged and stringing together garlands of white and yellow blossoms from piles of flowers heaped in front of them on the gray slabs. His mother had Ramanujan go over to them and he bought a finished garland for a few *paisa*. As his mother felt refreshed, the two of them entered the temple to offer the string of flowers to Namagiri Amman.

They stopped and said prayers at each of the images of the goddess and other gods to the side of the main shrine, and then approached the main deity. The form of the goddess was barely visible—she was draped in colorful silk cloth and garlanded with flowers. Incense sticks, oil lamps, more flowers, and turmeric and sandal powders were ceremoniously arranged before and around her. The priest chanted verses and accepted his mother's offering, passing an oil lamp before them so that they could be blessed by the flame which they gently fanned towards themselves. He placed a red *kumkum* powder *pottu* on each of their foreheads, and given an additional offering from his mother, he arranged a red and white garland over her bowed head and about her shoulders.

They next joined the majority of pilgrims and paid homage to Narasimha, housed in his temple carved into the solid red rock comprising the center of Namakkal. Ramanujan always felt conflicted with the sense of unease but awesome respect he had for Narasimha. Vishnu's incarnation as a lion-headed man had appeared magically to vanquish the evil Hiranya. The demise of Hiranya had been finalized by Narasimha draping Hiranya across his knee, disemboweling him, and pulling the entrails out with his clawed hands. All the statues Ramanujan had seen portraying Narasimha capitalized on this event, and the gory images never failed to capture his full attention.

The verses from Tirumankai Alvar about Singavel Kundram, Lion-Man Mountain had come to his mind.

The place of the Pure One who as a man-lion
Split the chest, blood gushing,
   of the demon while the world trembled,
Is Lion-Man Mountain where red-eyed lions
   take tusks of green-eyed elephants
And offer them with devotion, bowing low at his feet.

The place of the One with pointed claws
  who gouged out the chest of the murderous demon
As a fierce lion with sword-like teeth
  and a cavernous maw, quivering with rage,
Is Lion-Man Mountain where never ceases
  the shouting of bow-bearing hunters
And the thunder of their wide-mouthed war drum
  as they pillage embattled caravans.

He and his mother had stayed with a relative that evening, and he had socialized some with a distant cousin. But what made the trip stick in his mind was the combined look of anxiety—he understood it to be from her pregnancy—and of inner peace from the temple visit that had been on his mother's face as they sat in the small unfamiliar chamber and prepared for bed.

These memories found him pining for his mother who had devoted her life to her sons and sought nothing but their success and happiness with little thought for her own well-being.

CHAPTER 6.

It had been a full twenty-four hours since he'd last seen Amanda, who'd taken it upon herself as part of her daily routine to stop by frequently and update him on everything that had happened since her last visit. He welcomed the company, but also had to check his resentment at having his thought processes continually interrupted. He was accustomed to a full day of undisturbed work and had to remind himself that this voyage to England was not the same as being secluded at home—this was not only a journey on a ship, but also a transition from one way of life to another.

Ramanujan was finding it difficult to devote his full attention to mathematics, regardless. Normally, he could lose himself in an interesting problem for hours or days at a time with no mental cares or diversions. Here on the ship, however, he found himself bouncing between bouts of homesickness and yearning to be with his mother and his wife, concerns about what lay ahead for him in England, excitement at the possibility of meeting with others who lived and breathed mathematics, and continued efforts to learn about and fit into British society.

He rose from his deck chair and joined many others in the perpetual circuit up and down the cooler starboard side of the ship. On this occasion he was in search of either Amanda or her parents, Lord and Lady North. He took several laps and none of the family members were anywhere to be seen. To be certain that he covered all possibilities, he took additional walks along the boiling-hot port side where none but the very hearty ventured. He found no sign of them.

He ran into one of his fellow countrymen on the boat and had an amiable conversation with Dr. Chowry-Muthu who was on his way back to England to continue his practice in the treatment of tubercular patients. Ramanujan inundated him with questions about what to expect in England, and the doctor, answering the best he could, ended by saying that experience would be the best teacher.

Once they'd left the Indian coast, very few passengers appeared at the daytime lunches due to the blistering heat at midday, but the afternoon teas were much better attended. It was here that he finally found Lord North. Amanda's father was engaged in conversation with a couple at a small table, but Ramanujan took the initiative to interrupt them since he'd become increasingly concerned about the girl.

"Good afternoon, Lord North," he said. "I am sorry for the interruption, but I have a question if this is a good time."

Lord North turned to him with a worried look but then gave him a nod and a slight smile. "No, this is a fine time," said Lord North. "How can I help you, Mr. Ramanujan?" as the other couple also followed the conversation.

"Well, young Amanda has been a regular fixture for me on this voyage, and yet I have not seen a trace of her since around noon yesterday. I am curious and a little worried as to why she has changed her pattern of, well, activity," said

Ramanujan. "She is by far the most energetic and enthusiastic passenger among us."

Lord North frowned and the anxiety on his face was immediately apparent. "I'm sorry, Ramanujan, and I should've made you aware. Amanda has been stricken with a fever, and they're still trying to find the cause. She's been in the ship's infirmary, and may be there for another day if the damn fever doesn't break. My wife won't leave her side until it does. At least the doctor is convinced that it isn't malaria or cholera, but if she doesn't show improvement soon, he said that he may need to quarantine her until he finds out what it is. It could still be a cold or the flu, but we won't know for a while yet."

"I'm so sorry to hear that," said Ramanujan. "Please tell her that I asked after her, and I will keep her in my prayers."

"I will," nodded Lord North. "You know, she speaks very well of you and is always concocting some tale about you, so I'm sure she would appreciate that. We're hoping that in the next few days this will pass and she'll be able to have some visitors. Once her fever breaks I'll let you know. I'm sure she'd love to see you."

"I would like to see her too. Just let me know as to the appropriate time and I will be there."

"Thank you for your concern," said Lord North with a certain formality. "We'll search you out as soon as she can have company." And nodding in reply, Ramanujan left them to their tea and conversation.

Several days after his inquiries about the fevered girl, and still a few days out from the next port of call, Amanda was feeling well enough that she could take visitors. Since some friends of the North's were already in the cabin with her to give her their best wishes, Ramanujan waited outside and discretely prayed for Vishnu in his form as Dhanvantari, physician to the gods, to look after her and further her recovery. In his mind, he saw Dhanvantari enter her cabin, enveloped in healing vapors.

Illness was not a trifling matter, and the dire consequences were constantly on his mind having lost several younger siblings to disease. He was mentally reciting some verses when the couple emerged from the cabin and Ramanujan caught sight of the man's collar. *Ah,* he thought. *A Christian priest has been helping, too.*

Amanda gave him a quick if feeble smile when he entered the cabin. "Hi, Mister Rama," as Amanda had come to call him. "I actually think that now I've spent more time on this ship in bed, rather than out on the decks."

"Yes," replied Ramanujan. "And the entire ship and I have become very concerned about your health. How are you feeling? Is the fever reduced? Are you eating?"

Amanda shrugged her thin shoulders in reply. To Ramanujan she looked even more skinny and pale than she had when healthy and although she had a promising hint of color to her cheeks, he hoped that this flush wasn't the sign of a lingering fever.

"Do they know the cause?" he asked.

"No, but they said since the fever has broken, they aren't nearly as worried. Mummy hardly left my side, so now they're watching to see if she comes down with whatever it is, too."

They both sought to change the conversation and Ramanujan mentioned that they were due into the Port of Aden, at the entrance to the Red Sea, in two days.

"Oh!" exclaimed Amanda. "I must write a letter to my friend Mary before we land. Do you have any post cards I can use? Do we get to get off?"

"I do not know, and sadly, no, no extra post cards. I have some letters that I am anxious to post myself since I have found this voyage allows time for writing. But there is no real rush for you to write to your friend. I have been told that a letter from Aden will likely end up at its destination the same time as one mailed from Suez, or even Port Said for that matter. I have some ready to send and may write a few more. I can search up some post cards in Aden for you after we land if that is possible," said Ramanujan helpfully.

Amanda relaxed into her pillows. "Some cards would be nice," she murmured and closed her eyes.

"Amanda?" he asked after a long moment. "Would you mind if I sang you a song?"

"No, I wouldn't mind. What song?" asked Amanda, lazily opening her eyes.

"Well, I am still worried about you, even though you seem to be getting better, and there is a chant that we have that asks the Lord Vishnu to help you heal. Would that be all right?" Amanda nodded and then Ramanujan chanted:

Om Namo Bhagavate, Maha Sudharshana
Vasudevaya Dhanvantaraye, Amrutha Kalasa Hast-
haaya
Sarva Bhaya Vinasaya, Sarva Roka Nivaranaya
Thri Lokya Pathaye, Thri Lokya Nithaye
Sri Maha Vishnu Swarupa, Sri Dhanvantri Swarupa
Sri Sri Sri, O Ushata Chakra Narayana Swaha

"That was pretty," said Amanda when he'd finished, "but what does it mean?"

"It is asking Lord Vishnu in his form as Dhanvantari to use the nectar that he holds in his healing bowl to make you better. It is asking him to remove all of your fears and diseases."

"Thank you, Mr. Rama," said Amanda with a small chuckle. "That's almost exactly what the priest who was just in here was asking of Jesus."

She closed her eyes again and was quickly asleep.

He met the Norths sitting on lounge chairs not far from the stateroom door.

"Amanda must have had quite a day, she is now sleeping," he told them. "She said that she would like some post cards so that she can write to a friend."

"Ah, that would be to Mary," said an exhausted-looking Lady North. "We actually have some postcards from India, and I'll make sure that she has them available. Thank you again for visiting with her; I'm sure it lifted her spirits."

To Ramanujan this created an image of spirits rising up out of her and he said, "I hope she keeps improving, and I will continue to make prayers for a speedy recovery. Good day, Lady North."

They'd hit an unexpected patch of bad weather, and winds and waves had pounded the *Nevasa* from late that night until early on the following afternoon when the seas had suddenly subsided. Ramanujan remained in his cabin despite the ensuing calm. He wasn't seasick, but the fury of the winds had for a brief period made him feel as if he were under attack. And the storm had stirred to the surface some of the feelings that he'd previously suppressed in his eagerness to meet with the eminent scholars whom he knew could fully appreciate his work.

The correspondences with Mr. Hardy had not all been positive. The mathematicians in Madras had been unanimously amazed by Ramanujan's results, and so he'd come to see his findings as infallible. In casting further afield to England to the best minds in the Empire, however, he'd learned that some of the conclusions he'd drawn were not unique, and some, Mr. Hardy and his colleague Mr. Littlewood claimed in letters, were indeed in error. He knew he could explain his findings once he met with Mr. Hardy in person, but still, the rebukes had stung, and his stomach pains flared up as he thought of the harsh critiques and the possibility that their assessments were correct.

While he'd found the correspondences and their criticisms stressful back in India, alone in his cabin and sparked by the storm, his self-doubts had erupted. Nearly weeping at one point, he'd wondered if he'd blundered in revealing his work to English academicians and that, rather than being the proper course of action, this trip was instead the ultimate folly. Not waiting for the world to notice his incredible results, he'd uncharacteristically, for a Tamil, pushed himself to contact England—rather than having the world act on him as was his cultural upbringing, he'd realized that he had to act on the world in order to attain the validation that he knew he desperately desired. He became wracked with worry that his impatience was to be his undoing.

Finally, long after the storm had subsided, he remembered that he required peer acceptance of his work to be considered a mathematician of any standing at all, and this was why he'd pressed forward in the first place. That academic recognition was his ultimate goal and he hoped it would be worth the sacrifice because there was much he had to give up in its pursuit. Chief among the concessions he'd forced himself to make was the one to his religion. He was raised a strict Brahmin and so leaving India did not come easily. Meeting with Mr. Hardy in England had been his desire, but one did not act on mere wishes alone. The three days of fasting and prayer at Namakkal and his mother's dream of him living in England had shown that Namagiri Amman gave permission for the trip, but that didn't mean there wouldn't be personal consequences.

And the goddess was the root of the problem he had in answering the supposed errors that Mr. Hardy had discovered in his math. Many of the solutions he'd arrived at were based upon revelations from her that she'd given to him in dreams.

And how can I explain my findings beyond that? he wondered. Divine inspiration required no accounting. Not that hours and days of calculation and recalculation hadn't gone into his results. Even though they'd seemingly appeared as sudden inspiration, most were based on theories and equations that he'd studied before, especially those found in the Englishman Carr's textbook he'd devoured as a youth. He couldn't understand how some of his solutions could be wrong, but it now seemed possible that they might be if Mr. Hardy said they were.

His self-doubts remained, even as he poured over his notebooks and scribbled out some new results that had come to him in the midst of his own inner storm.

CHAPTER 7

Early the next morning he and the other passengers on deck began to make out land on either side of the vessel and as they neared the Port of Aden, the starboard side was dominated by a sharp semicircular ridge at the entrance to the harbor.

"I've never seen such a jagged mountain before, Charlie. Isn't it odd?" asked Ramanujan, as the man came up beside him at the railing.

Charlie had befriended Ramanujan after helping clean up Ramanujan's cabin during those horrible first days aboard. "That there's what remains of a volcano," said Charlie. "Do you see how it looks like a broken bowl with some of the side missing?"

"Oh, I have heard of volcanoes," said Ramanujan, "although I might not have been paying attention in class. What is it again?"

"A volcano happens when the hot lava in the earth spills out and layers up making a hollow mountain. This one is dead; it won't spew no more lava, so you needn't worry. I've seen Mount Etna in Sicily though, and it really puts on a jolly good show—especially at night. You can see smoke pouring out and red and yellow streamers of the lava tossed in the air. It makes red rivers run down the sides and is hotter than a furnace."

"I don't think we have anything like it in Tamil Nadu," said Ramanujan.

"I expect not, Mr. Ramanujan. At least I never heard of any there," said Charlie. A whistled signal blew from the bridge area. "Looks like I'd better hop to for the mooring," and he headed toward the bow of the *Nevasa*.

Stark, barren, and steeply gullied hillsides towered over sandy beaches to greet them as they anchored, and Ramanujan again marveled at the incredibly ragged appearance. *Our mountains are so much smoother and calmer,* he thought. *This one looks almost fierce – more like where a temple to Narasimha should be.*

The heat was oppressive for mid-morning, and even Ramanujan began to feel uncomfortable as sweat rolled down his back and the view of the town wavered in the distance. The passengers were discouraged from disembarking at Aden since the main purpose of the layover was to replenish both coal and water for the boilers. Despite this request, he and more than half of those on board elected to go ashore if only to stroll on solid land again. He enquired after Amanda from the Norths, also asking about their plans at this stop, and learned that they were remaining onboard and that Amanda was not yet well enough to write even a simple postcard. Once those going ashore alighted from the ship's tender at the dock, he joined in a slow stream of sweat-stained passengers asking for the way to the Post Office.

Two boys waving fans near the queue to purchase stamps barely kept the heat in check in the overcrowded room. Ramanujan suddenly reached out to steady himself. At first alarmed that it could be from the high temperature, he realized that he'd become accustomed to the steady rolling of the ship and he'd carried this motion with him onto the shore. He looked about and noticed that several others appeared to be in discomfort disproportional to the heat of the morning.

On his way back to the *Nevasa* he searched for a bookstore, going up some of the narrow lanes following garbled instructions but was unable to locate one. He did discover some postcards at a street-side stall, but the sellers spoke neither Tamil nor English. He was going to turn away, but remembering Amanda, managed, with sign language and fingers for counters, to trade some of his Rupees for a few worn cards.

To his amazement, he then stumbled upon a Vaishnavite temple entrance that he could pass into for prayers. As he stood in the shadows of the gate, he was suddenly dumbfounded. Kneeling down to untie and take off his shoes, he realized that this was the first time in his life that he'd needed to remove shoes to enter a temple.

He approached the priest and, putting his hands together in front of his chest, bowed slightly toward him. The priest reciprocated and said something unrecognizable to Ramanujan. "*Tamil pesuringula?*" asked Ramanujan, wondering if the priest spoke Tamil. Seeing no reaction, he asked, "Do you speak English?"

"*Kya aap Hindi bolte hai?*" asked the priest.

Ramanujan shook his head, but as he did so, he recognized the Sanskrit chants coming from deeper within the shrine. He was relieved to have made the trip across the water and to find blessings on the other side, and bowed again to the priest in gratitude.

As he was born and raised a Brahmin, there was a strict prohibition against him or any members of that caste crossing a large body of water. In India, there had never been a need for him to even contemplate disobeying this stricture and so it had not previously been a problem. Traders were meant to cross the water and the duty of Brahmins was to remain at home as a blessing to their community. Brahmins were the keepers of the knowledge of the religion, and it was not their place to leave in any case, as otherwise the populace would suffer their absence. Furthermore, it was known that the vast seas were the abode of the gods, and one should not disturb them unduly by a capricious ocean voyage, so why would one? And yet he had done just that.

And, of course, crossing the water meant living outside of his community's customs and protocol. Interacting with non-Hindus, or more specifically non-Brahmins, would mean that most encounters would lead to defilement. That was just the way of it if one chose to leave India. However, the modern world under the British Empire was changing the status quo, and there was greater need for people of all castes to travel, and more and more non-merchants, such as himself, were making the journey. He saw this trip, oddly, as a personal pilgrimage that was non-religious, an intellectual necessity that pushed uncomfortably against his acceptable boundaries—a step into the foreign and forbidden. And so, the voyage from India had so far been filled with hope, trepidation, and second-guesses. He would face the consequences from his fellow

Brahmins when he returned to Tamil Nadu, but it was the more immediate repercussions the gods might mete out that were the unknown quantity. Given all this, it was only after this blessing in a foreign land that his unease subsided, at least for the time being.

Walking toward the docks on his way back to the lighter, he found a stall that offered Indian food. The smell of the *pooris* emanating from one deep pan of bubbling oil was overwhelming and next to it balls for *gulab jaman* were being fried. He stood frozen. *This is not a Brahmin stall,* he lamented to himself. *But you are going to England where there will not even be Indian stalls, let alone Brahmin ones.*

He ordered *poori* with dry-fried *sabzi* vegetables, and a welcome cup of real Indian coffee. Sitting on a low wall under the blazing Red Sea sun, it seemed like this was the tastiest meal he'd ever eaten.

Part of the day had been spent in a foreign country, he'd crossed at least some of the water that he must, he'd received blessings, eaten real Indian street food, and as he re-boarded the tender for the short ride back to the steamer, Ramanujan felt a glimmer of inner contentment for the first time since leaving India.

Walking from his already sweltering stateroom and entering the shade on the starboard side the next morning, he was amazed to see Amanda wrapped in blankets and sitting alertly in a deck chair.

"Hello, Mr. Rama!" she said brightly as he approached. "It's funny that I used to think it was so hot outside and now I feel like I'm freezing in the morning air."

"Well, you certainly look much recovered today," said Ramanujan. "Are you feeling better now?"

"Oh, yes, much better," replied Amanda. "The doctor saw me this morning and said that I've really improved and that the fever has pretty well run its course. I only need to get my strength back up and I should be as good as new. Now I only have to worry about getting bored sitting in this dreadful chair."

Ramanujan reached into his jacket pocket and withdrew the postcards he'd purchased the previous day in Aden.

"Perhaps these will help fill in the time?" he wondered hopefully.

"Oh, thank you!" exclaimed Amanda. "I've been thinking that I should write, especially to my friend Mary. I'd promised to correspond with her weekly, and now she's probably begun to worry about me. At least now I have another life or death adventure to tell her about!"

Ramanujan winced internally that such words—referring to the imminence of death and announcing them loudly so that all, including the gods, could hear and take notice—should be uttered, but he also recognized the innocent exuberance behind her shout.

"Do you have a pencil I can borrow?" she asked.

He found one and handed it to her as he took a seat beside her. She wrapped the blanket more tightly around her shoulders as a slight breeze had come up and began to write on the back of one of the cards but was soon staring sleepily out across the deck.

His hair tickled his forehead in the light wind and his hand rose up to scratch. The sensation of then running his fingers through his thick hair was still odd to him. Short wavy black locks now grew from the front portion of his scalp, something that hadn't happened since he was a child. He gave the top of his head a vigorous scrub with his fingertips and then tamed the mop somewhat with his hands the best he could. Hair flopping onto his forehead was almost enough to make him question his sanity at times—he was constantly thinking that a mosquito was alighting on his head. However, he was slowly becoming numb to the sensation.

He fondly remembered his early morning baths in the Kaveri, joining all the other Brahmin boys and men in their morning ritual. Wading out into the river, the cool, cleansing sensation was always welcome even on the rare rainy mornings. His large body easily floated and instead of dipping into the waters, he would occasionally lie for a moment on his back letting the gently flowing water stream his hair out along the current. The older he became, the longer his hair, and once ready to leave the river he would flip his head around to expel most of the water in a long circular spray, and then use his hands to squeeze the remainder out. He'd quickly tie a knot at the end to keep the hair under control; make a prayer by cupping his hands, dipping them into the water, and letting the water drain out as he lifted his fingertips upward toward heaven; wrap his *veshti* around himself and then head for home. Several times a week he'd arrive at the riverbank early to have a barber shave any new growth from the front third of his head before taking his bath. The barbers also shaved his beard when he became old enough to grow one.

Back home with long hair that had dried in the sun, he'd then gather, twist, and coil the strands into a tight bun at the top of the back of his head. He was a Tenkalai Vaishnavite, so before morning *pooja* he'd use a white paste to place two vertical stripes down his forehead, joining them at the bottom to form a 'Y' and follow up with a red stripe between the top two. He'd then make his prayers and be ready for the day. In the evenings, he'd loosen his hair and comb oil through it until it glistened and again twist it into a tight bun. He'd then wash up in preparation for the evening ritual of Sandhyavandanam including the Gayatri Mantra.

Staring out across the ship's railings at the ruffled sea, Amanda asleep in her deckchair beside him, those days now seemed to have been lived by another person. His hair was shorn where it had once been long and grew where it hadn't been allowed since he was a small child. Still thinking of the Kaveri, he sang to himself as he rose and headed back to his cabin.

> The place of the faultless Lord who, as a swan,
>> saved the Vedas that day
> When the dense earth and land of heaven were hidden
>> in an impenetrable darkness
> Is Puḷḷampūtankuṭi where the Poṇṇi[1] River crashes

---

1 Another name for the Kaveri River.

bringing gold and jalap,
Bamboo pearls and nine jewels of shimmering light.

It was odd to be on the boat but not moving. Just off their port side lay a vast flat expanse of desert and the heat waves shimmered, blurring the horizon. With no motion and not a breath of wind, most of the passengers, including Ramanujan, were miserable and lemonade was being consumed by the pitcher. He sheltered under the starboard awnings, like everyone else, and had some more tea, something he rarely drank at home. Rather than allowing it to cool before sipping, he was used to drinking his beverages, usually coffee, as hot as possible, since this caused beads of sweat to form on his forehead, and the evaporation cooled him.

Seeing him sitting alone, Charlie stopped by on his way to help raise the anchor for the next segment of the journey through the canal.

"Hello, Mr. Ramanujan. Quite the heat, eh? I know it's hotter there, but come with me over to the port side—there's something I want to show you." Once the pair were on the opposite side of the ship he continued, "I don't know if you can make it out, but do you notice that little lake of water over there?" pointing at the flat expanse that stretched out before them.

Ramanujan squinted through heat waves and bright sunlight and thought he could just make something out—possibly a blue shimmering line. Nodding he said, "Yes, I think so."

"Did you know there was a canal here thousands of years ago—long before it was re-dug and opened by us some forty years past? That King Darius of Persia actually had a working canal going, but I heard it silted right up and became lost after a few hundred years. They say it ran through that there lake. Pretty interesting, ain't it?"

"I had no idea," said Ramanujan, wiping his brow. "Any clue as to when we are going to be moving again?"

"We're getting ready to weigh anchor right now. See that ship coming up to us? Once it passes, we'll be on our way." Just then both vessels exchanged blasts of their horns and Charlie said that he had to be up at the bow, "As quick as you like," as he made his way forward and Ramanujan returned to the shade.

It'll be so good to be moving again, thought Ramanujan, *I need air.* They were beginning the second day through the canal and had passed the Great Bitter Lake, but in his opinion, they still seemed to stop far too frequently in order that other vessels could pass.

Finally, they were beginning to move, and the slightest of breezes stirred to the relief of all onboard. Amanda came along the deck looking much more robust and she even showed the hint of some bounce in her step. Despite the blistering heat she still wore a shawl, however, and plopped down next to Ramanujan, slightly winded from the short walk.

"You're looking better, Amanda!" said Ramanujan.

"Thank you, Mr. Rama, but I'm just so bored now!"

"Maybe a puzzle would help?" asked Ramanujan. "How about working on a magic square?"

Amanda showed that he now had her full attention by leaning forward with enquiring eyes. "Magic?" she asked.

"Yes, in a way. A magic square is a grid made up of smaller squares. In a magic square, you see, no matter the dimensions of the grid, the sum of each row, each column, and each diagonal all equal the same number. No repeating numbers in the simpler squares are allowed. The most basic magic square is a three row by three column grid and employs the numbers one through nine once each." He drew a pencil from his pocket and on a crumpled paper scrap soon disentangled from another pocket he traced out a nine-cell square grid, filling it with numbers. "And this is it:" showing her the finished square.

6	1	8
7	5	3
2	9	4

"Do you see that every row, column, and diagonal all sum to the number 15?"

"Wow!" exclaimed Amanda. "How does that work?"

He looked at Amanda and smiled. "Magic. How would you like to try one?"

"Sure!"

"Alright, try one where every square must be an odd number and they all sum to 27."

Ramanujan sat on a deck chair with some papers and a problem of his own while Amanda went off to solve the puzzle. She was back in an hour.

"Well, it took some time, but I did it!" she exclaimed.

Ramanujan admired the completed magic square on the piece of paper she handed him.

15	1	11
5	9	13
7	17	3

"And well done, too!" said Ramanujan.

"Can I do another?" asked Amanda immediately. "How many are there?"

"Oh, there are many possibilities," said Ramanujan. "And the sky is the limit as far as the size of the square goes—of course they get increasingly difficult the larger they are. Just a moment, I want to go and fetch my notebooks and show you something."

Amanda at first gulped and then sipped the lemonade that her mother brought her just as Ramanujan was heading back to his cabin. She was staring out across the desert when he returned but remained bright-eyed instead of napping which had become routine for her over the past week.

Ramanujan carefully opened the top notebook to some of the first pages. Amanda put down her lemonade and shifted so that she could see.

"This may help you with future squares," he said and pointed at a small hand-drawn square.

C+Q	A+P	B+R
A+R	B+Q	C+P
B+P	C+R	A+Q

"Oh, my!" said Amanda, suddenly exasperated. "Do I have to solve that one to figure out the others?"

"No, no," said Ramanujan. "I have worked out a key that will be very helpful for you. This makes sense of the magic squares and works for any of them."

"But I thought that only one number went into each box, and now it looks like I would need to figure out two," said Amanda.

"Well, let me show you. Let's see the puzzle that you just solved, and compare it with this one in my notebook," said Ramanujan. "We don't need to worry about the actual values of the A, B,C's just where they lie.

"There is an arithmetic progression to the main cross and the diagonals—so, in the puzzle you just solved, the vertical center column progresses by 8, the center horizontal row by 4, and each diagonal by 2 and 6. See?"

And he traced each row, column and diagonal that he had mentioned.

"Now look at my matrix," said Ramanujan. "Since the letter B makes up one of the diagonals, we know that one of the diagonals in your square progresses by 2, and we can substitute 2 for B. You can now see that the A's, corresponding in position to the numbers 1, 5, and 3, also progress by 2, and the same is true of the C's—all in the same ABC class as B, they all progress by 2. We also can see that the letter Q is represented by the other diagonal and it progresses by 6. Now look at the position of the P's and the R's—they also progress by 6. Isn't that amazing?"

Amanda stared and then gaped. "Yes, but what's even more amazing is that you could see that pattern," said Amanda in wonder.

She glanced at the notebook and noticed even larger matrices populated with the A, B, C's. Some were square and some created large rectangles.

"Do you mean that you have this figured out even for these bigger squares?"

Ramanujan nodded and said, "Yes, the patterns somehow just came to me."

Amanda reached over and flipped a few pages more into the top notebook. They were filled with the most complex equations and formulae that she had ever seen. Part of what was under Chapter 4 of a second notebook looked like this:

$$\psi_1(n) = 1;$$

$$\psi_2(n-1) = \frac{1}{6}\left(\frac{1}{2} + \frac{1}{3} + \frac{1}{4} + \cdots \frac{1}{n}\right);$$

$$\psi_2(n-2) = \frac{n(n-1)}{72}\left\{\left(\frac{1}{2} + \frac{1}{3} + \cdots + \frac{1}{n}\right)^2 - \left(\left(\frac{1}{2^2} + \frac{1}{3^2} + \cdots + \frac{1}{n^2}\right) - \frac{1}{n} + \frac{1}{2}\right\};$$

$$\varphi_1(2r) = 1$$

$$\varphi_2(2r) = r$$

$$\varphi_3(2r) = r^2 - \frac{r}{6}$$

$$\varphi_4(2r) = r^3 - \frac{5r^2}{12} + \frac{r}{24}$$

$$\varphi_5(2r) = r^4 - \frac{13}{18}r^3 + \frac{r^2}{6} - \frac{r}{90}$$

$$\varphi_6(2r) = r^5 - \frac{77}{72}r^4 + \frac{89}{216}r^3 - \frac{91}{1440}r^2 + \frac{11r}{4320}$$

$$\varphi_7(2r) = r^6 - \frac{29}{20}r^5 + \frac{175}{216}r^4 - \frac{149}{720}r^3 + \frac{96r^2}{4320} - \frac{r}{2360}$$

She couldn't even recognize some of the symbols and they went on and on throughout the other pages she flipped through.

"I just noticed," said Amanda pointing to the letter *psi* ψ. "*Psi* looks just like the Hindu spears I saw—even that one stuck through that *sadhu*'s tongue."

Ramanujan looked to where she was pointing and chuckled. "They do look like Shiva's trident, don't they?"

Amanda nodded and before Ramanujan had the chance to begin explaining what she was seeing said, "I think I'll just struggle along with impossible old geometry next, thank you very much. How about another square puzzle?"

"OK," said Ramanujan. "Try a square where the rows sum to 36 and every number is even. Oh, and copy down this one with the A, B, C's to help out."

Amanda copied down the template and the problem and then hunched over her paper to work out the next magic square. Ramanujan leaned back in the inclined deckchair and closed his eyes against the shimmering heat. He found himself thinking about the strange probabilities that had brought him to experience this life, on this boat, next to this English girl, out of all the possible lives there were to be led. A long-forgotten scene had him momentarily back in India.

He smelled incense and heard a magpie somewhere above. Turning to the shrine, he watched an old woman rise with difficulty from a kneeling prayer. Her tiny weathered hand grasped a small lime and she approached and impaled the green fruit on the right curved and sharpened tine of Shiva's trident which stood imbedded in a square stone at the center of the shrine. He was afraid that she might cut herself as she both squeezed the lime and pushed it down onto the other, older limes that had been placed there before. The torn segments of the fruit were exposed, and their juice ran down the tine as well as along her hand and into the bangles on her wrist. He knew that the limes were a spiritually cool fruit and assuaged the goddess Mariamman's temper so that she would both bless and insulate the old woman from her wrath.

Ramanujan squatted on a nearby rock and watched the woman pray again and light a small clay oil lamp on a flat stone near the trident. Included on the stone were previous offerings including limes that had been cut in half and curled inward so that the outer skin formed the inner surface of a crude oil lamp with a pulpy exterior, powders for making *pottus*—the dot-like markings on the forehead, half-burned incense sticks, and some *bidi* cigarettes. Above the shrine hung closely packed brass bells of various sizes, and multi-colored cloths and strings hung from the same crossbar. The huge twining banyan tree next to the shrine was girthed by countless layered strings tied with various-colored cloth packets each containing a small stone in offering.

This shrine, he also knew, was used as a place of animal sacrifice during different festivals, or for special celebrations such as weddings, or on the occasion of a first birthday. Chickens and goats were killed, and the blood and meat were offered to the goddess, later cooked and partaken of by the worshippers. As a Vaishnavite Brahmin, this seemed as of another world, but still, had its place for some Hindus.

As the wizened woman finished her *pooja* and ambled on her way down the narrow path, he thought of the chances that had created this life for him. He could have been born a Shaivite and followed this woman through her prayers to the wrathful Shiva rather than the benevolent Vishnu, and this would have flavored his entire outlook on the world and on life. He would then have never known the goddess Namagiri Amman. He could have also been born into an entirely different, non-Brahmanic caste, and not have been steeped in the knowledge of the Vedas. Or, he thought, he could have been born as the magpie that dropped out of the tree to investigate the small shrine once the old woman had shuffled on.

Amanda was muttering to herself and Ramanujan turned to his notebooks, forcing himself from his sudden pondering of where this voyage would land him in his next life.

Finally clearing the Suez Canal, the *Nevasa* anchored near Port Said the next morning. Ramanujan had more letters in his pocket and was walking out of the galley after tea and toast, when he saw Amanda at the railing taking in the small city.

"Are you going ashore?" asked Ramanujan hopefully as he approached her.

"No," sighed Amanda. "Mother says that I shouldn't take on too much too quickly, and so she won't let me go. It's so unfair! But—she guarantees me that I can finally touch land again when we get to the next stop. Maybe we could go to shore together then?"

"That would be wonderful," said Ramanujan in full sympathy with her frustration.

"Would you mind posting a letter for me? It's for Mary." asked Amanda. "Oh, and I think I have the magic square figured out!"

She pulled out a piece of paper and the letter. She handed the letter to Ramanujan and smoothed out a folded page on the railing.

"Here's what I came up with first," she explained. "But I looked at it more carefully and even though it satisfies the rules for a square, it doesn't fit with the coded square you gave me. The rows and diagonals all work but not the A, B, C's."

14	2	20
18	12	6
4	22	10

"So, I spent some more time and finally got things to add up in this second square."

14	4	18
16	12	8
6	20	10

Ramanujan examined them and said, "Well, of course they are both correct, and you need not use my little codes, but I find them to be just a little simpler, I guess, which to me makes them more elegant."

"I think that the word 'elegant' probably only applies to royal courts and balls," said Amanda, "but I'm happy that you've found a new use for the word in dreary old math."

They both chuckled, and Ramanujan asked, "Is there anything you need from shore?"

"No," said Amanda dejectedly. "Oh! Wait! If you see any postcards with pictures of the pyramids, I would love one—no two—if that's all right."

"I was going to search for the same thing myself, so that will be easy," said Ramanujan and headed off to join the crowd awaiting shore transport.

CHAPTER 8.

The passengers began to comment on feeling some relief from the heat within hours of steaming into the Mediterranean, and as they neared Genoa, the climate entered the more temperate range which most of them welcomed. At night, Ramanujan felt what he perceived to be a nip to the air, but his shipmates were strolling about the deck in their shirtsleeves. The seas were also becoming rougher, something that Ramanujan hoped wouldn't last.

Charlie had come up to him while he was studying a map of Southern Europe that was posted on one of the inner passageways.

"Hello, Charlie," said Ramanujan as he was plotting their course with his finger. "I am having trouble with this. Can you explain why we are going all the way up to the tip of the—what is it?—Ligurian Sea, and Northern Italy, when the route to England lies," and he pointed to a more direct route, "this way?"

"Easy peasy," said Charlie with a grin. "We're not just toting passengers. We're also hauling cargo, and there is a god-awful lot that needs unloading in Genoa. Luckily, we'll have help getting it off of the ship, 'cause I don't right fancy doing it all on my lonesome."

"Ah, now I see," said Ramanujan. "Thank you, Charlie."

"Sure," said Charlie. "And, of course, all the passengers will be helping out, too."

Grinning that Ramanujan didn't pick up on his joke, Charlie filled him in on the jest and patted Ramanujan's arm as he headed off to his station.

Ramanujan was becoming familiar enough with the custom that he noticed but didn't wince at the contact by a non-Brahmin.

Heading back to his cabin, he saw Lord and Lady North out for an evening stroll and entered into a conversation with them about the relief from the heat, the expectations for the rest of the trip to England, and the stop to unload cargo and a few passengers at Genoa.

"Amanda had mentioned that she would be able to go ashore at the next stop," said Ramanujan. "I would be happy to watch out for her if you like."

"I think that would be wonderful," said Lord North, and Ramanujan noticed Lady North tug lightly at his sleeve as he said this.

"But we really need to see what our shoreside itinerary looks like, don't we dear?" asked Lady North.

"Well, I'm sure we can work around Amanda's plans," said Lord North.

"But we really haven't had time to help her with her plans, have we dear?" giving him a meaningful look.

"I'm sure something can be arranged, Ramanujan," said Lord North after a pause. "We'll have a chat with Amanda and coordinate all of our schedules for seeing the sights in

Genoa. How about if we let you know what we decide tomorrow morning?"

"That would be fine with me," said Ramanujan.

"Good night, then," the couple both said in unison as they turned and continued the conversation in whispers on the way to their stateroom.

Ramanujan wondered if the hesitation was due to an unknown issue regarding caste, or social status, as they would think of it in England. He thought about how difficult communication with the British on more than just the superficial level might turn out to be, and yet how well he knew his own people in the place he'd just left behind. *How easy is it going to be to make a true friend in England?* he wondered and suddenly drifted back to a memory.

Chandrasekaran squinted at the few coins in his hand and said, "Hey, Pillaiyar, can I have my glasses back? I can't even tell how much I have here."

Ramanujan nodded, slipped the glasses off his head, and handed them to Chandrasekaran. Chandrasekaran squeezed the frame of the glasses more tightly together and wrapped the temple tips around his ears and smiled. His family was a little better off than Ramanujan's and Chandrasekaran had been given glasses as soon as it was evident he needed them. Ramanujan was to wait another year for his, but it was fortunate that they both required the same corrections in order to read.

"Ah, there we go," said Chandrasekaran turning back to the sweets seller. "Two *laddu*, please." And he handed the man four *paisa*, who in turn scooped out two of the sweet balls and placed them in a rough cup made from *peepal* leaves. "Thank you," he said. Chandrasekaran and Ramanujan made their way to the shade of a nearby *neem* tree and shared the treat.

Chandrasekaran was Ramanujan's best friend and they'd just started school together. Ramanujan grinned inwardly that Sekar, as all of Chandrasekaran's friends knew him, had called him Pillaiyar. He was both pleased to have a new nick-name and resigned to the fact that this was yet another reference to his considerable bulk for a boy of his age. Pillaiyar was the large elephant god also known as Vinayakar or Ganesha, Remover of Obstacles, and a lover of good foods—especial-ly *laddu*. He just hoped that the nickname wouldn't spread through the school.

Sekar began tapping his foot and slapping out a rhythm on a nearby stone. He was thin as a rail and constantly moving—almost the exact opposite of Ramanujan. Where Sekar would want to be off on small adventures, Ramanujan would be content lying on his back, gazing at the clouds, and thinking. Yet the two had formed an inseparable friendship. Savoring the *laddu*, Sekar began singing one of his favorite verses about Krishna as a young lad, skipping some lines to make it more pertinent to the current setting.

> Sweets of red paddy and green pulse,
>   fragrant ghee and milk I made
> For the twelve-day Ōnam festival.
>   But I have long known this child!
>   "I want more," he said as he devoured it all,

and stood there looking innocent.
Please call your son, my lady. Yaśoda, this is only a part of it!

I had sugar candy and treats in a bowl with snacks
   and sesame seed balls.
I thought they'd be safe in my own house,
   but he sneaked in, took them, and slipped away.
He came back later and, spying my pots,
   found and ate my shining white butter.
Please call your son, my lady. Yaśoda, this is only a part of it!

They both had a laugh and then wandered over to the banks of the Kaveri and sat under another spreading tree in the cooling shade. After the normal six-year-old banter and throwing stones into the languid waters, they both fell into wondering what they would be when they grew up.

"I'd like to be a musician," said Sekar. And everything he said, did, and memorized made Ramanujan agree with him. Sekar had an incredible sense of rhythm and could sing or play on request every verse, tune, and pitch that he'd ever heard.

"I have absolutely no idea," responded Ramanujan. "It's like I think about all kinds of things but can't imagine what they'll form me into when I get older. I can't even fathom getting old. Can you?"

Do the British have friends like this? he wondered as the memory faded. *They never seem to really laugh or have any warmth.* But then he thought of the raucous laughter that sometimes spilled out of the tiny salon in the after-dinner hours, and the rowdy songs that he'd hear late at night on deck. *Maybe they do, but are more private about it,* he thought.

After promising his utmost vigilance regarding Amanda, the Norths agreed that she could spend the day in Genoa with Ramanujan which was her wish. "We're now considered to be boring," said Lord North with a sad smile. Lady North went off to help Amanda get ready for a day ashore. Pulling Ramanujan aside, Lord North muttered, "My wife had some misgivings about too much of an older man's attention to Amanda, if you know what I mean. However, I persuaded her that our daughter would be perfectly safe in your company."

Ramanujan was somewhat taken aback. "I am a married man, and anything untoward would be out of the realm of possibility, I assure you," he replied.

Seeing that Ramanujan had taken some umbrage at his remark, Lord North said, "Lady North really knows that you are a good person, Ramanujan. It's just that Amanda is getting to the age where it is something that we begin to worry about."

"I see," he replied. "Well, you can be completely confident in both my watchfulness and decorum."

"Very good," said Lord North, "I'm sure you two will have a grand time in Genoa."

Later, standing alone on the deck, Ramanujan stared out at the Lanterna lighthouse as the *Nevasa* was being secured to the dock. *So that's what the problem was last night*, he thought to himself, and realized that, of course, the same would be true in India for non-relatives. *I should've been more sensitive.*

Amanda was ecstatic to be getting off the boat and flew down the gangplank, waiting for Ramanujan at the bottom. Walking down Genoa's busiest street into the center of the city with her, Ramanujan was reminded of being with his childhood friend, Sekar. One was round, heavy, and slow; and the other was thin, quick, and animated. Noting that he was the darkest person he could see on the street and that she was still very pale, only added to the contrast of the pair. Still, Genoa was a cosmopolitan city, and they drew very few stares as they strolled along and gazed into every display window they passed.

After an hour of pleasurable wandering Amanda suddenly stopped before a storefront.

"Oh!" she exclaimed. "Gelato! We simply must have some!"

"What is it?" asked Ramanujan.

"It's a frozen, um, pudding that they put on an edible cone. It's absolutely fantastic!"

Amanda took a step towards the shop and paused. "Oh, and it is vegetarian," whispered Amanda.

Ramanujan thought about a frozen custard as they entered the shop. In India, there were cold foods and hot foods, although strictly speaking these labels had nothing to do with temperature—more like what effects they had on the body. Carrots, tomato, yogurt, papaya, some types of banana, grapefruit, and spinach were some of the hot foods. Beans, okra, chickpea, potato, pineapple, coconut, and orange were some of the cool foods. He had no idea what a frozen yogurt-type food would be classified as, but since he suspected it might be similar to the milk-based sweet *sri-khand*, he thought he would give it a try.

There were multiple flavors available and Ramanujan chose lime, a cool food. Amanda laughed out loud as he took his first taste. "You should see the look on your face!" she giggled. It was delicious, but he'd never had a food so cold before. They sat on some small chairs in the shade and chatted while they enjoyed the treat. Amanda gobbled up her cone, but Ramanujan couldn't bring himself to eat the shell that had been touched by other hands, and discarded the remainder, much to her chagrin.

Ramanujan marveled at the tall buildings and different architectures that appeared on every street. They strolled past the San Lorenzo cathedral, and Amanda wanted to go inside. Ramanujan was suddenly hesitant and said, "You can go on in, and I will wait for you right here, in this spot." He didn't want to tell her that he was suddenly nervous about not knowing the rituals that must be followed when one entered a church. *Do I remove my shoes?* he wondered about the constricting things the Europeans seemed to be so attached to. *Would I receive a Christian blessing? How would I respond to the priest as a non-Christian? Do I make an offering? What should it be?*

When Amanda emerged from the cathedral sometime later and they were making their way to the Piazza de Ferrari,

Ramanujan decided to ask about the customs observed on entering a Catholic or Christian church. "I hope this is not awkward, Amanda, but how restrictive are Christians about who may enter?"

"Oh, anyone is welcome almost any time," explained Amanda. "They won't mind, and even during a service a person can just sit and watch. Of course, there might be some stares at that, but it's not forbidden, or even frowned upon, for that matter. The main rules are to be quiet at all times, and stay in the back if there's a service or something. Oh, and I know from experience that they don't like it if you shuffle around or fidget too much in your seat."

She turned to Ramanujan. "Do you believe in Jesus?" she asked unabashedly. "I mean all of those brightly colored gods, gods with elephant heads, boar's heads, snake bodies, wings, fangs, and every kind of weapon—how can they be... they aren't a real person like Jesus, are they?"

They slowed their pace back to the docks. Ramanujan realized that he'd been expecting questions of this sort from his British hosts, and although he hadn't formulated any specific answers, he was also aware that he hadn't questioned what his own beliefs were from his first breath onward.

"I really know nothing of Jesus Christ," said Ramanujan. "Thus, it would be difficult for me to believe in something I know nothing about. There are many Catholic missionaries now in India, but I have never come into contact with any of them."

"Let us sit for a minute," he said and pointed to some benches along a small piazza.

"I have wondered how to answer questions about Hinduism, but you are the first to really ask," said Ramanujan. "Asking if I believe in Brahma, Shiva, or Vishnu—the source of all of those images you just listed—is like asking if I believe in life, or my hand, this bench, or you. From the time of our birth, the Hindu gods are part of who we are—especially us Brahmins who must know all the texts and rituals. We know not only every story about every god, but we can recognize any reference to any story about any god. It is part of who we are and not separate from us. Do you know what I mean?"

"So, like, every statue or carving on every temple—you know what they mean?"

"Of course!" exclaimed Ramanujan. "Take for instance, the ten incarnations of Vishnu. Everyone knows the stories that go with each one, and any text that makes even the slightest reference to them."

"Incarnations?" asked Amanda.

"Yes, incarnations," replied Ramanujan and thought for a moment. "They are sort of like individual lifetimes as that identity or form. Or a transformation into that form. For instance, Krishna is a part of Vishnu, or is Vishnu in another form.

"Periyalvar once sang:

The temple of him who was a divine fish and a turtle, a boar,
  a lion and a dwarf
Who became three Ramas and Kannan and
  who will conclude with Kalki
Is Srirangam of the river where a swan plays

swinging on the red lotus blossoms,
Embracing her mate on a flower bed,
   besmearing their bodies with red pollen.

"Kannan is another name for Krishna and is one of those ten descents of Vishnu. And in another example, there is Vishnu's incarnation as a dwarf. In this small form, he asked a king for a gift of as much land as he could cover in three strides. The king, seeing how small he was, happily granted the request. Then Vishnu transformed himself from a dwarf into a divine supreme being and encompassed the entire world and the heavens in three gigantic steps. So then to us, any reference to a dwarf immediately brings to mind Lord Vishnu."

He recited:

As one dwarf, he asked for the two worlds
   in three feet of earth,
   then trod the entire world in two steps one time long ago,
And said, "Give me one more."
   You who would clasp those feet of him
   who lowered his foot to put Māvali in prison,
Just go to Śrīrāmaviṇṇakaram in Kāḻi
   adorned with the riches of crowded street fairs,
The four collections of the Mysteries, the five sacrifices,
   the six sciences, and seven modes of music.

"Since we are under the British educational system, when I was in school I, of course, had to learn much of the history of

Britain. But for us in India, we don't keep track of history as much as we do of our religion. So instead of dates and facts, our minds are full of sutras, songs, stories, and legends. To us this is as real as the conquest of England by Normandy in 1066.

"So, when it comes down to it, I suppose it is not a question of belief for us—it is who we are and where our thoughts are continuously."

CHAPTER 9

The *Nevasa* was passing Gibraltar, and the passengers crowded the rails to view the immense white rock jutting up out of the green hills to the right and they could just make out the coast of Morocco to the left. As they entered the Atlantic, Ramanujan, who was already wearing his coat, could feel a definite chill in the air. Looking around to see if the temperature drop was only in his imagination, he noticed Amanda bundle her shawl more tightly around her thin frame, and his fellow passengers slipping on coats or sweaters as they took in the quickly receding coast of Spain.

The temperature seemed to plummet with every day that brought them closer to the British Isles. On this evening, only two days out from reaching England, he'd hurried back to his berth after a light dinner and was inclined to remain in his cabin given the chill. However, he'd noticed that the stars were brilliant as he left the galley, and more than the usual number of people were out on the decks to take in the evening air before retiring. Grabbing a blanket and wrapping it around his head and shoulders, he joined the others and gazed out at the mild waves below and the immense sea of stars above. He hoped no one noticed his shivering. *No wonder the*

shoes, he thought wistfully through the pain of wearing them. *If my feet were out in this, they would be frozen and useless.*

The purser had, as usual, announced any important news, status of the voyage, time to next port, and the temperature. He'd said that by the time they reached Plymouth, the last port of call they'd make before proceeding on to London, the high would be 12 degrees (54° F), and that this very evening the temperature would dip to 8 degrees (46° F). Ramanujan had sighed at this news—this was one of the hottest months in Tamil Nadu, but the highs that were expected in Plymouth and London were going to be far lower than the coldest weather he'd ever faced. He found it difficult to consistently maintain a train of thought without his attention being diverted to the climate and bitterness of the air.

They were due to dock in Plymouth the next day and Ramanujan was outwardly calm, but inwardly becoming more agitated. He'd arrived at several new theorems during the voyage and was excited to formalize and share them with Mr. Hardy and the other Trinity College mathematicians; he was anxious about what else lay in store for him when he reached Cambridge; and he felt like he was absorbing the anticipation of his fellow passengers as they neared England. He was also eager to hear news of home after an entire month at sea and hoped that there were letters waiting for him in either London or Cambridge.

At breakfast, Lord North asked if he could join Ramanujan at the table.

"Please, be my guest," said Ramanujan indicating the chair next to him. "You and your family must be very excited that you will soon be home and able to see friends and relatives again. Amanda told me that her aunt has been staying in your house while you are away?"

"Yes, my sister lives very nearby our manor and she's let her eighteen-year-old daughter mind her own house while she's been staying in ours. From what I've read in letters, it seems that this might have helped salvage relations between those two. Otherwise, yes, we're looking forward to the sanity of England."

Ramanujan was not sure what that meant about his own country, but suspected he was soon to find out. The waiter brought them both coffee, and Ramanujan had a banana and some yogurt while Lord North ordered an English breakfast consisting of beans, fried tomatoes, bacon, poached eggs, and a muffin.

As they each sipped at their steaming cups, Lord North said, "Mr. Ramanujan, I was wondering if I might make a proposal. I understand from Amanda that you'll be living in Cambridge, and that you'll be working on your maths with some professors there. You see, Amanda has not only taken a shine to you, but somehow has become interested in mathematics again. I never thought I'd see the day, but the girl has actually brought up the topic in conversation, and I find her scribblings on sheets of paper all over her room. What I mean to ask is this. Would you be amenable to perhaps coaching

Amanda in her maths over the summer? We live not far away from Cambridge, and I could arrange for her to meet you for an hour or so each week. Is this something that you might find to be in the least bit agreeable?"

"Oh, it is so good to hear that she is taking to the subject," answered Ramanujan. "I have no idea what my circumstances will be in Cambridge, but once I get settled, perhaps I could send word as to whether or not I am available?"

"Oh, yes, that would be most acceptable," said Lord North. "We must arrange, of course, for a public venue for these meetings."

Ramanujan paused with his cup at his lips and set it back in its saucer. "You have nothing to fear on any account," said Ramanujan. "As you remember, I am a married man."

He hesitated, fiddled with his spoon in his coffee, and then continued, "I have two things to inform you about before we enter into this agreement, and we will see if it is still acceptable after you have heard. Firstly, I married my wife when she was nine years old and she is now thirteen, no, she's just turned fourteen—about the same age as Amanda. This may seem strange to you, but in India, that is how these arranged marriages proceed. She lived in her own home for most of the three years after the wedding. And secondly, I did some tutoring in Madras before this voyage, and the comments I received back were not the most complementary. I must clarify these things up front and let you know that I am chaste and am obsessed with mathematics but am very prone, even so, to getting off the main track of the problem at hand."

Lord North smiled and said, "Married is married, and I have no qualms on that front. And, believe it or not, I'm not so much interested in what Amanda learns, but more concerned that she remains excited about the subject. If you can keep that small fire of curiosity burning, it will be more than worth it to me."

Lord North wrote down his address for Ramanujan, and they arranged that Ramanujan would be in touch after he was settled into his new situation. Amanda and Lady North soon joined them at the table and Amanda regaled Ramanujan with her excitement at returning home and anecdotes about her friend Mary. No mention of the possibility of him tutoring her came up, and so Ramanujan left it to Lord North to inform his daughter—if the arrangement maintained its appeal to the Lord once back in England.

The *Nevasa* docked in Plymouth and, as was the case in Genoa, the passengers continuing with the next leg were requested to remain on the ship. Ramanujan had no choice but to stay onboard, since departing passengers were required to pass through customs. Standing at the rail with Charlie as the ship unloaded, the deckhand had confirmed that approximately one third of those on board were scheduled to disembark at this penultimate port of the long voyage. To Ramanujan's eyes, it seemed that most of the cargo was being unloaded here as well.

The next berthing for him would be the end of his voyage, and the beginning of his life in England. He thought not only of the new experiences that awaited, but also of the adaptations necessary to assimilate into this foreign land. The list of these adjustments—from the insignificant to the profound—seemed to be endless. At home, each and every action he took was ingrained not only in himself, but also in his countrymen. He carried out all his duties as a Brahmin, and society in harmony reacted and treated him as a Brahmin in the proper manner. This would not be the case in England. And the impacts his arrival would have upon the rules and strictures that he normally followed at home went far beyond those minor inconveniences he'd experienced thus far at the dining table and in interactions with his fellow travelers. He mentally went over the Brahmanic rules that would apply to him while living in England and knew he would not be able to follow most of them. Luckily, rules about cows, sacred rivers, banyan trees, and relatives he doubted he would need to worry about since England had few of these in store for him. Plus, he was an Iyanger Brahmin and knew at some basic level that Vishnu would still bless him and that he would not be too severely impacted by any upcoming transgressions, but going against a lifetime of protocol would tax him mentally just the same.

However, were he a Smartha Brahmin like his friend Sekar, things would be even more complicated. Under those rules, he knew he must never see a sunrise, the sun at high noon, nor the sun at sunset without first offering prayers. He should not tread on the shadows of those—father, mother, god—above him, nor tread on the shadows of the base non-Hindus. He should never see his shadow in water. He should never blow out a flame or dowse it with water. He should never enter a dwelling by the back door. He should always wash his feet before going to bed and always avoid sleeping with his head facing north among a score of rules. The strictures that applied to dining alone were countless.

Ramanujan wore a sacred thread, bandolero-style around his torso which should be changed every four months, or sooner if necessary, through a sacred ritual. This was a favorite observance of his, and he'd enjoyed trips to the temple for this purpose. He knew that the sacred thread he wore would, in time, rot and fall away, and he would need to perform this ritual himself before it did so. He'd packed a box with the threads necessary to make the change. The thread was essential to being Brahmin, and he didn't know what life would be like without it.

Charlie broke his reverie by giving him a big slap on the back.

"You look a little down there, Mr. Ramanujan," said Charlie. "Cheer up, Old London Town will be just the thing to cure what ails you."

Ramanujan thought that Charlie had no idea what ailed him, but gave him a big smile in reply anyway.

They were no longer in the open ocean and the blue-green water had turned a muddy brown in the estuary. "Do you see the change in the color of the water?" asked his friend Charlie as they gazed ahead.

"Yes, it is brown now," said Ramanujan.

"That's the discharge from the River Thames, and London lays just ahead upriver." He took in a deep breath through his nose. "I can smell it even now." Ramanujan breathed in, but couldn't detect what Charlie seemed to notice in the air. "We won't be making it all the way into London proper because the channel just becomes too shallow for a tub like this. Instead, we make our berth some miles downstream."

"But how will we get to London then? How will people find us?"

"Don't worry, Mr. Ramanujan. That's just where we dock, and everyone knows it. You see, over the centuries, companies like the East India Company had to create side-channels off the Thames with docking facilities for the vessels in their fleet. Their boats had all become too big to make it to the downtown area. Now, all of those company docks have been taken over by the Port of London Authority, and they extend for miles. It's something else—just wait till you see."

"For miles?" asked Ramanujan.

"Not to worry, mate," Charlie said. "Your people will know London and know where to find you."

The further upriver they travelled, the more congested the waterway became. There were some steamships similar to the *Nevasa*, but there were also narrow and long canal boats, large two and three-masted schooners, barges, smaller sailing vessels, and painters and punts beyond counting. Staring out beyond the confusion on the water he found himself tracking the shore. Many of the trees were completely bare and most of those that had leaves were decked in a green that was more on the side of yellow than the lush green he was used to seeing at home.

"Are all of those trees dead or dying?" asked Ramanujan.

Charlie looked at him, gazed out at the banks of the Thames, and then back to Ramanujan. Suddenly he smiled and nodded with understanding.

"Ah, right," said Charlie. "You see, we live in a climate where the trees shed their leaves in the winter, to survive I suppose, and then sprout new leaves in the spring. In a few weeks and surely by summer all of these trees will be as green as grass, and then the leaves will turn color in the Fall and all drop off for the tree to make it through another winter." After a pause he said, "I would have thought your question strange, but realizing that you're a tropical gent, I knew that you might not really know about our seasons here."

"That is just remarkable," said Ramanujan. "I have read about the four seasons, but until now had no idea what that really had meant. To see so many trees that are just brown skeletal branches is sort of eerie, if you want to know the truth." He took in the scene again. "I am thankful for arriving in the spring with summer ahead, at least."

"I should say so. Well, I best get us ready for docking," said Charlie and waved as he headed toward his station, this time at the stern.

Focusing again on their path upriver, Ramanujan was amazed at the seemingly close calls between vessels with no resultant collisions. He'd trusted the captain thus far and was inclined to trust him until docking. It seemed that there was a hierarchy at work wherein the larger the ship, the more the smaller boats had to stay out of its path. *I would certainly make way for a cart or a water buffalo on the street,* he thought, *so this makes perfect sense.*

The clear air they'd experienced over the entire voyage was now becoming choked with all manner of smoke. He saw steamers trailing plumes, the houses now crowding the banks had smoke emanating from every chimney, and off in the distance, tall stacks spewed gigantic columns of the stuff. Visibility shrank the further upriver they chugged.

As they neared the docks, he could more easily make out the individual details even given the thick haze. Masses of people were crowding in all directions; horse-drawn carts, hansoms, cars, carts, small and large trucks wove through the populace; pulleys, levered booms, and powered cranes were lifting and moving assortments of baggage, crates, bales, and sacks onto the waiting carts and trucks.

Madras had some European-style buildings, there were some cars, and he'd seen new cranes moving stones into place in recent constructions. Ramanujan stepped back from the rail a pace and took in the hectic London panorama with some trepidation. Madras suddenly seemed quaint and pedestrian by comparison—London was going to be bigger, more modern, busier, and more complicated than he had ever expected.

CHAPTER 10

Amid the bustle of passengers and porters pushing carts swelling with luggage and crates through the narrow corridors and along the decks, he'd lost contact with Amanda as if she'd been carried away by the current. She'd wanted to wish him farewell before he left the ship, but the jumble and jostling on the deck had made the prospect of such a meeting hopeless. He'd tried to swim his way to her cabin, but saw that would be logistically impossible. He'd just made it to the safety of the railing overlooking the dock when he saw the Norths near the base of the ramp with their baggage being gathered around them. Thankfully he heard Amanda's voice not far away to his side.

"Here, Mr. Rama!" she said waving a kerchief above several heads.

He made it over to where she stood near the exit plank and they both stepped away from the crush of the crowd making its way down the ramp. She grinned and primly shook his hand and then offered a quick hug.

"I shall miss you ever so much and hope that we can somehow see each other again after we've gone our separate ways," she said with some formality and a little too brightly.

Her father hasn't mentioned the possibility of our meeting for math lessons then, thought Ramanujan. "It has been such a pleasure to meet and chat with you, Amanda," said

Ramanujan. "You have lightened the long voyage from my home considerably. I hope you do well in school, and your father has given me your address, so I will try and stay in touch."

"Oh, yes! I was going to give you our address, but completely forgot!" she exclaimed. "That would be absolutely fabulous! I hope that you settle comfortably into our country. As you said—we're all part of the same Empire. And you do have plenty of people to help you out... don't you?"

"Yes, in fact some of them are to meet me on these very docks, so all will be well."

"When you write, could you please send some more puzzles?" asked Amanda as her parents began shouting to her above the din from the docks below.

"Certainly," said Ramanujan. "And tell your parents again how much I enjoyed meeting them."

After a quick pat on his arm and several waves as she squeezed down the gangway, Amanda rejoined her parents and they quickly disappeared into the throng spreading away from the ship.

Ramanujan suddenly felt alone, and in turn, made his own way down the gangplank. He was not sure where to go and began making his way to what looked like a ticketing office or terminal when suddenly there was Mr. Neville standing right in front of him.

"I say, Mr. Ramanujan!" exclaimed Mr. Neville. "Welcome to England!"

Ramanujan was immediately relieved to find his friend, and so easily. Beaming, he shook Mr. Neville's proffered hand. "It is really good to see a familiar face here!" he said enthusiastically. Mr. Neville then placed his hands together in front of his heart and slightly bowed his head. A smiling Ramanujan reciprocated.

"How was the voyage? Not too rough I hope?" asked Mr. Neville.

"It was fine, once I got accustomed to the ship moving under my feet," said Ramanujan. "In a way, it was strange to be away from my home, and yet nowhere else in particular, really, either."

"I know the feeling, having just returned—only my disorientation happened on my way to India rather than on the way back. Oh, by the way, this is my older brother Alex," said Mr. Neville, gesturing toward a man who had been standing somewhat behind him, and Ramanujan shook his outstretched hand.

"It is nice to meet the brother of Mr. Neville," said Ramanujan. "You know he was just in India and met with me about my mathematics there? In fact, I believe he is the one who persuaded me, in the end, to come to England."

"So I have heard," said Alex. "Welcome to London, our..."

"Ramanujan, I simply must insist that you call me Eric, or at least E.H.," said Mr. Neville, interrupting. "Everyone does and we already know each other quite well. In fact, I believe that you are older than me, are you not? I was born in 1889?"

"Oh, I guess so," replied Ramanujan, mentally ignoring the suggestion to call Mr. Neville, Eric or E.H. "I was born in 1887—but late in the year."

Mr. Neville smiled. "That's settled then. Oh, I'm sorry to interrupt you like that, Alex," he said to his brother as he adjusted his thick glasses. "You were saying?" Alex shook his head and so Mr. Neville continued. "Well, I suppose we'd better get you to your room, Ramanujan. They recommend that new arrivals from India, students and such, stay for a few days at the National India Association on Cromwell Road. The plan is that after a short orientation there, you'll come to Cambridge and stay with my wife and me until we secure you some lodging. It should all be very exciting!"

Alex insisted on carrying his luggage and Ramanujan was led through customs and then to Alex's automobile. Once situated they drove from the docks into the very heart of London.

Ramanujan sat in the back seat and had a hard time engaging in conversation, although Mr. Neville kept up a running banter about the sights as they whizzed by. The automobile was loud and the city to him seemed out of control. Innumerable cars—more than he thought possible—sped down the roads giving way to huge lorries, then crept behind horse carts and hansoms, only to jump forward again to barely avoid pedestrians, hand carts, and as they got closer to the city proper, towering double-decker busses.

The bustling dockyards and crowded houses near where the *Nevasa* had berthed yielded briefly to some brown fields and open spaces to the right side away from the river. However, within minutes, massive buildings pressed on either side of the road, and although these crammed against one another, the occasional immaculate park would be miraculously revealed.

They pulled up to a four-story gray stone building and unloaded Ramanujan and his luggage. Mr. Neville went in with him, helped him get checked in, and made introductions to the administrators. One of them spoke Hindi, one Punjabi, and one Marathi, so since Ramanujan spoke only Tamil or Telegu from his native India, English became the obvious common denominator. He was to receive an orientation from two of them the next day. Once Mr. Neville had located and somewhat settled Ramanujan into his room, Mr. Neville shook his hand, assuring him that he would see him in a few days, and then departed with his brother. Alone and exhausted, Ramanujan stayed in his chambers for the remainder of the day.

He stripped down to his *veshti*, cleansed himself, and prayed for a long while. As the sun was setting, he was enticed to dinner by smells of Indian cooking and sat down to enjoy welcome dishes of *chapati*, curried peas and potatoes, *dal*, and cucumber *raita*, some of which he'd never eaten before. He, of course, did not partake of the curried chicken and lamb that was also offered. There were three other Indian students currently lodging at the NIA, and as they sat down to eat, one of them asked in English, "Welcome to England, are you going to stay here in London?"

"No," said Ramanujan. "I understand that I am going to spend a few days in this institute to become oriented, and then travel to Cambridge to meet with the professor who has invited me here."

"My friend Devinder and I also arrived recently, and we're heading to Oxford tomorrow," said the student who introduced himself as Gupta. "And this is Mr. Ramalingam, who has been in England for quite some time," indicating the third diner.

"I would suggest that you enjoy this Indian food. It may not be the best, but who's to say what will be available in Cambridge?" He then continued, in a lowered voice. "And try not to be overly influenced or offended by the 'orientation' you are expected to attend tomorrow. We have all been through it and are all in agreement that it misses the mark by a mile."

The table was replete with nodding heads. He ended up in a lively conversation with them, and it was a relief to be able to speak Tamil with Ramalingam, an engineering student who'd been residing in England over the past four years.

It turned out, as he'd been warned, that the meals and the fellow residents were the only positive aspects of his brief stay on Cromwell Road. Rather than uplifting his spirits for his impending residence in the country, the day of orientation clouded the duration of his visit in London.

During that first full day in the city, he'd met with the short Punjabi speaker, Akash, from Lahore and the lanky Hindi speaking Varma from New Delhi. They'd presided over a day filled with long lectures on the prohibitions and warnings necessary for the proper adjustment and meshing into British society.

"You must be diligent and not unconsciously revert to any bad habits while you are here," admonished Akash. "There is no urination in public, no matter how badly you have to go—and that means even by the side of the road or in the bushes. When you use the commode, as disgusting as it sounds, you should sit on it—and not squat with your feet up on the seat. These British don't use water to cleanse themselves either, but rather a ghastly paper—you will figure it out.

"No chewing of betel nut, of course, because it is very difficult to get here anyway, and definitely no spitting—even without chewing betel. When you wash your face and hands at a public sink, even then no mouth rinsing and then spitting. Drinking with a glass, your lips must touch the glass—no pouring into your mouth as we do; and don't worry the water and glasses here are very clean. Definitely never use your hands to eat, excepting that you can use a piece of bread to soak up a sauce or to push food around—and you should eat that bread after. The British find it very awkward if you squat on the ground while you are waiting or are tired. You must always find a bench or a chair to sit on, and no feet up on the chair in a squat position as well. You should sit with both feet on the floor and with a straight back. And avoid wearing anything but proper British attire, except you can..."

The list droned on and on while Ramanujan was amazed at the atrocities they thought him capable of unleashing on British society. After a break for tea, Varma took over.

"Now, Ramanujan," he began. "Many of us from India have found it very difficult to adjust to life here in England. Perhaps even Akash here is one of them."

A quick glance at Akash revealed a sheepish scowl.

"You see, we come from a warm, vast country filled with social people. England is a cold island and the people seem to mirror their country in many ways. If we are happy, we smile. If we are ecstatic, we laugh. If the British are happy, it might not be apparent, and if they are overjoyed, they might smile. On the other hand, you will rarely see a sad or stunned Englishman. They just do not seem to emote at all. Thus, you must not expect to find the same cues or reactions that you are used to seeing in social beings.

"So, on the streets, the society people will walk slowly, keep respectable distances, and nod in greeting to passersby, if they notice them at all, or nod and smile to a familiar face. It is not for us to approach, but rather to be approached; not for us to lead a conversation, but rather to be spoken to; nor for us to broach a subject that is not already under discussion.

"They say that they have no caste system here, but in actuality there is the caste of position and wealth. The higher the position, the more reserved the man. These are the people you will probably be interacting with. The poorer people and laborers are much more emotive, but unfortunately, we cannot mix with them.

"And although a tolerant society, it is a Christian society. It makes them nervous to witness prayers or *pooja*-related materials, so it is best to hide such things away. Some may be curious and ask questions, but try to remember that you represent India, and you do not want to reflect badly on our country. So, you should explain rituals, but not perform them. You know what I mean."

And this was another lecture that went on forever.

Ramanujan thought he understood. He'd just come off a boat and didn't want to convey the impression that he was still on one and not able to integrate. Still, he reflected on the voyage he'd just taken. Though he'd detected some side-long glances, his fellow passengers had been friendly and conversational to a fault. *Perhaps that was because they themselves had just been visitors in my country?*

All in all, the tenor of the lessons had been depressing, and to his mind, somewhat demeaning.

CHAPTER 11

Armed with a map and detailed written directions provided by his new friend Ramalingam, Ramanujan prepared to set out on the second day and visit the Kensington Gardens, Buckingham Palace, Westminster Abbey, and Big Ben and the halls of Parliament, or as many of those as he could reasonably manage. The controller at the Association had asked if he desired an escort or transportation, and he'd declined both. He was accustomed to walking and his horrid shoes were beginning to shape to his feet—or perhaps his feet were conforming to them.

He received last minute instructions from the doorman and stepped down onto the broad sidewalk outside the Institute. The cold wind pushing clouds that at times seemed to touch the buildings made him button his only coat as tightly as possible and wish for another layer. He'd wanted to visit a Hindu temple but was informed that, sadly, there were none in London, which probably also meant that there were none in the whole of England. Across the street from the Association building lay the imposing Natural History Museum which was of keen interest to him, however, after a solid month confined to a boat, he wanted to roam outdoors at will.

Once he'd crossed busy Cromwell Road, the perpendicular Exhibition Road was immediately much quieter as far as traffic was concerned, and to his right spread the Victoria and

Albert Museum, the entrance to which was full of peddlers selling postcards, books, and trinkets. Try as he might, he could understand only a few of the hawker's cries and come-ons. A man with a selection of black and white photographs of London and the museums approached him, but except for the initial 'Wotcha, mate,' he could barely catch a single word the man said. Varma had warned him about the varying accents, and now he understood how different the phrasings were from the proper English he'd learned in Kumbakonam and Madras.

Walking further than he expected and taking a right just before the Serpentine Lake, signage soon told him that he was now in Hyde Park which confused him, but he decided to keep going rather than retrace his steps and search out the Kensington Gardens. The lake was beautiful in the brief periods of direct sunlight, and there were several punts being poled about on the choppy water by couples doing their best to enjoy the blustery day. Once in the park proper, he found many more people strolling the paths than he expected, especially given the weather. Most of the women were dressed in ankle-length dresses or skirts, accompanied by long jackets that came down to mid-thigh, tight belts, and nearly always a decorated hat. The men wore suits often with vests, bow or neck ties, and either bowler or straw hats. Canes and parasols were everywhere.

He'd walked for ten minutes with the lake still to his left and began to feel uncomfortable. He slowed his pace and then stopped at a bench by the side of the path. *Why am I suddenly feeling so squeamish?* he wondered. He'd noticed that aside from the incomprehensible hawker at the entrance to the Victoria and Albert Museum, he had, as far as he could tell, not received a single nod, glance, or stare of any kind from anyone on his entire walk. It was like he was a ghost. Thinking about it, however, he realized that even this strange invisibility was not the cause of his mild distress.

It was the gigantic park itself. Nothing like it existed in Tamil Nadu—that he had seen, at any rate. There might be the odd pocket park in Madras or untended lots here and there, but all the rest of the land was either fully utilized or wild. For miles along flat terrain spread rice paddies, banana or palm groves, fields of maize, or plots of other vegetables. Beyond these, up in the surrounding hills, were the wilds—completely untamed lands with monkeys, tigers, snakes, bears, elephants, and deer. There was nothing in between.

Here lies a huge expanse of nothing, he thought. *And what's the purpose of these rows of arranged trees, manicured grasses, and occasional flower beds? The space isn't used by wild animals, and I don't see a single cow, sheep or horse grazing and making use of the grass. This could be built on, but it looks like it's been here as long as the old buildings that surround it. Where are the huts, children, herds, middens, cart merchants, or shrines that would immediately spring up in such an area back home? There are only people strolling.*

What a strange country is England! From what he'd read, the island had no snakes, no tigers, no elephants, in fact no real imposing wildlife of any kind. So, presumably, one could walk through forests or fields and be completely unmolested by nature. *Why maintain an area in the city that's exactly like any unpopulated part of the country on the outskirts?* he continued to himself.

I need to think more about this, he decided. *Although not when it's so cold.* And he rose from the bench to keep from freezing in the April weather. As he continued on his way, his mind immediately jumped back to a walk he'd taken with Sekar along a small road weaving through myriad rice paddies on the outskirts of Kumbakonam just at the beginning of the rice season. Vast level areas of hard red dirt filled with weeds and herds of goats during the dry season were being broken up into defined squares either laboriously by hand, or by oxen and plow. Some sections had already been flooded by water from the swelling streams, and he saw farmers in these working to form mud dykes that both divided the fields into smaller individual paddies, and diverted the water to other fields.

Using shovels with short handles that curved back just beyond the hilt of the blade, farmers dug into the wet mud and piled it onto dykes. Joining in endless patterns, the short dams were a yard across at the base, rose a yard in height, and were one foot across at the top. Mud was slapped into place and then smoothed with the outer edge of the shovel to make beautiful raised paths across the fields. As monumental as the paths appeared to be, however, Ramanujan had found that they could mysteriously appear, move, or disappear between the times he made his occasional treks out among the paddies.

As Sekar and he neared one of Ramanujan's favorite spots, he'd pulled Sekar off the small road they were following, suddenly aiming along a narrow dyke path toward the little shrine at its end. Sekar had been surprised by the change in route which led out to two huge shade trees growing in the middle of rice fields, well off the main road. To the side of the two *peepal* trees were imbedded two large vertical poles with a crossbar at the top. From the bar hung a dozen brass bells of different sizes and below the bells on a pedestal painted with vertical red and white stripes sat a statue of a *Naga*, or snake god. It was a sacred spot nestled among the fields.

"Why head over this way?" asked Sekar as they walked along the narrow, muddy dyke to reach the tiny island of tree and shrine.

"You'll see, it's just special to me," replied Ramanujan. "The way to get here seems to constantly change, but there's always a dyke that leads to it. And it's one of the most peaceful spots I've found—aside from the busy periods of the rice planting and harvest seasons, that is. No one is ever here otherwise, and I have plenty of quiet and shade to work on formulas."

They reached the spot and paid nominal respects to the spirit of the space. Where the villagers would ring the bells and have ceremonies, as Brahmins, they themselves merely respected the shrine. Then both grew quiet, sat, and gazed out over the surrounding fields, broken only by occasional palm and banana groves arising in the distance.

"You're right," Sekar had whispered. "This is a special spot."

Of course that's why they have these parks, Ramanujan now realized as he took in Hyde Park with a new appreciation. *A quiet space to think.*

Buckingham Palace had seemed grand, but hardly as imposing as Ramanujan had expected. To his mind, the Natural
History Museum had looked more like what he'd expected
for the exterior of the residence of a king. Staring through the
tall iron gates, he felt sure that it must be what lay within that
was of the most importance, since this was, after all, the seat
of the entire British Empire.

Miraculously, as this was a completely new city to him,
he'd then made his way to Westminster Abbey, only stopping
twice to ask for directions. He was anxious to witness the
devotion, rituals, and fanfare that went with the celebration
of the Christian god. Approaching from the west, he saw at
a distance the two towers that loomed over the smaller surrounding buildings. Nearing the main door between the towers, he looked up to see a clock on the left tower and a series
of carved statues above the entrance. It was very sparsely decorated from his point of view, with no color at all; at home he
was accustomed to parades of brightly painted images adorning the exterior of the entire temple structure.

Ramanujan was hesitant to enter, but saw many who didn't
appear to be British boldly push through the main doors. He
mentally prepared himself to be barred or expelled on entry,
just as a non-Hindu might be stopped from entering the inner sanctum of a temple. Trailing a large group, he worked
his way in and was immediately astounded. The height of the
ceiling equaled or surpassed the exterior of the gigantic *go-*

purams tiered above the entrances to the temple grounds in the major places of worship in Tamil Nadu, but there was no expansively open interior under the gopurams anywhere near approaching this. He craned his neck and stared up at the towering arches and where they met in intricate patterns at an incredible height. Staring ahead into the cathedral that stretched out under these arches, all the people and pews seemed insignificant, which, he realized, was undoubtedly the purpose.

He hung back near the doors to observe the devotees entering and leaving the abbey and to take note of their postures and progressions in order to see what might be expected of him. It appeared that all who entered immediately scattered at random and that no specific observances were due. He decided he wouldn't stand out, or even be noticed in this vast space, so he relaxed and began to cautiously explore, though with the niggling reminder that he was an infidel here.

Investigating some of the alcoves at the side, he was startled to hear the echo of his own footsteps. He was amazed at this for several reasons. First, other than a gentle padding sound, his feet had not produced noise inside a building for his entire life, and it was very odd to have the sound of clacking shoes magnified in such an immense and sacred space. Next, he recognized the strangeness that he should even be able to hear his footsteps in a place of worship. All the sounds in the cathedral were muted and hushed, and there was not a single bell, chime, chant, wail, drum, or song to be heard. And lastly, it came to him that the hollow sounds were at the same time echoing through what he felt to be his own cavernous loneliness.

He wandered in the cathedral and was pleasantly surprised to come upon something that he encountered daily in temples back home. People were lighting candles and then bowing in silent prayer over them. This was exactly like lighting a miniature oil lamp and offering it to the gods. Except at home, there would also be other offerings—flowers, bananas, incense sticks, and betel leaves. Then he and his fellow devotees would have an opportunity to put a red *kumkumam* on one's forehead, progress to the inner sanctum to receive a boon from a flame blessed by the god—or goddess—and receive a further mark on his forehead of sandalwood paste or colored powder. *It looks like people give offerings here, but where's the place where they get blessings in return?* he wondered.

He walked past rows of mostly empty chairs arranged along the middle corridor of the abbey and noticed what he understood to be the spot where the priest gave the blessings, far removed and above the seats.

Wishing he knew more about the ceremonies that went on here, he saw a list of services and sermons. There had been a service at 12:30 that day, and he had just missed a major celebration called Easter on the 12th. *I will be in England for a while,* he thought, *more than enough time to learn something of Christian practices.*

Seeing others sitting on benches to rest, he took a seat and was immediately enveloped by a memory from home.

235 steps: the distance from his front door to the Sarangapani temple entrance, and he counted this out every

day. At the temple, he'd walk through the gate beneath the giant *gopuram* bedecked with thirteen tiers, each packed with colorful god figures culminating in a gigantic lion head and a series of miniature golden domes barely visible from the ground. The well-worn stone slabs would feel smooth under his feet, and after continuing for a few meters he'd be out of the open courtyard and under the expansive portico with a massive flat stone ceiling supported by intricately carved square columns. These supports, though now weathered, were engraved with images of gods, the elephant-trunked *yali* creatures, and multiple ornate designs. He'd then step up, pass through the open secondary gate that was integrated into the surrounding walls and stone roof, and enter the inner temple.

The world shifted once inside the temple—dusty clay streets became the worn and cool surfaces of the massive stone floors; the heat of the sun, noticeable even in the early morning, became the cool gentle breezes circulating through multiple chambers and nooks; the bright colors so vibrant in the markets outside were muted here in the dark inner chambers; the initially high painted ceilings diminished in height to become stone passages that nearly brushed the head in the small opening leading to the temple deity, Narayana; the street noises and clatter became the echoing muted conversations and the chanted prayers of devotees and priests; and all of the random sights, sounds and smells outside the temple became those ultimately focused on the image of the god—the devotional chants with chimes and drums, and the emanations of offered butter lamps and incense.

This interior was an area contrasting in dark and light. The oldest structure at the center—created more than 2,000 years before—had sections that were accessed by narrow corridors and were always dark and temperate. There were also areas, however, that were bright as long as the sun shone—the covering portico surrounding the old shrine extended up to, but without completely touching the original structure, and in some spots the sunlight entered through these spaces in wide shafts. During the cooler morning hours, he preferred the sunlight and breezes provided by the openings to the sky and would sit off to the side on a raised platform contentedly calculating either on his slate, or on the surrounding stone surfaces with his chalk piece. When it was mid-day, he retreated into the more confined sections which were made of pale orange stone but stained mainly black from centuries of soot from oil lamps and offering fires. In places, the black surface became red or yellow from the blessing powders provided by the priests that had been rubbed into the stone by countless hands or lay in bright piles on ledges carved into the stones. The dark walls were not dull, but glistened from years of human touch or the oil from the small butter lamps. Either in the light from the sun in the mornings or in the darker more protected nooks, he enjoyed being across from the carved stone elephants and horses which symbolically drew the original temple as if it were a cart on beautifully sculpted stone wheels, the spokes of which were interspersed with human figures.

As a young man, Ramanujan had been drawn into this sanctum almost daily to pray, escape the heat, and to concentrate. Shaking his head now from this memory, his gaze slowly lifted to the immense vaulted cathedral arches so far out of reach. He expected flocks of birds or even clouds to float past at any moment.

CHAPTER 12.

Back in his room on Cromwell Road, Ramanujan was exhausted. He'd overestimated his endurance following a month of limited activity aboard the *Nevasa* and, after walking all day, the climb to his room on the third floor of the NIA had been an effort. He immediately pried off his shoes, and to his chagrin, saw that blisters had formed. It was just approaching sunset, and so he quickly walked to the washroom down the hall and brought back a basin of water. Ramanujan stripped, washed, and donned his *veshti*, then removed some small statuettes from his suitcase. He'd plucked a flower near the end of his walk and, setting it next to the small oil lamp he kept with the idols, he held a *pooja* and made offerings to the tiny figure of Lakshmi. Singing the prayers softly to himself, he knew that Namagiri Amman, as Lakshmi, was there in his mind to soothe him and open even more mathematical doors.

He then dressed again for the meal, this time without his shoes in spite of what Akash or Varma might think. The dinner offering was *dal*, rice and curried vegetables of some sort, so he was in luck—being famished from his outing, he cleared his plate and was requesting a second helping when he was joined by Ramalingam, the fellow Tamil he'd met earlier. "How was your day out in the city, Ramanujan?" asked his new friend.

"Very interesting, I must say," replied Ramanujan. "I saw the Kensington Gardens—no, the Hyde Park, the Buckingham Palace, and the Westminster Abbey, but they are much further apart than I expected, so I'm exhausted."

"Yes, London is a huge city. One must really use the busses and trams to get around, otherwise it's just too much to cover—especially in a single day. You should try them the next time—they're so convenient and really a joy to use. Oh, and everyone here calls me Ram, so you might as well, too."

"All right, and do you like it here, Ram? Do you feel comfortable here?"

"Yes, I should say so, Ramanujan. Why do you ask?"

"It may be just the climate that I find so oppressively cold, but that's my impression of the entire city—these huge stone buildings and paved streets and walkways. It's populated, but at the same time it seems empty to me."

"What do you mean?" asked Ram.

"Well," Ramanujan paused and thought for a moment. "It feels barren, doesn't it? Except for the Hyde Park, where is the dirt? Where are all of the sellers and stalls? Where are the cows, chickens, dogs, and goats? Where are the shrines and bells? It just feels like it's packed with buildings, but there's nothing here."

"I know what you mean," said his friend, "but your opinions of the place will improve. There are so many positive things in this country that will soon outweigh what you're starting to miss. This society is so well organized, and the machines run to perfection."

"But the people seem so cold. I felt like I was a ghost wandering through a desert of… no, I felt like I was the only human walking through a city of ghosts—that's it."

"Ah, but remember that you haven't made any friends here yet. Once the people get to know you, they're very kind and civil indeed. And you'll be living in Cambridge—the pinnacle of mathematical studies. I think you'll fit right in. Don't worry too much about England based only on the first day or two. And remember, this is just London, they're even more friendly in the outlying towns." Ramanujan looked doubtful, but nodded back.

The conversation turned to other subjects, and Ramanujan asked about the strange vegetables he was being fed, the accents he'd heard on the streets, and any information Ram had about Christian church rituals. Ram was forthcoming with answers, admitting that much of Christianity was still a mystery to him, and explained about services and the sanctity of Sundays.

"Only Sundays? They don't go to temple… church every day?" asked Ramanujan.

"Not that I know of, unless it's a special holiday," replied Ram. "I think there are daily services, but most people seem to only go on Sundays."

"But why the huge temples for only one day a week?" asked Ramanujan. "I have a lot to learn."

Once back in his room, Ramanujan sat on a chair in the darkened space and gazed out over the gas-lit street. Suddenly chilled, he walked over and switched on the room light and sat cross-legged on the floor with a shawl over his shoulders.

It was now obvious to him that he had no temple to attend with familiar daily rituals, no mother here in London to say prayers with, no sacred flame to provide him blessings, no friends other than Ram to speak the same language with, and no one with whom to discuss the intricacies of his religion. This would have made him despondent after such a day, but he somehow recovered and was so imbued with the substance of Vaishnavism that had been his life and breath, that Vishnu and Lakshmi were both there in front of him, and the room was full and warm.

He sang to Rama, and felt at peace:

All of your heroic deeds without omitting one,
I have inscribed on the sides of the walls of my heart.
Prince Rama who on his right bears the king-conquering axe,
Now that you've come to me, Lord, where else is there to go?

As Ramanujan lay on his bed contemplating his visit to Westminster Abbey, he closed his eyes and reflected on temple visits he'd made throughout his life in India: excitement, intimacy, camaraderie, and a feeling of complete belonging had been part and parcel of every single one.

On one trip they'd made south of Kumbakonam, his mother, his younger brother, and he had visited Alakar Koil, a major temple outside of Madurai. This had been the final resting place of Periyalvar, or the Great Alvar whose songs he and most Vaishnava Brahmins knew by heart, and who had died in the gardens there in the ninth century. They'd made the trip to view and be blessed at the temple, but especially because his mother had a great love for Periyalvar, and she wanted to pay tribute to his memory at his temple. Ramanujan had desired a pilgrimage to Nupura Gangai spring which lay two kilometers up a steep winding hillside from Alakar Koil. This was too long a hike for his mother and brother, and so he had made the trek alone, or as alone as one could be with so many enthusiastic fellow worshipers on the same footpath.

The trail followed a streambed up the untamed mountainside dense with ground vegetation and trees: banyans, various towering trunks supporting hanging vines, scattered bands of monkeys, bursts of white or yellow flowers. An increasingly thick mist permeated the spaces between the trees the higher up the hill he climbed. He remembered feeling elated—trekking in the wilderness, but still on a path that had been so well travelled by fellow devotees. He could occasionally make out the dim shapes and pick up snatches of conversation from those both ahead of and behind him. Pilgrims on their descent would appear, pass by, and then disappear back into the fog. This flow of humanity had reassured him, but he'd also been frightened at the same time—in the swirling mists how would he ever make out a tiger in time to flee?

He eventually reached an open area at the top of an alternate route wide enough for vehicles, where hired carts and hansoms, and the occasional automobile, let off the more well-to-do. He joined the busy line of pilgrims climbing the remaining long flights of steps leading up to the shrine. The stairs were enclosed by short mud walls on each side, painted in wide alternating red and white stripes. Monkeys with their frisky babies sat along the walls the entire length of the stairway anticipating the nuts or fruits the worshippers gave as offerings.

At the top of the steps was the shrine—a large square structure with a small dome at the top. Of the two possible entrances, he joined the larger, slower crush of worshippers awaiting entrance on the left. For a few *paisa* more, the corridor to the right allowed a quick entrance and a privileged route through the shrine, but he had been barely able to afford the trip as it was, so he was happy to take his time.

He was here at a *tirtha*—for a water cleansing—at the natural springs which had flowed continuously for thousands of years, as attested in ancient Tamil songs. Herded in through the entrance, he followed the progression along a series of columns and diversions and eventually came to a large square well with a dozen steps leading down to the flowing water. Like others, he held the water in his hands, took a sip, and then quickly ducked below the outflow to immerse himself in the blessings of the springs. Climbing out, he'd stopped and bought a small pot of waters from the springs for his mother, and then began the slow but joyous trip back down the hillside. He came to learn the entire family history of an older gentleman who'd just made his second pilgrimage to the springs during the long but easy walk downhill, with the mist clearing to glorious sunshine as they neared the bottom and Alakar Koil.

Honking horns jolted him back to the present, and he wrapped the shawl tightly around himself to try and get some sleep in this cold, unfamiliar, modern world.

He awoke the following morning still fatigued from the previous day's outing. Ramanujan's thighs ached and his blisters, although thankfully much better, still prevented him from easily squeezing back into his shoes. Shuffling down to the dining hall barefoot after prayers, he and his friend Ram enjoyed a breakfast of *idli*—an unexpected treat. One of the cooks had heard that both he and Ram were from Tamil Nadu and had prepared an *idli* batter the night before. It was a welcome change to the normal menu and even some of the staff partook. Ram was heading to the south of England that afternoon and so he and Ramanujan exchanged mailing addresses and farewells after breakfast.

Even though refreshed from the morning meal, Ramanujan had decided to remain in his room for the day. *It is just as well,* he thought looking out of his window. A dense and odorous fog had settled during the night and he couldn't make out the opposite side of the street let alone the museum that lay beyond. Like the fog, a vague sadness hovered over him as he felt England stealthily infiltrating and blurring some of his memories and dulling the familiarity of home and country. He already found it difficult at times to fully recall his new wife's face.

Following morning prayers on the *Nevasa*, he'd tried to immerse himself in his equations and deductions on a daily basis—either pursuing a previous line of enquiry or following the inspiration given to him by the goddess in dreams the preceding evening. However, he'd also made sure to observe routine stops for tea, meals, and conversation, and so his mathematics had suffered. Today, he concentrated on his maths and did not resurface until dinner. He wanted to be prepared for his upcoming meeting with the eminent Mr. Hardy.

Given the ebb and flow of students moving through the National India Association quarters, he seemed to have arrived for dinner at an ebb. He was the only guest present, and it was a very plain fare of boiled potatoes and beans. He idly wondered what had happened to Ravi, the cook who'd made the Tamil breakfast that very morning.

CHAPTER 13.

The next day was merely cloudy, and Mr. Neville greeted him cheerily in the lobby when he came down. Together they hailed a cab to take them to King's Cross station where they were to catch the train to Cambridge. Ramanujan marveled at the prominent twin protective glass domes which allowed natural light in but, at the same time, protected passengers from any inclement weather—a good precaution in London. As Mr. Neville went to check on the next train departure and purchase their tickets, Ramanujan surveyed the immense structure and realized that the station mirrored his impression of London—the only things that occupied the vast space were the scattered passengers and some newspaper and cigarette sellers, even though it was the busy time of day. In India, there would be crowds waiting for the next train, families camped out and building a small fire to prepare a meal, tired travelers laid out on the benches or along the floor catching up on sleep, huts and small shelters extending out from the station as railway workers or the poorest sought shelter near where they could work, collect, beg, or be near the center of transportation. Here there was no one.

Once aboard the train, Ramanujan was surprised that they were given individual cushioned seats with plenty of room between passengers.

"How was the stay on Cromwell Road?" asked Mr. Neville.

"Well, quite unexpected, I would say," murmured Ramanujan. "I actually found myself somewhat depressed following the orientation."

"Oh, no, we can't have that," said Mr. Neville. "What was it that was so disagreeable?" And Ramanujan described the tenor of the lectures he'd been given.

"Why, that's deplorable, Ramanujan!" said Mr. Neville. "It's hard to imagine people from your own country treating you like a heathen. I'll try and make sure that some words are said. And you mustn't take any of that claptrap personally. The English are a proud and dignified people, but that doesn't mean that we don't have a heart, for God's sake! I'm sure that you'll be welcomed in Cambridge with open arms. I know that my wife Alice and I are looking forward to your stay, and that will be the same with Mr. Hardy, Mr. Littlewood, and all of the others who are anxious to meet you. I'm really sorry that we didn't bustle you off to our house immediately, but the Association was so adamant that arriving scholars be introduced slowly into our society."

"Well, I feel fine now," said Ramanujan. "And did I say that I was able to see the Buckingham Palace and the Westminster Abbey?"

They talked more about the sights of London and, responding to Ramanujan's questions, Mr. Neville briefly explained about the establishment of the Church of England by Henry VIII, the directions provided in *The Book of Common Prayer*, the sacrament, and holy communion, all of which Ramanujan did his best to follow. During a break in the conversation, Mr. Neville rose to go check on the tea service, and Ramanujan stared down the carriage, again marveling at the sumptuous and orderly décor. The surprisingly familiar sounds of the rails and the rocking of the car brought him back to pilgrimage trips he'd taken by train, as he briefly closed his eyes.

The train was not just full, it was overflowing. People lay down in the overhead racks, between the feet of passengers in the crammed benches, and in the cubicles between train cars. The assigned seats were useless, but he and his mother managed to find two spots together after some cajoling on his mother's part. This was an especially short and congested segment so that not only the rooves of the cars were full, but pilgrims were even hanging off the sides of the train—the open but barred windows providing an ideal spot to grip and hang on for dear life, but he feared for them with the sudden lurches the uneven tracks caused.

The words, "Here, Ramanujan," snapped his eyes back open to the quiet, staid carriage. "I've found us a cup of tea," said Mr. Neville as he carefully set a tray on the small table he'd pulled out before them; the elegant, formal tea service suddenly made Ramanujan laugh out loud.

"What's so funny?" asked Mr. Neville with a smile as he took his seat.

"Oh, I was just thinking about Indian trains and how different this one is—so quiet, so formal."

"I've never traveled by train there, but I hear the trips are quite interesting."

"Oh, yes. As the main way to get around, they are heavily used—quite the experience, even for us."

"How so?" asked Mr. Neville.

"Well, it seems like the mood is always festive, because besides those of us trying to get from here to there for personal reasons, there are always excited groups of pilgrims who cluster together throughout the cars. Women in red saris with bright yellow borders will sit together for the trip along with their babies and squirming toddlers. And there are always proud shirtless men in either black or orange *veshtis*. Each of these different troupes is making the rounds of the pilgrimage sites."

"Red saris and black *veshtis*? What are the purposes of those?" asked Mr. Neville.

"Oh, they identify the different sects the pilgrims belong to. Each one is going to different temples, especially at the time of holy festivals," and Ramanujan paused. "Now that I think of it, there is always a holy festival going on," and they both laughed.

"And besides the pilgrims, the corridors hold a constant stream of men selling spiced and roasted chickpeas, peppery *murukkus*, dried fruits, and other snacks, and they have to weave and twist their way down the central aisle since it is always so crowded. Sometimes the carriages are so overflowing with people that the brave ones have to hang on outside." Mr. Neville shook his head at the thought. "And each new station brings a mob of vendors crowding the open windows selling an even bigger choice of meals and snacks." Ramanujan suddenly mimicked, "'*Vadai, vadai, vadai*'; '*chai, chai, chai*';

'café, café, café'; '*dosa, dosa, dosa,*'" at different pitches, and Mr. Neville chuckled.

"I also noticed that the stations here are so neat," Ramanujan continued, describing his impression on entering the King's Cross station. "Plus, if you had been to a train station in India, you would have seen that the rail bed under the platforms and out into the railyards is littered with the smashed red unglazed clay cups used for chai and coffee, so that there are piles from years of folks tossing them out as the train leaves the station."

"Well, we won't be tossing these," said Mr. Neville as he arranged Ramanujan's cup before him. Ramanujan took a welcome sip and leaned back in his cushioned seat.

"Quite festive," he murmured as he continued in a lower voice. "Besides all the chatting, groups in the rail cars will sometimes break into song, and musicians usually parade down the aisles, enlivening the crowds and taking donations along the way. Sometimes, a pair of Hijra—men or boys dressed as women in half-saris—will clap loudly three times at each bench and we give them a boon for the blessings they offer."

Just then the uniformed conductor came by and punched the tickets Mr. Neville handed him. Ramanujan smiled and took another sip of tea. "Sometimes our ticket takers are practically lost in the hubbub and confusion on a trip. This is nice and sedate—and so clean."

Mr. Neville gave him a questioning look.

"Well, if we were on an Indian train, by the time we arrived, our white *veshtis* and shirts would turn to near black in spots—especially around the armpits and down our chests and backs, or wherever we sweat. The smoke, small cinders, and sometimes even clinkers from the coal-fired engine stream back over the train and settle into the cars through the open windows." He shook his head and pretended to wipe off his suit. "I can feel the soot between my toes, in my eyes, and in my scalp even now. No wonder the pilgrims take dips in the sacred pools or line up to be doused by buckets of water at blessing stations in some of the temples."

This left Mr. Neville nodding his head in agreement. "I suppose it is a hot country, after all. Luckily, here we get to keep the windows closed!"

Alice immediately helped Ramanujan get settled into his room—gigantic to Ramanujan's eyes. After stowing his suitcase, showing him the basic layout of the house, and conversing about his trip, Alice became focused on his immediate requirements. "What would you like to eat, Ramanujan? I assume it must be vegetarian? Are you familiar with our vegetables here? Is there anything you don't care for?"

"Oh, I'm sure anything vegetarian would be fine, thank you, Mrs. Neville," said Ramanujan as he was mentally still adapting to the idea of being the guest in the home of a British family.

"Please, Ramanujan—just Alice." she admonished. "I honestly won't respond to any other name. Now, how would you like your food prepared?" she asked. "I don't have a cookbook, but I've been asking around about Indian recipes, and Eric has come back with some from India, too. He also brought back pounds of spices with him, since he loves the food so much, but I have to admit that I don't know what half of them are or how to use them."

"Really, anything would be fine," replied Ramanujan, a little overwhelmed at the questions.

"Now, now, don't stand on politeness," said Alice adamantly. "I want you to feel at home here, and I'm excited about being able to prepare something for you that you would enjoy eating."

After fifteen minutes of furiously writing down some recipes and procedures dictated by Ramanujan, she set off for the kitchen, Ramanujan in tow. He immediately took to Alice, and she reminded him of a sister he never had. After he'd helped her identify the spices and explained how each was used, she released him again into Eric's hands. Eric was just about to show Ramanujan around the house and backyard when Alice appeared again with a tray of tea and biscuits, insisting that they both go outside to enjoy the day and then quickly disappeared into the kitchen to prepare dinner.

Mr. Neville carried the tray out to the garden, "since it's so nice and warm." Ramanujan didn't want to say anything, but hoped that the slipping on of his coat went unnoticed. He was freezing, and yet everyone was exclaiming about the good weather. He cradled the hot teacup in his hands and chose the seat on the patio that was fully in the sun. In a short time, the tea and sun both helped warm him and he did agree that this was a pleasant afternoon after all.

Following tea, they took a brief walk, crossing Chesterton Road on the opposite side of the house to a narrow strip of park between the road and the River Cam. As they strolled along the lazily flowing waters, Mr. Neville pointed out the bridge that he would cross on his walk to the campus the next day, and from their position they could just make out some of the college buildings poking out above the trees. *I've actually made it to Cambridge!* thought Ramanujan on glimpsing part of the university. Some small boats were out on the river and people were using poles to push the punts about.

"What is Mr. Hardy like?" asked Ramanujan as they turned back towards the house. "I have corresponded with him, and you have told me about him in general terms when you were in Madras, but I am wondering what sort of man to expect. I mean, could you describe him?"

"Well," said Mr. Neville, "he's certainly highly regarded at Trinity. He's a member of the Royal Society, and an outstanding professor—I highly respect him. When it comes to his mathematics, I'd use the word 'rigorous' to describe him overall. I know that he loves cricket, he's not married, and he has private accommodations on campus. He's thin, and, dare I say, handsome. He can be tenacious about any issue he's passionate about. All together a true academician. You'll have to judge for yourself when you meet him, which he is very much looking forward to, by the way."

"I am, too," said Ramanujan as they made their way back to the house.

They were greeted with the smell of something burning when they entered the main hallway. "Not to worry," said

Alice as she appeared out of the kitchen wiping her hands on her apron, "a minor mishap, but that will not be what we'll be eating tonight."

As it turned out, the dinner was highly passable. The rice was cooked perfectly, the okra dish was spicier than even Ramanujan was accustomed to, and the sambar was, although including ingredients unfamiliar to Ramanujan like zucchini and a pepper that was not hot, nearly acceptable—to Indian tastes.

"I am forever in your debt for such a fine meal," said Ramanujan, now with higher hopes for British cuisine despite what he'd heard from others abroad.

That evening, alone in a strange, elegant bedroom, Ramanujan unpacked and arranged his papers for the next day. Sitting on the comfortably carpeted floor, he thought about the circumstances that had brought him to England, of all places, and how it seemed that the path of mathematics had been chosen for him.

When he was fifteen or sixteen, it had seemed that there was nothing he couldn't accomplish with numbers. Where most of his fellow students had struggled with the subject, he seemed to find the material and solutions to problems came easily to him. He was at a loss for an explanation, although he basked in the rewards.

He remembered a day after school when he'd perched on the steps to a nearby shrine in a patch of welcome shade from the afternoon sun. He'd pulled out his homework, completing the assignments in no time, when he'd glanced up and seen a small group of classmates—including some from the upper level—standing waiting for him to finish.

"What's this?" asked Ramanujan.

The student nearest him looked sheepish, but said, "My friend Kumaran said that you could solve any problem, and I'm absolutely stumped by this one," he said holding out the math primer. Ramanujan took one look and knew the answer. As he tried to explain the method for arriving at the solution, the impatient student had interrupted, "Please, Ramanujan, just the answer? I hope it doesn't offend you, but my friend also said that you were rubbish as a tutor since you say much more than is needed for the problem at hand. I'd be grateful for the answer, or a meaningful hint in the right direction, but otherwise I doubt I'll understand what you have to say."

This was the first time he'd heard this sort of bluntness about how others perceived him, and he was momentarily taken aback. Looking at the four students huddled around the first all nodding their heads, he sighed and gave them each the answer they sought.

He'd later mentioned this encounter to his friend Sekar, and the fact that all mathematics came so easily to him. Sekar had shaken his head and said, "Well, I think it's all due to your peculiar interests."

"Peculiar interests?" asked Ramanujan.

"Yes," replied Sekar. "It's peculiar that you're only interested in the Vedas and mathematics!" he said laughing. "All of the other lads are interested in music, like me, or cricket, or football, or girls, or English, or—well, anything else. You, not so much. I think it's your focus that's makes you a legend in school. Look, you even took top honors for the district, again!"

"Well, maybe not a legend," Ramanujan had said, although he was inwardly pleased by the praise.

CHAPTER 14.

Ramanujan was nervous as he accompanied Mr. Neville to Trinity College for the first time, and the cool wind on what Mr. Neville described as a beautiful morning added to the shivers that ran up Ramanujan's spine. It was a long walk, however, and Ramanujan warmed up midway through, as they left the broad expanse of open parks in Jesus Green and Midsummer Common and entered the complex of buildings that comprised Cambridge University.

Mr. Neville had gifted him an old leather briefcase in which to carry his notebooks and papers, and Ramanujan clutched it lightly, constantly changing hands. He'd wanted to be polite and so had accepted the bag, but being a Brahmin, the impure cowhide only added to his feelings of unease that morning. Mr. Neville was explaining the steps necessary to register and be officially recognized as a scholar in the school, but not much of this was able to penetrate Ramanujan's consciousness. He soon became lost in the maze of courtyards and short-cuts as he followed Mr. Neville on the path to Mr. Hardy's office.

Finally, at the top of a flight of stairs and down a creaking wood-floored hallway, they stopped in front of a solid-looking door, and Mr. Neville rapped on the oak panels, waited for a space, and then they entered.

Mr. Hardy glanced up and then rose immediately, greeting the pair with a welcoming smile. He rounded the desk and approached them; however, he didn't reach out to shake Ramanujan's hand as was the usual British custom. Hand shaking was not common in India, so Ramanujan had no preconceptions and took no offense. He'd later learn that it was a peculiarity of Mr. Hardy's that he didn't greet people in this manner.

"Welcome, Mr. Ramanujan!" exclaimed Mr. Hardy, arms thrown open wide, but obviously not for a hug. "How was your trip? We're so glad that you've finally made it to Cambridge. We have so much to discuss."

"It is such a pleasure to meet you at last, Mr. Hardy," said Ramanujan, shifting the briefcase under an arm and unconsciously bringing his palms together in front of his chest. "And it is so kind of you to pay attention to me in your letters and then bring me to England. I don't think I will ever be able to thank you enough."

"Oh, no, that is nothing compared to being able to share some of your ideas both with me and with the other fellows at the University," replied Mr. Hardy. "Please, take a seat." Ramanujan sat with the briefcase across his lap next to Mr. Neville with Mr. Hardy settling into his chair behind a desk piled high with papers. "And you're well situated at the Neville's?"

"Yes, Mr. and Mrs. Neville have been very helpful and welcoming," replied Ramanujan.

"Well, really, it's the least we can do," said Mr. Neville, "and we're happy to have you."

"Well, good," said Mr. Hardy quickly, and then leaning forward. "I'm extremely interested to hear about how you arrived at some of your results, Ramanujan, both in the letters you sent and in the notebooks that you've described. For instance, I had some questions about these equations in your first letter," and he pulled the scribbled sheet from a small pile and pointed partway down the page. "Take this integral of dx over the square root of log x plus rho of x..." Soon the two were at a blackboard and scratching out the beginnings of a derivation. Somehow Ramanujan could tell that Mr. Hardy was relieved to get right down to work rather than spend time on pleasantries.

"You see, Ramanujan," said Mr. Hardy when they arrived at a critical juncture. "I don't mean in the least to be condescending, since you've come up with some brilliant work in the letters here and in your notebooks, I'm sure, but I can't help but both lament and rejoice that you were only self-taught in your pursuit of these theorems. I see such sparks of genius, and frankly, have no idea how you were able to come up with some of the results I've seen. That being said, however, if you'd been properly trained you would've known that some of these have already been solved, or proved to be false, by some of the best minds of their times. Rather than repeating their work you would've been able to stand on their shoulders and reach even higher, so to speak, or not have wasted time duplicating their mistakes. And all that you've recorded here still needs to be proved, step by step. I'm not saying that your approach is wrong, and don't be discouraged in the least, but until each point can be verified and confirmed based on existing or new proofs, they're interesting but not yet useful results."

Ramanujan wore an enigmatic smile, trying to process what he was hearing.

"And, I might add," Mr. Hardy paused with a barely audible sigh. "You rely, perhaps, overly much on your intuition, without thoroughly investigating all of the implications. For instance, in your letters to me dealing with prime numbers, and concerning the zeta function which you know is an important component of the equation for estimating the count of them, you skip over the ramifications inherent in where the function leads to zeros. There are, of course, the trivial zeros of the function—it goes to zero at all the even negative numbers, as you are well aware. You've been out of touch, however, with the very thread concerning the non-trivial zeros that originated with Euler and Gauss. The heart of the issue was dealt with a century ago when Riemann made the hypothesis, as part of the estimation of the number of primes along the number scale, that, indeed, all the non-trivial zeros of the zeta function occur along the critical line where the complex number $\frac{1}{2} + xi$ has the real part one half and an imaginary part for some value of x. We're just beginning to finally delve into the values that lead to those zeros. Since the zeta function is used in an integration, these zeros are critical, and cannot simply be ignored, as you have done."

Mr. Hardy moved from the chalkboard and pointed to a picture of a dark-haired man with round spectacles and a thick bushy beard hanging on the wall behind his desk.

"This is the estimable Mr. Reimann," he said, and continued. "The thing is, his hypothesis has never been proved, and so it's like your intuitive results. Yet the Riemann hypothesis is so important, so pivotal, that mathematics is evolving around it regardless of the evidence of proof. I, myself, have just completed a paper titled 'Sur les zeros de la function $\zeta(s)$ de Reimann' proving that there are, indeed, an infinity of such numbers for x that lead to zero, but I can't prove the Reimann hypothesis itself—we should go over my paper at our next meeting so that I can take you through the steps I took to get there. So, you see, I understand the value of intuition but, except in rare cases, I feel that we must provide all the steps that others will need in order to follow and build on what we've done. We don't want to make a supposition, as did Riemann, without providing access to its secrets."

Looking at Ramanujan for a moment, he added, "Or, perhaps in Riemann's case, we do."

"Yes, Mr. Hardy," said Ramanujan, outwardly portraying the picture of calmness. "I look forward so much to working with you to, as you say, be more rigorous in detailing all of the steps."

Inwardly he was absolutely crushed, but he grasped at the parts that were more positive in what he'd just heard than those that were negative and didn't slip into the feelings of dejection that would occasionally overwhelm him.

Sensing his discomfort, Mr. Neville interrupted and said, "Perhaps we should take care of some of the registration paperwork now, and then you two could find some uninterrupted time later on to discuss all of these intriguing issues."

"Ah, yes, of course, of course" sighed Mr. Hardy wiping chalk from his hands. "Why don't we have some tea sent up and we can fill out these forms and then Neville can take you around and get you settled before we get started on more important matters."

They completed some paperwork and enjoyed tea that had been brought in. "Do you follow cricket at all, Ramanujan?" asked Mr. Hardy, and Ramanujan shook his head. "Well, of course not—India doesn't even have a team. I just thought that some of the British chaps might play some local games. No?"

"No, Mr. Hardy, I'm not even really sure what cricket is."

"Well, it is the most fascinating game, and I must introduce you to it at our pitch sometime," and then he began to describe the rules of the game and the status of teams in the area.

After tea, Mr. Neville took Ramanujan in for registration, and then gave him a quick tour of the colleges so that Ramanujan could get his bearings. Ramanujan asked if they were going back to Mr. Hardy's office, but it was mid-afternoon and Mr. Neville explained, "I don't think we'd find him in his office even though you're here and he's excited to meet with you. He has a habit of walking and taking in a cricket match, or playing tennis in the afternoon, and today is a cricket match he was especially keen on watching."

So, the pair were back at the Neville's by teatime and he and Mr. Neville went over a problem that Ramanujan had solved the previous day. Mr. Neville said that much of it was beyond him, but he followed Ramanujan's explanations with interest anyway.

Ramanujan had quickly settled into a comfortable routine. After his early morning cleansing and *pooja*, he'd join the Nevilles at breakfast and enjoy a fare that he'd found to be agreeable—some toast with mild cheese and a banana. Together over tea, or the rare cup of coffee, they'd discuss the news and plans for the coming day, and then he'd leave for the University, usually accompanying Mr. Neville. After arriving at Mr. Hardy's rooms and following a brief exchange of small talk with Mr. Hardy, he'd arrange his papers while the customary morning tea was served again there. Mr. Hardy would finish reading the early edition paper with the cricket scores from the previous day, and then the two would set to work. Often, they'd be joined by Mr. Hardy's closest colleague, Mr. Littlewood. They would break for a late, or sometimes very late, lunch, and then Mr. Hardy would spend the afternoon outdoors while Ramanujan would remain in the rooms and either continue his own work, follow a line of investigation laid out by Mr. Hardy, or resume a session with Mr. Littlewood.

At the end of the second week, however, something had changed. Mr. Neville had already left for his office and yet Ramanujan was still lingering over breakfast.

"Aren't you going to be late for your meeting with Mr. Hardy, Ramanujan?" asked Alice as she came into the dining area and began to clear the dishes from the table.

She'd caught him lost in thought, and he startled slightly at her question. "No, I may not go to my meeting today," said Ramanujan.

Thinking that he looked somewhat down, and detecting the same thing in his voice, she said, "Why? Is something wrong? Homesick perhaps?"

Ramanujan shook his head and stared at his empty teacup.

"What is it then, Ramanujan? What can I do to help?" asked Alice becoming concerned and sitting down across from him.

"Oh, it is nothing," he said.

"Well it's certainly something—you were so excited to be here and excited to meet Mr. Hardy, and now you may skip a meeting with him? Are you feeling ill? Should I take you to a doctor?"

"No, Alice," said Ramanujan and then hesitated. "You see, I do not think that Mr. Hardy is pleased with me or my work."

"Whyever do you say that?" asked an astounded Alice.

"Well, I thought he was happy with my coming here at first, but now all I am hearing about are the mistakes I have made on a divergent series and that he wants everything spelled out on other equations where the results are right there, staring him in the face. He is simply not satisfied with what I have shown him."

Alice smiled slightly and said, "I believe that is just Hardy being Hardy."

Ramanujan raised his eyebrows and asked, "What do you mean?"

"First off, I want you to know that Hardy and Littlewood are ecstatic to have you here and are raving about your work. Eric told me so again just this morning," said Alice. "From what I know of Hardy and from what Eric's said, he's obsessive about the details—that's just him. It's probably not what you've come up with, but how you've presented it that's the problem for him. I wouldn't worry about the quality of your work based on Hardy's reaction to some of those details."

"But he is saying that it appears to be inferior work to him," said Ramanujan sadly.

Alice thought for a moment and then said, "I know—perhaps it's like this. You speak English, and very well I might add, isn't that right?"

Ramanujan nodded and said, "I try my best..." at the compliment.

"But you do speak it with a foreign accent, don't you? You can't help it—that's just how you speak our language, it's how you learned it."

Ramanujan nodded again.

"I think that Hardy, Mr. Hardy, is happy with your English—your equations, if you see what I mean, but is just trying to convert them from Indian English into proper... British English. My guess is that the meaning is solid, he's just trying to get it into the form that everyone else is used to hearing. Does this make sense?"

Ramanujan was about to protest, but then slowly smiled. "Yes, when you put it that way, I think I see what you are saying. That may be exactly what he is doing. Thank you, Alice—I think I understand." He somewhat formally folded his napkin and stood. "Well, I had better be going now or I am going to be late," and he carried an air of renewed confidence to Alice's eyes as he headed for his coat and briefcase near the door.

On his way to Trinity College a few days later, the late-blooming yellow daffodils along the walkway seemed bright enough to blind him. Above them, the blossoms on the cherry trees filled the branches to bursting with a subtly pink version of white. Each intake of breath provided a new scent of some flower or bush in bloom. The smells from the newly opened lilacs were incredible. He was amazed at the numbers and diversity of flowers that he saw planted in boxes on window-sills, in gardens, and growing seemingly wild along the paths and in the fields, and he took these all in as he made his way toward Mr. Hardy's office.

He'd thought that India seemed to be full of flowers, but there were really very few varieties, and they never approached the profusion that he saw all about him in Cambridge in the spring. At home, there were frangipani, lotus, hibiscus, water lilies, magnolia, *ashoka*, many types of jasmine, marigold, and roses. Most of these he saw as already plucked blossoms in the markets or temples, but rarely growing in front of someone's house. Spring was definitely a time for nature's showy displays, and England was awash in the spectacle the gardeners had obviously so carefully tended and prepared in the previous seasons.

Noticing a splash of red flowers leading up to a doorway took him back to Navratri, the festival of nine nights—three nights dedicated to each goddess, Lakshmi, Durga, and Saraswati. At each sunset during Navratri he'd stroll past displays of oil lamps set along courtyard walls and enter the small shrine nearby their house that held an image of Durga and watch the *poojas* being made to her. Nostalgically, he remembered a temple elder grasping a gigantic paddle and stirring a huge vat of festival rice being made for the worshippers. Each day of the festival, the temple had been filled with red hibiscus and rose flower offerings to the goddess. It was forbidden to destroy the flowers, and so the petals that eventually fell from the garlands or displays were swept into a pile on some banana leaves that had been laid out at the base of the goddess. By the end of the festival the mass of red and green petals and sepals reached up to the feet of the Durga image positioned on a small platform a yard off the floor.

Ramanujan gazed out across a multi-colored carpet of flowers in the nearby park and wondered what sort of celebrations accompanied these gorgeous springs in England.

"Hello, Ramanujan," greeted Mr. Hardy as Ramanujan took off his coat. "How was your walk this morning?"

"Oh, very good, Mr. Hardy," replied Ramanujan. "I was just thinking how much the flowers here remind me of home, and yet we have hardly any of these same types. There is such a profusion here."

"Yes," said Mr. Hardy. "I understand it is a bit of a cliché—you do know that word, don't you?"

"I do not believe so," said Ramanujan, shaking his head.

"Well, it's nothing that a mathematician would need to know, unless you were a public-school teacher, perhaps, but 'cliché' is a French word for something that's not only well known, but even a bit overdone, if you see what I mean. So, it's a bit of a cliché that the English love their gardens. In fact, gardening is even the retirement goal of many people here."

"Well, I love looking at them even if they are clichés," chuckled Ramanujan, and then picked up a piece of paper he'd brought. "I believe you might find this very interesting," said Ramanujan, and thus began another day.

After his initial misgivings, Ramanujan was relaxing and becoming more optimistic that he'd made the right decision. He'd loved Alice's analogy and kept it in mind when working with Mr. Hardy. He'd come to a foreign country where his English was passable, though not perfect nor proper, and was speaking to a person who knew no Tamil. In the language of mathematics, however, they were both completely literate, although they expressed themselves with slightly different accents. And Mr. Hardy seemed to be very interested not only in his work, but also in helping to assure that some of his findings were published—in the standard tongue.

It was apparent to both that they came at the problems from what always seemed to be completely different directions. Ramanujan had difficulty in explaining how he'd arrived at a result—many of the answers had, after all, been revealed to him by his goddess, or given to him in very real and compelling dreams. He quickly learned that this was not an acceptable source of inspiration to the Western mathematics community, and so he was left struggling to provide the tedious links between initial proposal and inspired result.

Mr. Hardy, on the other hand, and to his immense credit, was very much a stickler for rules. He had explained several times that the entire foundation of mathematics was built on the ability to prove—in intricately verifiable steps, no less—how one got from the first to the final point. "One missing step means," Mr. Hardy had tried to emphasize, "that no journey has, in fact, ever taken place." Those words and his emphasis that 'mathematics was not trust; it was verity' were slowly drilled into Ramanujan's head.

CHAPTER 15

"Are you all right?" asked an alarmed Mr. Neville, slapping Ramanujan on the back. "Here, drink some of this," he said holding a glass of water up to Ramanujan's lips.

The personal contact, a glass on his lips, and it being held in Mr. Neville's left hand all went by in a blur as Ramanujan fought for breath.

Coughing, he was finally able to say, "Yes, I am fine. It was only a piece of food eaten too hastily."

"And you are healthy, aren't you?" asked Mr. Neville once Ramanujan had recovered and was able to continue with dinner. When answered with a questioning stare, he added, "Well, I worry about the health of your entire colony. I've been meaning to enquire, and this may be indelicate of me, but is it possible that most of the people in Madras and the rest of India have tuberculosis?"

"What?" asked Ramanujan. "Why do you ask that? We are a very healthy and robust country—for the most part, of course."

"I was afraid to raise the question when I was there," said Mr. Neville. "But I became so concerned and unnerved when I saw all of the blood being spat onto the ground. Everywhere I looked there seemed to be big splotches of red on the roads, and I even saw some people spitting out blood. I was fearful that I might contract something, so I made sure to keep my shoes outside of my room every night and washed my hands constantly."

Ramanujan thought for a moment and then laughed. "Ah! I see!" he exclaimed. "No, you have misinterpreted what you were seeing."

"Well, bloodshot eyes and red lips and tongues from the blood is hardly a mistaken observation…" began Mr. Neville.

"Yes, but it was not blood," smiled Ramanujan. "It was betel."

"What?" asked Mr. Neville incredulously, and after a long pause, "Oh, I've heard of betel, of course, but does that cause their mouths to bleed? I thought for sure that the cause was TB."

"It was not blood; it was juice from chewing betel. I of course don't chew, but I have seen it many times in the shops. The sellers lay out a betel leaf, smear it with lime paste, add some areca nuts, saffron, clove, tobacco, and other things and then wrap the leaf into a little packet. When the people chew it, it creates a red spittle that goes everywhere—it must cause them to salivate like hungry dogs because they spit all of the time."

"What a relief!" exclaimed Mr. Neville. "I was worried for your entire race."

"I assure you that I am as healthy as…" said Ramanujan and hesitated.

"We say as healthy as a horse." smiled Mr. Neville.

It was a Sunday, and, as such, he was not to meet with Mr. Hardy. Alice and Mr. Neville were going to a noon church service and had asked Ramanujan if he wanted to accompany them, but he'd declined. As interested as he was in learning about Christian rituals, this invitation had seemed like too much of an intrusion into the private lives of the couple. He was also now aware that Sunday was the only day of the week the pair had to worship, and to him it was of paramount importance not to interfere since they didn't partake in daily rituals.

Alice was excited for him to be introduced to western classical music, and so had set up the phonograph to play some selections by Mozart while they were away at church. He'd heard some western music in India since several popular songs had made it to Madras and Sekar had sung quite a few, including "Bill Bailey, Won't You Please Come Home." Naturally, formal British concerts were performed in Madras, but he'd never had the desire, status, nor the money to attend. Then there was the uniformed brass band that performed at civic functions—easy to discount as music and hard to ignore as noise.

Ramanujan had to adjust his ears to even begin to enjoy the music as the record began. There was no percussive beat to follow, but the strings often created some occasionally complex rhythms as part of the melody. And an even bigger adjustment was needed in order to try and understand the very strange but pleasing overlay of notes all being played at the same time. To his ear the music sounded odd, but he could see where he could grow to like it.

Our music is much more based on rhythm, thought Ramanujan, recalling a concert that featured his friend Sekar after he had become proficient on the *mridhangam*—a long drum with two heads on opposite ends. Held sidewise on the lap, both ends could be played simultaneously. Sekar's teacher had clapped out the eight-count beat while a tambura played a slow series of four notes in the background. Sekar had been just marvelous. Starting simply, he'd progressed into the most complex rhythms—but each time ending the solo with a final beat that matched the eighth beat of the overall pattern. Before the end he had been getting cries of appreciation from the audience as he resolved his improvisations precisely on cue. The crowd had gone crazy at the end of the performance. He thought proudly that Sekar was on his way to becoming a true, highly acclaimed musician.

The recording concluded, but Ramanujan had Sekar's *mridhangam* pinging away in the back of his mind.

CHAPTER 16.

It was the beginning of the summer, and Ramanujan took in his new rooms on campus with a mixture of both contentment and sadness. He'd let it be known that he wanted to be located nearer to Mr. Hardy to be able to spend more time with his advisor and, now, colleague. But truthfully, since he spent the bulk of most days with Mr. Hardy anyway, it really came down to the walk from the Neville's house to the college as the reason for the move. Ramanujan was not averse to the exercise, and in fact would walk for miles to reach a shrine or ceremony at home, but here in England it was different.

His feet were still not adapted to the shoes he wore to reach campus, giving him constant pain, and indeed he often flopped about in a pair of fleece-lined slippers the Neville's had found for him when shoes weren't absolutely necessary. So, the daily journey to the college had become stuck in his mind as some kind of torture, and adding to it, the weather was not usually the best. Plus, he felt that he was somehow wasting time on the walk to Trinity College even though he often found himself with productive thoughts during the hike.

Unfortunately, in making the move onto campus, he also carried with him a pronounced regret at leaving the Neville's. Here was a loving couple who'd become like a family to him. Alice, especially, was as attentive to his needs as a mother would be and anticipated nearly all obstacles and smoothed any of the social bumps he'd encountered. He truly felt that he could relax around them both, and the three enjoyed each other's company immensely. Still, they were a couple, and he knew that the days he spent in the house were an intrusion on their privacy and that they had their own lives to lead and interests to pursue.

Mr. Neville was instrumental in procuring the rooms for him on Whewell's Court that lay along the outer edge of the college, and Ramanujan reiterated how grateful he was when Mr. Neville had helped him with the move. It was a shame that Mr. Neville's mathematical field did not coincide with his own, because he was a good mathematician, and the two of them got on famously.

They'd agreed beforehand that Ramanujan would join the Nevilles for Sunday breakfast or dinner when he could, and they'd stressed that he was welcome at any time to stop in for tea.

As happy as he was to be nearer to the heart of his work, Ramanujan felt cold and empty the first nights in his new lodgings despite the mid-summer warmth. The sparseness of his rooms, populated with only a study desk and chair, an eating table with two dining chairs, a small kitchen alcove, a bed, a dresser, and a side table, seemed bare and hollow compared to living in the Neville's comparatively grand house. And yet, these new lodgings were in many ways more spacious than his home in India. His apartment was nearly the same size as their entire house in Kumbakonam, and here he had all this space to himself.

He'd been amazed at the number and variety of possessions held by the English. Alice and Mr. Neville kept a beautiful home and populated it with multitudes of pleasing objects. Carpets on the floors, pictures on the walls, amazing light fixtures hanging from the ceilings. Alice had a cabinet for all the china, glasses, and silverware needed to make dinner an elegant affair. She also had two special cabinets with glass doors that kept lovely figurines and cut-glass dishes safe from dust. Several small tables had the sole purpose of holding vases or providing a spot to put down a drink. The marvelous phonograph machine itself was wrapped in a gorgeous wooden cabinet with beautiful floral inlay.

A small library was overflowing with books of all types, and Ramanujan had spent hours thumbing through the volume—Mr. Neville's mathematics books, especially—but also many of the volumes that consumed the varied interests of him and Alice.

The kitchen was filled with utensils, most of which left him clueless as to their purpose. It also contained tubs of grains, jars of spices, and even a special cabinet for pies and breads, all these helping fill a space cluttered with an enormous variety of pots and pans. There was, incredibly, an ice chest for storing meats and cheeses and small stands for holding dishes above a flame to keep them warm.

He'd quickly become accustomed to the feeling of luxury and prosperity that emanated from each room, and it was somehow humbling to move back into confines much more similar to his sparsely decorated home in India.

He'd also privately wanted to move closer into the campus to reduce the unpleasant encounters his old route had sponsored. On one particular day, he'd been nearing the Queen's Gate that led from Great Court to Trinity Lane, his usual path from the Neville house to Mr. Hardy's rooms in the New Court, when a group of students had veered toward him. He'd kept to the side of the walkway near the grass, feeling somehow wary but not threatened. He'd been aiming for the gate when one of those passing him had yelled, "Hey, Fakir!" which Ramanujan had heard as "Hey, faker!" since he didn't speak Arabic, and was unfamiliar with the commonly used term. This shout had been immediately followed by "Where's your flute and your snake in a basket?" The pack had halted his progress by forming a semi-circle around him and had then laughed at his confusion. One or two had suddenly lunged at him and even given him a little shove. Unsure what to do, Ramanujan had stood still and kept his eyes on the ground. Another burst of laughter, some jeers, and then the group had continued on its way. They hadn't hurt him physically, but to him, it was the same as if they had.

His heart had raced as he'd entered Trinity Lane and stopped to think, *What did that mean, 'faker'? And the comment about a snake?* Then he'd realized that they'd thought he should be a snake charmer with a cobra in a woven basket. But a faker?

Oh, he'd thought. *They think I am faking being British and lying in my reason for being at this University. Or, what if they think I have misrepresented myself and my qualifications to Mr. Hardy?*

Seeing himself as somehow exposed and vulnerable, this had set off a tumultuous series of doubts and self-criticism that had festered for days. He'd previously been called "Big Black Sambo" which had made no sense to him at all, except that he was big, and to them, black. He'd asked Alice, who was furious upon hearing this, what the moniker had meant, and she'd explained that a very popular children's book named "Little Black Sambo" had come out about fifteen years before and was about a South Indian who'd fooled some tigers into turning themselves into butter. *Not such a bad story after all,* he'd thought, but it had still stung. And then there had been the sneering senior who twice had sung to him in some tune he didn't recognize, "Hindooooo man, go back to Hindooooostan."

On the day of the 'faker' insult, he'd calmed somewhat when he'd reached Mr. Hardy's offices, and knocking at the door and opening it, had taken off his coat and hung it shakily on the coat stand.

"Welcome, Ramanujan," had greeted Mr. Hardy. "I was just thinking about the convergence of this series...."

It had taken a while for Ramanujan to work himself back into mathematics. The faces of his taunters had floated before his eyes, and he'd been at a loss to find the emotions to deal with them.

He'd sent a letter to the North's residence once he had a reliable return address at the Neville's. After Ramanujan had moved into the rooms at Trinity College, Mr. Neville stopped by on his way to his own office bearing some mail.

"Hello, Ramanujan!" he exclaimed, glancing around the room. "It looks like you're settling in well here. How are your kitchen staples doing? Have you been able to prepare meals?"

Ramanujan laughed. "You are just like an Indian, Mr. Neville. The first thing out of your mouth is 'Have you eaten yet?' Yes, I am doing fine, and you must thank Alice for the delicious breakfast on Sunday."

"Of course, and you know that we miss you in our house, and that you're welcome back at any time if this doesn't work out," said Mr. Neville. "How is your stomach today?"

"I think it is much better," replied Ramanujan. "I used to get terrible side-cramps in Kumbakonam just like those I had at your house on Sunday, and I'm sure it is nothing."

"Well, that's good to hear, but we can also arrange for you to see a doctor if you think you need one. Do you want me to set something up? Our own doctor is very good and has an office nearby."

"No, thank you. I am fine."

"Well, this isn't the first time you've been hit by these pains, so let me know if it gets worse." Ramanujan nodded in reply. "Oh, and here are these," said Mr. Neville, handing Ramanujan a bundle he'd wrapped in paper. "I've brought some paperwork that the College had sent to you at our address, as well as some mail, including packets from India and a letter from the Norths. Would this be the Amanda North that you told us about from your voyage over here?"

"Yes, that is her, and thank you for bringing the mail by," said Ramanujan. "If you don't mind, I can read her letter now and let you know what it says. We are arranging for Amanda to meet with me for math tutoring."

Mr. Neville nodded, and Ramanujan read the letter quickly to himself.

He sighed. "Apparently, Amanda has had a relapse of the illness that afflicted her on the *Nevasa*. The doctors are now at a loss as to the cause of the fever. She is not quite well enough to travel here, but the Norths are wondering if I might be able to come and visit them during the Christmas break."

"That sounds wonderful," said Mr. Neville. "We're also hoping to spend time with you over Christmas, but can adapt to any schedule that you have."

"All right then. I will write to them and accept their invitation and let you know what days they have planned," said Ramanujan.

He again thanked Mr. Neville as his friend continued on to his office, and he sat down to read his mail and to compose a letter to the Norths.

He eagerly sifted through the remainder of the mail in the small pile. Among the letters he received from India was one from his friend Rao, one from his mother, but none from his wife. He quickly scoured the letter from Komalatammal for any mention of Janaki. He'd asked specific questions of his mother about his wife, but once again there was no mention of how she was—not a single word. *She's driving me crazy!*

he thought as his imagination began to spin with possibilities. *What's going on with them?*

Lately, if he wasn't thinking about mathematics, his mind found itself going back over the well-worn paths of speculation about the condition of things at home. He sent letters and money to Kumbakonam regularly, and he heard back all sorts of trivia and reports of his parents and friends, but news of Janaki was conspicuously absent. Since he received no communication from his wife, his mind was free to imagine and worry about what was really happening with her.

He wrote letters to Janaki almost weekly, but hadn't received a single reply other than two brief notes when he first arrived in England. In his attempts to fathom the cause of her stony silence, the most frequent explanation he came to was that she was disgusted with him no longer being a pure Brahmin. He was sure that in her eyes, he'd been defiled by this entire venture of coming to England, and since he no longer followed his precepts as a Vaishnavite, she was having nothing more to do with him. In every letter, he made sure to emphasize his strict adherence, or as strict as he could find possible outside of India, to his caste and his religion. He only ate vegetarian food, now cooked mainly by himself, and engaged in no other unseemly practices.

He also often stewed that perhaps she was ashamed of his lack of success in England. So, in his letters he routinely included the status of his studies and chronicled the papers he'd written that were already published or were due to be put into print. He wasn't a failure here, but he wasn't sure that she was aware of the fact.

Now, after several months with no communication, Ramanujan was slowly awakening to the shame of possibly losing a wife due to his journey to Cambridge. He reread the letter from his mother and caught himself up on events including the lives of his father, brother, and others in Kumbakonam. The mail stack also included many letters from friends who were excited upon learning of papers he'd published, and they included descriptions of the compliments and exultations they'd heard from members of the academic community back in Madras. *I'll read them again later,* he thought, as he absentmindedly dribbled the papers back onto the table. He went to the small fireplace, built a fire, and sat huddled on his haunches gazing into and through the flames. Perhaps it was because of his recent talk with Mr. Neville, but the pain in his side seemed to become suddenly worse as he thought of home.

Both Mr. Hardy and the Nevilles had urged him to eat at the dining hall with the rest of the college. "Not only does it make cooking unnecessary, but it's also an excellent chance to socialize and meet some of the other lads," Mr. Hardy had said. So, Ramanujan had decided that since he was now settled into his new lodgings, he'd try the meals there and he joined the stream of Trinity scholars making their way to dinner one evening.

The huge hall was filling with students, and he could make out Mr. Hardy and Mr. Littlewood already ensconced and engaged in conversation with other professors at the head table under the beautiful wood paneling and scrollwork running up the end wall. He found a spot on a bench near the rear that was not yet full and took a seat as two underclassmen squeezed in on either side of him. "Mallory," said the one on his left and "Fitzgerald," said the student on his right as he introduced himself and shook their hands. "I haven't seen you here before," said Mallory slowly and distinctly, "which department are you in?"

"I'm working with Mr. Hardy on mathematics," said Ramanujan, not going into the fact that he wasn't, strictly speaking, a student.

"Hey, you're English is very good," said Mallory, "wasn't expecting that. We're studying Latin under Housman." A blank look from Ramanujan prompted, "A.E. Housman? *A Shropshire Lad*?" When Ramanujan shook his head, Mallory said "Oh, for God's sakes," and then began to talk with Fitzgerald about the difficult translation they were working on as if Ramanujan wasn't sitting between them.

Goblets were set in front of them and red wine was poured from a large silver pitcher into each glass. Taking a break from their discussion, the two boys offered to toast with Ramanujan, but knowing it was alcohol, Ramanujan refused to touch the cup. "Too good for us?" asked Fitzgerald.

"No, no, I just can't drink wine," said Ramanujan, reaching for his water glass. "Will this do?"

"I suppose," said Fitzgerald, "but you don't know what you're missing!" The two touched their glasses with his and then continued again with their conversation, speaking louder and louder as the din from other's voices and clinking silver-ware filled the cavernous hall.

What an odd custom, clinking glasses, thought Ramanujan as plates were finally set before their table. In a reflex reaction, he nearly pushed the plate away. Roast beef, glistening potato, and boiled spinach lay before him, the juices from the roast running under the vegetables. *I suppose I can try the potatoes,* he thought since he was suddenly very hungry. He speared one with his fork, but noticed some brown bits clinging to it. "Excuse me," he interrupted Mallory and Fitzgerald, "do you know what these brown pieces are?"

"Well, I suppose that's the bacon," said Mallory, spearing a potato himself and taking a bite. He nodded, "Yep, it's bacon."

An expression of relief crossed Ramanujan's face and Mallory asked, "Just what you've been waiting for?"

"No, actually, I'm not feeling that well today," said Ramanujan. "I think I'll return to my room."

"But you haven't even tasted it," said Mallory.

"No, I think that will only make my stomach worse," said Ramanujan, secretly glad that he'd thought to ask about the potatoes. "It was nice meeting you," as he got up from his seat and headed for the exit.

"What an odd duck," he heard Fitzgerald say as he was nearly out of earshot. "Yeah, and a very black one at that," said Mallory.

Ramanujan had mixed emotions as he returned to his apartment. He hadn't felt welcome at the table, but at the same time he could see how everyone else fully enjoyed the camaraderie, food, and wine. Thinking back to some of the crowded tea stalls he'd eaten at in Madras, he could see how they all felt right at home, and once more he became achingly homesick.

"So, if you won't eat in the dining hall, who's feeding you?" Mr. Hardy had asked after he'd heard that Ramanujan had shown up but left before the meal had even begun.

"Oh, I cook for myself or sometimes have friends over and have them join me for tea or a dinner," Ramanujan had replied.

"And you can find the time for this? The dining hall provides excellent meals, you know, Ramanujan."

"Yes, I know, but to tell you the truth, there is a lot of meat served at the hall, and I am a strict vegetarian," Ramanujan had replied.

"Well then, what about fish or chicken? Those are often on the menu," Mr. Hardy had asked.

"I'm sorry, but I don't take fish or chicken either," Ramanujan had said.

"Really? Only vegetables?"

"Yes, but Indian food is delicious if cooked properly, and that is what I am accustomed to," Ramanujan had said. And then on an impulse he'd invited Mr. Hardy to join him and a small group of friends in his quarters a few nights later for an Indian vegetarian meal.

Back in his apartment, Ramanujan thought about how perceptive Mr. Hardy had been in worrying about the time it took to prepare meals. Food preparation had expended first his mother's and then also his young wife's constant waking moments. It was so time-consuming that they'd arise before daybreak to begin the daily ritual of bringing food out for each meal.

The early-morning delivery of milk, either straight from the cow led to the front door or delivered in a brass pitcher, would be divided so that some could later be boiled to make coffee, and the remainder could be set aside to make yogurt for the meals. The milk destined to become yogurt would be poured into a pot to which some of the previous day's yogurt culture had been added, and by dinner, the pot left sitting out in the heat of the day would provide the fresh yogurt for that meal and breakfast the next day.

Spices were essential and took time to prepare—cumin and coriander seeds, peppercorns, chilies; cardamom pods either whole or broken open, stripped of the inner seeds and ground; turmeric—and, if they were lucky, saffron—cloves, asafetida, fenugreek, nutmeg, bay leaf, and curry leaf would each be ground dry into powders, ground together in required amounts into pastes, or individually added to dishes as they cooked. The combinations of these spices into each designated mixture were either family secrets, common blends, or rarer specialties formed from countless permutations of ingredients.

His mother was especially proud of her sambar recipe. Made of vegetables—snake gourd, tomatoes, green beans, and others—some water, her special sambar spice mix, lentils, and fresh tamarind water, the ingredients would simmer all morning until done. The resulting delicious odors would permeate the house and create a heavy anticipation for lunch or dinner.

Sambar would go over *idli* or *dosa*—but especially over rice with different sambar recipes used for each dish. Both *idli* and *dosa* were the lovely fermented rice/*urad dal* main dishes—*idli*s, a steamed ovoid cake, and *dosa*, a crispy thin pancake. His mother never said but he suspected that both came from the same time-consuming batter. In the morning, she'd soak a few handfuls of *urad dal* and of rice in separate bowls. In the afternoon she'd drain the *dal* and put it in the large stone mortar and pestle grinder that had been with her since she was a young wife. Adding back some of the drained liquid, she'd grind until the *dal* was a soft mass. Next, she'd do the same with the rice and then mix these two together in a large bowl, throw in some salt, and cover it overnight. Late the next morning the fermented batter would be ready to steam as *idli*s in pieces of cotton cloth, or fry on a *tava* for the flat *dosa* pancakes, and he'd be ready for brunch, the first real meal of the day. She'd also have made a coconut chutney with cilantro to go with the *idli*, or perhaps *idli podi* powder mixed with oil—either way he found that he had no trouble keeping in a fit round shape with his mother's cooking.

Ramanujan was nervous. As he was making friends on campus, and word of his notoriety was spreading throughout the

Indian community, more and more people were showing up at his door to socialize, and he'd occasionally prepare dishes for them. However, he'd never cooked for his mentor and wondered how Mr. Hardy would receive an Indian meal. Mr. Hardy was joining them in a simple dinner Ramanujan was hosting to celebrate the engagement of his new friend, Chatterji, who was bringing his fiancé and a friend of hers, and they'd agreed to provide some snacks. Ramanujan spent the day making *rasam* soup with a side of rice and was going to follow up with some sweet *pongal.*

Chatterji and the two ladies arrived first, and they were just settling in for some tea beforehand when Mr. Hardy knocked at the door. Ramanujan showed him in and made the introductions.

"Ah, Mr. Chatterji, you're doing well in Bertie's... ah, Mr. Russell's philosophy lectures, isn't that right?" asked Mr. Hardy.

"Why, yes," replied Chatterji, "but how ever did you know?"

"Oh, Bertie's a good friend of mine, and when I've talked to him about our Mr. Ramanujan, he said that he also had a bright Indian student in his philosophy class." He turned to address them both, "So you're each a shining example of your country!"

Both Ramanujan and Chatterji bowed their heads and smiled at this. "Tea?" asked Ramanujan, "Indian style?"

"Sure, why not?" replied Mr. Hardy. After taking a sip from the offered cup he said, "Mmm, this is delicious, but I could see where it would fit a dessert course even better."

Ramanujan gave no reaction but was suddenly worried that he'd served something at the improper time. They sat and had their tea and the spiced chickpeas that Chatterji and his fiancé had brought and then Ramanujan went into the cooking area to make the final preparations of the *rasam*.

Mr. Hardy was in a conversation with Chatterji and the two ladies were having a side discussion in Punjabi when Ramanujan brought out the soup. They sat cross-legged on some cushions Ramanujan had set round a newly-acquired low table, with long-legged Mr. Hardy trying his best to copy them. He soon adopted a semblance of the position as Ramanujan served the *rasam*. "Why, Ramanujan, this is delicious," said Mr. Hardy. "A little peppery, but that's what I love."

"Thank you, Mr. Hardy," replied Ramanujan, inwardly pleased as both Chatterji and the ladies also complimented him on the soup.

Unnoticed by the others, Mr. Hardy had discovered the sole red chili Ramanujan had used to spice the soup and bit down on it out of curiosity. His eyes immediately flew open wide, and he began fanning at his mouth while shakily placing the bowl back on the table. After a moment of incomprehension, Ramanujan raced into the kitchen and brought back a bowl of yogurt and a glass of water to help cool the burning effects of the chili.

By now, Mr. Hardy was laughing and the rest of them couldn't contain themselves either. "By god, Ramanujan!" he howled. "You certainly know how to heat up your soup!" and the laughter continued for minutes as Mr. Hardy vacillated between wiping his streaming eyes and downing spoonsful of yogurt.

Once they were all resettled, they talked about Chatterji's upcoming marriage and the preparations that were being made for the ceremony, and seeing that everyone's bowls were empty, Ramanujan offered seconds. All were happy to have more, and Mr. Hardy was interested that the friend of Chatterji's fiancé was studying ethics in a Cambridge college outside of Trinity. When the conversation turned to the international situation, they all joined in with opinions on the moral ethics of government, and Ramanujan could see that everyone was enjoying the discussion. He was delighted that Mr. Hardy was fitting in so well.

Ramanujan offered another helping of *rasam*, but this time only Chatterji desired another bowl. Ramanujan ladled out some of the soup and brought the serving dish back to the cooking area where he set down the bowl with the intent to next serve some of the *pongal*, when he was suddenly consumed with doubt. *Maybe the* rasam *wasn't that good, and they were only being polite,* he thought. *What if the* pongal *is worse? What will they think? Is Mr. Hardy really happy or just joining in the conversation to ignore the meal? And he burned his mouth so!*

Ramanujan began pacing about the alcove and his doubts soon morphed into an overwhelming feeling of inadequacy. He picked up the *pongal* and took a few steps towards the lively debate going on in the next room when he froze. He resolved on the spot that couldn't face his guests again, especially Mr. Hardy if there was the slightest chance that he was unhappy with the meal.

Setting down the *pongal,* Ramanujan quietly slipped on his shoes, grabbed his coat, making sure it had a little cash in the pockets, and then snuck out the back entrance. The cool air felt good on his hot cheeks and by the time he reached the purser's stand he was feeling much more in control. *Should I go back?* came to him, but he stubbornly ordered a cab, directed it to the train station, and he boarded the first train bound for Oxford.

Settling into the railcar, yet feeling oddly detached from the entire experience, he was suddenly flooded with memories of the events surrounding his lonely escape up to Visakhapatnam.

He alit from the train at the Visakhapatnam station and spent several hours wandering the village streets in despair and sitting at the beach staring forlornly out to sea before finally summoning the courage to go to the door of a relative and beg for lodging.

"Ramanujan! What are you doing here?" asked his cousin Krishnasamy looking past him. "Where's your mother? Is she well?"

"Yes, yes, she's fine," muttered Ramanujan despondently. "I'd rather not talk about why I'm here, but I was wondering if you could find your way to putting me up for a couple of days?"

"Oh, of course you're welcome to stay here, but you must tell me what's brought you all the way up from Kumbakonam," said Krishnasamy. "My wife will arrange dinner and you may have the room in the back where the cook sleeps."

Ramanujan could not be induced to give the reason for his unexpected visit to Visakhapatnam for several days until, finally, in tears over tea one hot afternoon he told his cousin of the disgrace that had led to his impulsive trip.

"I don't understand what's happened," he sighed and wiped at his tear-streaked face. "My friends admired me, and now I can't face them. I've disgraced my mother, and I've ruined my life."

"Come now," sympathized Krishnasamy. "It can't possibly be that bad—you have good health and a family—that's all that really matters isn't it? What's happened?"

"I've failed at school, and the entire town knows about it," said Ramanujan. "I can see it in their faces and in how they act toward me now. It won't be long before they'll shun me altogether."

"But I hear that you're a brilliantly shining star, cousin—that you know more mathematics than practically anyone in the country. Word of your achievements has even reached your family way up here in Visakhapatnam. How could you have failed?"

"Things have suddenly become difficult," Ramanujan replied with effort. "When I was younger, I could conquer any subject, and especially the maths came so easily to me. Now the only thing I care about is the mathematics, and I'm a failure at everything else. I had a scholarship to attend the Government College in Kumbakonam, but they took it away because I failed in English. Now, without the scholarship money, I can't help provide for my mother and father, and I can't advance in college either. I'm lost." He held his face in his hands and was wracked again by sobs.

When he'd calmed himself a little, he continued in a weak voice, "I left home without telling my parents where I was going, and now I'm too mortified to face them when I do return, plus I'm too humiliated to see my friends who used to look up to me. What should I do?"

Krishnasamy consoled him and assured him that things were not as bad as they seemed, stressing that he was welcome to stay as long as he liked. Several weeks with his cousin had improved Ramanujan's outlook, and during that time Krishnasamy had secretly sent word to his parents that Ramanujan was with him and would soon be returning home.

"Ramanujan, you should have said," declared Mr. Hardy when he saw the remorseful Tamil the next week. "I would have sent the funds to Oxford, or even hired you a cab."

"I know, Mr. Hardy, but after I left it was difficult for me to show my face again. I had convinced myself that you all hated the meal."

"Well, I must say that that is absolutely preposterous," began Mr. Hardy, but then in a gentler tone said, "It was a very good meal, and we were all worried about you after you disappeared. I even had the mind to call the police, but Chatterji convinced me that you'd turn up, and you have."

Ramanujan nodded staring down at his hands. "I actually had to ask him for enough money to afford the train trip back."

It was Mr. Hardy's turn to nod. "So I heard." Then after a pause. "I say, Ramanujan, you really are a sensitive soul, aren't you? You should tell me if something is bothering you or if you're unhappy. That's the only way I'll have in knowing that anything is amiss. I find I can't read you otherwise. You always seem fine to me, and this came as a total surprise."

"Yes, Mr. Hardy, I will," said Ramanujan as he opened his notebook to the section they'd been working on.

Mr. Hardy looked at the equation, back at Ramanujan, and sighed. "All right, then," as they both turned to the task at hand.

"So, Ramanujan," said Mr. Neville. "Now that you're settling in, are you feeling a part of the fabric of the college here in Cambridge? Was it worth it to make that long journey from Madras and to devote your time to study here at Trinity?" They were sitting in the Neville's garden and catching the final rays of sunlight after a late Sunday dinner of curried cauliflower and peas.

Ramanujan felt that he didn't need to burden Mr. Neville with details of the disastrous meal with Mr. Hardy if he hadn't already heard. "Mr. Neville, it has been beyond my greatest expectations," said Ramanujan with an inner sigh at his duplicity while sinking back into his wicker chair. "Mr. Hardy is always so enthusiastic, and we are making great strides. He is also teaching me the 'formal' mathematics that I had missed out on by not learning under the English school system. I thought that I was learning under that system, but apparently it is much different in India. I am quickly catching up on the time that we feel I have lost, though."

"Hardy is the right person for you, Ramanujan," said Mr. Neville heartily. "Once you've passed his threshold tests, which you appear to have done remarkably well, he's a champion and a life-long friend. If you'd been in contact with anyone else in England—or the entire mathematics community of the world, for that matter—I fear that you wouldn't have gained an advocate anywhere approaching his mettle."

"Threshold test?" asked Ramanujan with a measure of trepidation apparent in his voice.

"Oh, no! Not a formal type of exam of any kind," stressed Mr. Neville. "I just meant that Hardy doesn't suffer fools kindly." At an uncomprehending look from Ramanujan, he further clarified, "Hardy is the sort of person who has certain internal standards by which he grades people. If you don't meet those standards, he's still as pleasant as can be when he meets you, but he'll not devote much energy in your direction. If you do meet the benchmarks as you have, however, you become a person worth reckoning with in his mind."

"Oh, that is so good to hear, because I also have the highest respect for him," said Ramanujan. "I never thought that I would find someone who actually understands what I am saying so easily." He hesitated and then added quickly, "mathematically, that is."

"By the way," started Mr. Neville. "I must tell you that Alice told me all about the problems you were having with some of the junior students harassing you. I was, of course, as upset as Alice, and took the matter straight to Hardy."

Ramanujan was surprised and embarrassed by this news, but Mr. Neville went on. "When I told him about the matter, Hardy suddenly became livider than I thought possible and stormed about his chambers. We had tea brought in, and discussed the issue at some length, and he became resolved. Somehow, through his connections, and his interest in cricket as it turns out, he discovered that the students who'd treated you so badly were on the second-string cricket team. 'Thank God for that,' he'd said. 'I'd hate to lose our decent cricket team of firsts.'"

"Anyway, apparently he met with the Dean of their college and then later gave the lot of them a thorough dressing-down. He compared them to a bunch of chimpanzees jumping up and down and yammering at Charles Darwin. He was not happy, and then they were not happy, and have been suspended from cricket for the remainder of the term. You should have no more problems on that front."

Mr. Neville could read the discomfort on Ramanujan's face. Having spent enough time in India, he recognized the distaste for conflict and direct confrontation ingrained in Indian society. He was also aware of the fear of public ridicule that was common to all cultures.

"Put your mind at ease, Ramanujan," he said. "Cambridge isn't the sort of place where thugs lurk in the dark waiting for retribution. And to make certain of that, knowing the student culture as he does, Hardy made it well understood that not even a whisper during evening meals would be heard concerning this incident. Hardy has your back, as they say."

Ramanujan didn't know how to reply. He was moved by Mr. Hardy's defense of him and sensed that he'd have to somehow let Mr. Hardy know of his deep appreciation for his actions. Oddly though, he found himself worrying about the fate of the students Mr. Hardy had disciplined, and these thoughts lingered as he and Mr. Neville watched the sunlight vanish through the highest tree limbs as twilight approached.

"Let's hope Fairbairn does better than Calthorpe," said Mr. Hardy as there was more applause from the Oxford section of the spectators. "It's not looking good for the Blues."

"The Blues?" asked Ramanujan.

"Yes, the Cambridge cricket team," replied Mr. Hardy with a little irritation. "Haven't you been paying attention?"

"Ah yes, Cambridge," said Ramanujan.

It was a warm July day, and Mr. Hardy had brought Ramanujan to see his first-ever cricket match. Ramanujan had tried his best to follow the rules as explained by Mr. Hardy, but soon became lost as Mr. Hardy fell into terminology that was totally foreign. After a series of comments including 'leggie', 'Yorker', 'popping crease', 'stumps', and 'Bunsen', Ramanujan had mentally abandoned the running commentary and stared listlessly out at the field. He'd tried to grasp the point of the game, but it just seemed to be a series of groans or cheers from the bleachers, with no apparent action on the field, or moans and shouts when there was a burst of sprinting between the two wickets.

"I'm sure you'll warm to the game once you get to know it," Mr. Hardy was saying when his attention was diverted by the next bowl on the field. "Come on, lads!" he shouted from the stands.

"This has been interesting, Mr. Hardy, but perhaps I had best return to my rooms and work on our paper," said Ramanujan during a break as the teams switched sides.

"Ah, yes," said Mr. Hardy sympathetically. "Cricket can be a bit wearing on the uninitiated." And before Ramanujan could get to his feet, he continued, "You do know that none of the boys who taunted you are on the field? Don't you?"

"Yes, Mr. Hardy," said Ramanujan, somewhat abashedly. He looked down at the empty scorecard he was holding. "I don't know how to thank you for speaking up for me, but I never would have told Alice if I thought it would make it back to you and cause those boys to be shamed."

"Shamed?" asked Mr. Hardy in surprise. "They should be ashamed by how they treated you. We simply can't condone that type of behavior in our university."

"No, but now they are the ones being looked down upon and will have a hard time showing their faces. Some may even have to leave the university."

"What? Nonsense! I don't know how they do things in India," said Mr. Hardy, "but here I think most would agree that those addle pates were let off lightly for their stupidity."

"But it must be the same as in India," said Ramanujan. "People want their name well known when they have accomplished something, but even a whisper of shame can devastate a person."

"Ah," replied Mr. Hardy, gazing at his friend. "So, there is a difference after all. Don't you worry, Ramanujan. In this country you'll see that I haven't been too severe. With the bluster and bravado of the lads on this campus, their discipline will probably be worn as a badge of courage or pride. No amount of browbeating will really harm any of them, unfortunately."

"Ah, that is good," said Ramanujan. "Then thank you again for defending me."

"It's my pleasure," said Mr. Hardy. "And I want to reiterate that you can come to me anytime with any troubles you might be having. We've spared no expenses to get you here, and I want that personal attention to extend to your private life—so that it's free of any cares. We need to keep you in tip-top shape for mathematics."

"Thank you, Mr. Hardy, I will try," Ramanujan promised as he stood and made his way out of the stands and back to the college while Mr. Hardy roared when a ball was hit high into the air.

CHAPTER 17

During his first spring term in Cambridge that year, much of the focus of the school, the community, and the country had been across the channel towards Germany as an arms race of several nations was becoming more and more apparent. The grounds of the Cambridge campus were mostly empty during the summer recess, but when the news broke, it still echoed off the deserted rooms and courts. War had been declared in Europe on July 28, 1914, a month after the assassination of the Archduke Ferdinand of Austria; and a week later Britain joined the conflict on the mainland.

Mr. Hardy had become increasingly preoccupied with the buildup for war and regretful of not being able to spend all of his time with Ramanujan. "I'm sorry, Ramanujan, but I must rush off to a meeting," said Mr. Hardy with a shake of his head during one of their sessions. "This country is out of control and simply reacting to events. Instead of mapping out an open public agenda, it's marching ahead with all the critical decisions being made behind closed doors. It's almost as if those in charge were waiting for this war to erupt so that they could lock down every bit of dissent and grab all of the power that they can."

He was flushed and more animated than Ramanujan had seen him.

"If the matter didn't involve the lives of normal people, and only embroiled the wretched military, that might be one thing. But we're talking about the future generations of our country, and I can't stand by and watch good and brilliant minds—on either side of the conflict—being tossed aside as if they counted for nothing."

As he took his boater off the hat-stand, he unexpectedly had a grim smile on his face. "And to be petty about all this, cricket has been suspended for the foreseeable future." He gave a sigh as they both stepped out of the room.

Ramanujan had been concerned about the entry into war, of course, but had been focused on mathematics and hoped that everything would become resolved by calm diplomacy. As he descended the stairs and walked out into the courtyard, the gravity of the situation to himself personally began to dawn on him. *Two years,* he thought. *I told Janaki that I'd be gone for two years. Now they are saying that shipping channels have been threatened and that nothing but troop transports will be traveling to India. What if this goes on longer than they are projecting?* He found after his conversation with Mr. Hardy that he, too, would become obsessed with the newspaper reports and the statistics that began to stream in daily from the battlefront.

Ramanujan had been wary of Mr. Littlewood when they'd first met, largely because it seemed to him that Mr. Littlewood was the one who'd sponsored much of the criticism he'd received in the letters he'd exchanged with Mr. Hardy prior to his voyage to England. However, except for Mr. Neville, it turned out that Mr. Littlewood was one of the most engaging of all the fellows he'd met at Cambridge and he came to enjoy their sessions together. Surprisingly, for a man of such standing in the mathematical community, Mr. Littlewood was only a few years older than Ramanujan himself.

It was becoming evident that the primary lesson Mr. Littlewood was trying to convey to Ramanujan was the same concept of mathematical proof that Mr. Hardy had lectured him about. After a time, even Ramanujan could detect some of Mr. Littlewood's frustration at him not being able to stay on task and exasperation would occasionally bubble up through Mr. Littlewood's calm demeanor. But Ramanujan was unable to constrain himself to the matter at hand despite his new friend's best efforts. They would begin patiently working through the steps of a problem, and suddenly Ramanujan would see another angle and excitedly start mapping that out, or an entirely new problem would jump into his mind, and he couldn't help but launch himself into that intriguing new possibility.

At one point, just as his frustration was beginning to show, Mr. Littlewood sat back and chuckled, shaking his head. "Yes," he said. "That certainly is a very interesting idea, but that too will require proof. Now I know what it's like to be a cowboy."

"A cowboy?" asked Ramanujan, with visions of a small boy leading a hefty Kangayam bull down a narrow lane and between rice paddies.

"Yes. In America, there are men on horseback who try and guide huge herds of cows. They spend all their time rounding up strays and trying to keep the rest of the herd on track. That's how it is sometimes working with you, Ramanujan. But, we'll eventually get there.

"Here, let me give you a concrete example about proofs," said Mr. Littlewood reaching for a journal on the table. "I don't know if you've seen my recent paper—'Sur la distribution des nombres premiers', in the *Comptes Rendus de l'Académie des Sciences*? The title in English means, 'On the distribution of prime numbers'?"

Ramanujan shook his head and was about to describe his own investigations into the estimation of the number of prime numbers, up to any given prime, but wisely stopped himself. He knew that he needed to hear what Mr. Littlewood had to say.

"Well, I know of your keen interest in prime numbers, and that you're aware that the true number of prime numbers up to any given integer is based on the prime number counting function $\pi(N)$, so that, discounting the number 1, at $N = 2$ the function gives the value of 1 since 2 is prime, and then at $N = 3$ the value changes to 2 since 3 is prime, and that it remains at $\pi(N) = 2$ until $N = 5$ where it changes to the value of 3, since 4 isn't prime, but 5 is, and so on. This is, of course, a function that can't be used for prediction, but only to keep track of what we've already counted.

"As you, yourself, have investigated, we can't reasonably count the number of prime numbers by hand, unless one is willing to become very old and very dull. So, our best estimation, to date, has been the log integral function:

$$\int_0^x (1/\log t)\,dt$$

which we know as Li(N). The estimation of the count of prime numbers by Li(N), compared to the actual count of prime numbers in π(N) has resulted in a very small error which is equal to Li(N) - π(N) or the estimated count minus the actual count. As far as we've gone in our enumeration of the prime numbers, the difference has always been small but positive, so that the integral function always slightly overestimates the actual count of prime numbers. This error has been a positive value as far as we've been able to verify."

Ramanujan nodded, and again held his tongue about some discoveries he'd made.

"My paper," continued Mr. Littlewood, "through logic and meticulous proofs, shows that the error term will, in fact, eventually become negative, or the estimate will actually be less than the true value. And, furthermore, I prove that the error term will change signs an infinite number of times, jumping from positive to negative and back again. I've proven this without being able to state the actual value where this first sign change will occur. And yet the results are incontrovertible. Someone, someday, will be able to come up with the exact number, but that's irrelevant. Through careful steps I've proven that it must be so without needing to state the value at which this occurs."

They are really serious about this, thought Ramanujan. *This is exactly the lecture Mr. Hardy recently gave me about proofs.* He was also not surprised, given their interests and collaboration, that the two had in fact published papers on prime numbers in the same journal and in the same year.

"You, on the other hand," continued Mr. Littlewood, "come up with some amazing results, but without any kind of logical rigor behind them, and, unfortunately, you're unable to show precisely how you got there. In mathematics, we must be able to follow the leader, step by step, to all arrive at the same place, otherwise the answer, however brilliant, is an inherently meaningless result. It's a stray cow left out in the wilderness."

Given this lecture from Mr. Littlewood that augmented the one from Mr. Hardy, Ramanujan resolved to become more alert and better at staying on track in the future, but he was not, when the inspiration hit him, ultimately successful in his resolution.

CHAPTER 18.

He awoke with a start and sat up suddenly, blinking his eyes in the dark room.

What was that? he thought trying to orient himself. *Or rather, where did that come from?*

He'd had a dream unlike any other that had previously been given him, but the emotions it produced were familiar. He commonly received dreams of home, religious dreams, but also dreams of mathematics. Often, he awoke with the thread of an equation slipping away, numbers in odd series, or Namagiri Amman giving him an unexpected insight into a problem. But he also often had dreams reflecting his anxiety about exams, and at the heart of it, this dream dredged up that common fear. At the surface, however, this dream was different from any of the others. It was as if he'd experienced the dream of someone else.

In the dream, he was in a hurry. There was an exam that he was scheduled to take, and he was late. Every turn he took seemed to end up being on the wrong path, and he was constantly interrupted by people in the way or stopping him to help them solve some mathematical problem. Finally, he arrived at his destination. The setting was academic—a classroom or a library—lined with tall bookshelves and filled with evenly spaced desks. He was the only one present in the room and was in the middle of taking a test. He'd opened a plain-covered, thin book that was clean, neat, and typeset with regimented paragraphs and equations. In his dream, he'd read a chapter and had just turned a page to find the following problem:

> Set up a puzzle like 'The Three-tiered Hanging Garden.' Use a divergent series and prime numbers in your solution.

He'd panicked. In the dream, he had no recollection of what he'd read or of any problem resembling 'The Three-tiered Hanging Garden,' and had not recalled seeing any suggestions or solutions involving a divergent series, nor prime numbers in the book. He had the oppressive feeling that he was expected to provide a solution or fail, and yet he had no clue where to begin. He went to the front of the book and saw that it was written by a Swiss mathematician with a name he didn't recognize and was edited by a friend of the author living in Bern, another unfamiliar name. Then he'd awoken.

He sat with his back against the wall and thought about how odd the dream had been. It was completely English in flavor with no hint of anything even vaguely Indian even in the background. He'd of course seen numerous rooms like this in Cambridge, but had never encountered such a simple text of mathematics. His dreams almost always set up solutions to problems instead of problems that were unsolvable in themselves. *And what is a hanging garden?* he wondered. *What was the problem associated with it? How could it be solved using a divergent series? Who was the author of the book, since I have no recollection of the name I've just read?*

Ramanujan was strangely in awe of this dream. It had caused him anxiety, which was rare when it came to mathematics but common when it came to exams. It had been in a completely foreign environment. And it had provided a puzzle that could not be answered, whereas he was used to finding solutions. *If one doesn't know the nature of the problem,* he wondered, *how could it be solved?* And there was not a hint of Namagiri Amman anywhere in the dream, which was perhaps the most bizarre aspect of all.

Am I finally becoming British enough that I now only have dreams of England? he wondered. *I hope not.* He arose in the early dawn and washed up, went through his *pooja*, ate some cold rice and vegetables, and prepared for his daily visit with Mr. Hardy. He'd analyzed the dream and realized that his fear of exams had again been on full display, but his grasp of the mathematics was, for the first time, elusive. He endeavored to uncover more about the Hanging Garden problem.

Following their morning session, he'd asked Mr. Hardy if he knew anything about hanging gardens.

"Do you mean the little hanging fuchsia baskets ladies set out each summer?" asked Mr. Hardy.

Ramanujan didn't want to reveal much of the dream, since it was so curious to him in the first place, and so he said, "I am really not sure—I heard someone talking about a hanging garden, as if it was something noteworthy, and I wondered what it was."

"Well, the only thing that comes to mind in that context is the legendary Hanging Gardens of Babylon," said Mr. Hardy. "I don't know much about it, but I seem to recall that it was listed as one of the Seven Wonders of the World. I'm sure the library would have some information about it."

On his way back to his rooms, Ramanujan made a detour to the Wren Library and was directed to a section containing books on world history. He found that the Hanging Gardens were described by historians, but the site of their physical location had not as yet been discovered, leading some of the authors to even speculate about the likelihood of their ever having existed.

The historians noted that the Hanging Gardens were reputedly built by Nebuchadnezzar II for his homesick wife. She'd come from a mountainous area, and he'd built the gardens out of the flat expanses of the plain to please her. The dimensions of the square base were said to be 360 feet per side, and tiers rose from this base to a height of 75 feet. The plants overhung the edges of each tier, and various walkways and pavilions were described. One source said that the gardens were watered by a conveyor of buckets, and another mentioned a screw device to lift the water from a nearby canal.

Ramanujan sat back and stared out across the nearly empty library. The only thing that seemed like it involved a mathematical problem of any kind would lie in the physics describing a screw mechanism, and envisioning the likely equations in his mind, he saw no connection with a divergent series, nor with prime numbers. Without knowing the problem, or even the context of the puzzle, Ramanujan decided that the dream had served no real purpose, after all, other than to highlight his underlying fear of exams.

Back in his room sometime later, he recalled his discussions with a newly-arrived Mr. Neville in Madras in which the gentleman had been trying to persuade Ramanujan to make the journey to England.

"There are two things I must insist upon before I can make a decision," said Ramanujan. "The first is that there will need to be funds made available to support my family, since they will have no other means of providing for themselves if I am away. And the second is that no exams will be required for me to enter or remain at Cambridge," said Ramanujan.

"I can definitely guarantee the first and would think that the second won't be a problem, but I'll relay these both to Mr. Hardy in my next letter to make sure," said Mr. Neville. "May I ask why the subject of examinations is so important in making your decision?"

"I may not remain long in England if I must take any tests," lamented Ramanujan. "To tell you the truth, examinations have become my biggest fear in life, and I cannot describe the anxiety I face when one is eminent.

"You see, when I was young, and, as it turns out, fearless, I came out at the top of every examination that I took in every subject and, with one exception that still stings, I was always the first in mathematics—even for the entire district. Then it suddenly was not so easy for me. I understand now that my total focus on mathematics led to the neglect of most other subjects. Coincidentally, at the same time that I could not meet the standards in other subjects, the tests themselves became more and more important. And then I became paralyzed. I could not even pass the entrance exams into college, and each new trial was worse than the previous one. I finally had to resign myself to the fact that I would never obtain a degree, and so I had to seek employment instead of attending school—whence I settled in as a clerk here in Madras.

"So you see, if testing is a requirement, I will not be staying long in England, and it would not be worth the trip in the first place. I am afraid your Mr. Hardy will need to take me as I am, or not at all."

"I can assure you that Mr. Hardy is looking forward to meeting and collaborating with you and wouldn't wish you to return to India any sooner than you, yourself, desire," said Mr. Neville. "There's really no need to worry, and you should rest assured that it will not be his desire to cause you any undue anxiety."

CHAPTER 19

Ramanujan made a trip to London to visit the zoo in the early Autumn. This was yet another Sunday when he was not meeting with Mr. Hardy, and Ramanujan wondered about this particular Christian day of the week. *Perhaps Mr. Hardy just needs to take off one day a week for rest*, he thought, *as Sundays in England seem to be sacred to others—but they don't appear to be so for him.* His new colleague was not in the least bit religious and had a list of many complaints about those who were. Ramanujan had learned, early on, to leave personal beliefs and any mentions of his dreams as the source of his inspiration out of their conversations.

The knowledge he'd gained on his initial train trip up from London with Mr. Neville, combined with information provided by his new Indian friends on campus who frequently rode the rails to London, had convinced him that such an excursion was common, or at least easily done. The train was full of young men in uniform, but he was lucky enough to find a seat by a window and enjoyed the scenery on the trip down.

Regent's Park, which held the London Zoo, was within tolerable walking distance of the King's Cross station, so he had no need for the extra complications of a cab ride; besides, the day was fairly clear with only occasional high scudding clouds, and it was still warm for the season. Once at the zoo entrance, he waited his turn in the queue—a practice with which he was becoming accustomed. In India, there was no such concept as a line, and one simply joined the crush to purchase a ticket or to gain entry through a door—the longest arms reaching through or over the crowd, or the cleverest shoves or maneuvers won the day. Often the loudest voice could end up being the game-changer. Standing back and awaiting a turn led to absolutely no advantage in India. He heard people behind him complaining about the crowd of people on a Sunday at the zoo, but he noticed only open spaces. He balked a little at the entrance fee, but then remembered that while he was not rich, he was not poor either, and was being well compensated in his Cambridge position.

The People's Park Zoo in Madras was the first zoological garden constructed in India, and he'd visited it many times when he lived there. He'd found wandering the paths around the lakes and observing the animals to be very soothing. He was already noticing a distinct difference between the Madras zoo and this one, however. Here, people were relatively hushed and stood and viewed the animals with little or no attempts at interaction. In India, around the tigers and bears especially, there were continual yells, shouts, and gestures to try and get a rise out of the animals or to look for some kind of reaction in them, as if the people sought a one-on-one relationship with the beast. And they possibly had less respect for the animal, now that he thought of it and was in a more British frame of mind.

He came to the large elephant enclosure and lingered. The other visitors came and went, but he just stood mesmerized and enjoyed watching and being near the huge mammals.

He also loved the tigers and the monkeys and realized that these, too, had probably come from India. On the train trip back to Cambridge, he felt heartened that there really were so many creatures from his country, himself included, living in England.

Staring out of the train window on his return from the zoo, he thought back fondly on the temple elephants in his home country. He'd retreat to the temples for worship, of course, but also for the cool and quiet corridors, and would spend hours in alcoves scratching out his formulae on his slate. But often too, he'd slowly wander about a temple complex lost in thought. A favorite destination for him was to walk out of the main temple, through the adjacent courtyard, and over to the housing for the temple elephant. He'd stand to the side in the shade and watch the huge pachyderm being fed, being washed, as it slept, or being adorned for an upcoming celebration.

The elephant was adored by the community and was kept mainly for processions. It would be elaborately decorated with garlands, headdress, cloths, and colors, and would carry the priest and an idol through the streets to the accompaniment of music, dancing, and thrown flower petals. Surrounded by throngs and in the middle of a huge parade, the elephant was the center of the celebration and provided blessings for all.

He also cherished memories of visits to temples where the elephant was available for individual blessings. After praying to the main deity, there was often a station just off the path through the maze of narrow corridors leading to the exit where the elephant stood waiting, shifting patiently from foot to foot. Ramanujan would hold up a one *paisa* coin, and the elephant would reach over with its trunk and nip the coin from his hand and drop it into a bucket. Then the huge trunk would arch up over him and the tip would hover for a moment poised above him. The elephant would then drop the tip of the trunk onto his head, the shaved front half of his scalp feeling the thick bristles near the end of the trunk and then he'd receive the sudden hot puff of breath from the elephant. The temple elephant's warm blessing would flood through his body and in a daze, he'd make room for the next awaiting worshipper. The touch from that elephant, which had actually borne the deity on its own back, always felt so personal and so lastingly intense—sometimes more so than any blessing given by the priest.

CHAPTER 20.

Mr. Hardy held up the paper[2] that Ramanujan had written and pointed to it as he read aloud, "It was proved by Dirichlet that

$$\frac{d(1) + d(2) + d(3) + \cdots + d(N)}{N} = \log N + 2\gamma - 1 + O(\frac{1}{\sqrt{N}})$$

"And, just down the page you quote my proof where I state that..." and he continued reading from the article of which they had just received the publisher's draft.

"There, you see?" asked Mr. Hardy when he finished. "This is an excellent result, and you're exploring completely new ground. You've written a well-referenced paper that now has a foundation in the publications of those who went before, and you're building on a solid platform. This is a true mathematical paper, written with much rigor, and it will soon appear in the *Journal of the London Mathematical Society*. You're getting published, Ramanujan, and you should be proud! Not only that, but we both know this is only a harbinger of great things to come."

Ramanujan gazed at the finished manuscript on the table before him. He subtly breathed in until his lungs could take no

---

2 S. Ramanujan, 'Highly Composite Numbers,' *Proc. London Math. Soc. Serie 2 14 (1915), 347–400.*

more, and then slowly exhaled, suddenly feeling extremely re-laxed. *I'm being published—and in the London Mathematical Society Journal no less!* He looked over at Mr. Hardy and grinned. He'd been so caught up in the details of this, and other papers, that he'd not taken the time to step back and appreciate what he'd accomplished. This was, after all, what he'd come to Cambridge—to England for. He thought of his mother in their house in far off Kumbakonam and of how proud she would be of her son.

He looked over at Mr. Hardy and gave another smile.

"Yes, I am very happy, Mr. Hardy," said Ramanujan, barely containing his emotions. "And I think that this was a paper that I could not have written alone. You have taught me so much already. I cannot thank you enough."

The idea of highly composite numbers was an invention of his own and had inspired an investigation that had come to some substance after all. These were numbers that had jumped out at him as having many more divisors than any of their neighbors. For example, the number 36 was highly composite and had nine possible divisors: 1, 2, 3, 4, 6, 9, 12, 18, and 36 whereas its nearest neighbors had few divisors—those for the number 35 were 1, 5, 7, and 35, and those for 37 were only 1 and 37, since it was prime. The highly composite number preceding 36 was 24 with eight divisors, and the next after it was 48 with ten divisors. He'd seen this as just another of the myriad interesting ways that numbers presented them-selves—more of a conversation topic, but Mr. Hardy had con-vinced him that no, this sort of observation was something that needed to be shared with the world.

There was a warm moment of shared silence, and then the two began pouring over the most recent problem that had caught their attention—number partitions.

The leaves on most of the trees had begun to turn color and they were set aglow by the incrementally weaker afternoon sun. Ramanujan had taken to walking the university grounds nearly every afternoon to absorb this spectacle of yellows, oranges, and reds that he'd not known lay hidden beneath the summer green of all the various leaves. What amazed him as much as the transformation of the trees was that the ground changed color beneath them as the fallen leaves created a brightly colored circle under each one.

So much is changing in Cambridge, almost like this autumn season, he thought after he'd picked his way through the tents and sheds that had plopped down in nearly all the small squares on campus. A line of lorries was in constant movement—bringing in freshly wounded soldiers or taking away the recovered or deceased. Cambridge had become a hospital for the multitudinous casualties of the war. And it was sending off new recruits daily from the training grounds that had been set up on the outskirts of the university. The dining hall had become a mess-hall for the soldiers and medical staff, and Ramanujan was glad that he had no reason to enter the packed space.

He walked along the banks of the river now continuously dotted with men bandaged in various and sometimes hideous configurations, ferried about by nurses carrying stretchers or pushing wheelchairs. A man with a thick compress over one eye nodded hello and joined him in gazing up at the leaves. "I never tire of this sight," the man said, "and I thank God that I'm still able to see it after what I've been through. Still, I hope I can do something to keep fighting after this bandage comes off."

"Yes, we must all do what we can, and thank you for what you have done already," said Ramanujan, although he was not sure what he himself had contributed or could offer to the war effort.

He was fascinated by the news coming in from Europe—the battle reports and the number of deaths involved in the gigantic conflict were staggering. The newspapers were flooded with pictures, stories and data, and conversations always centered on this single topic of war. Just recently the Germans had been stopped after a massive and lightning-fast push towards Paris. It was reported that six hundred Paris taxis had been enlisted to drive French and British troops to the front at the Marne River and they had done the trick in halting the advance for the time being.

Many of his countrymen living in England were joining the army to help in the fight, and he heard that there were troops from India being moved to the Middle East and to Europe in an attempt to halt the advances of Germany and the Ottoman Empire. Many of the students from Cambridge had already enlisted, packed up, and shipped off, and several professors were also due to leave. Mr. Littlewood expected to depart soon to join the artillery units, and he said that he hoped to help with their ballistics calculations.

Ramanujan thought of what part he could play, and his solution was to spend more time in his morning and evening *poojas*, praying to Vishnu for the, welfare of the soldiers. The soldier with the eye-patch wandered away and Ramanujan sang to himself as he watched a boat punt slowly along the current, a bandaged soldier laying at its bow.

> Devaki's child, he with war weapons,
>   compelled time to elapse,
> Standing in front of the kings who were waiting,
>   counting the minutes.
> There are those who saw him next to the well-armed warrior
> Who made Jayadratha's head roll on the field
>   when the Lord hid the sun with his disk.

He'd crossed the Cam via the Bridge of Sighs and wandered a little to the west through St. John's College when he stopped and watched some tractor-drawn carts move slowly past, piled high with the harvest of wheat and barley from the summer crops. They seemed to be moving in another world and in a time far removed from war, and he thought wistfully of the rice harvest back home each year in Tamil Nadu. As an Iyengar, his non-farming family never celebrated the harvest, but he loved to walk through the neighboring villages and observe, nonetheless. The peak of the harvest culminated in the four-day festival of Pongal, named after the sweet rice dish that was made in celebration of a successful rice crop. Small village squares would be piled high with the light-brown harvested grain, and carts coming in from the fields would be full of the pale rice stalks headed for the threshing ground. Roads and pathways during harvest often saw the rice stalks laid across them so that passing carts and footsteps would help separate the grain from the stalk, and the rice would be winnowed into piles. Burlap sacks would then be filled with the grain, moved, stacked, and stored in the paddy owner's house for later use or sale.

Ramanujan remembered the contentment that seemed to emanate from every village at harvesttime—the gods had provided them food for another year, and the celebration allowed them to express their thankfulness in return. The evening before the main celebration day of Pongal, mothers would set up a prayer station for *pooja* and the family would gather and sing verses and songs around the small family shrine. Then in gathering darkness with various oil lamps in hand, they'd head out to the entrance of the house and make a *kolum* on the walkway or road in front of the gate. The *kolums* were meant to be on display and trod upon by passersby the next morning to cleanse them from bad karma. Each *kolum* consisted of various geometric shapes made by filtering fine lines of powdered rice through fingers, and during Pongal the shapes were always of stylized *pongal* pots and sugarcane leaves. Some mothers would also incorporate the actual leaves from the sugar cane, real flowers, and flower petals into the design for additional color.

The morning of the main celebration found women in houses, courtyards, and at the local shrines, in the process of making *pongal* to give thanks to the family deity. Metal pots were set above tended fires throughout the town, and Ramanujan envisioned the various stages of the process: Some women were just in the act of bringing the fire to life to heat the mixture of water, sugar, milk, and cardamom; others were attentively tending the pot until it boiled; and still others watched as the foaming pot began to overflow with the boiling mixture. All through the town, and at various times, the families gathered around the pots would ululate at the moment the foam streamed over the lip of the pot, at which point the rice was added to make the *pongal* pudding. A fortune was told from the direction in which the over-boil had occurred, the favorable directions often helped along by a subtle tilting of the pot during cooking. The finished *pongal* with a buttery sheen would then be ladled out onto short banana leaves and enjoyed by the celebrants.

Ramanujan remembered as a child wandering the streets to see as many of the animals as he could on the third day—Mattu Pongal, or 'Cow Pongal,'—the blessing of the livestock. Goats would be dotted with colors, and he once saw a young boy trying to dot his sheep, which ended up having the entire front half of its body coated in a deep pink. Venturing out of town he'd passed a farmer walking his cows into town for a blessing. The old man was in the middle of the tiny herd and prodded the five animals, each with a rope running through its nostrils and over the head, and he was pulling the rope this way and that to keep them all in control. Each cow had a series of purple and red dots running the length of the animal, from nose to tail. Barefoot and dressed all in white, the farmer had flashed him a proud, toothless grin as he headed to temple. It seemed that every animal Ramanujan had encountered was decorated in colors or garlands, and he could see that each was truly blessed.

How pastoral this seemed to him now, living in a modern, mechanized, urbane country wracked by war. The memories of home kept him grounded, although he could feel that his recollections of India were lately not as sharp as they once were, becoming more like the foam flowing over the lip of a *pongal* pot.

It was dark, and his fingers gripped the end of the sheets and blankets near his chin. He could feel himself physically relax as his body heat slowly warmed the mattress and blankets, and for the first time since the balmy summer months, he drifted off to a comfortable and uninterrupted sleep.

His friend Mahalanobis had visited that afternoon. It was an enjoyable pattern: after a session with Mr. Hardy and working through computations in solitude afterwards, to return to his lodgings and have friends stop by for chats that would sometimes evolve into spirited discussions that lasted well into the night. He was feeling much more at home with so many extended friendships among compatriots and he liked hearing English spoken just as he spoke it—that is when the conversations weren't possible in his native Tamil or the neighboring language, Telugu, in which he was also fluent.

After offering Mahalanobis tea and seating himself as close as possible to the fire he'd just built in the small fireplace alcove, his friend had asked jokingly, "How are you dealing with this wretched damp cold that seems to permeate our bones most of the year on this frigid island?"

Ramanujan chuckled. "Oh, I don't seem to notice it much during the scant daylight hours, since Mr. Hardy's offices are warm, and I bundle up as much as I can when I'm outside. It's just that the evenings and nights are so brutal—who knew that the daylight could become so short? In those dark hours when my mind isn't engaged in other things, I find that the cold can become so very oppressive. How do these British ever manage to sleep at night?"

"Isn't your fire able to warm the room enough?" asked Mahalanobis, now becoming serious. "Do you need more wood or coal?"

"Oh, no," replied Ramanujan. "This room stays warm well into the early morning. The problem is that the bedroom never really heats up enough. I've tried sleeping in front of the fire, but the floor is so hard that sleep is impossible even though I'm warm. I suppose I must buy an extra set of clothes or a coat to stay warm at night."

"You don't have enough blankets?" asked Mahalanobis. "Surely they'll supply more if the ones you have are insufficient. Let me have a look." And he walked into Ramanujan's bedroom and examined the bed.

"This should be more than enough," said Mahalanobis. "And I must say that you keep a very tidy bed. This one looks like it has never even been slept in—the sheets are so crisp and starched. They must have just changed them."

"No, I sleep there—shivering—every night," said Ramanujan.

Mahalanobis looked his friend up and down, and then back towards the bed, with a dawning realization. They walked back out to the sitting room and drank some more of the now cooling tea.

"Ramanujan," said Mahalanobis. "I hope you won't think this insulting, but I believe that there's a custom or way of doing things here in England that you haven't yet adopted. You know in India how important it is to stay as cool as possible at night? And we simply lie down on top of a mat or wooden cot with a minimal amount of covering?"

Ramanujan nodded and said, "Yes, I am beginning to miss those warm evenings to the extreme lately."

"Well," continued Mahalanobis, "Here in England the goal is to be as comfortable as possible in order to be able to sleep. Do you seriously think that the population of this entire island is joining you in freezing every night?

"The bedding here is designed to keep you warm. You must pull back all the blankets until only one sheet is exposed above, and another below, and then crawl in between them with all the blankets piled on top of you, not you on top of them. Then you'll find that you'll be warm enough to sleep blissfully except on the coldest nights when you simply add another blanket to the top."

Ramanujan stared at him for a moment in embarrassment. "What?" he suddenly exclaimed. "Why didn't anyone tell me? Like those idiots at the National India Association, for example!" Later, he'd heaped his friend with praise and plied him with extra biscuits and tea before he left for the evening.

Slowly emerging from sleep the next morning, wrapped in warmth, he could picture his house and his mother, possibly at this very moment. She was sweeping the brick floors, using a bundle of long twigs and grasses bound by hemp cording at one end that also served as the handle. The shape of the broom was causing her to stoop over through her sweeping chores as though she was in the fields cutting rice stalks. The dust deposits from the outside breezes would have covered everything and needed to be brushed away daily. She was now ushering him out of the house so that she could sweep up the detritus and take up a pot of water to nestle against her hip, dip in her hand, and then sprinkle the floors with vigorous flicks of her wrist. The room was now cooling from the dampened floors and helping to mitigate the relentlessly growing heat of the day.

At her beckon, he was reentering the family home in Kumbakonam which lay open to the world. Sounds, smells, and breezes passed freely through the small rooms. This was a natural state of all houses in India due to both the heat and the society. To maximize the benefit of breezes, one rarely closed the shutters to the windows, and glass was unheard of in any but government offices. There were bars on any window openings facing the street, to discourage thieves at night, and strangers or other castes were never allowed in the house, but still, the barrier between the exterior and interior was seemingly non-existent to nature. Even the gentlest breath of wind could help cool down the interior of their home, and the house was opened up in welcome—including a portion of the narrow middle section that became a small courtyard with an open section of roof to allow in wind and rain.

And, just as the interior of the house welcomed nature, the outside world embraced those within. He remembered that for him, as with most Indians, there was no difference between the outer and the inner. His time in the temple was like sitting with his mother in his house, and his family in the home embraced the community as his family. He could wander freely between the two and each was included in the other. From an early age, his mother had no worries about him going to the temple alone, and this trust soon expanded to the entire town. A trip to a different temple or a trek to a neighboring shrine was the same as wandering about in his own house. The *pooja* prayers out in the fields at a roadside shrine were just as if they took place in the inner sanctum of Sarangapani temple.

He now slipped out from under the warm covers and into the cold room, still picturing his family staying as cool as possible in the night by keeping low to the ground and rolling out first a mat and then a thin mattress over the bricks. In the summer months, shutters open, they required little if any bed coverings—perhaps a thin gauze at the most. To him it was the oddest juxtaposition to now be building a small fire to try and bring some warmth to his room after being bundled in blankets all night.

CHAPTER 21

Amanda and Ramanujan had exchanged several letters during the fall, and she was now much recovered from her lingering illness. In her most recent letter, she'd said that she was back to her old self, and he thought it peculiar that he was beginning to feel unwell himself lately with a nearly constant pain in his side. Amanda was excited that he'd be coming to visit over Christmas, and Lord and Lady North had even included money for Ramanujan's rail tickets in one of her letters. The Norths had a small manor in Shotteswell near Banbury, and it was arranged that they would pick him up at the Banbury station for the short drive to Shotteswell upon his arrival.

The train station was filled with soldiers and troop transports, and it took him some time to locate his train on a side-platform. He boarded at 9:00 am on his birthday—or at least he was fairly certain this was his birthday—December 22nd, although the records and recollections from his parents were somewhat sketchy as to the exact date. December had been very cold and wet, and low clouds pressed down on the gray countryside. There were no more colorful leaves to be seen and every tree was bare, almost skeletal it seemed after the lushness of summer. He was told to expect snow this winter, and he wondered what that would be like, if it came.

Staring out of the train window during the three-hour trip, his thoughts were mainly on a math problem that had been consuming his attention of late, but he also had time to reflect on turning twenty-seven. This had been a tumultuous year for him; however, reviewing his accomplishments, he was certain he'd made the right decision in coming to England and collaborating with Mr. Hardy. England represented a complete contrast for him after living a simple life in Tamil Nadu, and Mr. Hardy had emerged as his polar opposite.

Here was a man who to him was tall, slim, and handsome, where he knew that he himself was overweight and had a face pocked from smallpox. Mr. Hardy was reserved and refined, taking every bit of news or new problem in stride, whereas he could not contain his excitement or exuberance over a new achievement or be crushed by a failure. Mr. Hardy was comfortable in his status and position and knew every person on campus, whereas Ramanujan knew a several of the Indian students but only a few English—Mr. Littlewood, Mr. Neville—and Alice. Mr. Hardy was areligious to the point that Ramanujan thought he may be an atheist, whereas he himself was a devoted Vaishnavite and worshipped Namagiri Amman from whom all of his gifts sprang. And—Mr. Hardy studied mathematics rigorously and based every step he made on all the previous works others had proved, whereas he felt that the answers sprang up from some fountainhead granted by the gods.

Ramanujan marveled that they got along as well as they did.

The train pulled into the station, and he could make out Amanda through the now-rain-streaked windows as she stood on the platform with another girl, huddling together under an umbrella and scanning the cars for him. When he stepped down from the carriage, she and her friend came running up to him. "Hi, Mr. Rama!" she exclaimed while giving him a hug. "How was your trip? It is so good to see you! This is my best friend Mary Cartwright. Mary, this is Mr. Rama... Mr. Ramanujan."

"Mr. Rama is just fine," grinned Ramanujan. "It is an absolute joy to see you again, too, Amanda!"

Mary was eagerly shaking his hand, and then the two led him to the waiting car, where they climbed in for the trip to the manor, chatting all the while. "Mary gets to stay with us for a whole year!" Amanda told Ramanujan as the two girls settled into the rear seats.

"Why is that?" asked Ramanujan fearing a sickness in the family.

"Her father is a minister and had been asked to run a parish in Africa until next Fall. Her mum was keen to go, but they didn't want to disrupt Mary's schooling this year. Luckily for us, Daddy asked if she could stay with us—and they said yes!"

"Well that sounds like it was a good solution," said Ramanujan. "Do you miss your family though, Mary?"

"In a way, but the North's have always been like a second family, so I'm glad I didn't have to go."

"And I get a sister!" said Amanda to a little squeal from the both of them.

They drove west through the refreshingly small town of Banbury and then headed north the four miles on Warwick Road through the fields to the even smaller village of Shotteswell, then back east through Shotteswell to Mollington

Road and the manor. Ramanujan thought that the manor was the two-story stone building that spread along the Mollington Road as it headed out of town, but they pulled into a long driveway and he discovered an even larger building lay behind it.

As they drove up, Lord and Lady North were there to greet them, and hustled them inside as a lashing sleet fell.

Ramanujan later found that he couldn't fully describe the feelings resulting from his stay at the manor. The experience for him was completely alien, taking place in a foreign country, with people not his own, and yet he felt the most at home during this short visit than he had on any day during his entire stay in England except, perhaps, for those first weeks with the Nevilles. The Norths had engaged Sujatha, a cook from Bangalore who lived in Banbury with her family, and every meal was delicious South Indian cuisine—minus most of the chilies that made all the food from home spicy hot to the extreme.

"Isn't this delightful?" asked Lady North when they gathered around the table on the first evening after they'd settled Ramanujan into his own room in the spacious mansion. "We're so ingrained with the idea that we have to prepare our traditional English fare at Christmas—and I hope you don't mind if we have a ham with cloves to the side on that day, Ramanujan—but we found that we've actually missed all of the food from your country too, which took so long to get accustomed to, but is so hard to forget once you've had it. So, we thought—why not have Indian feasts while you're here and make an occasion of it?" The most wonderful smells wafted out of the kitchen while she said this and then Sujatha began bringing out the mouth-watering and colorful dishes of his home.

Ramanujan was overwhelmed, and constantly thanked the Norths, getting up to personally thank Sujatha once during the meal. The Norths all laughed at some of his animated expressions and exclamations as he sampled the dishes. Mary, who at first showed trepidation with each bite of each new course, was soon asking for seconds of every dish and laughing as Amanda tried to show her how to ball up the rice and eat it with her right hand.

Following dinner, they chatted at length about India, and about how he was adapting to life in Cambridge. He'd started to describe his work, but immediately sensed that this wasn't the time nor company to carry on about equations. But he did mention his difficulties in fitting in with British society. "For me, you are the exception, rather than the rule in finding acceptance into the lives of the people here. Other than the Nevilles and Mr. Hardy, you are the only real contact I've had with any English families since my arrival."

Lord North began to huff with umbrage at the suggestion that the English would be unwelcoming, but Lady North placed a hand on her husband's arm. "I wish I could say the reciprocal were true, but we were treated very well by everyone we met when we were in India. You are some of the warmest people we've encountered." She thought for a moment. "Then again, it may have solely been due to our status... I hope you've not been treated too poorly here, Ramanujan."

"No, no," he replied sensing that they were drifting into uncomfortable territory. "I think it is just that I am having a difficult time making English friends. But I do have plenty of countrymen who are stopping by frequently and so I do not lack for companionship."

Later, everyone retired to the drawing room which was normally the domain of only the male guests after dining. Lord North continued the tradition as if the women weren't present, and the two girls sometimes weren't—running off to play a game of tag or bringing in a set of cut-out dolls to keep themselves entertained.

"Blast this war!" he exclaimed, swishing a snifter of brandy and sinking back into an over-stuffed leather chair, but with eyes ablaze. "This damn thing's going to end up consuming all of the resources—in both capital and men—that this country and every other country, for that matter, have available! And all because of a power grab by the Germans! Britain simply must protect the Empire and its allies; but it comes at such a cost that we may not be able to pay in the end."

He puffed on a cigar after offering one to Ramanujan who politely declined. "They told us that the war would be over in three months," he said. "Pfft. From what I've heard, things are just settling in for the long haul. I think we're protecting Paris, but poor Belgium was overwhelmed within days. And burned to the ground! And who knows what Russia is up to?" He looked over at Amanda and Mary and lowered his voice. "I don't mind telling you that I, personally, might be called on to aid the effort. This is going to cause no end of problems, but I see no other way to keep my family and the rest of the country safe other than to join in if it becomes necessary."

Ramanujan said that he had several countrymen who were either in the European conflict or were in the process of joining. He didn't mention that he expected to play no role at all. One look at him and Lord North would have called him unfit for duty in any case.

They were all leaving the study and in the main hall when Sujatha emerged from the kitchen on her way to her temporary quarters. "Oh, Sujatha," said Lady North, "I must formally introduce you. This is Mr. Ramanujan from…" and she thought quickly, "Madras? In Tamil Nadu."

"Pleased to meet you," said Sujatha in English, "and thank you for the many compliments to my cooking."

"No, I am the more pleased due to your excellent skills," complemented Ramanujan again. Then he asked her how she was, this time in Telegu. The two spent the next fifteen minutes learning about each other's families and histories in a foreign language while the others started preparing for bed. Sujatha was staying in the carriage house during his visit and was met at the door by the chauffeur holding up an umbrella in a driving sleet storm, and she grimaced as she headed out with him.

Ramanujan's room was on the second floor with a view of the fields, but it was too dark, and the windows were too wet, for him to see out as he prepared for bed.

That night he had another dream about the Three-tiered Hanging Garden, which, he thought later, had probably been brought on by staying in unfamiliar surroundings.

In the dream, Trinity College Great Court was empty, and he was hustling as fast as he could to make it to a room in a building across the compound. He had the answer to the Garden problem grasped in hand, although he could not exactly recall what it was at the time, and he needed to be present for an exam within ten minutes to write down the answer as required.

With every step towards his goal, the once empty court became more and more crowded, and even though he'd made the proper turn to reach the exam room in the Wren Library, he found that he was headed in the wrong direction. The crowds jostled him, and he saw Mr. Hardy at the far end of the courtyard and started to call to him. Suddenly a student stopped in front of him, shoving a paper into his hands. "You must help me," said the student in anguish. "I don't know the answer to this mathematics problem."

Ramanujan had taken the paper and quickly became absorbed in the equations, eventually writing the answer down for the grateful undergrad. Looking up he found that he was late for his own exam, and no longer remembered where he was supposed to be to take the test. And to his chagrin, he realized that he had also forgotten the answer to the Garden problem. He looked down at the sheet of paper in his hand, and it was blank.

His eyes flew open and he lay staring at the dark ceiling for what to him seemed like hours. The cool room and warm blankets, however, eventually had him back to sleep again.

He awoke to snow. He'd sensed that the light filtering in through the curtains seemed somehow different or brighter, and when he pulled them apart and stared out of the window, he was amazed. Six inches of white fluff blanketed the yard, bushes, and surrounding fields. To Ramanujan it was captivating—it made the world look soft, rounded, and suddenly in high contrast composed only of the darks and the whites. Since he knew that it must also be very cold, however, he somehow saw it as a shroud of death, a blanket that would never warm up.

Downstairs, Amanda and Mary were absolutely bursting at the seams with excitement. "Have you ever seen snow before?" asked Amanda breathlessly.

"Only in a picture," replied Ramanujan.

"Well, hurry! We want to take you outside—it's fresh!" said Amanda. They tried to rush Ramanujan through breakfast, but he still took his time to savor a welcome cup of Indian coffee and a delicious *aval* dish made by Sujatha. As soon as he put down his empty cup, the pair of girls bundled him into his coat, a borrowed hat and pair of mittens, and hustled him out the back door. They'd also provided him with a muffler for good measure and part of it trailed in the snow until he gave it another wrap around his neck.

He could barely keep his eyes open, the snow was so bright, and yet the sun was still partially concealed behind a thin layer of clouds. He took a few steps, and the snow packed and crunched under his shoes making each movement quite slippery, and he threw out his arms at one point to maintain balance. Amanda and Mary showed him how it could be packed, and they all made a lump of snow in their fists. Soon snowballs were flying, but they spared the Indian from too many direct hits, pummeling each other instead. A laughing, wet-faced Amanda took a huge bite out of a snowball in her hand and said, "Try it!" Ramanujan reached down and brushed the top layer of snow aside, took up a clean handful, and then tasted the cold, flavorless mass. "Not as good as gelato, though," he said with a grin.

They began to walk across the yard when Amanda and Mary suddenly flung themselves onto their backs.

"Watch, Mr. Rama!" yelled Amanda as she began moving her arms up and down and her legs as far apart as possible and then back in. "Here, pull me up." And he reached down awkwardly and grabbed her mittened hand, helping her to her feet without stepping on the shape she'd made in the snow. Amanda then pulled Mary up.

"See? Snow angels!" exclaimed Amanda. And peering at the shapes he could see figures that did barely resemble some of the drawings of angels he'd seen.

Bending over in unison, Mary and Amanda then began pushing a small snowball around until it gathered enough mass to be a huge roundish ball. He did his best while slipping to help with another and they soon had three large orbs, each a little smaller than the first. With some effort, they soon had them stacked on top of each other.

"A monument of snow!" declared Ramanujan.

"No! A snowman!" exclaimed Amanda. "See?" she asked.

Ramanujan stepped further back and said, "No, I cannot see a man."

"Well, wait here," she said while she and Mary ran off laughing into the house.

Ramanujan stood looking at the beautiful, but cold and hushed, landscape. The winter air seeped deeply into his clothes and any exposed skin felt its frigid touch. His feet began to ache, but he realized that it was the cold rather than his shoes, for once, that was the cause of the pain. Amanda and Mary were soon back, carrying a bundle of items. In no time, the three large snowballs had coal eyes and mouth on the uppermost ball, and coal buttons down the front of the middle one. A carrot nose, stick arms, a muffler, and a stocking cap were applied where needed. Ramanujan stepped forward and smiled at the face grinning back at him.

"Ah, yes, I do see a man," he smiled. "And a very odd man at that."

They'd just begun to warm up inside when Lord North announced that he'd had a horse and sleigh rigged, "Just in case this all disappears," he explained, and took them all out on a short trip across some of the neighboring fields. It was incredible to Ramanujan to be pulled across an utterly white surface, except where the horse's hooves dug into the partially frozen mud underneath. They trotted through a quiet world that strangely muffled even the bells on the horses and the songs and laughter of Amanda and Mary, gliding across a frozen scene that bit at his cheeks, eyes, and lungs, but included the unexpected warmth emanating from Lord and Lady North who sat on either side of him.

"What kind is this?" asked Ramanujan as he held a small round nut up so that Lady North could see it.

"That's a hazelnut—you should try one of those too," said Lady North handing him the nutcracker.

Ramanujan wrestled the small but slippery nut into the jaws of the nutcracker and tasted the meat when the shell had fallen away.

"These are also very good," he said with a smile as he returned to his task.

It was the morning of Christmas Eve day, and he was helping Lady North fill cloth sacks with nuts, berries, dried fruit and a piece of chocolate to distribute at the church on Christmas. Amanda and Mary had both been helping, but were called away when two other friends appeared at the door and wanted to go sledding. Ramanujan's job was to fill each of the square cloths and tie it closed with a piece of string while Lady North cut pieces of red or green ribbon and finalized the little packages with a fancily tied bow.

"You said you've made a lot of friends, Ramanujan?" she asked as she chose a green ribbon and cut several lengths off with an angled slice of the shears.

"Oh, yes, and more every week it seems," he replied. "The contacts among the Indian students and other Indians living in England seem to spread wider and wider all the time. Plenty of people drop by or invite me over. To tell you the truth, sometimes I have to say no because of all of the work I need to complete."

"And so, you're not too lonely or homesick in Cambridge then? That's a good thing."

Lady North was one of the first English ladies he'd become acquainted with on the *Nevasa,* and he'd liked her since they'd first met. In his eyes, she became the standard of all British women—feminine and reserved, but also strong and forthright. But still, he'd never felt like he knew her that well because of the social and cultural distances between them. On this visit, however, he came to see that she was very warm and perceptive underneath her more reserved and calculated exterior. She reminded him of Alice, but wearing finer clothes, moving more slowly, and being more guarded in her relationships—to him, the perfect English gentlewoman.

Ramanujan nodded but then said, "Yes, I do have friends who drop in, but the homesickness is sometimes difficult to keep away."

"Oh, yes," replied Lady North, "I can imagine it must be terrible to be so far removed from your family." She paused as she tied another ribbon. "I'm sorry to bring it up."

"No, that is fine, Lady North," said Ramanujan, "it cannot be helped."

"But at least you have your correspondences. I know that while we were in India, the letters I received made home seem not so far away."

Ramanujan was frozen for a moment with a walnut in one hand and a sachet in the other. "Ah," he said sadly, "but something has happened with them."

"What do you mean?"

"I do receive letters from my mother and from many friends, but the ones I miss the most are the ones from my wife. For some reason she has stopped writing to me."

"Oh, I'm so sorry to hear that," said Lady North sympathetically. "Why ever did she stop do you think? Was there an argument if you don't mind me asking?"

"I have no idea," replied Ramanujan. "I must have done something wrong, because the letters just stopped." He finished wrapping up a bundle and then looked over at Lady North. "I think my biggest mistake was in not bringing her with me to England. I hadn't been here before, you see, and so it seemed somehow very... threatening for a young Indian woman. Now I see that there was no reason for concern, and that she would have fit in well. Or if not, at least we would be together. We would have each other."

Lady North stared at him for a moment and then reached over and touched his sleeve. "I too am sorry that things haven't worked out for you as well as you'd have liked in your marriage. It must be very difficult." She turned away momentarily and out of the corner of his eye Ramanujan thought he saw a kerchief as she raised her hand to her face.

"Now," she said, turning with a smile to the table full of small decorative packets, "we simply must get these done before the messenger comes to collect them at lunchtime!"

They decorated a tree in celebration of the season that afternoon. One of the manor staff had chopped down a fir tree from a neighboring copse and he and another helper had set it up on a stand of crossed wood. To Ramanujan it was strange but beautiful to have such a needled and rugged tree displayed within the house during the middle of the winter when nothing but this type of tree was green, and everything that was normally lush appeared to be brown and devoid of life.

He watched Amanda, Mary, and Lady North pull out boxes of ornaments and begin hanging them on the tree. Amanda picked up the angel clad in a flowing gown and brought it over to Ramanujan. "See, Mr. Rama?" she asked. "This is the angel that goes on top of the tree. I thought you looked confused yesterday. Doesn't it look like the angels we made in the snow?" Ramanujan finally understood the figures that Amanda and Mary had made and nodded. The three ladies also set candle holders with small candles randomly about the tree on the branches that stuck out the farthest.

He'd been warned that this was going to be a long evening. After another fabulous South Indian dinner, the family moved back to the great room containing the tree. A roaring fire had been made in the fireplace, and they all encouraged Ramanujan to sit in the chair nearest the blaze. He watched as Amanda and Mary used long matches to light all the candles on the fir branches while Lady North dimmed the other lamps in the room. Then they all sat back admiring the tranquil display.

"Ah, this is like Navaratri," thought Ramanujan aloud. "The candles are just like the oil lamps set out each night, and the tree is holding all of the figures in tiers just like the *golu* erected in most houses in our town."

Lord North seated next to him looked over and nodded, but had obviously never seen a *golu*. "Every house and every shrine sets up a *golu* during Navaratri." Ramanujan then explained that a *golu* was a tiered stand of multiple levels, some reaching several yards in height. The stands were draped in cloth, and on each tier were arranged small figurines or objects of fired clay, all painted in bright colors. There were miniature ceramics of the gods and goddesses, figures of men and women at work or in prayer, figures of different fruits and flowers, and of animals, carts, or many other every-day objects. Miniature scenes were also arranged on small side-platforms—subjects kneeling before a king, scenes from stories of the gods, women planting rice in a field. The shrines held the largest *golu* and these were fabulously populated in intricate displays, enticing the entire community to turn out and enjoy them. As he finished his explanation he thought, *The feelings people have during Navaratri are just like these here during the Christmas season. I've missed Navaratri, but it's followed me here to Shotteswell.*

A servant brought eggnog to all in the room, and Ramanujan and the girls shared in cups that contained no brandy, but had plenty of nutmeg. To him, it was ambrosial, and he momentarily closed his eyes in utter contentment.

"And in a similar way we set up scenes called nativities that sound just like the ones you described in the shrines," began Lady North, but Ramanujan had dozed off and they gave him time to take a nap by the fire.

As it neared midnight, the North family, Mary, and Ramanujan bundled up and walked along the now-slippery road lit by staggered streetlamps and the glow cast from neighboring houses. They slowly progressed to the base of the hill leading up to the St. Lawrence church, joining the string of people headed in the same direction. Ramanujan fell twice at the bottom of the long slope, and the others couldn't help but laugh when he said, "This is impossible! I can never make it up that hill!"

Amanda came immediately to the rescue. "Here Mr. Rama," she said taking an arm. "The trick is to not lean too far forward when you're walking uphill, or too far backward when you're heading downhill. You also need to take smaller steps, like this," and she walked stiff-backed for a few yards looking to him like a toy soldier waddling like a duck. He suppressed a grin as Mary took his other arm, and the three of them advanced up the hill with no further mishaps. There were several stops as he received numerous introductions to friends of the North's they encountered along the way.

Amanda had reassured Ramanujan that he'd be welcome and wouldn't disturb the service in the slightest. The experience was not in the least what Ramanujan had expected. After his visit to Westminster Abbey with its cold interior and vast expanses, he'd expected the same at this church. However, the evening turned out to be surprisingly warm and intimate, and not so far removed from his own expectations of a religious celebration at home in Kumbakonam.

Rather than a forbidding distance between people and an abundance of empty space, he found a packed church warm with cloaks, bodies, and filled to the point that many had to stand along the walls at the end of the aisles. The church was brightly lit with multitudes of candles, including those in the chandeliers, and at one point, lit candles were passed throughout the crowd so that each worshipper held one, most reverently. Ramanujan felt that the blessings of Vishnu were entering through those flames, although this was an Anglican service and the priest spoke only of Jesus and the Trinity.

Contrary to the silence that he'd expected, there was almost continual singing and he was impressed that all present, except himself, knew the words by heart—just as a good Brahmin would know any of the songs being sung during prayers. These were people who were well versed in their hymns, knew the scripture, and obviously took time and effort away from their everyday lives to become immersed in and enjoy these celebrations.

When the time came for communion, he was brought almost to tears watching the intimate connection between the priest and the worshippers—each person touching the cup, each person receiving a wafer from the hand of the priest. The bowed heads and clasped hands were heartfelt displays of devotion. It was just as the offerings of the sacred flame of Vishnu blessed by the priests in temple. He was suddenly extremely homesick and at the same time deeply touched by the service. He hoped that his damp eyes and emotions wouldn't show, but he was nearly moved to burst into song himself.

> On whatever day it was written
>   that we are your servants, great Lord,
> On that day we in your family of servants
>   gained salvation and were saved, you know,
> One fine day, you appeared in Mathura
>   to break the bow, my Lord,
> And to leap on the serpent's five hooded heads;
>   to you we proclaim, "Many years!"

> "Many years!" – these heartfelt words said to the pure Lord,
> Supreme Being, Ruler with the Sarnga bow,
>   words by Vittucittan of Villiputtur, -
> Those who repeat them with practice in all years,
>   saying, "Namo Narayana,"
> Will dwell for many years near the Supreme soul,
>   praising him with "Many years!"

The entire household rose late the next morning. Gazing out of the multi-paned windows on the way down the stairs, Ramanujan could see that there was little left of the snow from the previous day, and that the snowman was sagging horribly. He almost wanted to run back to his room and say a *pooja* for the poor man. For breakfast, Sujatha had made perfect cups of Indian coffee, and had deep-fried some *vadai* to accompany them. Everyone at the table was subdued, but content, from the late-night services on Christmas eve.

He was invited into the great room where he noticed a small pile of brightly wrapped packages on display under the tree. He excused himself momentarily and climbed back up to his room. Mahalanobis had told him about Christmas traditions, and mentioned that a gift exchange might be appropriate. He reached into his bag and pulled out a small parcel he'd brought for Amanda.

Downstairs again, the family took its time opening gifts, and Ramanujan presented Amanda with a copy of Loney's *Plane Trigonometry* he'd purchased for her in Suez. "I wanted to give this to you on the *Nevasa,* but realized that it was probably more advanced than the level you were at in school at the time. I hope it is appropriate now."

"Oh, it certainly is," said Amanda. "This is our math subject for next year, so I'll have the whole summer with it to help prepare."

"I should say so," said Lord North. "Mr. Ramanujan has agreed to help tutor you during this coming summer, so it will be very appropriate indeed."

"What?" asked Amanda excitedly. "Really, Father?"

"Yes, he's agreed to see you once every two weeks to help you stay focused on mathematics. You can easily take a train to and from Cambridge for a nice outing."

"Can Mary come, too?"

"Why, that would be a great idea!" said Lady North, glancing with a smile at her husband.

Lord North looked to Ramanujan who nodded back, and said, "Yes, I don't see why not."

The two girls shrieked at the prospect of regular trips to Cambridge. Ramanujan noticed that their excited conversation over the next few minutes made absolutely no mention of mathematics.

Ramanujan opened his gift from Amanda. It was a blue knit wool hat. Putting it on his head immediately warmed him, and he found that he'd wear it daily well into spring.

They sat down later to a Christmas dinner, once again expertly prepared by Sujatha. In the center of the table was a ham stuck through with cloves and glazed with honey, a plate of baked yams with spices, and several plates of Indian curried vegetables and biriyani rice. Lord North began to proudly carve up the ham, and all the others were happy to take a slice while Ramanujan began to have doubts about his meal. Just then Sujatha stepped out from the kitchen and they all immediately complemented her on the dishes and their presentation. She bowed, smiled, and said, "Thank you very much, it has been a pleasure to cook for you." Then she addressed Ramanujan in Telegu. "Don't you worry, big brother, I cooked the ham on the opposite side of the kitchen and in a separate oven," giving a big grin.

"Thank you, little sister!" exclaimed Ramanujan in relief and in Telegu, tucking into the biriyani as she disappeared back into the kitchen.

CHAPTER 22.

1915

In a way, the trip to the North's over Christmas had been like going home, and he'd relished the food Sujatha had conjured up for each meal. Now he was back to his own cooking, and it was terrible by comparison.

He wondered vaguely whether he'd made a mistake. He'd recently moved to new chambers that were even nearer to Mr. Hardy's and were like the first rooms he'd occupied on Whewell's Court. The accommodations were fine, but the food was not. The remaining students and professors still took advantage of meals in the dining hall, but his one miserable experience there had ruled that out as an option for him.

He'd chosen proximity to Mr. Hardy above all other considerations. Many of his Indian friends were in boarding houses and said that while the food was not the same as that cooked in India, it was vegetarian, nourishing, and didn't require any effort for preparation on their part as the host provided it. They all highly recommended the arrangement and said that adding chutneys or spicy pickled condiments made almost anything tolerable. He was now finding that obtaining and preparing food was not as easy a thing as he'd first imagined, and so his variety and quantity in meals suffered badly.

The market was a long walk from his new rooms, and in the cold, wet British autumn, winter, and springs, he found it very difficult to force himself to make the trip. And of course, the food selection once he was in the market seemed, by his standards, to be abysmal. The tomatoes were larger and much juicier or meatier than in India, so that when he used them, it took much longer to cook anything down to the proper consistency. He recognized the bell peppers now, and came to like them, but there were absolutely no chilies to be had in the entire town. The potatoes were not the same texture he was used to, and he could almost not abide how mealy they were. The carrots were quite good, and he found that *courgette* was similar to snakegourd without the pithy interior and he quite liked it when it was in season. There was no *aubergine* to be found. Otherwise, the other vegetables were mainly foreign and unpalatable or not amenable to Indian cooking.

The rice was another thing he disliked—it was sticky after being cooked which worked well for some dishes, but horribly for others. At home there was a wide variety of lentils, or *dal,* available, but here in England there was only one type, a large brown/green-colored bean which was difficult to find at the best of times, and now nearly impossible during wartime. There was no *moong dal, toor dal,* or *urud dal,* although he could occasionally find garbanzos or *channa dal.* So, the brown/green lentils went into nearly every *dal*-based dish, meaning that nearly every recipe tasted the same to him. Naturally, not even the most basic Indian spices were available in the markets.

Thank goodness, he thought, *that I have some supplies arriving from back home.* Friends and family had sent packages—some at his urgent request, of *dal* flours, some rice, spices, pickles, chutney and many other necessities. Shipping large quantities of the prized South Indian rice and the various *dals* he desired was prohibitively expensive, and so he discouraged any of these being mailed to him.

All of the time and effort spent preparing marginally acceptable meals was taking him away from his mathematics. And sometimes the mathematics made him forget about eating altogether, so that his diet was beginning to suffer. The sporadic abdominal pains that had plagued him back home were becoming both increasingly more frequent and intense, and in addition to his daytime aches, he'd begun to suffer from night sweats that affected his sleep. Lately, he began to wonder if his lack of proper meals was connected to the state of his health, but there was nothing he would do to change his eating habits regardless. He vowed to maintain his strict Brahmin diet, just as he would back in Tamil Nadu. Substandard meals seemed to him a small sacrifice to pay as he was driven to devote all the time possible to furthering his mathematical career.

Over a pot of boiling rice, Ramanujan thought back wistfully to what now seemed like idyllic times. He had been poor, unrecognized, jobless, and without prospects when he'd failed in the college entrance exams. But after reconciling with his failure he had, on reflection, been in the happiest state he had so far achieved in his life.

He remembered awakening late one morning after a long night spent at a nearby temple discussing the Vedas, astrology, and, of course, mathematics. He'd been so energized from the discussions that he'd had a difficult time falling asleep when he did return home and had dreamt vividly when he'd eventually dropped off. Even now, he recalled the dream: he'd been deep in the heart of a temple, when a door had opened and Namagiri Amman had appeared, effortlessly scribing equations into the solid stone pillars of the shrine. On waking, Ramanujan had begun chalking down what he could remember of the equations onto a slate and rubbing out the previous results as he continued the derivations of the formulae.

"You arise so late in the morning—and look at you already with a chalked-white sleeve!" Janaki had joked, carrying in a cup of coffee as his mother followed with a tray laden with breakfast fare, including *idiyappam*, one of his favorites.

Ramanujan had given brief greetings to them both, but then forgot about breakfast, and the world around him, as he continued with his work. Without noticing, except for drinking his coffee, he had eaten his entire breakfast, solely by being hand-fed by Janaki as she hummed in a subdued tone, watching him scrape symbol after symbol onto his slate.

Later that day, the three of them had taken afternoon tea and were joined at dinner by his father. The specifics of this meal escaped him, but he remembered sitting back against a cushion and savoring the cool of the evening and the warmth of the interactions with his family. There had been a spat between his mother and Janaki barely out of earshot, but he'd also embraced this as being part of a dynamic family arrangement. Ramanujan had been amazed at how well provided for he was, and how supported he was in his studies. He'd been fed meals that were flavorful and nutritious—all without his conscious interaction unless he'd desired. This, to him, had been heaven.

CHAPTER 23

In late May, Ramanujan greeted Amanda and Mary at the Scholar's Lawn. They'd been dropped by taxi on Queens Road and walked the short distance along The Avenue and across the walking bridge over the River Cam to meet him. It was a beautiful sun-drenched afternoon, and Ramanujan strolled with them towards the Wren Library.

"How was your trip?" he asked as they stepped from The Avenue onto the expansive green lawn.

"This is so much fun!" exclaimed Amanda. "And it's so much easier than I expected to get here. Wow, this is a beautiful campus."

"Yes," said Ramanujan. "And just think—perhaps one day soon you will be attending school here."

"Well... maybe." said Amanda. "Oh, before I forget, this is for you," handing Ramanujan a cloth-wrapped packet. "We've been working hard in the garden and these are some of the early green beans and some unripe tomatoes. Mum started them in the house, and she says to just put the tomatoes in a windowsill and they'll ripen pretty quickly."

"Thank you," said Ramanujan. "And how are your parents?"

"Good," said Amanda. "Mummy, Mary, and I volunteer to cut and sew bandages once a week at the church, and she's really focused on the garden. Daddy's thinking more and more about volunteering, but hasn't so far."

"Oh!" exclaimed Mary in a hushed tone as they walked past a row of wounded soldiers sunning themselves in front of the library, and both she and Amanda tried without success to keep their eyes averted. After they entered the building, Ramanujan found a small alcove to the side of the main library stacks where they could talk quietly.

"I'm still pretty scared of this trigonometry," said Amanda.

"Not me!" said Mary. "I'm excited to get started! Come on, Amanda, how hard can it be?"

"Mary's right," replied Ramanujan. "Maybe I can explain some things that will set you two off on the right foot, or feet in this case."

Amanda and Mary both nodded, so he continued.

"Do you remember learning about triangles in geometry, and how there were a few facts you could discover just by knowing the basic rules? Such as all three angles sum to 180 degrees, so that if you know two of them you automatically know the third, and using the Pythagorean Theorem you can find the length of the hypotenuse opposite the right angle?"

Again, the girls nodded.

"With trigonometry, you can find out even more, even if you have just a few pieces of the puzzle. Years ago, people noticed that there is a relationship between a circle and a triangle. I won't go into that now, but let's say that we have one of the simplest right, or 90 degree, triangles you could make, and that it has each side next to the right angle equal to one unit—say a yard. We also know that each of the two other angles must equal 45 degrees. Then the hypotenuse would be calculated from the Pythagorean Theorem."

And he drew on the paper:

"$a^2 + b^2 = c^2$ and $1^2 + 1^2 = 2$ so $c = \sqrt{2}$, the hypotenuse is equal to $\sqrt{2}$."

"Now those old mathematicians noticed something very interesting. The ratio of either of the sides, or 1, to the hypotenuse is equal to $1/\sqrt{2} = .70710678...$—and they called this sine, one of those numbers that goes on forever. They also noticed that the ratio between the two equal length sides is one to one, or 1, and this relationship is the tangent. So, they began the study of trigonometry based on these ratios and others like them and they used terms like sine, cosine, tangent, and cotangent to refer to those ratios. All of the values of sine, cosine, and tangent for any angle are available from tables in the back of your book, and these will change as the length of the sides, and degrees of the angles change, and so they are useful for any problem.

"Let us say that we are interested in measurements of the steeple on the St. Lawrence church in Shotteswell, but we don't have a tall enough ladder. The tangent works well for this because we can know the length of one of the sides of a triangle we make, or the distance we walk away from the base of the church. If we went out in the churchyard and walked 100 feet from the base of the steeple, and measured the angle back to the top of the steeple with a protractor or another instrument and saw that the top was, say, 30 degrees, we would find in the tables that the tangent of 30 degrees was, .577 or so, then using the ratio: $.577 = height/100$ ft and multiplying both sides by 100—to isolate the height value in the equation—we would know that the steeple was 55.7 feet tall. Next, if we wanted to know the straight-line distance from us to the top of the steeple, or the hypotenuse of the right triangle we have made, we could use the cosine of the angle 30 degrees which is approximately .866 as you can see in the tables. Here we have:

$$.866 = \frac{100}{hypotenuse}$$

And rearranging to solve for the hypotenuse we end up with:

$$hypotenuse = \frac{100}{.866} = 115.5$$

So, 115.5 feet and we know all we need to know about the triangle we have made—all from just knowing the tangent value of 30 degrees and how far away we were from the church when we make that measurement."

Ramanujan patted the textbook and got up to give them time to absorb the lesson. Mary had an amazed look on her face, and Amanda quickly copied this formula down and then they both began reading. Ramanujan let them explore and answered questions as they came up. Mary in particular kept up an intense series of questions on their way back to The Avenue. Amanda's eyes were slightly glazed, and Mary's were glowing as they approached the stand to wait for a taxi to take them back to the railway station and home.

When he'd first arrived in Cambridge, he'd occasionally catch sight of a biplane in the skies to the north or hear one of their sputtering engines off in the distance, and these occurrences were becoming increasingly common since the outbreak of the war. Ramanujan had once examined a biplane up close in Madras. He'd never seen one in flight, but had paid 15 *paisa* to have a look at the famous airplane that had flown over the city a few years before he'd settled there in his clerking job. It had, by all reports, caused a sensation. He'd needed his imagination to envision the thing in the air, but as it turned out, his imagination nearly matched reality, except that airplanes turned out to be much more maneuverable, and much noisier, than he'd expected.

Choosing a clear afternoon, he found the bus stand for the transit to Cottenham, a village just a few minute's bus-ride to the north of town. He got down at the only bus stop in the village, and walked for several minutes toward the aerodrome, soon reaching the wire fence that surrounded the air corps station. A bench was situated along the roadside which skirted the confines of the RAF air strip, and he joined an old man sitting there gazing across the field.

The thin, gray-haired gentleman with a hooked nose looked over as he sat. "Well, hello," the old man rasped. He examined Ramanujan suspiciously, and then his eyes followed a biplane as it approached for a landing. "This is apparently how I'm ending my days then. The world has blown up, there are flying machines in the sky, and now a black man sits down next to me on a bench. Did you know that before the outbreak of the war, I was in a peaceful village, I'd seen very few biplanes, and very few—what is it you are? Indian?"

"Yes," said Ramanujan. "I am from Southern India and researching at Cambridge. I have come to watch the airplanes."

"As have I," said the old man. And then after a little hesitation, "You're welcome to share my bench."

"Thank you very much," said Ramanujan. "Oh, here comes one now!" pointing as the biplane buzzed over their heads, and they followed its progress as it turned and landed on the strip.

"That was an Avro 523 Pike," said the old man.

Ramanujan turned and stared at him in amazement. "What?" he asked. "You know their names?"

"Oh, certainly," the old man replied. "Comes from sitting on this bench day after day, don't you know?"

Together they watched a Bristol Scout, a Sopwith Pup, and three Sopwith triplanes take off, perform some maneuvers, and then land. The pair entered into a lengthy discussion about the aerodynamics and stability of biplanes versus triplanes, and the old man was much more knowledgeable about planes and flight than Ramanujan had at first thought. As the sun was near setting, the old man said he needed to head back to his cottage for an early supper.

"Early to bed and late to rise," he told Ramanujan with a grin. "Makes an old man sleep more than half his life away. It was good to meet you, Ramanjin, and I hope you come back to Cottenham sometime soon. I'll be at this bench, God willing," he said, mispronouncing Ramanujan's name and rising somewhat shakily.

After the old man shuffled down the road, Ramanujan thought back to India. The skies were always empty and quiet there, except, of course, for the birds and countless insects during the day, and the fruit bats that filled the air at dusk—huge silent flyers. The only other entities that could occupy the air were the gods, and these were legendary, and therefore not commonly seen by man. Now, in Europe, machines flew in formations and intricate patterns—not only that, but machines now also managed to cram the roadways, and bob in and across the oceans. There were also reports of horrible machines—armored tanks, machine guns, and flame throwers, not to mention the very non-mechanical gasses that were being used, all for the sole purpose of killing more people.

He focused again on the airplanes. These at the Cottenham aerodrome were the first planes that he'd watched in flight up close, and he realized that he was already accepting this as something commonplace in the skies. Ramanujan sat back and watched a plane perform loops and barrel rolls. All he soon saw were the possible mathematics behind each twist and turn as the sun began to sink into the fields.

"Ramanujan, I was wondering if you're engaged this evening?" asked Mr. Hardy as they were finishing up and arranging papers for the next day. "Only, my sister has come for a brief visit, and I thought I'd throw a little party and introduce her to some of my friends."

"No, I have no plans tonight, Mr. Hardy. I would be honored to attend," as the word 'friends' rang in his ears.

"Well, then, we'll expect you around eight?"

"Yes, I will be there," said Ramanujan. "Thank you very much."

Ramanujan was mildly shocked to be invited to a social function with Mr. Hardy. He'd eaten lunch with him on numerous occasions and had invited him to an awkward dinner, but had never socialized or been with him in a large-group setting. At eight o'clock precisely, Ramanujan knocked on Mr. Hardy's door and soon learned that he was the first to arrive.

"Ramanujan!" said Mr. Hardy happily, showing him in and taking his coat. "This is my sister, Gertie... um, Gertrude, Gertrude Hardy."

Ramanujan bowed slightly and said, "It is a pleasure to meet Mr. Hardy's sister, Mrs. Hardy."

"Now, that's awkward, isn't it? First of all, it should be Miss Hardy, and second of all I won't be addressed by anything other than Gertie! It's a pleasure to meet you, too, Ramanujan. I've heard so much about you."

Mr. Hardy had just hung up Ramanujan's coat when there was another knock at the door and soon people began to stream in, all happy to greet or meet Gertie and to accept one of the G&T's that Mr. Hardy began to hand out. The two main rooms were soon full of laughter, smoke, and the clinking of ice in glasses.

The company slowly divided into small groups, and Ramanujan found himself near a corner of the room against a credenza with two other students from India who were in a heated discussion about the politics in Calcutta, of which Ramanujan knew little. Unexpectedly, Gertie had joined them. She gazed over at her brother and said, "He certainly can be the social animal when he wants to be, can't he?" They watched Mr. Hardy tell a joke and slap another chap on the back as the circle he was part of broke into laughter.

"It seems to be so," said Ramanujan. "This is the first time that I have been with Mr. Hardy in such a social setting, so I really would not know. Did he not organize this party for you?"

Gertie turned to him and said, "More like he put it together for himself because he didn't know what to do with me. He sometimes finds it awkward when I show up for a visit."

Ramanujan had previously noticed something awkward with her eyes and again found himself staring. "One glass eye," said Gertie.

"Oh! I am so sorry!" exclaimed Ramanujan. "I did not mean to stare, only something did not seem right, and I could not make out what it could be."

"Don't worry," said Gertie. "I've had this eye since I was little and am very comfortable with people being uncomfortable about it."

"Not uncomfortable, just curious," said Ramanujan. "You forget that we have plenty of blind or partially blind people in India. Only, no glass eyes."

Gertie laughed. "Well, I must be upper class then!"

"Very much so," said Ramanujan. And after an awkward pause he ventured, "What do you do, if you don't mind my asking?"

"I teach art in a town called Cranleigh where Godfrey and I grew up. It's a little south of London."

"Godfrey?" asked Ramanujan.

"Hardy, of course," replied Gertie. "G.H."

"Ah," said Ramanujan. Then, "You are very fortunate to have him as a brother."

"Yes, I agree," said Gertie. "He and I are lucky to be very close, especially since our parents have passed. Although he usually does this."

"Does what?"

"We have very lovely, intense and intimate discussions on the first day or two when we get together, and then he feels the need to fill the space with other people, which is something that I never do. Thus, the impetus for this party."

"Oh, and I should let you go over and be with him," suggested Ramanujan.

"No, I'm fine right here, and am enjoying being away from the crowd."

"Do you mind if I ask a question, Miss Hardy?"

"Goodness! It's Gertie as I said! No, ask away."

"Oh, yes, Gertie," stammered Ramanujan. "I was wondering, had Mr. Hardy ever married?"

"Hardy?" asked Gertie stifling a laugh. "No, he hasn't yet."

"He seems to be so eligible, but I have never dared ask him about it."

"Well, Ramanujan. He is not really a lady's man. More of a… You see, he is so consumed by his work," said Gertie by way of explanation.

"Yes, I can understand that," replied Ramanujan.

Laughter broke out again across the room and Ramanujan and Gertie caught snippets of the lightning-fast barbs and jokes being traded around the circle containing Mr. Hardy. Watching Mr. Hardy nod at a joke with a broad smile on his face and then explode with laughter, Ramanujan thought that he'd never seen his friend in this light—a carefree, quick-witted, jovial side he hadn't known existed. He suddenly felt much closer to Mr. Hardy without having exchanged more than a word with him all evening.

"You see," he was explaining to the girls at their next meeting. "The trigonometric functions, like sine and cosine, are at their heart a means of measuring a circle, or even more importantly, a cycle or a wave. After one revolution, they end up back at the same place, if you imagine it as a circle, or back to the same spot in a wave as it moves up to the top of a crest, down to the bottom of the trough and then back to its resting place.

"As it happens, degrees, like on a compass, are handy in telling us where we are as we move around the dial, but they are actually a little messy when calculating the motion of things like waves. So, mathematicians have come up with a corresponding measure that is much easier, and it is called the radian. You know that the circumference of a circle is $2\pi r$. Well, if we make the radius equal to one, we have what is called a unit circle, and the circumference is then 2π radians, or 6.28319 radians. A radian is the ratio between the distance of an arc on the outside of the circle and the radius. So, it would take a distance of 6.28319 radii, of unit one, to travel around the outside of an entire circle. Ninety degrees, or ¼ of a 360-degree circle in radians is ¼ of 2π, or $\pi/2$ radians. 30 degrees would be $2\pi/12$ or $\pi/6$ radians, and so on. The tables in the back of your book will show you the sine value in either degrees or radians.

"The reason that I love radians is that they allow the mathematics to shift into something I am very interested in. There is a way to calculate the value of the sine of an angle without looking in the tables in the book. It can also be calculated by an infinite series that looks like this if we are measuring x in radians, and he scribbled out the following:

$$\sin x = \left(\frac{x^3}{3!}\right) + \left(\frac{x^5}{5!}\right) - \left(\frac{x^7}{7!}\right) + \left(\frac{x^9}{9!}\right) - \cdots.$$

and

$$\cos x = 1 - \left(\frac{x^2}{2!}\right) + \left(\frac{x^4}{4!}\right) - \left(\frac{x^6}{6!}\right) + \left(\frac{x^8}{8!}\right) - \cdots.$$

"Those exclamation marks indicate that the value is factorial which just means that 3! = 3x2x1, and 5! = 5x4x3x2x1. And those dots at the end mean that this series goes on forever in the same pattern."

"But you could never calculate all of those in a million years," pointed out Mary.

"I agree," said Ramanujan. "But usually the first five or so terms are all that is necessary to come close to the right answer.

"In your trigonometry class, you will mostly be using sines and cosines to calculate the value of a missing side of a triangle, and you can use the tables to find what you need. But I have fallen in love with the underlying math that allows us to know the values as extremely interesting series that go on forever. The deeper you dig, the more intriguing series and patterns pop up. They actually tell me all I need to know about the world." And Ramanujan stopped there sensing he was losing them, not wanting to frighten them away from the math.

They spent the rest of the afternoon going to a nearby tea shop with the girls catching Ramanujan up on the wonderful world of teenage gossip and relationships.

The visits from Amanda and Mary continued biweekly throughout that summer, and it became apparent over time, that Amanda's interest in mathematics was waning, while Mary's interest was on the rise. Mary, however, had to discontinue her trips to Cambridge a month before the school terms started in the fall, because her mother was returning from Africa and they were moving to another district where she would be attending a different school than Amanda.

In the last visit by Amanda before her own school term began, she again met with Ramanujan in the Wren library. "Well, Daddy's done it," she breathed out heavily. "He's enlisted in the army, and we're just beside ourselves with worry!"

"Oh, he had said that he thought he might need to join up," said Ramanujan. "I'm sorry for you that it has come to that."

"What does he know about fighting?" asked Amanda earnestly. "And here he's going to lead a newly formed brigade against the Germans in France?"

"He is brave to do so," said Ramanujan, shaking his head. "And I know that the country needs smart men to lead the others, but still..."

"I know it does, but who will lead us?" asked Amanda. "Who will look after our family if something happens to him? Hang the bloody war! And Mummy agrees—she's made herself almost sick with worry," and it took some time for Amanda to calm down as Ramanujan consoled her and they talked about Lord North's preparations and his sudden eagerness to become part of the war effort.

Once the lesson started, Ramanujan veered immediately off course, diverted by an interesting result based on the sine function, when Amanda stopped him by saying, "That's all well and good, Mr. Rama, but I have a question for you."

Ramanujan looked up, and now guessed that this last meeting would have very little to do with mathematics. "About your father?" he asked.

"No," and she suddenly looked abashed. "I know that you're from a different culture and all of that, but there are some things that are not that easy to figure out, even in our own society," she said, and flipped the pages of her book. "Well, this is a little embarrassing, but—how do you, or how does a girl, that is, know when a boy is interested in you? What are the signs? They must be the same everywhere?"

Ramanujan was momentarily taken aback by the question, but then replied after some thought. "Well, cultures may actually make a big difference about this. In India, we rely heavily on our parents finding the right match for us. They arrange everything based on kinship and astrology, and we just assume that they have done their best. We marry before interest or love even come into the picture, if you see what I mean."

"Oh, well, thank you very much, but that is going to be of no help then," said Amanda with a sigh. "In fact, even though I like him, I don't think that my parents would consider this guy to be the 'right person' by any stretch of the imagination.

"He's the cutest boy, he really is, and has this curl of hair that he continually has to flip out of his eyes, which are a very pretty blue, by the way. He's taller than me and can run like the wind. He doesn't dress very well though, and all of my friends call him a 'rough boy,' but I'm just mad about him. I simply can't tell if he's even interested in me though. I catch him staring at me sometimes, but when I try and talk to him, he'll say a few words and then find an excuse to be off. In a nice way though. It's just so frustrating. And I don't know of any way I could introduce him to my parents—especially

Daddy! When I think of a tea with him and Mother, I just picture an absolute disaster."

Ramanujan walked her out to the taxi stand as they continued to talk, and he listened to Amanda's schemes to ferret out whether this boy liked her or not.

"Enough about him!" said Amanda, when they reached the taxi. "This has been a fantastic summer and thank you ever so much for tutoring me. My parents said that they are in your debt, and I shall miss you so much this school year." She gave him a quick hug, and as she climbed into the taxi, said, "Goodbye, and make sure you eat well," with a smile. Then she was off, waving through the rear windscreen.

Amanda is definitely growing up, thought Ramanujan as he made his way back to Trinity College.

The next day he took a late-afternoon stroll through Fellow's Gardens, along the graveled paths, and past the multitudinous flowers that grew between the walkway and the garden wall. A young enlisted man and nurse sat on one of the curved benches secluded by hedge breaks and as he sauntered by, the woman, whose eyes were locked on her male friend, put her hand gently up under his chin and brought her head forward for a lengthy kiss. Ramanujan didn't linger, but didn't hasten away either, as the pair conversed in low hushed voices.

How extraordinarily different our two cultures are, thought Ramanujan as he admired the flowers and watched the passersby. He noted another couple holding hands as they entered the garden path.

In India, such public displays of affection were never witnessed. A man and wife walked with a respectful distance between them, and they never touched in public. The only signs that they were together and married were her *tali*, the necklace she was adorned with by her husband at her wedding, and her toe rings. There was no hand holding, no linking arms, certainly no hugging—no contact of any kind. Kissing in public would be beyond thinking. Only in the confines of the home was any familiarity allowed to be expressed, and never when company was present.

He'd run into Alice at the market that morning. "I had my last math tutoring session with Amanda yesterday," Ramanujan had said as they made their way along the sidewalk heading to their respective homes. "She was understandably upset that her father is going to fight in the war after all."

"Yes, I would be, too," replied Alice. "I'm becoming worried that Neville might be called up even though he is practically blind without his glasses and a pacifist, but I suppose we must all do our part in some way—God knows everyone else is."

"Yes, Mr. Neville has mentioned his hatred for this war, but that he was feeling frustrated at the same time," Ramanujan nodded, and after they'd walked a little further he said, "Amanda was more interested in my opinion about something else than she was in trigonometry."

"Oh, what about?" asked Alice.

"Well, to my surprise, she expressed her interest in a young man and sought my advice about how to gauge his interest in her. I have to say, I was a little taken aback by her speaking so plainly about her affection."

"Ha!" Alice laughed suddenly. "It looks like Amanda will soon be the object of someone's attentions," and, to Ramanujan's raised eyebrows, she'd then explained courtship with all its subtle and not-so-subtle rules and signals to the baffled Indian.

As Alice highlighted some of the complexities of British romance, Ramanujan's thoughts turned to his own situation. He was married, and yet had never really known his young wife. Janaki was, after all, barely fourteen when he'd departed for England. And now their marriage appeared to be in jeopardy. His daily attempts to ignore the chasm that had ripped open between him and his young wife were rarely successful. The final upshot of this had been his decision that summer to halt all further communications with his family. The distress that the lack of response from Janaki continually aroused in him made it not worth the effort to reach out to any of them.

As he'd realized when he'd talked earlier with Lady North, he should have brought Janaki with him to England after all. Before he left, she'd asked and wanted to join him, but he'd said that she was too young, and that Britain was too foreign for someone so innocent. He was now aware that the time they could have been together would probably have prevented a rift from developing in the first place. And he was positive that she could produce better meals with the most meager of supplies than he could with the best available.

Listening again to Alice, he was surprised that he'd also absorbed most of what she'd said while they walked, and he bid her a very good day as their paths diverged.

He returned to his lodgings in a somber mood, not because of the subject matter of his discussions with Alice and Amanda, but because of his dark broodings about home. However, that temper was suddenly buoyed by an unexpected letter from his childhood friend, Sekar. In the letter, Sekar had written of Kumbakonam, some of their mutual friends, and that he was going to America to play *tabla* with a travelling musical group as soon as the war was over! Another Brahmin crossing the water—and seemingly ecstatic about the prospect.

CHAPTER 24

Ramanujan detected a hint of concern in Mahalanobis' voice as they sat at the small dining table in his apartment. "Ramanujan, you've adapted so well to Cambridge," his friend was saying. "You have a circle of friends here, and countrymen who make the trip from London or Oxford to meet you and discuss your mathematical findings. You've published many papers with Mr. Hardy, and have become a trusted co-researcher of his. You're part of the academic community here. Now you must adapt even more to British society and eat something, or you will waste away. I can't help but notice that you're losing weight, and that can't be healthy."

"But I'm being poisoned," replied Ramanujan frankly.

"What?" asked Mahalanobis in surprise. "Whatever do you mean?"

"Virtually everything in this country has animal products in it. Did you know? They include the remains of dead animals in almost all foods that you can buy in the shops."

"Again," asked Mahalanobis. "What are you talking about?"

"I was happy with the fried potatoes, chips, when I first arrived—until I found that they are fried in animal lard instead of butter or vegetable oil. Who would do that? Why ruin a perfectly good vegetable? I had to purge my system and offer *pooja* for a week after I learned this."

"Surely that was just an isolated incident."

"No—have you ever read the labels? Unless you trust the cook, or buy it fresh, you can't eat anything that comes from England—or any of Europe for that matter. They have a love of eating meat and use it for cooking almost everything. I had a flavored milk that I liked—Ovaltine—but when I read the label, I found it contained animal byproducts! I'm still not sure that I have the possibility of becoming pure after drinking that! It's part of their culture, and, meaning to or not, they are defiling us."

"I'll try and see that you get more foodstuffs from our country, but you can't possibly refuse to eat all foods from here simply based upon those two incidents."

"I can, in fact, refuse those very things," Ramanujan maintained, adamantly jabbing his finger into the table. "As the great Periyalvar sang," and he chanted:

Kannan, Primal Cause, Dark One,
You who created the four-faced Lord,
On a day that I do not eat at all, I, your servant, feel no hunger.
But a day that I do not revere the Rig, Yajur or Sama Veda,
Or a day that I fail to approach your feet with flowers,
That day is a fasting day for me.

"All I really need for nutrition are my religion and my mathematics, and I will never give up on either of those two," he said, pointedly ending the topic under discussion.

Seeing his stubbornness, Mahalanobis then suggested that they go for a punt on the River Cam, and the two spent an amiable afternoon that stretched into the early evening, poling up and down the serene stretches of the river.

"Well, depending on how you look at it, perhaps we've both turned out to be lucky in these unluckiest of times," said Mr. Hardy. "You made it to England before the damn war made such travel nearly impossible. And I've failed in the Derby Scheme."

"You have failed at something?" asked Ramanujan incredulously. "Wait, I have heard of this proposal, but given it little notice. What is the Derby Scheme again?"

"By now you must be aware that I'm against this bloody war, and it just goads me that all of our supposedly great unthinking leaders have led, and are still marching, some of our finest minds—even those marvelous German scientists and mathematicians—to slaughter. It's like a campaign to set us back intellectually into the Stone Age. So, even though it seems a contradiction, I signed up under the Derby Scheme, but failed on medical grounds! Can you imagine? I play tennis—very well, I might add, and cricket. Not eligible? Well, anyway, the Scheme is to test how many able-bodied men would be willing to go to war voluntarily without the need for conscription. As against the war as I am, I couldn't stand the thought of some young talent needing to enter battle against his will just because I failed to stand up."

With a sigh, he continued. "It looks like I failed the Derby Scheme, and the Derby Scheme has failed England. There's to be a conscription after all. Maybe it was purposefully designed to fail in the first place," and he shook his head in disgust.

They resumed working on the stepwise proof of an equation that Ramanujan had posited to help with a paper they were submitting for publication. Mr. Hardy had been scratching out something on a sheet of paper when he slowly put the pencil down and regarded Ramanujan. Ramanujan noticed his gaze and looked up.

"I must say something that may not come across as obvious to you, Ramanujan," began Mr. Hardy. "This war has been incredibly difficult, well, obviously, and it's been a drain on our society in so many ways—manpower, energy, foodstuffs, supplies, and life. Those who support the war have left the country to fight in it, and those who oppose the war spend what seems like an inordinate amount of time banging on doors that never open. I know you also see how dark these times have become. The campus seems nearly deserted of students and is now plugged to bursting with the wounded."

Mr. Hardy stared out of the windows at the rain pouring down on the drab gray tents in the courtyard below.

"It has, of course, affected me personally," he continued. "I've lost a good friend and scores of men that I know socially. Littlewood and all the remaining good minds are not dead, yet, but are in the field which is a cause for constant worry. I work tirelessly to try and bring this madness to a halt, but the huge wave of politics is against pacifism. Even some of the best cricketers are in the war, and there are now barely enough feeble bodies to even carry on a decent match.

"But in spite of this," he seemed to rally, "your presence here has been like a day of sunshine in this dreary season of war. I know that being here and enduring this upheaval has also brought hardship on you, but without our daily meetings, I want you to know that I'd probably be in a deep depression, or worse, by now."

Ramanujan nodded and said, "It is so strange that the highest point of my life, coming from the East, corresponds with the lowest point of times here in the West. Everything since I came to England has had that odd element of opposition." They both became silent again and resumed laboring through the steps toward a proof.

When they were finished for the day, Mr. Hardy spent another half-hour regaling Ramanujan with the latest cricket scores from Australia and his thoughts on the best remaining prospects from England. To Ramanujan, this was an extremely odd obsession, but it was one that he enjoyed hearing about, nonetheless.

Walking back to his room after his sports lesson, Ramanujan realized that Mr. Hardy and he had many conversations each day, but this was the first time that Mr. Hardy had expressed his feelings of appreciation that he was England. He also realized that he'd come to describe Mr. Hardy to himself, without any negative connotations, as Winter—something he'd not experienced until setting foot on the island. Once he'd become fully acquainted with the season, he'd thought that this was the perfect description of the man. On the outside he was cold, and parts of his personality were either clearly defined like the contrast of snow on dark branches, or aspects of him were muffled as if he were obscured by flurries and frost. On the interior, however, once the doors were opened, he was warm and inviting, though not venturing beyond the comfortable confines he'd established. He kept a neat house and the fires were always well tended, good friends were always welcome, and the discussions around the fireplace centered on a singular topic—mathematics.

CHAPTER 25

1916

Perhaps, he thought, *I'm looking at this the wrong way.* He'd been pondering his odd Three-tiered Hanging Garden dream on and off during the last few months and had pulled out his notebooks to look through them. *It may be that the point of the dream was to find an equation resembling a tiered problem of some sort, and I'm supposed to discover that.*

He flipped through his first notebook seeking a layered equation of some kind or one that resulted in discrete or stepped values, and then immediately forgot his purpose. Instead, he found himself reminiscing about the discoveries he'd made and paths he'd followed as he'd recorded the notebook entries; some scribbled out now eight and more years previously. He came to the section on Bernoulli numbers. He'd published a paper based on his findings in the *Journal of the Indian Mathematical Society* before he'd even thought of travelling to England.

Ramanujan proudly recalled his submission of the paper, 'Some Properties of Bernoulli's Numbers,' and its broad acceptance by the Indian mathematics community. In the paper, he'd presented his technique for calculating the Bernoulli numbers in many fewer steps than had previously been required. He'd also outlined some of the properties he'd discovered about these numbers—coefficients first derived by Bernoulli, and used in the summation of integers raised to some power. He'd shown that the denominator of each Bernoulli number contained the factors 2 and 3, only once each, and hence every denominator was divisible by 6. He'd also described the interesting relationships between the ranks of the Bernoulli numbers and the location of prime numbers in either the numerator or denominator. He'd written a list of the first even Bernoulli numbers in his paper:

$$B_0 = -1, \quad B_2 = \frac{1}{6}, \quad B_4 = \frac{1}{30}, \quad B_6 = \frac{1}{42}, \quad B_8 = \frac{1}{30},$$

$$B_{10} = \frac{5}{66}, \quad B_{12} = \frac{691}{2730}, \quad B_{14} = \frac{7}{6}, \quad B_{16} = \frac{3617}{510},$$

$$B_{18} = \frac{43867}{798}, \quad B_{20} = \frac{174611}{330},$$

$$B_{22} = \frac{854513}{138}, \quad B_{24} = \frac{236364091}{2730}, \quad etc.$$

As he scanned the figures, his eye for some reason went back to the twenty-second number, $B_{22} = {}^{854513}/_{138}$. He'd used this number in several examples in his paper, and in one example showed that since 22 factored into the two primes 2 and 11, ${}^{854513}/_{11} = 77683$; and 77,683 should thus be prime. Something about this number didn't seem right and kept nagging at him, so he pulled out a table of prime numbers and began to calculate.

His stomach tightened as he looked at his results, and the niggling pain which now constantly lingered in his abdomen was suddenly magnified tenfold. 77,683 was not prime. It was the result of two smaller prime numbers, 131 times 593.

Ramanujan looked again at the numbers, and then squeezed his eyes tightly shut. *I've made a terrible mistake!*

He dropped his pencil, stood suddenly, and began a panicked aimless pacing about the room. *What will people say when they find out? Should I tell anyone? How could I have been so stupid?* He found it difficult to breathe and his side burned as the questions and self-blame cycled through his brain. Gradually, however, he slowed his pace, calmed down, and eventually became resolved. *I'm not going to tell a soul. I'll just have to deal with the consequences when the time comes.* And he consoled himself with the realization that many of the greatest mathematicians in the world had been found to have made errors—usually discovered only after new techniques or reexaminations revealed the mistakes. *And often they were dead before these were found out,* he thought, which also somehow comforted him.

In this state of anxiety, he couldn't eat, but did manage to make a cup of tea, and the warm mug helped keep resurging feelings of doubt and disappointment with himself at bay.

As he sat gazing out at the gray day, he pondered how his eye had been drawn to that particular number, and what it was that had caused him to suspect that there was something not quite right about it. It was almost as if Namagiri Amman, unseen, had focused his attention on that small detail, out of all the numbers and equations in all of the pages of his notebooks. She had led him to many of the results in the paper, and now she had shown him his error.

It could be due to his darkened mood, but it seemed to Ramanujan that she was visiting him less frequently as he worked with Mr. Hardy to become more rigorous in his methodology and to carefully detail each step required in arrival at a final proof. And it was Mr. Hardy who patiently pulled him back as he started down some undiscovered path while they were trying to lay the foundation of a road already under construction—a path that Namagiri Amman would have guided him safely along.

He'd now published several papers with Mr. Hardy, and some very significant findings were in the works. None of their results could have possibly found acceptance within the academic community without absolute accuracy and verifiability, so he was spending more time on the process that explained the old, rather than on the creation of the new. His sadness grew as he felt himself even more cut off from home and the joyous communion with the goddess whom he now felt he'd so taken for granted.

"Are you by any chance Mr. Ramanujan, the great Indian mathematician?" asked the injured soldier who'd come up to him as he'd paused in his stroll and stood gazing out over the River Cam.

"Um, yes," said Ramanujan, sheepishly, "But perhaps not that great."

"No, no," replied the man. "Hardy and the others have nothing but praise for you."

They stood for a moment in silence.

"Let me introduce myself," the man said, stretching out his left arm with some difficulty to shake Ramanujan's hand. "My name is Ralph Fowler, and I've been a student of G.H.'s—or, well, Hardy's for some years now."

Ramanujan hesitated but then clasped the man's unclean left hand with his right. It was obvious that the man's right arm was severely wounded, and that he'd had no choice but to offer his left. It had not been proffered in offense but in friendship, and so Ramanujan briefly shook it.

"So, you were here at Cambridge before the fighting broke out?" asked Ramanujan, unable to take his eyes off the thick bandages on Mr. Fowler's shoulder and elbow.

"Yes, but then I enlisted and tried to help out at Gallipoli. I'm sure you've heard how that turned out?"

Ramanujan nodded with a wince. "Yes, the news reports were dreadful—the deaths, and so much illness. I am glad you made it through alive, but I am also sorry that you were wounded. Are you going to stay in Cambridge when you have healed?"

"Well, not at the present time. I'm still an officer, you see, and have recently been asked to join the Anti-Aircraft Experimental Section, or AAES."

"I have not heard of this," said Ramanujan. "What is its purpose? I assume it has something to do with anti-aircraft defenses?"

"Yes, it does. As more German zeppelins and aircraft invade our airspace, we need to become more accurate in the calculations that guide anti-aircraft weapons against them. Here in Trinity, I was a theoretical mathematician under G.H., ...," he hesitated again, "Mr. Hardy, and now the government has a great need of those skills. They've called me into service in the Section—once I'm healed up."

"Do you perhaps know Mr. Littlewood?" asked Ramanujan. "He is a colleague of Mr. Hardy here, and a friend of mine, but was also called into service."

"Yes, of course!" said Mr. Fowler. "He's brilliant and helped me in my research in college. I understand that he's also aiding the army with artillery ballistics, though I haven't heard much of or from him recently."

"Nor have I," said Ramanujan. "I know that Mr. Hardy has corresponded with him, and so the two are in touch. Thus far I can relate that he is well. So, you will be working on ballistics?"

"Yes, in a fashion," said Mr. Fowler. "With anti-aircraft projectiles there are so many variables at play that we'll be working out calculations to deal with as many as we can—projectile weight and propellant, wind speed, altitude of the enemy aircraft, speed of the enemy, and other factors. Then there is how to time the fuse so that it goes off when and where we need it to. Multiple calculations need to converge at the right point in time and space."

That was all that Ramanujan needed to hear, and the two spent the next three hours hunkered over bits and scraps of paper filled with conjectures and avenues for exploration.

Becoming settled in with a small but extended community of friends in Trinity and southern England often left him feeling conflicted. All that he really desired was to have quiet time to work on number theory, but his notoriety among Indians living in England made it so that he occasionally had what seemed to be floods of visitors stopping by. On many evenings his rooms were filled with the local Indian students and even some professors, all engaged in animated conversations that could go on well into the night. He was simultaneously both energized by their warmth and attention to him, but also left feeling drained and unfulfilled by not being able to continue an avenue of investigation he'd been following. And his exhaustion was being exacerbated by the now-common nightsweats that often woke him from fitful sleep. Still, he realized that to be so admired was something to show appreciation for, and he really did enjoy and become engaged in many of the sometimes deep, sometimes funny, conversations that sprang up in the evenings.

Then there were those who came to visit but were not scholars, nor interested in mathematics or other intellectual pursuits—they simply wanted to meet the person they'd heard to be the famous Indian mathematician. The Patels, for example, came for a visit from London and stayed—and stayed. At one point he'd needed to take a trip to London for a few days, and they'd boarded in his rooms while he was away—with his blessings, of course. But when he was back in Cambridge the next week, the couple wanted to spend all of their time with him. They were pleasant enough and of some standing—the husband being a barrister—but even with Mr. Patel's humorous stories from the London courts and his wife's news from back home and the war, he still began to subtly resent the precious time they demanded and of which he had so little.

Well into the second week of their stay, he'd gone out for a punt with them on the River Cam to enjoy the warm summer day. He'd come to love poling about the river on lazy afternoons, usually to lose himself in his own thoughts. He didn't know what got into him that particular afternoon, but he'd become more and more animated during the punt and began to sit, and stand, and move about the small vessel. Perhaps he was becoming overly confident with his abilities on a punt, or perhaps, on later reflection, he should have gone for a walk on solid ground instead. Before anyone could react, first he, and then all the others plunged overboard into the cold river as the small boat finally capsized. They came up sputtering and startled, but by the time they were helping each other up the slippery grass slopes of the bank, they were all laughing at the mishap. It took forever to calm Mrs. Patel down and stop her hysterical laughter. Whether it was a coincidence or not he never knew, but the couple ended up leaving the next day.

CHAPTER 26

He was picking his way through the Great Court in the autumn of 1916 and became aware that he was the only person associated with the university in the entire courtyard. When he'd first arrived, the campus had been bustling with young scholars, but in the year following the outbreak of war, the crowds had thinned to a handful of students. Now the squares still bustled, but with the wounded and medical personnel rather than with academicians. The proportion of Indian students among the scholars remaining on campus had risen dramatically, mainly because of the low representation of English students—they were instead populating the battle trenches of France. The preponderance of faces he saw in the halls of Trinity were now Indian friends of his, and in numbers they dominated the participants from England taking the annual exams.

That morning, he'd picked up the local newspaper and read more about the Battle of the Somme—the tallies of the dead and wounded were beyond comprehension. Nearly 60,000 troops had died on the first day of the battle, by far the worst day in July, and the numbers of casualties had mounted daily since then.

As he made his way through the courtyard, he thought about the taunting he'd received at this very spot two years previously and wondered what had happened to all those young men. Perhaps brought on by this memory, he had a nightmare later that night with fierce gods and demons rending apart human bodies and the faces of his deriders floating up out of masses of corpses to torment him again. He awoke in a sweat and remained awake as the first light of dawn was filtering into his bedroom, the pains in his side seemingly even more extreme than normal.

He performed a *pooja* that morning with prayers for the welfare of the nation. As if the dream from the night before had been an omen, he retrieved his mail, happily opened a letter from Amanda and found, to his immediate grief, that Lord North had been killed in the Battle of the Somme. He wept for the loss of a friend, another British casualty in this horrible war, and for Amanda, now fatherless. He sighed and performed an additional *pooja* for the welfare of the family, and then sorrowfully penned a letter of condolence to Amanda and her mother.

Where has the time gone?, thought Ramanujan. *I told Janaki that I'd be gone for only two years and yet here I am still... And, where is she?* Tired of living as a bachelor and especially disgusted with his limited diet, he'd approached Mr. Hardy late that summer to try and bring his wife to England. He'd finally realized that he hadn't thoroughly considered the impacts of not having a constant close companion when he'd made his plans to come to Cambridge. Three major hurdles had materialized when he'd uncharacteristically, for him, decided to take the necessary steps to have her join him. The first was the collection of trip funds—the cost was far beyond his meager savings, and after several independent inquiries, both he and Mr. Hardy discovered that the war had obliterated any chance of extra monies being available for such an expense. The second, which should have been glaringly obvious, was the war itself. Nothing but essential travel was permitted through the Mediterranean and the Atlantic, and that journey was perilous even for battleships. And the third and most insurmountable obstacle was the disappearance of his wife. He'd received no letters from her, his mother was uncommunicative on the subject, and two of his friends in Tamil Nadu had been unable to track her down.

The paper he clenched between his outstretched hands quivered as his arms shook with emotion and Mahalanobis couldn't tell for the moment whether Ramanujan was upset or angry. It looked like Ramanujan wanted to rip the letter to shreds, but that some unseen force had grabbed his arms and was holding him back in some internal battle. They'd been talking about home and Mahalanobis' family when Ramanujan had confessed, "I haven't written home in quite some time, Mahalanobis. It was just becoming an exercise in futility."

"How so?" his friend had asked.

"It does no good to write when there is either no response, or direct questions are ignored," Ramanujan had sighed. "Janaki has written only one letter other than the two I received when I first arrived, and that most recent one was horrible. On top of that, Mother refuses to answer any questions I pose about my wife."

"What horrible letter?" Mahalanobis had asked, "I hadn't heard of this before."

"No," Ramanujan had responded, "I didn't want to burden you with my personal problems, but since we are talking about family, I may as well tell you."

"Yes, perhaps it will help me understand your difficulties," Mahalanobis had sympathized.

"Difficulties?" Ramanujan had asked, working himself up. "More like a nightmare of some kind! Here, let me find the letter," and he'd risen and agitatedly begun shifting piles of math papers and correspondences until he'd finally pulled one from the stack.

He now held it in his trembling hands. "She shows no emotion or care for me at all in this! Just listen," and he read aloud with a thick, bitter voice.

My Dear Husband,

I hope this letter finds you well. My brother, Srinivasa Iyengar, is getting married soon, and I have moved back to my family home in Rajendram to help with all the necessary arrangements. We are hoping for a very auspicious occasion, and the astrologers all agree that it will be so.

We are struggling, however with all the necessities for such a celebration. My brother cannot support me and make arrangements at the same time, so I am asking if you could send me money for a new sari so that I do not shame my brother at his wedding? And also money so that I can buy him the wedding gift.

Sincerely, Janaki.

"So, do you see?" asked Ramanujan, almost painfully relaxing his grip and fixedly placing the paper on the pile with the others. "She doesn't ask how I am, or what I am doing. She only cares about the money I can send her. And what is she doing in Rajendram? Why isn't she home? How long has she been there?"

"I'm afraid I don't know, Ramanujan," said Mahalanobis, "perhaps she..."

"And then I received this letter from my mother a few weeks later!" cried Ramanujan as he sifted papers again and came up with another worn letter. "Listen to this part!"

Why are you brushing me aside, son? Why have you stopped responding to my letters? I know in my heart the reason why. You are now corresponding solely with Janaki and are shutting me out. I have done nothing to deserve such treatment and am saddened that it should be so. Please open your heart and write to me again.

"What do you make of that?" Ramanujan questioned in near despair. "I receive nothing from Janaki for years, until a letter appears as if from the heavens, and I open it in rapture only to read that she has left home. And then comes the letter from my mother who says nothing of Janaki or her move away and then suspects that I correspond only with Janaki? Has my family gone mad? Or am I the crazy one?"

"For some reason this reminds me of some stage play where there is a huge misunderstanding by all of the parties," said Mahalanobis. "There must be something that is missing."

"What could be missing, besides me back home in Kumbakonam?" asked Ramanujan in despair.

"I don't know," said his friend. "I hope it's a simple misunderstanding. We want this to turn out like one of Shakespeare's comedies in the end, don't we?"

"I don't think this is an English play," said Ramanujan shaking his head. "Especially not a comedy. I now see that I should have either brought Janaki with me or stayed at home in India and none of this would have happened."

"Staying home wasn't a real option though, was it? Then Cambridge and Hardy wouldn't have known you, or you them," said Mahalanobis, "and that would have been the tragedy."

Ramanujan rearranged the papers on the desk and sat down heavily on the chair next to Mahalanobis. "Perhaps you're right," said Ramanujan with a sigh. "I would not have missed meeting Mr. Hardy or Mr. Littlewood for the world."

After his friend had departed, Ramanujan's renewed fury at Janaki and his mother gradually subsided, and he thought back to his first real connection with his young wife.

In the months before coming to England, he'd returned from Madras to Kumbakonam for a spell and, after taking a walk through town, had just reached the steps leading down to the Kaveri to sit and chat with some of the other men when he spied Janaki walking out across the dry riverbed to the small remaining channel along the opposite bank. She had a brass jug balanced casually on her hip, hips that had just developed since they'd been married, and set it down when she reached the water's edge. She took a moment to arrange her sari, and then squatted down next to the river along with several other women busy gathering water or washing clothes. Grasping the straight-sided brass jug by the squat, wide mouth, he saw her dip it into the river and then set it aside again on the riverbank. Taking a cloth object from her head, he watched her unfold the material until the straw ring within was revealed and then rewrap it snugly into a cushioned circular form. Replacing this on her head, she then lifted the jug upwards in two motions: first to her hip, and then, dipping down while raising her hands high above her, she lifted the jug onto the ring atop her head. Straightening, she then swiveled and began walking back to the steps he sat upon, holding the jug steadily in place with one upraised hand, and clasping the end of her sari in the other.

Ramanujan met her at the top of the stone-slab stairs and fell in step with her as they walked back towards the house together.

"I'd heard you were coming," said Janaki with a smile.

Ramanujan grinned back. "But why have you come all the way to the river to get water? Why not draw it from our well at home?"

"Mother said that the well is low and that I should go and fetch some water for washing. It seems a long way to go for water that we already have, but what do I know?"

"Perhaps the dry spell is affecting the well, then," said Ramanujan.

"That must be the case," said Janaki, "although it seemed fine the last time I drew water. I'm so glad that you're back from Madras if even for a few days, husband. Have you heard again from the English gentleman?"

"Yes, I received another letter from Mr. Hardy, and he was very encouraging about my work and interested in my discoveries. I also spoke with his colleague, Mr. Neville, who is lecturing in Madras, and that is one of the reasons I've come back to Kumbakonam for this week."

"What did they say?" asked Janaki.

"They want me to go to England to meet Mr. Hardy," said Ramanujan.

"What?" cried Janaki, nearly spilling the brass urn on her head.

"Yes, they want me to come to a town called Cambridge and show my results and to work with them."

"Oh! What about me?" asked Janaki. "Can I come too?"

"I think not yet," said Ramanujan. "The funds seem to be limited, and besides, you are so young."

"Not too young to be your wife," said Janaki. "You need someone to look after you there!"

"Be that as it may, the idea of your joining me was never offered."

"But how will you survive without us, and we survive without you?" asked Janaki.

"Oh, I will be able to provide for both you and Mother, and Father too, of course. I made sure that was a stipulation before I'd even think about going."

"Maybe I could come after you get settled?"

"Maybe, we'll need to wait and see."

"And I could get new bangles and a new sari?"

"Possibly," replied Ramanujan, "but we needn't plan too far ahead."

"I would look my very best," said Janaki. "I've been wondering—how does a British lady put the flowers in her hair when she wears a hat? Is there room left to affix them?"

"I have absolutely no idea," said Ramanujan.

"Oh, but everyone wears flowers in their hair on special occasions and for celebrations," she replied. "There must be a way."

Ramanujan nodded as they trod up the dusty road nearing their house.

"You must be so excited to be finally having money," she said.

"I'm happy that you may have some, but I'm really only interested in the mathematics," he replied with a slight smile.

"And I'll have something better than money as well," said Janaki.

"Oh, what's that?" wondered Ramanujan.

"I'll have a husband who's a world-famous mathematician."

Returning from his reveries, he now gazed with sad eyes at the letters on top of the mail stack. Theirs had been an arranged marriage and that day had been the first time that Ramanujan had truly felt the stirrings of real love for his young wife.

CHAPTER 27.

1917

He heard unfamiliar noises and slowly opened his eyes. *Do I have visitors I forgot about?* he wondered vaguely. To his great surprise, Alice was standing over him next to a woman who appeared to be a nurse, and who was currently taking his pulse. He quickly realized he wasn't in his bedroom and, instead, pale light was streaming through the tall narrow windows in what appeared to be a ward lined with rows of beds.

"Alice?" asked Ramanujan, now blinking. "How strange to see you—but why are you here and...where am I?"

"In hospital," said Alice, gently patting the hand that had just been relinquished by the nurse. "Do you remember that you were complaining of stomach pains recently and of high fevers during the night?"

It took Ramanujan a while to think this through, and then he nodded in reply.

"Well, it seems that you woke up yesterday morning and staggered into Mr. Hardy's office, covered in sweat, and you nearly collapsed. You were mumbling something about some foreign names, and, I gather, raving incoherently about some equations. Mr. Hardy knew immediately that something was terribly amiss. The staff brought you here straightaway, and you've finally woken up again this afternoon. How are you feeling now?" she asked.

"The same as I have always been feeling," said Ramanujan after a pause. "Cold, and in a foreign country with terrible food."

Alice smiled as he smiled back. "At least you still have your sense of humor," said Alice.

"But where is this?" asked Ramanujan scanning the room, "Where are we?"

"In the small university hospital a few blocks from your apartment," Alice replied. "I think this will be a good place for you to rest and make a recovery."

"I assume a doctor has seen me?" asked Ramanujan. Alice nodded and then he asked, "What did he say was wrong with me?"

"He thinks that it's a gastric condition, perhaps gastritis, or that maybe you've brought some disease with you from India. They're also not ruling out food poisoning at this point," she said.

What I really need is a good Ayurvedic doctor, or some family and friends with a temple nearby to perform a pooja *for me,* he thought. He was suddenly aware of the huge gulf that lay between this ward and his home, and he wasn't sure that Alice and the British doctors to whom he granted a grudging trust, would be effective, depending on what was wrong with him. *What if the illness isn't just in my body?* he wondered.

"You know, my friend, that you've not been eating properly for quite some time—you've even stopped coming to our house on Sundays. And with the war going on, even non-vegetarians are having a tough time eating a healthy diet. Do you really think you can get proper nutrition the way you've been starving yourself?" asked Alice.

"Ah, but the most important thing is to only eat the foods a good Brahmin would eat. Vishnu will provide," answered Ramanujan.

"Well, there I sadly beg to disagree," sighed Alice. "You really must take better care of yourself, Ramanujan. As we say here: 'Health is not valued until sickness comes'. And now, I fear, you are very sick. Why didn't you seek out a doctor or tell us that it was getting so bad?"

Ramanujan's head fell back on the pillow and he stared at the ceiling for some time. "I suppose it is because there was no one to tell me to," he said looking over at Alice.

"Whatever do you mean?" she asked.

He thought about it some more and then said, "I hope that you will not take offense at this, because you are like family to me," said Ramanujan. "But you are not family." Another pause. "I know it is not how things are done here, but in Tamil Nadu, you only speak of really personal things with your immediate family, your priest, or your doctor. Here in England I have none of these. I did not know I was so ill because I have been so busy and except for brief mentions to you and Mr. Hardy, I have discussed my pains with no one— so I had no one to tell me that I was so ill. Of course, I have no family or priest here, but I also had no doctor to discuss things with—I did not know I needed one."

"Well, I think that's going to change now," said Alice.

"I suppose so," said Ramanujan, looking up at Alice. "I am glad that you are here."

Sometime later he awoke in a slumbering ward. In the dim light, he noticed that he was in strange clothing, and could make out his shirt and pants folded on a small stand beside him. He instinctively reached up to his chest for his sacred thread and felt that it was still there beneath the starched hospital gown.

Just a month ago, he'd taken a similar thread, wrapped the six disintegrating strands around a rock, and then ceremoniously thrown it into the River Cam. This was part of the religious requirement when the thread could no longer be worn—the deteriorating bits must be discarded in water. He'd then chosen some cotton strands, twisted six together for his new sacred thread, and performed the necessary ritual in the proper manner. But still, the personal ceremony didn't feel right.

When he was a youth, he'd been given his first sacred thread in the Upanayanam ceremony. The thread was made up of three strands, and later when he was married, he'd doubled this to six strands to indicate his marital status. The renewal ceremony for the thread, performed every month or so to maintain it in good condition, was a simple ceremony that he cherished. It not only helped keep the tradition alive, but each time it also felt like a renewal of himself. With an urn of water next to him, and sitting cross-legged on the red clay ground of Kumbakonam, he, often along with many others, would follow the procedures: sprinkling themselves and the thread with water and chanting; putting on the new cord which had been prepared ahead of time and secured with a knot; removing the old thread; and washing his feet at the conclusion. Bare chested in the sun of the day of the new moon, he'd follow the ceremony he'd performed since the thread had first been granted to him. As flowed the river, the remains of cord after cord from his life were wrapped about stones and placed into the Kaveri.

On his first ceremony, his father had sat next to him holding the thread knotted into a continuous loop—one hand-held high and one held low to form the cord into a long oval. Ramanujan with his mother standing behind him had worn a garland of red and yellow flowers around his neck and chanted with the priest as he performed the ritual. Accepting the garland and then moving his hands over the flames of the sacred fire, the priest had blessed the cord, and then his father had passed the thread over his son's head, onto his left shoulder, and under his right arm. He'd undergone a ritual rite of passage that day and had begun daily prayers from then after. He'd kept to the faith since then by the constant renewal of the sacred thread—three strands when he was a youth, and six strands when he'd been married.

The gods are omnipotent, he thought now from his hospital bed, *but still, I'm thousands of miles away from the temples of home and the Kaveri River.* He worried that the ceremonies he carried out for thread renewal would not be efficacious. *Am I losing touch with the gods in far off India, or are they disapproving of me being all the way here in Cambridge?*

It was summer, and he was becoming familiar with the new routine—nightly sweats and poor sleep, daily lassitude and an inability to concentrate, and frequent sharp pains in his abdomen. He'd been in the small Cambridge University hospital for months and began to despair of recovering or moving back to his own rooms—every time he began to feel improved, they refused to discharge him from their care—then as they predicted, he would backslide.

He was allowed strolls along the Cam on most days, and often the staff had to send a nurse to fetch him from Mr. Hardy's office if he failed to return to the hospital on time. His productivity had slowed but he was still able to focus enough on maths that he was coming up with new ideas and able to collaborate with Mr. Hardy on several papers. Try as he might, he could detect no apparent disappointment emanating from Mr. Hardy, although he was certain it must be there.

On a lazy summer afternoon following a horrible previous night, a visitor was announced. He turned expecting to see either Alice or Mr. Hardy, but instead he saw Amanda walking across the ward for a visit.

"Hello, Amanda!" Ramanujan beamed. "How good to see you!"

"Hello, Mr. Rama," smiled Amanda. "I'd say that you're looking somewhat better than my visit last month. Remember when it was me who was confined to bed all the time? And now it is you."

"Yes, I remember," replied Ramanujan, "and I'm so glad you are better now. I'm also certain that some of my condition could have been my continuing sorrow at your father's death—that combined with the theory that they are now propounding... they think I may have been suffering from tuberculosis all this time. Anyway, regardless, I have been so worried about you and your mother, but you look like you are somehow still managing. How is Lady North?"

"Oh, Mum is fine," said Amanda. "And I'm getting better—day by day. I didn't want to tell you before, but I feel like I suffered two losses rather than just the one of my father when we learned of his death."

"How is that?" asked Ramanujan.

"Oh, I was caught up in a relationship with a boy before Daddy died. And afterwards he ended up being a right rotter and hurt me, especially when I needed his support the most. I felt such a fool at the time that I didn't want to tell you about our involvement, but I'm squaring with that now, and I'm ready to plot a new course—without being nuts about boys—I can tell you that."

"I am sorry to hear that you had distress beyond the loss of your father. If there is anything I can do, just let me know."

"No, your friendship is more than enough," said Amanda with a smile.

They talked for a while about her mother, the estate, and her friends.

"And I've decided that I should like to become a teacher," Amanda announced. "I'd thought of going into literature, history, or mathematics, but then I realized that to become a teacher I must know quite a lot about all of those subjects. So, I'll be starting my courses for a degree in Education at King's College in London this fall."

"That sounds fabulous!" said Ramanujan.

"And, of course, you remember Mary?" asked Amanda to an immediate nod from Ramanujan. "She's been such a rock since Daddy died and has made several trips up to visit me. She said that she should like to see you again, and so maybe she'll join me on a visit sometime. Anyway, she's been trying to decide where her direction in college should be, and I think she's chosen history as her discipline of choice. Although, I would say that she still has a keen interest in mathematics, thanks, I think, to you."

"Well, the world can certainly do with more mathematicians," said Ramanujan, "As I do not seem to be able to keep up my end of it right now," he joked.

"Oh, come now, Mr. Rama," said Amanda, patting his hand, "a little more rest and help from the doctors and you'll be back to your old self in no time."

Mr. Hardy and Ramanujan were sitting in the warm sun enjoying a game of cricket. Ramanujan was there for the sun, and Mr. Hardy, of course, was there for the cricket. There were very few, if any, university sponsored games played, but several times a week soldiers and medical staff found enough able bodies to put teams together for a match. Ramanujan scanned the viewing area, noticing that nearly every spectator sported a bandage of some sort. Although not a fan himself, he and Mr. Hardy had fallen into the habit of watching games on nice days, especially on those days when Ramanujan was too frail to be up in Mr. Hardy's offices concentrated on their work. Given the quality of the cricket play, Mr. Hardy would often bring a pile of papers for review or academic articles to read, and Ramanujan would close his eyes and let the sounds of the game and the heat of the sunshine wash over him.

Ramanujan suddenly gripped his belly in pain, and Mr. Hardy looked over in alarm.

"Are you alright, Ramanujan? Should I fetch a nurse?"

"No, I am fine, Mr. Hardy," said Ramanujan after his teeth had unclenched. "It was just one of those spasms."

"I must say," said Mr. Hardy, shaking his head, "I thought that you'd bounce right back after they admitted you to hospital. This must be more serious than they thought."

"I don't understand either," said Ramanujan. "All of the treatment and rest, and I seem to be getting no better at all."

"Perhaps the staff is too overwhelmed by all of the war casualties to give you the proper attention that you deserve," said Mr. Hardy. "I'll need to ask them about that."

"I think they are doing their best," said Ramanujan, trying to put his friend at ease. "A doctor came up from London last week to treat other patients and they had him examine me when he finished his rounds. I did not hear exactly what he said but, apparently, he was also extremely curious as to what my problem could possibly be. It is just so depressing to not know the cause of this illness."

"I think that as long as you keep your spirits up, you should get through this just fine," said Mr. Hardy encouragingly.

"Yes, I suppose so," sighed Ramanujan.

"I have to tell you, confidentially, that I've been trying to get you a Fellowship at Trinity, but so far there are several voting members who just won't budge on the issue. I shouldn't say this, but I suspect that it's simply the color of your skin that's holding them back. The thing is that they won't come out and say their real reasons for their objection and so I have no means to protest. If it was based on merit alone, I had hopes that this would show you how valuable you are to our department, but you'll just have to take my word on it for now."

"Thank you so much, Mr. Hardy," said Ramanujan, "I had no idea that my name had been submitted." He paused a moment. "At least I have my Bachelor's degree, and we do have several papers out. I'm sorry that work on the others has slowed though."

"Not to worry, Ramanujan. You'll be right as rain soon enough, and then we can continue."

"I certainly hope so," said Ramanujan, and they both settled back into the sun and the game.

CHAPTER 28.

How mysterious the gods are, that they've set me on this path, he thought, *and how inexplicable that they should land me here. My journey has become so very strange that I think now I just want to go home.* He would never have imagined that he'd suddenly be so far from Cambridge, or home, as he had unexpectedly come to call it. He was far from Mr. Hardy, Alice and friends, and yet still in England. It was even stranger yet that, seemingly so far removed from anyone he knew, he should immediately recognize and begin a friendly conversation with his doctor.

"How are you feeling this morning, Ramanujan?" asked Dr. Chowry-Muthu as he entered the ward where Ramanujan lay in bed.

"I was just thinking how extremely odd, or perhaps destined, that I should know someone here, of all the places in England," said Ramanujan. "I was so surprised to see you when I arrived yesterday afternoon. And where is 'here' again?"

"I'm surprised to see you too, Ramanujan. And I'm sad to say that you don't appear to be in the same spirits and health that you enjoyed when I first met you on the *Nevasa*. You've been placed under our care for a period here at the Mendip Hills Sanatorium," said the doctor. "You must remember the long train trip you took yesterday?" Ramanujan nodded, and

Dr. Chowry-Muthu continued. "We're actually fairly near to Portsmouth where the *Nevasa* first landed in England. That's where I disembarked and made my way here. We're near the town of Wells in Somerset County, far west of London and close to Bristol."

"You told me on the *Nevasa* that you were a specialist in tuberculosis, and I never would have guessed that I would end up in your care," said Ramanujan. "Perhaps this is a sign from the gods that you can make me well again."

"That's certainly our goal, although I must warn you, a disease like tuberculosis can take quite some time to treat and to cure," said Dr. Chowry-Muthu.

"As I keep hearing again and again... repeatedly," said Ramanujan dejectedly. "I'm sorry. I know that I am ill—there is simply no escaping the fact. But I think some of the pain I feel is really due to my inability to fulfill the goals that were expected of me when I came to England. The Trinity College must be wondering what they were thinking, to pay so much to bring me to the University, only to have me lay in bed for months on end. I fear my sponsor, Mr. Hardy, must be beyond disappointment, and yet he carries on as if it was of no great issue."

"Ramanujan, you must concentrate on becoming well and not on the limitations your sickness has caused," said the doctor. "It will not help in the least to dwell on them. We must see that you stabilize your condition and begin to gain some weight. Without that, your prognosis cannot possibly improve."

"Speaking of gaining weight," said Ramanujan immediately. "I hope that since you are here, that this means they know something about cooking Indian food. I think that is another cause of my ill health—there is simply nothing acceptable to eat in this entire country."

"Alas, I have nothing to do with the cuisine offered here, especially since the war has dragged on and supplies have become constricted... no, nonexistent," lamented the doctor. "And," he whispered confidentially, "I never take my meals here—my wife provides for me. Unfortunately, I'm not allowed to share with the patients, since the diet restrictions for all of you are very strict."

Of course, thought Ramanujan with a sigh.

Dr. Chowry Muthu consulted a clipboard he'd brought with him. "While we're on the subject of food, I can at least make a diagnosis of the reason you have lost so much weight and are wasting away," said the doctor. "My colleagues in Cambridge report that you apparently refuse to eat everything that is offered to you."

"Not every bit that is offered," said Ramanujan. "But the rest is—now here is a word I recently learned and is so aptly applied here—insipid."

"Be that as it may, good nutrition, or any nutrition for that matter, is exactly what your body requires," said Dr. Chowry-Muthu. "I know that you're a mathematician—of some repute, I understand—and must be able to grasp the concept of an equation. What's on one side of the equal sign must be of the same quantity as is on the other side. You must have at least the amount of nutrition going into your body as your body requires to maintain itself. Otherwise you lose weight. And the weight balance is currently your personal equation of highest priority. Even more quantity must be added to one side of the equal sign if your body is to become healthy and gain some weight on the other side."

"You are forgetting the variable of belief, however," said Ramanujan flatly. "It does the soul absolutely no good to intake any amount of impure foods. What the body gains, the soul will soon suffer for."

"Yes, but pure or impure, a departed soul is a departed soul," said Dr. Chowry-Muthu. "And we don't wish yours to depart this earth any time before it should. Anyway, I've also come to discuss your underlying condition. You know that I specialize in tuberculosis, and I'm an expert in its treatment. I must tell you, however, that your case is very perplexing to me. You show some of the symptoms of tuberculosis, but I am still not entirely convinced that this is the true nature of your illness. You have fevers that spike every evening, and yet these high readings are either gone or diminished during most of the day. You've lost a significant amount of weight and have pain at the bottom of your ribcage. All of these signs can be consistent with a diagnosis of tuberculosis; however, other indicators are not consistent in the least. The pain in the lower chest could be tubercular, although this is not necessarily a symptom of the disease, you show absolutely no difficulty in breathing, and there's not the normal coughing or bloody mucus that results from the cough. I have to say, that if you are tubercular, you're on the outer edge of the range of normal symptoms, and if it is not tuberculosis, I've no clue what you could be suffering from."

Ramanujan studied Dr. Chowry-Muthu. "Since you are from the same country and know our culture intimately, could it simply be my coming to England that has caused this illness?" he asked. "Could the gods be angry? After all, I have broken countless rules, crossed huge bodies of water, eaten unspeakable things, violated every Brahmin stricture. I cannot pray in the temple, nor be blessed by Vishnu's flame. I am an outcast."

"No, no, Ramanujan," said Dr. Chowry-Muthu vehemently shaking his head. "There are illnesses that can be caused by the mind, but yours is definitely not one of them. Some agent, unknown as yet, is attacking internal organs and causing fever, pain, and weight loss. I'd say that you most assuredly must calm and free your mind of all such negative thoughts. There are countless individuals from our culture who have made the trip to England and very few end up in medical institutions. The mind, as you know, is a powerful thing and, while it can't cause such a disease, it can certainly exacerbate the situation. My advice to you is to regain your strength through a good diet, calm your mind about breaking taboos, and concentrate on mathematics."

"Perhaps you are right," said Ramanujan. "But as soon as I try to think about mathematics now, I also think of the disappointment I have caused Mr. Hardy, and of my failures in meeting his expectations."

"Failings?" asked Dr. Chowry-Muthu. "I've heard nothing but of your great accomplishments. You'd been heralded by the Indian community even before you arrived here. I absolutely can't see you as a failure at all."

"Oh, but I have been turned down as a fellow at Trinity College and am likely to never see the approval of my mathematical peers. My prospects are dimming in the field in which I thought I was destined to shine."

"Again," said Dr. Chowry-Muthu. "You simply shouldn't be so hard on yourself."

"Then the gods should not be so hard on me," said Ramanujan as he turned away from the conversation.

Again, he found himself exiled miles away from Cambridge, however, this time he knew not a single soul. And, again, he was in an institution, this time in the Matlock House Sanatorium, in Matlock, Derbyshire County—the very center of England. *I have another name for this place,* thought Ramanujan soon after arriving, *Macchal House*—as he knew it in Tamil—'death house'. The treatments at Mendip Hills under Dr. Chowry-Muthu had come to nothing, and so within a month it was decided that a different regimen would be more beneficial to his health.

"But it is the middle of winter, and you are saying we cannot have a fire?" a freezing Ramanujan had asked one of the nurses.

"No, Mr. Ramanujan," she'd replied. "And you'll see that it's for your own good, too. We're following the recommended course for the treatment of tuberculosis—the rooms are to be kept chilly with plenty of fresh air—it is the best treatment we know of, especially for the lungs."

And so, he perpetually shivered with the cold and slept badly. During the days, he and his fellow residents wandered about the open rooms with shawls and blankets draped over their shoulders. He was absolutely miserable. *I know what it is,* he thought, and nearly believed, *German agents have snuck into England and are torturing its citizens. I've been captured by them and am undergoing some bizarre form of diabolical mistreatment. They're somehow involved in the terrible penance that I must pay—and they're all under the guidance of the evil Dr. Ram.* Here was another fellow Indian, who, in sharp contrast to the personable Dr. Chowry-Muthu, allowed no familiarity at all, and, in fact, was a dictator.

Soon after he'd arrived at Matlock House, some of the staff had thrown out papers he'd been working on, thinking of them as scribbles. In a panic, he'd scoured the room, even looking under his mattress for his prized possessions, and then under the mattresses of others as well. "Where are my notes?" he'd yelled at the first available nurse. "What have you done with them? I was near a solution! Mr. Hardy has been waiting for this and I nearly had the answer!" In a white-hot anger, he'd then stood in the middle of the large floor and screamed, "Where are my papers?!"

The tirade resulted in several nurses running for Dr. Ram.

"What is the fuss, Ramanujan?" asked Dr. Ram as he strode into the hall. "We can't have disruptions like this in our facility!"

"Fuss?" cried Ramanujan, continuing in a raised voice. "This is my work, my life work—and it has been taken or destroyed! It is not only my property, but also that of Mr. Hardy. It is not a fuss; it is a demand! My papers must be returned to me, or..." unfortunately he had no plans for recourse immediately at hand.

"I see," said Dr. Ram. "I have, of course, heard of your reputation as a mathematician, but I do not believe my nurses were aware of your standing, or that this is your occupation." He stared firmly at Ramanujan. "I will instruct my staff that they are not to disturb your work, as long as your work does not interfere with your treatment. But I will brook no more outbursts in my facility. Is this acceptable?"

"Yes, thank you Dr. Ram," said a more subdued and contrite Ramanujan.

After this episode, the papers began to pile up next to his bed, and he was able to once again engage in productive correspondences with Mr. Hardy.

He received four visitors over the Christmas holidays. Alice, his most frequent visitor, had baked him a completely vegetarian fruitcake. "Thank you so much, Alice," he'd said. "It certainly has an interesting flavor."

"It's my mother's recipe, and her mother's before that," Alice had explained proudly. It had contained an odd flavor from dried fruits and some spices he didn't recognize, but he'd eventually and gratefully consumed the entire cake.

"How is Mr. Neville managing?" he'd asked.

"Not very well, I'd have to say," said Alice. "All of his efforts to oppose the war seem to be working against him. You would think that the leadership in the University would be enlightened, but instead they all seem to be pro-war conservatives. It's like they're too old to serve in the military themselves and feel their own impotence, and so they lash out where they can instead. They're even beginning to threaten his tenure because of his pacifism."

Mr. Hardy also had called on him in Matlock House, bringing with him a fresh supply of pencils and paper, and they'd spent three intense days going over an article that they were finalizing for submission to a mathematics journal. Ramanujan had been both invigorated and exhausted by this visit, but he was ecstatic at the opportunity to work again closely with the mind most like his on the entire island.

And, he'd received a visit from Amanda and her mother.

"Lady North! Amanda!" Ramanujan exclaimed. "How wonderful to see you!"

"Well, Mr. Rama—we could hardly leave you alone up here at Christmas, now could we?" asked a smiling Amanda.

"But it is such a long journey, and in this weather," said Ramanujan.

"No, it was a pleasant trip," said Lady North. "And besides, my brother lives in Chesterfield, not far from here, and so we're making a small tour of friends."

"Oh, thank you so much for including me," said Ramanujan. "I must say, again, how sorry I am for the loss of

Lord North. He was such a good man, and very approachable by people from all walks of life."

"Well, that's part of why we wanted to visit with you," said Lady North. "The Christmas that you visited us is so tied up with our memories of my husband during the holidays that we just had to come and spend some of the time with you. Your visit actually meant a lot to him, and he loved his trip to India, so now, India and Christmas are forever linked in our minds. And Amanda and I both agreed that we didn't want to just sit in that cold mansion and celebrate the holidays alone.

"Look, we've brought you some treats, made by Sujatha—and she sends her greatest affection with them." She set a basket on his bed and began pulling out tins and jars of wonderful-smelling dishes. "We can have a Christmas picnic."

"And, we brought you presents," said Amanda happily pulling them from a small bag.

Lady North had brought Ramanujan a scarf she'd knit, and Amanda had made him a stitched notebook with a cloth applique cover featuring an image of an elephant.

"I'm sorry that I don't have any gifts for you..." began Ramanujan when he was cut off by Lady North. "Don't be silly," she said. "How would a person suffering from tuberculosis in a sanatorium possibly go shopping or be prepared for unexpected visitors? It is absolutely our pleasure to be able to come and visit you."

They took the picnic treats to an atrium with many tall open windows, and Ramanujan wrapped the scarf around his neck, the old familiar hat given him by Amanda still on his head. They ate and chatted for several hours, much to

Ramanujan's delight, and caught up on each other's lives. He could tell that there was much concern about the ability of the mansion to remain in the North name for much longer. The war had taken its toll. They'd lost Lord North, and the resources to maintain the estate were dwindling—monetary reserves, available estate workers, food stuffs and supplies, and the will and ability to keep it all afloat.

CHAPTER 29.

1918

He was beginning to think that this eagerly anticipated trip to London had been a mistake. He'd jumped at the chance to leave '*Macchal* House' when the staff had offered him the opportunity of a brief visit to the city, but now he questioned the wisdom of his choice.

Matlock House felt like a prison to him. There, he was isolated in an unpopulated and, to him somewhat wild, region of England, and the sanatorium was cold, stark, silent, remote, overseen by the tyrannical Dr. Ram, and was nearly driving him mad. It was as if he'd entered a bizarre land that was the exact opposite of India in nearly every possible way. Spartan conditions he was very familiar with, but to be assigned to a huge room with doors and windows open regardless of the weather, seated in chairs arranged along a frigid stone wall, was agony—especially with hacking tubercular patients as fellow inmates. If the same space had been filled with numerous families busy with cookfires and conversation, with a gentle breeze blowing through on hot days, he would have wanted to stay for months. A trip to London had seemed like the perfect break from the daily tedium and isolation that had become nearly unbearable in its constancy.

But London had changed so since his first arrival: along the streets were jumbled bricks where buildings had once stood and stacked sandbags attempted to protect the others; there was no more casual strolling—everyone scurried seriously about on their business or hid indoors out of sight; gone were the flowered hats, parasols, and fancy gowns—uniforms and sober work-clothes now dominated fashion; out were the bright city lights—the entire area became absolutely black at sunset; the smoke that rose was not from the workings of happy industry, but from munitions factories and bombed buildings, with barrage balloons dotting the air between the plumes; women, of all people, were taking tickets and driving buses, and the lack of men in most jobs was noticeable; and the buoyant mood of the capital of an empire was now as gloomy as the trenches in France.

As he neared the Natural History Museum, Ramanujan noticed a group of three smudged children in torn clothes huddled in an alcove off the road, and one tentatively held out a tiny hat. He dug into his pants pocket and offered up ten pence. The toddler barely broke a smile as the coin disappeared into his pocket. Watching him crouch down again with the other waifs, Ramanujan thought of all of the families that had been destroyed in this city alone over the last three years. London suddenly seemed so gray and forlorn—seemingly reflecting his own mood over the past year—almost as if he'd created this scene out of one of his own mental projections.

Ramanujan hesitated before entering the museum, turning to glance across Cromwell Road at the National India Association building where he'd stayed on his first arrival in

London. *Everything had seemed possible then,* he thought. *But what have I actually achieved? Next to nothing.* He sank down for a moment on the hard marble steps. *A bachelor's degree and a few papers.* His recent election to the London Mathematical Society had briefly lifted his spirits, but instead of appreciating the honor, it had made him even more aware of the awards that had not been granted him.

In a rare moment of introspection, he realized that he'd expected to be raised up on a pedestal when he arrived in England. He'd expected to be showered with awards. For some reason, this conjured up the picture of Reimann hanging on the wall in Mr. Hardy's office. *I think that's what I expected,* he thought, *to have my picture someday hanging on the wall next to someone like Mr. Reimann.* A feeling of failure and defeat overwhelmed him as he rose and entered the museum, barely noticing his surroundings or the approaching exhibits.

In the unfamiliar London lodgings the previous evening, he'd had a vivid dream in which Namagiri Amman had been unable to see him. He was standing right before her, hoping for her attention, but it was as if he were an invisible wraith. A simple *sadhu* had walked past him in the dream, and she had bestowed countless blessings upon him, while appearing to ignore Ramanujan completely. He'd never felt so shunned and utterly alone as when he'd awoken.

The Natural History Museum would normally cheer him up immensely with the intricacies of the world on display, but the impacts the war had exacted on the city and seeing the desperation of the motherless children outside had brought his barely dormant broodings to life. *Most of these animals are now extinct,* he lamented, *never to grace the earth again – the dodo and passenger pigeon are gone forever, never to fulfill their true purpose on the planet. And now I know what it feels like to be one of them.*

He'd intended to take the tube to King's Cross, and from there to buy a ticket further on to Cambridge by train—to somewhere that felt more like home. The walk from the museum to the tube station barely registered as he made his way down the endless flights of stairs and onto the platform. Sandbags and piles of supplies reminded him that this was also a refuge from the bombs—he'd heard and seen the results of one only the day before. Somehow his vision had become as narrow as the tunnel, and he felt that he could barely see, let alone think of anything other than the strange darkness that seemed to have descended over him. Suddenly, the tube train appearing out of the gloomy tunnel looked amazingly like the brightly shining and extremely elegant solution to his problems. With an unexpected flash of resolve, he took two quick steps and launched himself into the air and onto the tracks. Feeling the sharp stings to his body when he landed, hearing the screech of the brakes, he was assured that he'd passed on—to finish out the rest of this life as a ghost. His troubles were over until his next rebirth, however low that may be.

Regaining consciousness with a crowd of staring faces peering down at him was not what he had had in mind at all. In a daze, with shouts and whistles blowing in the background, all he could think about were his reasons for the jump. Several hands pulled him further from the tracks, and he could glimpse the legs of people boarding the train he had unexpectedly interrupted. Different people were shouting questions at him and someone placed something soft under his head. He could feel the ground tremble and hear the high-pitched screech of another approaching train. *This time...* he thought as his attempt to rise was counteracted by several hands pushing him firmly against the hard granite platform.

He gazed at his hands, still bloody with creosote-coated splinters driven into the palms. Below his hands, he could see his pant legs torn and soaked in blood from the shins on down. Both his hands and legs screamed with pain, but he felt numb to it. His head hung and he couldn't bring himself to look up at those around him, nor at his surroundings.

He'd been questioned several times and was being held in a small, but open, cell near the central area of a police station. Near him sat a cold cup of tea that he'd refused to drink when it was brought to him.

Ramanujan first saw the man's feet. "My, God, Ramanujan!" exclaimed Mr. Hardy as he stepped up near Ramanujan and then gently lay a hand on his shoulder. "What have you done?" he murmured more quietly.

"I cannot really recall anything," said Ramanujan, shaking his head.

"Well, I can tell you what we've compiled through witness reports, since this one is unwilling to discuss it," said a sergeant in Scotland Yard who'd accompanied Mr. Hardy into the cell. "Let's see," he said thumbing through a notebook. "He was in the South Kensington tube station, and among the things found in his pockets was a ticket for the Piccadilly line to King's Cross. He also had a cancelled ticket to the Natural History Museum, as well as a small amount of money. We assume he walked from the Museum down into the Tube and was waiting for the train. No one really noticed him until, moments before the train pulled in—he dove onto the rails in front of it. It was only for the fast hand of a station guard at the switch that stopped the train in time, and then a trio of soldiers on leave from their base leapt down onto the tracks and dragged him back up off the rails. He was sobbing when the police arrived, but hasn't recalled the incident for us. He's one lucky man caught in an unlucky act, I can tell you. In my humble opinion he needs to be protected from himself and be either locked up or committed to an institution. However, it's not in my power to decide what happens to him—that will be left up to my superiors or the courts."

"Ramanujan, don't you fret," said Mr. Hardy. "We'll have you out of here in no time."

"Now, to whom must I speak?" asked Mr. Hardy as he followed the sergeant out of the cell. "Ramanujan is a mathematician of international repute, and with the keenest mind of a generation. It simply will not do to have him locked away.

He's suffering from tuberculosis and has been in a weakened state..." And the two disappeared into the clamor of London police activity in the busy station.

Ramanujan found himself back in the National India Association building on Cromwell Road. The police had agreed not to hold him at Scotland Yard, but had stipulated that he must be under constant supervision until they sorted out what to do with him. He mostly chose to stay in his room, but once his legs had begun to heal, an attendant would accompany him across the street to the Natural History Museum. He generally stuck to the displays of minerals, fossils, and birds, although he also found himself drawn to the butterfly collection.

A week after the attempt, there was a tentative knock on his door, and before he could rise from his bed, the handle turned and his friend Mahalanobis peeked in around the edge. Ramanujan sat up and gave him a sad smile while Mahalanobis hesitantly entered the room and took a chair opposite him. Both remained silent for several minutes with Ramanujan staring fixedly at the floor in front of him. Finally, he raised his eyes towards his visitor and asked, "So, you have heard about my mishap then?"

Mahalanobis nodded and stated frankly, "To me, it sounds like more than a mishap."

Ramanujan suddenly sat up straight at the thought that all of Cambridge was now talking about his suicide attempt. "Who else knows?" he asked in a panic.

Mahalanobis gave him a comforting look and said, "No one but Mr. Hardy and I... so far," and before Ramanujan could react, he added, "and we are not telling anyone."

Ramanujan looked relieved. "But how did you find out?" he asked.

"I had tried to ring your hotel because I was thinking of coming to London, and they said there had been some kind of emergency, so I phoned Scotland Yard, and they told me a little about it. Then I went and saw Mr. Hardy when he returned."

Ramanujan nodded.

"Surely things can't be that bad—can they, Ramanujan? Why ever did you do it?"

Ramanujan stared at the floor again and refused to answer.

"Really, Ramanujan, you simply must speak to someone about this. I know you've become terribly ill, and that you've been living far away from your friends, but surely things can't have been that desperate, can they?" His friend remained silent. "Can I at least know some of your thoughts, so that I can try and understand and not worry about what you might do after I leave here?"

Ramanujan closed his eyes against sudden tears and his mind again became focused on what had brought him to that desperate moment. He was silent for a time and then began to slowly speak at a level just above a whisper. "This is hard for me to say. I feel foolish now, but I have to tell you that it was for so many reasons at the time." His breath caught as he fought for control, but then coughed before he continued, "I've been wasting away in so many ways, Mahalanobis—to the point that no one sees me anymore, not even my goddess who seems to never appear now. Mr. Hardy can rarely make visits of any quality, especially when I've been exiled to far flung sanatoria. My academic peers can't bring themselves to see me as an equal and have refused to admit me as a Fellow at Trinity. Much of my work has become vapor since I've either got it wrong or covered areas that others had long ago explored. I'm now invisible to my family—especially to my own wife who never writes to me and has seemingly disowned me. I'm seen as an outcast to most of this British society whose peerless members either ignore me or offer disdainful sneers—you know their attitudes as well as I. The pall of war hangs over this country and its resources and spirit are grim or lacking to the point that I think I've absorbed that feeling of defeat. And possibly the worst thing: I'm no longer a member of my own Brahmin caste, and will be shunned and excluded from many ceremonies, should I ever return home." He sighed heavily. "Which now seems highly unlikely."

Mahalanobis rose and walked over to sit on the bed next to his friend, placing an arm across his shoulders. He began to tell Ramanujan that everything would be all right, and that many of his perceptions were not as bad as they seemed, but sensed that now was not the time. He simply sat feeling the shoulders under his arm convulse with the sobs that Ramanujan was now allowing to flow freely.

Sitting later in his bare room at the NIA and staring at the wrappings on his shins, he reflected again on his awkward leap onto the tracks. He'd merely managed to damage himself in his attempt, and he thought back to the two truly broken men he'd befriended in Kumbakonam when he was preparing to enter college. The first, most people saw as mad. He was not a *sadhu*, but was more of a lost soul, caught up in his own form of Hinduism complete with its own cosmology. Since Ramanujan loved numbers and the strange results that could be found in them, he marveled at many of the connections and weird interpretations that Kuppasami, or 'garbage fellow'—the only name that anyone knew him by, spouted as he walked along the Kaveri.

Kuppasami followed a daily circuit, the bulk of which traced the banks of the Kaveri River upstream and ended at a small shrine upriver from town sometime around dusk. How he happened to begin his trek in town near the Sarangapani Temple again every morning was a matter of much speculation. He knew a few words of English and wore a British military jacket that he'd somehow acquired, his long stringy hair cascading down the back. His rantings included revelations about the British spies that were among them, the fall of the British Empire, the next incarnation of Vishnu, his alleged childhood growing up in the Cotswolds, and the paths of the stars affecting men. It was the paths of the stars and planets that most intrigued Ramanujan, and he'd walk along the riverbanks sometimes in deep, but also deeply disturbing, conversations with the man. Kuppasami lived in Kumbakonam, but was also somewhere else, much removed from the rest of society.

The other broken person was nameless to all who saw him, and his given name was never divulged to Ramanujan, even though he'd inquired repeatedly. He was referred to as 'Avan', or 'that man,' by any of the worshippers at the temple who noticed him. Avan had legs that were small, disfigured, and as thin as sticks. He wracked them under his body and scooted around mainly on his rump, using his arms to propel himself forward. He'd find different stations around the temple to beg for alms and, otherwise, he went through life unnoticed by the community. He often sat near where Ramanujan would retreat from the heat of the day to work out math calculations on his slate, and the two of them had entered into a light friendship. Ramanujan would share his lunch with Avan, and he was fascinated by Avan's insight into human nature—an area comprised of layers of subtly that Ramanujan himself found increasingly difficult to appreciate or fathom.

Here were two people trapped in Kumbakonam. One couldn't leave because he was mentally in two places at once and, for the other, travel was a physical impossibility. Yet each was a prisoner under house arrest in some manner—each at home with where he found himself. *My suicide attempt could severely infringe on my own freedom,* he suddenly realized, *and I'll be interred a very long way from home!*

In a mild panic, his cheeks burned, and his immediate impulse was to deal with this humiliation in the same way that he'd dealt with others in the past. He'd simply flee. He even stood up in the bare room and headed for the door in reaction, his shins screaming in pain at the sudden movement. After failing exams to remain in the Government College, he'd snuck away to stay with his cousin Krishnasamy. After the failed dinner party in Cambridge when he thought that Mr. Hardy and the other guests didn't appreciate his cooking, he'd snuck out the back door and fled to Oxford straight away. And now he'd just attempted and failed in the ultimate escape, and his instinct was still to take wing. However, under watch and in his current state of complete disgrace, there was no longer the capability of flight. He'd need to face his humiliation directly and he wasn't sure that he'd be up to the challenge. He looked down again at the bandages on his healing hands and legs. *It's just possible that I'm as broken in body and mind as my two distant friends in Kumbakonam.*

Suicide was not unheard of in Tamil Nadu. But it was by no means condoned either—the deed set one backwards on the karmic path where escape from the constant cycle of rebirths was the ultimately desired goal. The majority of historical suicides had been *sati*, where a wife would throw herself on the funeral pyre of her dead husband, so that the two could be together for the next stage of the journey. *Sati* was not common, but it did occur, and now happened even less frequently since it had been outlawed under British rule.

He knew the fate of one who committed suicide from what was written in the Vedas—"But what becomes of one who has tried to commit the act and failed?" he worried aloud. This recent desperate attempt, he realized, was only adding to the list of Brahminic strictures he'd broken.

He'd been attempting to remain a good Brahmin with all his might during his stay in England, but circumstances and the foreign environment had made conformity nearly impossible. He'd tried to monitor and restrict his diet, but had unknowingly consumed what was not to be eaten; he had no access to temples or priests and had managed to worship and to conduct ceremonies to the best of his abilities; and he'd lapsed in his attention to prayers and the Vedas, since he was so involved in his mathematics. In India, there had been a harmonic balance between his studies and prayer, but here in England he'd mainly concentrated on his studies.

Sitting in limbo and awaiting word on what the police had planned for him, he now worried more about what would become of his soul. *Have I gone too far to be saved by Narayana, or will the Lord recognize my efforts and still offer me the possibility of salvation?* he wondered. Unbidden, fragments from Periyalvar floated into his head.

> He heard cheers when he smashed the angry elephant
>> and the wrestlers,
> The wheeled wagon, Pralamba, the evil horse
>> and the laurel trees in the dark grove.
> Through the realm of fiery rays dispelling darkness,
>> he raises his devotees in grace,

Then removes the ladder [to rebirth]
   to accept them as servants;
   the city where he dwells is jeweled Srirangam.

Hopefully my fate is through the grace of god, and not my own feeble attempts at salvation? Will Narayana take me in? Or have I doomed myself further by what I've done? he wondered. *But there is a route for the pious,* he remembered hopefully, *perhaps I should concentrate even more on my worship—then Narayana might protect me after all.*

Of goodness and evil, I know nothing –
   nothing but to ever say, "Narayana"
This is not just scheming flattery, you know,
   spoken emptily to you.
Tirumal, I know no way to perceive you,
   I who incessantly say, "Namo Narayana"
Real strength is the strength of a Vaisnava
   living in your temple, you know.

I was growing weary and sinking on the far side
   of the sea of Pointlessness.
By the grace of your name, I climbed out on this side.
   With, "Don't fear!" you stretched out your hand,
You with the disc, wide hands and wide eyes,
   with a golden-colored raiment,
You whose hue is of the red evening sky,
   My Father of Tirumaliruncolai.

CHAPTER 30

Back in Matlock House weeks later, convinced he was an outcast, weak from illness, he had nothing but time on his hands and found that he was incessantly reciting the songs of the Alvars to himself.

Help me, Pure Lord. Committing as many sins as exist,
    I am weary and worn.
Nor have I ever been able to continually worship at your feet.
Father of the great Vēnkaṭa Mountain,
    encircled by thick copper-hued peaks,
I, your slave, come here to take refuge.
    Have mercy; receive me as your servant.

My body, scored with scars, I grow weak,
    weeping; I am weary and worn.
Lord who is the earth, water, fire, wind,
    and the cloud-shifting atmosphere.
You of sacred Vēnkaṭa Mountain
    whose tall summit fills the heavens,
I, your slave, come here to take refuge.
    Have mercy; receive me as your servant.

His small collection of miniature gods and items necessary for a proper *pooja* had been left in his Cambridge rooms, and he had no means to make his required Brahminic observances here in the open, sterile place, in any case. He could only recite the Vedas and the poems of the Alvars to himself as any form of piety. Ramanujan lacked the energy for anything else, regardless.

He'd tried to end his own life purposefully, but now Ramanujan felt that he may be truly dying anyway. His abdomen ached severely, he shivered constantly during the day, and suffered from fevers at night. His only diversion, when not praying, was still found in his equations. Despite poor food, no heat, and lack of sympathy from Dr. Ram and his staff, he could still, with effort, focus on his mathematics and make the rest of the world disappear. The duration of his periods of total concentration were much reduced, but he found that even with mental wanderings, trying to focus on a problem kept him from noticing his surroundings. This anesthetic, more than anything, prodded him to continue on his course. Mathematics became his medication, and he relied on it as much as prayer.

The only redeeming feature of his long stay in the sanatorium was the concession of twice-weekly trips to the baths. Matlock had a natural thermal hot-springs, and thus a wonderful spa had been built around it. The institution took advantage of this and allowed even the tubercular patients to spend an hour or two lounging in the warm waters after all the other patrons had vacated. Ramanujan welcomed this warming respite and would lie with his head supported on a brick edging, floating his body in the pool until: He could see them—people lounging on the banks of the river, parrots flying overhead. And he could hear their chatter and the temple bells clanging in the distance. The refreshing waters of the Kaveri flowed around and over him like a balm. He felt thoroughly cleansed and the waters awakened him in body and spirit. He could feel the soothing river running across him as he lay out in the gentle current, immersing his entire body in the mild warm flow. The water was the same temperature as the air, and it was an odd feeling to dunk into water that he could barely feel—as if floating briefly in space.

He suspected that part of the reason he'd been sequestered at Matlock House had been his state of depression. There had, of course, been the matter of his attempted suicide, which, as he now saw it, was a momentary lapse into desperation framed within a long period of dejection. Ramanujan was not given to deep personal reflection, but even he could see that his mental and physical health were conjoined twins, like those he'd once seen at a circus in Madras. At the time, he'd wondered if one of the pair always had to do what the other willed, and now he knew.

So, given his deteriorated state, he had at the outset not quite known how to accept the news that had arrived by letter from Mr. Hardy. The words on the page: 'You have been made a Fellow of the Royal Society...' didn't immediately sink in. In fact, he'd fallen asleep upon scanning the letter, and it was only on the second reading that the realization had hit him. *A Fellow!* he thought, *at last!* And then, *But I'm not even there to receive it...*

Spring had finally arrived, and he was out in the garden sitting on a small bench facing into the sun, wrapped in a shawl, and wearing both the wool hat Amanda had given him years before and the new scarf knitted by Lady North. It was near mid-day and the Brahminic rules said that he should not gaze upon the sun at noon. It had been such a long, and to him, severe winter that he didn't care. Just to be somewhat compliant, he closed his eyes for half an hour, and simply soaked up the radiant warmth.

He was no better, but the weather made him feel as if he were partaking in all the healthful herbs, baths, ointments, and medicines that he would have received at home under an Ayurvedic doctor's care.

In Kumbakonam, he had once acquiesced to being treated by Western medicine, and though painful, it had helped his condition immensely. He'd had a badly swollen scrotum which the doctor had called a hydrocele, and it had become uncomfortably large, making normal walking next to impossible. None of the home remedies had helped, nor had the Ayurvedic treatments. He'd been lucky that a Western-trained doctor had insisted on the necessary operation at little cost to the family, and after a few months, he was much relieved of the problem and able to walk normally again.

Later in Madras, on the other hand, he'd contracted what he subsequently discovered was a case of amoebic dysentery that had laid him low for months. Being far from Kumbakonam, he'd relied on friends and relatives in Madras when he was so ill and had seen a Western doctor who had not affected any change in his debilitating symptoms. It was only upon returning home and benefitting from the care of his mother, his new wife, and an Ayurvedic doctor that had made the difference in his condition. He'd gradually recovered enough to return to Madras, and his improved health allowed him to acquire a much-needed position with the government as a clerk.

Thus, he had no great expectations while exiled here in the center of modern, yet wild, England that Western medicine would be able to provide the cure for whatever it was that was ailing him. Instead, he imagined the strengthening spring sun as a Vedic flame passing over his head and prayed for its blessings.

Taking in the views provided by the Matlock House terrace from the same bench each day, he realized that since his arrival in England, this was the first time that he'd taken the time to carefully observe the unfolding of spring. The crocus that he'd been so enthralled with only days before were already wilting, and he knew that he'd need to pay close attention to each day's changes so as not to miss any of its marvelous gifts.

Those trees are amazing, he thought from his solitary perch. *The wood that looked dead, and no different from the logs that they throw on the fire – far too infrequently,* he added ruefully, *is now sprouting buds and new leaves. How is this possible – new life from apparent death? How could a plant go dormant so that all life seems to be gone, and then revive itself on its own to begin again?* In India, this was an uncommon sight. Apart from the almond that lost red leaves at the new year, most stayed green year-round. The life in the large tropical plants continued throughout the year, perhaps with periods of slower growth, but always with growth. *Where do these English trees get the energy to begin anew?* he wondered.

Thinking of the ability to revitalize from within gave him hope, and the rejuvenating spring sun revived him. At least, in spirits.

Ramalingam, the Tamil friend he'd met when he'd first arrived in London also looked in on him at Matlock House. His friend had visited him occasionally in Cambridge, and they'd kept in close contact through letters. Whereas none of the other visitors had commented directly on his condition or his appearance, he could tell at first glance that Ramalingam was appalled.

"How good to see you again, Ram," said Ramanujan, enjoying being able to speak in Tamil. "I can't thank you enough for making the trip up here—how was the journey?"

"It was long, cool, and wet, but what trip in England isn't? Anyway, I'm here now, and I want to both visit with you and see what I can do to improve the conditions you've described in your letters," Ram said. "I'd sent you some ghee and pickles that you wrote you could use—did those arrive alright?"

"Yes, thanks so much for sending them. The thing is, the cook we had here who was just barely passable in her culinary skills has recently departed—oh, not died—she went on to other employment. But her replacement can't even boil rice. So, no matter what foodstuffs I have to contribute to the kitchen, they'll probably be destroyed by a glance from the new cook. It's absolutely hopeless here as far as food goes. But enough of that! Where are you staying while you're here?"

"I enquired with the administration as soon as I arrived," said Ram, "and they've been good enough to provide me with a room out of the few they have available here in Matlock House, so I'll be right around the corner!"

"How good it'll be to have a friend nearby!" said Ramanujan with relief. The pair then launched into long discussions about Ram's adventures in the war, his new duties, friends from home, and homesickness for India—all in colloquial Tamil.

After several hours and several breaks, it was nearing Ramanujan's time to visit the spa baths. Ram became quiet and then suddenly stared intently at his friend.

"Ramanujan, I hate to say this, but you look horrible," said Ram shaking his head, "absolutely horrible. I simply must find out what's been happening with you here. What have they done to you? There's no vitality left in you at all." Ramanujan opened his mouth to reply, but Ram stormed on. "What's the status of your medical condition? Who's your doctor, and what does he say? How can it be that you've lost so much weight? They must be feeding you, but probably not enough would be my guess."

Over the course of the next several days, Ramanujan found that his friend had spent hours talking to the doctor and his staff and at the same time he'd also corresponded with Mr. Hardy. This was all in an attempt to find the cause of Ramanujan's decline and take any possible actions necessary to remedy the situation.

They ate breakfast together in the large open commons the day Ram was scheduled to return to London and continue his service in the Army.

"I hope you don't mind if I speak frankly?" asked Ram, apparently trying to screw up courage as he asked.

"No, we're friends," said Ramanujan. "Tell me whatever's on your mind."

"All right then. I've done some serious investigation into your stay here—especially about your diet. And I find that not all of the fault lies with the cook. Some of the problem is with you, yourself. You're simply too picky about what you eat. They're not trying to poison you here, you know, and they're trying very hard to meet your requirements. But you must be flexible too. As I understand it, you're not even eating grains like oatmeal, or having much dairy."

"It's not the nourishing food of Madras or Kumbakonam," replied Ramanujan a little testily. "So even if I consume it, it can't possibly make any difference—it's like eating paper."

"Nourishing," said Ram, "is anything that'll make you strong and keep you from becoming even more ill. Even meat, for that matter, could help your poor body recover. I sent you two jars of ghee, but I see them there, still sitting unused on your shelf! You simply must try and eat more, even if it's the British cuisine. Is there anything local you find even remotely acceptable?"

"Well, I do like that dish they serve sometimes," said Ramanujan. "It is called macaroni with cheese. Only now they've run out of cheese."

"What? In England?!" Ram was incredulous. "That's simply not possible. And even before I leave this morning, I'll look into this supposed cheese shortage."

Ram also promised to be his conduit for good Indian foodstuffs, especially once Ramanujan was able to leave the inflexible confines of Matlock House.

CHAPTER 31.

He felt free. His sentence had been commuted and, to his utter joy, he was out of the wilds and back in London. Even though the air quality was much worse, every liberated step he took seemed like a breath of the fresh country air he'd just left behind. The city felt different to him than on his last visit, and although not forgotten, memories of his suicide attempt were for the most part kept at bay. He was in good spirits, but he made it a point to remain in his lodgings should he feel his mood darken, and he resolved that he would sit in silent chanting if the black cloud ever descended upon him again.

Ramanujan reveled in his new-found freedom. He was staying in a hotel-like facility for patients under observation, but could come and go as he pleased. Dr. Ram, in consultation with other physicians, had agreed that the severe treatments for normal tubercular patients were not being effective in Ramanujan's case. In fact, it appeared that the spartan environment of Matlock House had exacerbated the decline in his health. Other doctors had concurred that he was curiously asymptomatic for one suffering from consumption, and he was now in London to consult with several specialists in advancement of his health. It had been three weeks since his arrival, and already one of the specialists, Dr. Lawrence, remarked that he seemed to be in better spirits and had gained two pounds in weight.

Ramanujan sat for long afternoons in the curiously-circular Fitzroy Square Garden just off his lodgings, wandered slowly and idly around nearby Regent's Park admiring the swans on the boating lake, visited some friends in the area by cab, and, of course, made numerous trips to the Natural History Museum. He was also regaining his interest and ability in mathematics. He'd loathed his hiatus from concentrated study, but now he felt that he had the strength and mental acuity to resume his investigations. Mr. Hardy had also been delighted with his return to London and had already made two trips to the city to go over some lines of enquiry with him. Ramanujan was beginning to feel like his former self, however, without the stamina and wide-eyed enthusiasm that he'd enjoyed in his health.

"I do not know how to explain it," Ramanujan had said. "The pattern just jumped out at me from Major MacMahon's table of results." Staring back at him, Mr. Hardy had just smiled, shaken his head in wonder, and then encouraged Ramanujan to write an additional article detailing his unexpected findings.

After multiple drafts, they'd finally published 'Asymptotic Formulae in Combinatory Analysis' in *the Proceedings of the London Mathematical Society*. The paper had presented formulae for calculating the number of partitions for any given number. The number five, for instance, had seven different partitions, or ways that it could be uniquely divided into subparts: 5, 4+1, 3+2, 3+1+1, 2+2+1, 2+1+1+1, and 1+1+1+1+1, and they had devised a computational means of deriving the number of partitions without actually dissecting each integer and counting the number of its component parts by hand. Major MacMahon had painstakingly provided a table of actual counts by which they could compare the results of their formulae. Glancing at the Major's table, Ramanujan had suddenly noticed a pattern and soon arrived at some new insights. Somehow, he'd noticed that the number of partitions for the numbers 4, 9, 14, 19, etc. were all divisible by the number 5. He'd then seen an easy means to generalize this pattern as a mathematical expression. Any integer put into this equation for symbol m resulted in an answer for which the number of its partitions would be divisible by 5 with zero remainder:

$$p(5m + 4) \equiv 0 \ (mod \ 5)$$

If m was zero, the result was 4 and that number had five partitions, if m was one, the result was 9 which had 30 partitions, and so on, each result being evenly divisible by 5. And similarly, he'd seen a pattern for the number seven that resulted in the following:

$$p(7m + 5) \equiv 0 \ (mod \ 7)$$

The number of partitions for the numbers 5, 12, 19 and 26 were all divisible by 7. And he'd found comparable results for several other numbers of partitions as well.

Where he'd noticed what to him had seemed like interesting patterns, Mr. Hardy had pressed that they were more than just interesting—this was another of Ramanujan's insights that needed to be conveyed to a broader audience. Ramanujan had been taxed by the paper, but he was also extremely gratified that now more and more of his ideas were being presented to, and accepted by, the mathematical community at large.

Ramanujan occasionally had difficulties in reading people and deciphering more than just the most obvious outward signs, but even he could detect that Mr. Hardy felt awkward on this visit upon finding him still convalescing in bed, a situation which was becoming more common than not of late. And he could also see that Mr. Hardy was searching for some connection or item of small talk to bring up before he delved into the most recent math problem they were tackling.

After describing his trip down from Cambridge as pleasant and mentioning that it appeared momentum was moving in the favor of the allies in Europe, Mr. Hardy, grasping for a topic, said, "Otherwise, I have little of interest to tell you. Even the cab number from the ride today was rather dull—1729."

Whereupon Ramanujan suddenly brightened. They were both now speaking a language he knew in some depth. He could read numbers, if not people. "Oh, no, Mr. Hardy," said Ramanujan. "Quite the contrary. 1729 is, in fact, a very special number. It is the first number, in the series of positive numbers, that can be expressed twice by cubes. It is the sum of both of the cubes $12^3 + 1^3$ and $10^3 + 9^3$. So, you see, it holds a distinguished position after all."

Mr. Hardy shook his head and grinned. "Alright, Ramanujan, I don't know how you do it, but you uncover what no one else is able to tweeze out. It is, after all, a very special number, indeed.

"Do you know," he continued after a pause. "Before we roll up our sleeves on this paper we're working on, I wanted to tell you something."

Ramanujan raised his eyebrows as an indication to continue.

"The doctors tell me that you're improving, and that you've actually gained some weight lately. I believe, and I don't pray to God, but I hope that I'm correct in feeling that the war with Germany will be over very soon. And there's good news from Madras, too. Not only will you have the Fellowships in the Royal Society and Trinity College here that have just been awarded, but you will also receive one in the university there. In fact, Madras is offering a very sizable remittance, and the fellowship includes the ability to easily come and research with us again in England whenever you desire. All in all, a very satisfactory and salutary outcome from all the advancements you've made in Cambridge.

"What I mean to say..., and this is not easy for me to admit..., but it's probably the right time for you to return to India—to convalesce and to finally conquer whatever it is that's laid you so low. We won't have this immediate contact, of course, but don't you agree that our friendship and working relationships are now so firmly established that we'll be able to continue our collaborations through the mail system rather than in person? I shall truly miss being able to see you and talk to you directly, but this is only a temporary situation until you're back on your feet."

"India," sighed Ramanujan, lying back on his pillow. "I am not sure what awaits me back home." He closed his eyes for a moment. "But I also know that I have been lingering during the last two or three years here without any true improvement. It surely cannot hurt to return. It is fortunate that knowing you has made the choice of whether to travel home or to stay here appear as equal sides of an equation. Here or there is not important; it is our work together that matters to me the most, and it will continue as usual. Of that I have no doubt."

Unwilling for the moment to meet Ramanujan's eyes, Mr. Hardy nodded, pulling out the papers from his briefcase, and then the two immersed themselves in the problem at hand.

"Oh, Mr. Rama!" said Amanda in a mildly distressed tone and rising as Ramanujan approached her table. He'd tried to put a spring in his step but ended up shuffling instead. As she hugged him lightly, she said, "In your letters, you said that you were doing much better, but to me you look worse."

"Hello, Amanda!" greeted Ramanujan as he let himself be hugged and then sank into the nearest chair. "No, I am much improved, but the walk here was much longer than I expected," as he took some more quick breaths.

"Oops, I meant that I expected you to look better, not that you look horrible now," explained Amanda, embarrassed.

"I know what you meant, but I also know that I am much different than when we first met on the *Nevasa*, am I not? And look at you—you're taller every time I see you."

"So much has happened since we met on the boat, hasn't it?" asked Amanda. "They say that the war is almost over, and maybe we can all get on with our lives soon." Just then the waitress arrived. Amanda had invited Ramanujan for tea at a fairly upscale restaurant, by wartime standards, and ordered Earl Grey tea and cucumber sandwiches for the both of them.

"I'm so glad that you're in London now," she continued. "Are the doctors here able to help you?"

"They seem to be. I have gained back some weight, and my endurance is improving somewhat. I think that once I am back in India, I will be able to fully recover."

"India?" asked Amanda. "You're thinking of heading back home?"

"Yes, I just recently learned that this would be possible, and Mr. Hardy thinks it would be a good idea, especially once the sea-lanes are free again."

"Oh, but we will miss you here!" said Amanda, "Although, I'm sure that your family misses you terribly by now, too."

"I hope so," said Ramanujan. "I haven't heard too much from them lately. I will need to contact them and let them know to expect me."

"I should say so," said Amanda as the tea service was set before them and Amanda proceeded to pour.

"How is your mother, Amanda?" asked Ramanujan, taking his cup and sipping his tea.

"Mum is doing fine, but things are not going so well with the estate. She just wrote me, though, and said that she's heard from the church. They need a new rectory and have inquired about the mansion as a possible site for both a rectory and for a hostel housing either nuns or priests. She says that she isn't sure how it will turn out, but that this could be the answer to our problems. She said that she told them that it could be offered to them at a very reasonable price."

"But where will she stay if she sells the house?" asked Ramanujan.

"She and my aunt—Daddy's sister—have become very close since Daddy died, and Aunt Claire says she'd love for Mummy to move in with her. They both feel that they're living in spaces that are way too big for them since I'm no longer at home, and my cousin has married and moved to Yorkshire."

"I am glad that your mother has maintained close ties with your aunt," said Ramanujan. "Keeping those bonds strong is very important." He took a bite of a cucumber sandwich and found it acceptable. "How is school progressing?"

"Very well, indeed, and I love my professors. Thank goodness I've received a stipend from the army to help me continue. Daddy would have been proud."

"I'm sure he would have been," said Ramanujan, "I know that I am."

"And I must tell you that I've met the nicest man, Mr. Rama. His name is Edmund, and he is so sweet and kind. He was in the same battalion that Daddy was in and was injured in the Battle of the Somme, but is healing well. He lost two fingers on his left hand, but they thought, at first, he might lose the entire arm. Anyway, he is two years older than me and was a medic in the war. He's now studying to become a doctor. I would so love for you to meet him sometime."

"I would like to meet him, too," said Ramanujan.

"Edmund's parents lived in India for two years, and when I mentioned I was meeting with you, he said that he'd love to make the voyage and see all of the sights that they talked about. If you return home, perhaps we could visit you sometime?"

"That would be excellent!" said Ramanujan. "We will need to keep in touch, because I expect to be back in England once I recover, too. Mr. Hardy is very anxious that we continue our research and wants this to just be a temporary visit."

The two enjoyed their tea and sandwiches, and Amanda had even more to say about Edmund and school.

Eleven, Eleven, Eleven, thought Ramanujan. *Eleven is a palindrome, the same backwards and forwards. So is eleven squared – 121, and eleven cubed – 1,331, and eleven to the fourth – 14,641; 11111 times 11111 is 123454321, and so it goes.*

He was reading the Tuesday headlines from the morning *Guardian*—"The War is Over!" and the first paragraph, "London, Monday Night. The maroons that in the bad nights of the past beat like blows on the drum of Fate gave the news to London at eleven o'clock this morning and sounded the overture of rejoicing."

November 11th at 11:00 the previous morning, the city had erupted. The guns had made a terrible booming, and then the bells in every steeple went wild. People had begun rushing into the streets, and soon there was no more room—people clung to statues and stood on cars and busses. The party had lasted all that day.

The still, overcast sky had been a cheerless dull gray, but the mood was as if the sun was shining brightly in the middle of the summer. A smile was on every face, and Ramanujan had never seen such hugging, back slapping, and kissing in public. He'd been out for a walk and was six blocks from his room—the most he could manage lately—when the news broke. There had been some early reports of a treaty from a few days before, but the country had remained quietly skeptical of that news. Yesterday, however, peace was certain, and they'd celebrated. He himself was embraced numerous times as he'd made his way back to his lodgings to watch the crowds from the safety of an upper window, and it took him nearly an hour to make the journey.

He'd seen some drinking back in India—especially among the poor laborers who were to be found lolling about on some of the back streets in Madras. Here in England, every native to the island seemed to drink some amount, and probably daily—but he'd rarely, except for some student parties in Cambridge, seen people actually intoxicated. Yesterday, however, the entire nation seemed to be reeling as beer, wine, and spirits flowed out of the houses and taverns and into the streets.

He felt well and rested the next morning as he ate breakfast and read the newspaper alone, served by a groggy-looking waitress. He guessed that he'd be one of the few in the entire city, for a change, who didn't feel 'under the weather' on this day.

C H A P T E R   3 2 .

1919

Perhaps it's not so odd that I should feel so at peace, he thought. *I made it to England and worked with Mr. Hardy; I've published some of the best mathematical results I could; I'm a Fellow; I've battled illness; the horrible war is over; and now I am going home.*

He *was* composed—no matter how roughly the waves pounded the hull of the *Nagoya*, he wasn't bothered and felt safe. This time he had full knowledge of the length of the voyage and settled into it. The food was in fact better than he'd eaten in some time, and the cook was able to produce Indian dishes that were more than palatable. His collar didn't strangle his neck. His shoes were comfortable, and he barely noticed that he had them on. The cut of his hair felt natural. His clothing hung loosely on his frame rather than bursting at the seams as it had on his trip to England. He managed a knife and fork with aplomb and was conversant in all the topics of discussion that had previously been indecipherable to him. And, instead of being one of a handful of Indians on the initial voyage, half of the ship was peopled with his countrymen, returning, mainly wounded, to their homes. With his fevers and aching abdomen, he was, in fact, no better or worse off than most of them.

Freshly arrived from India five years earlier and disembarking from the *Nevasa* onto the busy docks in London had been seemingly into chaos. Now, as they were anchoring in the Bombay harbor, the clamor and activity seemed almost staid by comparison. London had been bustling with people in strange dress and jammed with the latest in modern transportation, and the crowds and automobiles had all intertwined in an incomprehensible web, filling a city of unexpected size and breath-taking architecture. And he had come to find that strange new pace and efficiency within apparent mayhem as comfortably routine.

Today, on a balmy, tropical morning, he took in the Bombay shoreline. Though busy with activity, the movement was slower, the profile lower, and the setting more natural—a rural city. Rather than intensely concentrated commerce, there were carts, a few lorries, and a few cranes; rather than multistoried buildings as far as one could see, there were luscious plants and palm trees peppering the landscape dotted with low-rise buildings merging into the greenery; rather than choking smoke from numerous factories, there was a refreshing breeze off the ocean. He was nearly home.

It was a short ride to shore on the ship's tender, and he could already smell wood-smoke in the air, as well as the odors of cattle dung and drying fish. As they approached the dock, he could even detect the whiffs of an early curried lunch being prepared somewhere in the huts along the beach. He thought of Charlie picking up the scent of London as they'd steamed into the Thames and chuckled to himself, wondering what had become of the sailor.

He alighted from the tender and joined the other passengers slowly climbing the wooden planks up to the level of the docks. Winded, he stepped to the side at the top of the ramp. They were waiting for him—his mother and brother stood among an immediately familiar crowd of people who looked just like him.

He launched into Tamil and thrilled at hearing it echoed back in the intimate manner of family. "Mother! Brother!" exclaimed Ramanujan, holding his hands together in front of his face and bowing slightly to each. "You don't know how good it is to see you again!"

"Ay oh, Ramanujan!" exclaimed his mother, replying with her hands flying up first to her own cheeks and then to his. "How you've changed! I knew that you were unwell, but I had no idea how poorly you've become. We must get you home immediately, and we need to have doctors at our doorstep when we do. Look at how much weight you've lost! Look at how pale you are!"

Ramanujan pulled out the loose waist of his jacket and shrugged his shoulders in the now spacious suit. "Yes, Mother," he said. "I've been quite ill, but I'm not yet dead. And I've come home to do something about it. I would've returned sooner but for the bloody war, and I needed to get to the point where I was strong enough for the voyage. All will be well once I'm home."

"Yes, and we'll head there as soon as possible," said his mother watching with anxiety as he gripped the railing for support, "although, I think Madras would be even better. Kumbakonam won't have the doctors who can treat you. We'll need to check on the next available train for Madras. I'd thought that an immediate cleansing ceremony in Rameswaram would be best, since you've polluted yourself in so many ways in journeying to be among the English, but this, I see now, won't be possible. We'll need to change our tickets..." and she hesitated. "Because, I must say that for you to survive the journey to Rameswaram and then back up to Madras might even be beyond the helping of the gods."

"Come now, Mother, it's not that bad," said Ramanujan. "I'm nearly home."

His mother, Komalatammal, and brother, Lakshmi Narasimha, quickly became involved in the changing of train reservations and in finding suitable lodging if no train was immediately available. They left Ramanujan, to his uttermost contentment, in the nearest coffee stall where he had deliciously sweet and flavorful Indian filter coffee for the first time in years, a plate of freshly fried *murukku*, and some spicy fried vegetable balls.

There'd been little opportunity for more than pleasantries between his arrival and the hurried arrangements for a new train connection, which, they discovered, would be a few days out. On the way to the lodgings obtained by his brother, his mother had prattled on about the meager funds they had available, the state of his father who was becoming blind—first in one eye and now the other, and the many requests she'd had from Ramanujan's friends wanting to meet him when he arrived in Madras. She was both proud and energized to have him home again and to be in charge of his well-being.

After they'd settled into their room in a small hostel, they found time for a more meaningful conversation. "Honestly, the main thing on my mind right now is Janaki," said Ramanujan. "Where is she?! She wrote only a few letters to me at the beginning, before I even reached Cambridge, and then the letters stopped completely. I'm worried about her!" not mentioning the single additional plea for money Janaki had sent him seeking help with her brother's wedding. His mother remained silent but gave him an odd look that slowly transformed itself into a barely discernable smile. He continued in an anxious tone. "Why isn't she here? What could be more important than meeting with her husband again? Especially after such a long absence and considering my state of health? Where is she? Is she unwell?"

"She's not really family, now is she?" asked his mother. "At least not one of us when it counts, and she was so young when you left. From what I hear, she's been busy seeing to an ill father, and hasn't cared to be around us in Kumbakonam for quite some time."

"What do you mean, not around?" asked Ramanujan. "I left her with you, and she should have stayed. Is her father in dire circumstances? Where is she now?"

"Oh, she's off with her family, and you shouldn't be concerned, especially given your own condition," said his mother. She then diverted the conversation in other directions until Ramanujan nearly collapsed from fatigue and frustration, and his brother helped him into bed.

She's not family, he thought repeatedly. *Then what is family? What had happened to Janaki's father that's so serious? For Janaki not to be family is a very curious and very damning statement, yet Mother threw it off as if it meant nothing.*

He now had time to think about it as he lay exhausted on the cot. Given his mother's unsympathetic attitude towards Janaki when they'd first been together, he wondered if more was going on between his mother and his wife than his mother was letting on.

The family visited the nearest Vaishnavite temple early the following morning which was a long walk for him and yet only a few blocks away from the hostel where they boarded. Before his trip to England, Ramanujan had both enjoyed and taken for granted observing *pooja*s with his mother. Now, he felt a curious disconnect. After receiving his first blessings in years in the temple, his only thought was to be alone.

His stomach still hurt him terribly, now even more so, probably from the spicy foods that he'd eaten the day before. Nevertheless, after *pooja* they found a stall near the temple and he ordered some delicious vegetables, sambar, and yogurt with rice. He also couldn't resist a small bowl of *aval* with cardamom and cashews. He savored the meal and the coffee, and tarried, sharing small talk with his mother and brother.

"Mother, I'm feeling tired, and it's so nice and cool in the temple," mentioned Ramanujan as the others were rising to head back to the hostel. "I don't think I'm quite yet re-accustomed to the heat. I've decided to linger in the temple and perhaps wait for the noon prayers before I return to the rooms. Why don't you and Narasimha go on with what you have planned and let me rest in the cool interior?"

"Oh, but we have so much to catch up on," lamented his mother. "Why don't we go stroll through that nearby market?"

"I'm too exhausted to even make it to the gate," he said. "You should enjoy yourselves here in Bombay, and we can talk more on the train tomorrow."

Soon he was back in the temple. The worshippers ebbed and flowed around him, and it came to him that he felt like a solitary rock being washed over by the turbulent sea.

No, that's not quite correct, he thought. *I'm more like a small punt from the River Cam adrift on the Indian Ocean. Here, but not here. An odd thing in a usual spot. I'm not even feeling at home with my own family.*

He found a nook in the temple wall and sat watching the passing worshippers, hearing vague phrases in Marathi. Familiar scents of incense, sounds of bells and prayers, and people all of an old, familiar dress and color washed over him and soon he was asleep.

He awoke sometime later and reached out for his slate and piece of chalk, but there were none at hand, and he had no paper. He had no important equations in mind to write down in any case. It had been a force of habit. *How things have changed*, he thought, as he fell asleep again with his head resting against a cool stone pillar.

CHAPTER 33

"Really, Ramanujan—you shouldn't be so short or cross with me," complained his old friend Rao. "I've only come to wish you well and to help see to your needs. Are you in such pain that you tear into me so?"

Ramanujan shook his head angrily and was set to lash out again and demand that Rao leave when he instead let his head fall back and took a deep breath.

"I'm so sorry, Rao," said Ramanujan. "I'm in pain, but it's no worse than normal. Can you please close the door?"

As Rao closed and softly bolted the double doors, Ramanujan patted at the side of his bed and Rao, searching Ramanujan's eyes all the while for clues, sat where indicated.

"I've just realized," said Ramanujan, "that I'm not cross with you, old friend—I'm cross with the world, and it's made me cantankerous. Now that I think about it, my time in England has not only made me ill, it's also given me the time and acquaintance with what the English call 'introspection'. We know that word here, of course, but there are aspects of its meaning that are foreign to us. Here in India, all that we say or do is straightforward and for God. Whereas, the people and doctors there in England are prone to self-examination and look for the underlying meanings of anything anyone says or does. Did you know that they have a secret message system that they use based solely on the type of flowers they send to someone? And there is a Dr. Freud who's all the rage in Europe with his 'psychoanalysis' which looks even further into hidden motivations."

Rao nodded, but the head bobbing also contained a question. "Yes, I have heard of Dr. Freud, but have never really read anything by him," he said.

"Here is my take on what might be his psychoanalysis of me," continued Ramanujan, "even though I really know nothing about it. I'm cross because I can't help it. I'm ill, and I think that I'm actually becoming sicker by the day. I'm either fevered, or ache all of the time, and thus I can't sleep or concentrate. I've committed grave sins by traveling to England and as a result I couldn't even attend our friend Kumaran's recent funeral! But you know what? I'm even more sorry that I've had to leave my proximity to the great Mr. Hardy with whose help I gained publications and membership into the Royal Society, of all things. And now I'm back home, or rather back to a place that doesn't feel like home anymore—besieged by family who, honestly, only seem interested in money or bickering, and by friends who only care about my good name and not me."

Rao turned his gaze to the floor.

"Oh, of course I didn't intend to include you, Rao! Nor the many friends who stood by me and helped me achieve great things without thinking anything of themselves."

He lay his head on the crook of his arm and closed his eyes for a few moments. Then he partially sat up and raised his hands pressed together in front of his heart.

"Bless you, Rao," he said sincerely. "I've never had a better friend than in you. I hope you understand that I'm flailing like a damaged English biplane looking for a safe place to land over a now foreign soil. I love India, but I think I'm looking at a rough landing."

Rao nodded and pressed his hands together as well.

"I understand, Ramanujan, and wish you well," he said. "We're clinging to a vision of your old self and pray to the gods that that healthy version re-emerges in all its glory."

"Janaki! Your smile is just the same, so I'd recognize you anywhere!" said Ramanujan as he held onto the door for support.

"And you, husband, look far too thin!" said a now worried-looking Janaki in reply.

It had taken some time and much effort through family connections, but finally Janaki had arrived at his doorstep. He'd left behind a child-bride of barely fourteen, and now standing here in front of him with her brother beside her was a comely young woman of eighteen. This first greeting quickly became awkward since Ramanujan couldn't disguise his conflicting feelings—his delight at seeing Janaki again, and his disappointment in her lack of contact while he'd been away.

The family was currently renting a small Madras villa, and Ramanujan was feeling increasingly fatigued at the constant stream of admirers and well-wishers who came to the door at all hours since he'd arrived. He'd renewed many friendships, but also endured many who'd only come to see him because of his new-found reputation. He was having a bad day, but had managed to stand and walk slowly to the door in order to greet his wife.

After the initial formalities, Ramanujan returning to his bench, and Janaki settling once again into the household, they finally had a moment alone and had begun a more friendly conversation when his mother swept in and ushered Janaki out.

"Can't you see that he's unwell?" asked his mother. "We need to keep this house clean, and dinner hasn't even been started. What do you think you're doing? Don't you want the best for your husband?"

"Mother, really," said Ramanujan. "We were just catching up, and..."

"Well, there'll be time to catch up later," she said. "There's work to be done. Now, go and do your duty, Janaki."

Janaki gave him a strange look, and meekly went off to sweep out the house and begin the preparations for the evening meal. Ramanujan had issues with this, but was too weak at the moment to offer more than the most meager protest.

"There, isn't that better?" asked his mother as she herself was walking out of the room and shutting the door. "Now you just rest, and I'll see to everything."

Ramanujan had found that it was nearly impossible to spend any time alone with Janaki while his mother was in the house, and a few days later he hired a rickshaw to take the pair to a nearby pocket park—much to his mother's strident protestations. Even the minimal moments they'd managed to be together were strained by the mood in the house. Whenever guests were absent, small arguments and petty conflicts seemed to erupt. Ramanujan knew that he wasn't in the best mood and apt to lash out or lose patience himself, but there were also frequent outbursts between his mother and Janaki.

Ramanujan was in no condition for a long walk, but had said that he needed to take in the fresh air. The pair alit from the rickshaw, paid the driver, and then started out along a path leading to a central gazebo with surrounding benches. Janaki had kept a respectful distance, sometimes a bit behind him, when he heard her muffled weeping. He halted his slow shuffle and turned to face her. "What is it Janaki?" he asked. "Why are you so upset?"

Janaki hid her face with the end of her sari and was eventually able to stutter, "Why... why did you never reply to my ... my letters? Why didn't you take me to... England with you?"

Ramanujan stood struck, utterly dumbfounded. *Letters? How could this be?* he thought. *She'd written to me?*

"What do you mean, you'd written?" he asked, somewhat crossly. "You're talking about the two letters when I first arrived in England?"

Janaki was now shocked. "I... I wrote to you every week for a year—and you never replied," she said.

"What do you mean?" repeated Ramanujan. "I was the one who wrote letters weekly until I couldn't stand the lack of response anymore!"

"What? You wrote?" asked Janaki, her eyes welling again with tears.

They both stared at each other in bewilderment, and then Ramanujan, unable to cross the distance to the gazebo, slowly crumpled onto the meager brown grass of the park.

"How could this be? Did you get the address wrong?" he asked. Janaki sat a small distance from him with her head bowed. "Just exactly how did you write to me, Janaki?" he asked.

"Well, I didn't really write, since I'm only just learning my scripts. I told your mother what I wanted to say, and she wrote down the words."

He sighed, and feeling suddenly exhausted, desperately wanted to lie down on his own cot. "I apologize—this trip to the park is more than I'm able to manage right now. But I must ask the obvious question—who collected and opened the mail each day?"

"Well, your mother, of course," replied Janaki.

"So, my mother was supposed to be the conduit of our letter exchange. Now it looks to me like she was a python—constricting our correspondence."

After a long pause, he said, "I'm so sorry—you can't know the bitterness I felt in not hearing from you—and now I find that all my anger was misplaced."

They couldn't hug in a public space, nor even show the depth of the emotions resulting from these revelations. Pointedly looking at the ground, Janaki whispered, "And I was foolish enough to think that you no longer wanted me for your wife."

The tips of the willow branches brushed the water's surface and he edged the punt in beneath them. The deep shadows under the trees made this section of the Cam look like cool dark pools and he was just thinking about diving in when he was suddenly awake. The bickering had started in the morning, and now in preparing lunch, a full-blown row had erupted between his mother and Janaki in the kitchen. His head reeling from the effort, Ramanujan pushed himself up off his cot with a purpose and shouted, "Stop! Stop it you two this instant! I can't take it anymore!" And just as quickly he dropped back down in exhaustion.

"This simply must change," he said in a tone just above a whisper.

Wiping her hands on a rag and stepping into the room with a concerned expression that slowly changed to a pleased look on her face, his mother said, "Well, now finally you see the poison this one has spread. It's time for her to go."

Ramanujan stared at his mother for a long moment and then calmly and deliberately said, "No, Mother, you don't understand. I'm not the same person who left here five years ago, and no matter how ill I am, I'm claiming my position. The position that I built while I was in England, and now demand here, too."

His mother stared back with a confused look, and then began a tirade about the failings of Janaki.

"Mother!" shouted Ramanujan. "I'm not your little boy any longer! I'm a fully-grown man and a capable husband, and my household now consists of my wife and me. You're allowed to remain as long as you are civil."

His mother was taken aback. Beginning to weep she began, "How could you, after all that I've…"

"No, how could you?" demanded Ramanujan with his eyes closed. "How could you block the correspondence between Janaki and me while I was away? How could you allow my wife to leave our home? How could you only care about the money and not the household? How could you say that Janaki wasn't family?"

He opened his eyes again and leveled them at her. "Well, I'll tell you now to your face that you and I no longer share the same definition of family. The family that I desire is to have my loving wife by my side, to have a calm household where I can continue my work and recovery in peace, and to have respect shown to all in it. Since you don't have the same views, you're simply no longer in charge, and should feel lucky that you're allowed to remain—as long as you are respectful."

It was clear that his mother was poised for another outburst, but instead ran weeping from the room. Janaki who had been standing in the doorway with downcast eyes, slowly raised them toward him with a warmth he had not felt before from another person.

1920

His mother brought in the mail and read the return addresses to Ramanujan as she sifted through the pile. Ramanujan stopped her when she said, "Amanda North." She lifted the letter out of the stack. "Would you like me to read it to you, son?" she asked helpfully.

"No, thank you," said Ramanujan. "If you'd open it, I'll read it for myself." Komalatammal slit open the envelope, unfolded the letter and laid it carefully on the top of the stack. "That will be all for now, Mother, thank you."

As Komalatammal pulled shut the door to the room, Ramanujan, sat up with some difficulty, adjusted his glasses, and read.

Dear Mr. Rama,   *January 12, 1920*

I hope you are finding the recovery that you wished for and are well on your way to full health. Your last letter was very encouraging, and so I hope you continue to improve. It sounds like you have had many visitors and have stayed active with your mathematics, so that is all for the good.

I am writing with some exciting news. Edmund and I are getting married. He is the medical student that I spoke to you about in London, and things have only become better between us. He proposed when we were both visiting Mummy over Christmas, and Mum is ever so enchanted by him, as am I. The wedding date is set for August 12 of this year, and we hope that you will be able to attend. If not, Edmund says he would like to come and visit you as soon as we are finished with school, as he may also have some job prospects in India.

Mum is just fine, and did I say? The estate was sold to the church after all. It has enabled her and Claire to live very comfortably and both are so happy with the arrangement.

Please give my affection to your mother and wife.

The very fondest regards,

Amanda

Ramanujan lay back with his head on the pillow and the letter draped across his chest. "Yes, I'll try and make it," he said quietly, "but I'll need to write the reply letter a little later." He drifted off to sleep with sudden memories of cold snow and a frigid wind on his cheeks.

Blisteringly hot days, sweltering nights, and a perpetual fever left him continuously bathed in sweat. The only cool things he seemed to find now were Janaki's light hand and his mathematics.

The math was becoming more like a trance to him, and he couldn't easily distinguish between the dreams he had of equations and the functions he was writing at the moment—he seemed to fade from one into the other and back again. However, this was during the worst periods—he would also have extended periods of extreme lucidity.

He continued his pursuit of the idea that the levels or tiers implied by the Three-tiered Hanging Garden problem intimated a solution composed of discrete values—no matter what was put into the equation, within defined limits, only certain integers would appear as results. And he was specifically interested in an equation which resulted in only three distinct outcomes, either in the coefficients of the equations or the results.

And now he felt that had something that was a close approximation—at least compared to not knowing what the problem really was in the first place.

He'd created something that he called a 'mock' theta function. These 'mock' functions held strong similarities to a true theta function, but differed in their asymptotic expansion. Ramanujan was intrigued not only by the equations themselves, but also by their coefficients and the equation that generated these coefficients, which was:

$$(-1)^{n-1}\frac{\left(\exp\left(\pi\sqrt{\frac{n}{6}-\frac{1}{144}}\right)\right)}{2\sqrt{n-\frac{1}{24}}} + O\left(\frac{\exp\left(\pi\sqrt{\frac{n}{6}-\frac{1}{144}}\right)}{\sqrt{n-\frac{1}{24}}}\right)$$

Previously, he had discovered a mock theta function as follows:

$$p(q) = \sum_{n=0}^{\infty}\frac{q^{2n(n+1)}}{(1+q+q^2)(1+q^3+q^6)\cdots(1+q^{2n+1}+q^{4n+2})}$$

For this equation, the coefficient-generating equation above it provided the following coefficients in order: 1, -1, 0, 1, 0, -1, 1, -1, 0, 1, -1, 0, with the thirteenth coefficient = 2, and all of the rest beyond the thirteenth, unfortunately, straying from 1, -1 and 0.

Now he had discovered another mock theta function which expanded the string of three distinct coefficients even further:

$$\chi(q) = \sum_{n=0}^{\infty}\frac{q^{n^2}}{(1-q+q^2)(1-q^2+q^4)\cdots(1-q^n+q^{2n})}$$

He found the following values for the coefficients from the generating equation, in order, before they devolved to include other integers: 1, 1, 1, 0, 0, 0, 1, 1, 0, 0, -1, 0, 1, 1, 1, -1, 0, 0, 0, 1, 0, 0, -1, 0, 1, 1, 1, 0, -1, -1, 1, 1, 0, -1, -1, 0, 1. So, n in the generating function had to reach 37 before the coefficients varied from these three values.

The coefficients stayed within three tiers, the equation was divergent since parts—the cusps of the ellipses—went off to infinity, and it was loosely connected to the prime number equations he'd been working on. *Perhaps with each step I'm coming closer to solving the mystery of the Three-tiered Hanging Garden which has appeared so often in my dreams,* he thought.

He cried out as demons slashed at him. He jumped to the side, but snakes struck at his legs. He was dying of thirst, but he felt that his throat had shrunk to the size of a straw. He was just placing his mouth into a fetid puddle, trying to draw up even the smallest amount of liquid, when he awoke with a start.

Janaki was there immediately and had brought an urn filled with water. She poured a cup, and tilting his head back gently, directed a small stream into his mouth until he felt sated. He gave her a weak smile and managed, "You have no idea of the dream that I just had—and it bears no repeating. Thank you for the delicious water."

"So, it was not a math dream then?" she asked jokingly.

Shaking his head ruefully he said, "Oh, I wish it was."

Janaki gently removed his wet *veshti* and bathed him with the cool water. Suddenly the time and space felt very intimate, and they were alone. In what was becoming a rare occurrence, they behaved as true husband and wife. Afterward, Janaki bathed him again and helped him into fresh clothes.

She left to prepare the lunch, and he turned on his side to continue the derivation of some new equations he'd been intrigued with. When she returned with a light meal, Ramanujan was asleep with his mouth drooling somewhat on the paper he'd been using for mathematics. She moved the paper and gently shook his shoulder. He was dazed and took a long moment to sit up. His head still in a fog, it took him some effort to decipher the new entries he'd written on the page.

"Oh, Janaki," he lamented, "What am I going to do? I can hardly hold my head up or concentrate for more than a few minutes anymore."

He took a few spoons of *rasam* and then lay back and gazed across the room.

"I never thought that these verses from the Alvars would begin to take on some meaning for me," he said as he sang in a soft, raspy voice:

When one becomes weakened, the strong whom he entreats
    will surely be his saviors.
So even though I'm undeserving, I reach out to you
    who once saved the elephant.
When I'm suffering from fatigue, I won't remember you at all,
So I'm speaking up right now in advance,
    Sleeper on the serpent in Srirangam.

When Yama's lackeys snatch and push me,
    send me crashing with, "Move on, Flesh,"

I won't be able to think of you, I,
　who know nothing of your great mystery.
Lord of the heavenly celestials, great Mayan born in Mathura,
Whatever happens, you must protect me,
　Sleeper on the serpent in Srirangam.

"I only hope the Lord will accept the poor, defiled thing that I've become, and see that I did the best that I could, when I could. Mathematics is the language of the gods, so he must be forgiving."

He tried his best, but he couldn't move, he couldn't speak, he couldn't swallow. His eyes were open, and he could see the sunlight on the floor, feel a gentle breeze, and hear someone in the kitchen cleaning or cooking. A few flies buzzed in the empty air, and there was no other sound.

He somehow sensed that he was going to sleep for the last time, and his thoughts were not on mathematics, but on the verses of the Alvars and they came to him as though someone else was singing them on his behalf:

Don't sleep, don't sleep, bright shining disc!
　Don't fall asleep, Oh, conch!
Sharp well-wielded Nandaka sword, lovely Sarnga bow,
　Oh, mace!
Protectors of the eight directions who never know destruction,

Don't fall asleep, Oh, King of birds;
  watch over this bedchamber.

Before your time arrives
  when you can't even open your mouth,
When questioned all around you with, "Tell us!
  Is there stuff you've stashed away and forgotten?"
Fix the god, Madhava,
  in the temple that you build in your heart.
Those who offer flowers of love will be spared
  torture by snakes.

Before your family clusters in bunches,
  lauding your feats, leaving out your faults,
Before they cover you in a shroud and lament
  while they put you on a bier
Like a pot of honey for a pack of jackals,
  let your heart rejoice and join him,
Govinda, the kaustubha-jeweled,
  then escape past that notorious place.

He tried to call out for Janaki. He tried, but then found he
could no longer take a breath.

CHAPTER 35

It was a warm day under a brilliant sun, yet a cool breeze kept the temperature pleasant. He found himself gazing at a magnificent garden with paths that disappeared into mists on either side and, as he stepped forward to the walkway's edge, found that he was at an altitude and could make out innumerable levels above and below. The plants around him were animated – strangely in motion even when the gentle wind subsided.

A figure was walking toward him up the sloped path. At first, he thought that it was Namagiri Amman but, as it neared, it resolved through the mist into a man in European dress with a dark hat, spectacles, and a bushy black beard. There was an ecstatic smile on his face, and Ramanujan felt an outpouring of love both to and from this man.

No words were exchanged, but he knew who this was: Mr. Riemann whose photograph he had seen hanging in Mr. Hardy's office and who had made a famous though unproven conjecture about the zeta function he'd created to refine the prime number theory. They gazed at each other and then both lifted their eyes skyward where Ramanujan marveled that the garden continued in levels as far as they could see, rising like a living temple gopuram. Plants sprang out from every tier. Someone in the distance sang the songs of the Alvars.

Ramanujan realized that, somehow, the zeta function created the very path on which they walked and the garden in which they stood. Each non-trivial zero in Reimann's enigmatic equation produced a new shoot that became a fascinating and intricate plant. He stepped up to a flower on the nearest vine and marveled at the mathematical expression revealed within it. Mr. Reimann moved past him to continue up and onward, and after breathing in the flower's essence, Ramanujan turned and followed until the next plant momentarily beckoned. Mr. Reimann paused and waited until they both continued up the path, and Ramanujan sensed that his next life might lie just up ahead.

ACKNOWLEDGEMENTS

The translations of the Alvar poets were provided by Dr. Lynn Ate, either from her book *Yasoda's Songs to Her Playful Son Krsna*, or from her unpublished works. Invaluable edits on Indian/Brahminic culture and religion were provided by Dr. V.A. Vidya and Rema Raghu of the Chella Meenakshi Centre for Education and Research Services in Madurai, Tamil Nadu, India. Helpful comments on a first draft were given by friends Todd Broadman and Paul Rasmussen, and an invaluable editorial assessment was provided by Jessica Hatch of Hatch Editorial Services. Helpful feedback by the beta readers at Entrada Publishing was also gratefully welcomed.

The section symbol ௐ used in this book is the Tamil script for OM.

Srinivasa Ramanujan (his last name pronounced 'rah mah new gen' with the emphasis on the second syllable), was a mathematical genius whose works and enigmatic notes are still being studied and unraveled by generations of mathematicians. His life is largely as outlined in this novel in which I've tried to portray the struggles he must have undergone in dealing with contrasting cultures, British imperialism and attitudes, and debilitating illness. He died at the young age of 33.

G.H. Hardy and J.E. Littlewood were world-famous British mathematicians and both knew, mentored, and collaborated with S. Ramanujan. E.H. Neville was also a mathematician of repute who encouraged Ramanujan to come to England from Madras, and he and his wife, Alice, provided Ramanujan his initial home base in England. I have invented the name of Mr. Neville's brother.

Mary Cartwright became famous for her work in chaos theory. She studied for her doctorate under Hardy and collaborated with Littlewood. There is little chance she actually met Ramanujan, but her age in the book is accurate.

Ralph H. Fowler, among other things, explained field electron emissions and became well known in physics and astronomy. He was at Trinity College at the same time as Hardy and was a cricket player. He did get wounded in Gallipoli and worked on anti-aircraft ballistics.

There was a Lord North who owned a manor in Shotteswell, England, but that is the only association with this work of fiction.

Ramanujan had a cousin in Visakhapatnam, and I have taken the liberty of naming him Krishnasamy. Ramalingam, Mahalanobis, and Rao were good friends of Ramanujan's, and Drs. Chowry-Muthu and Ram were his actual physicians in England. Ramalingam went by the name A.S. Ram while in England. Dr. Chowry-Muthu was on the *Nevasa* with Ramanujan. Ramanujan's wife, Janaki, and mother, Komalatammal, are portrayed largely as described in his biography, *The Man Who Knew Infinity* by Robert Kanigel, as are most of the strictly historical events that occurred in India and England. The remainder of the people, places, and circumstances are of my own invention.

My purpose in writing this novel is to highlight the changes and struggles that must have been encountered by Ramanujan in the last years of his life when he made his journey to England. Here was a poor, religious, and largely rural Indian growing up in Kumbakonam which 100 years after he lived there has a population of 170,000 people. Before he traveled to England, he lived in Madras (Chennai) on and off for several years, and so was accustomed to a bigger city (estimated to have a population of 500,000 or so in 1910). Still, I feel that the accounts of him, even by G.H. Hardy, seem to brush aside the enormous adaptations he must have had to make in moving to Cambridge, a town probably of a similar size to Kumbakonam at the time, but situated in a modern, industrial, insular, Christian, cold, wet, England just at the outbreak of the First World War. This would have been difficult enough for anyone even without facing severely declining health and estrangement from those he loved. So, my intention here is to focus on Ramanujan and his culture rather than on G. H. Hardy and his Cambridge society.

SOURCES AND SUGGESTED READINGS

Ate, Lynn. Unpublished papers.

Ate, Lynn. *Yaśodāa's Songs to Her Playful Son Kṛṣṇa*. SASA Books, Woodland Hills, CA, 2011.

Berndt, Bruce C. *Ramanujan's Notebooks. Part 1.* Springer-Verlag Inc., New York, 1985

Berndt, Bruce C. and Robert A. Rankin. *Ramanujan: letters and commentary*. American Mathematical Society, 1995.

Derbyshire, John. *Prime Obsession: Bernhard Riemann and the greatest unsolved problems in mathematics*. Plume, published by The Penguin Group. New York. 2004.

Hardy, G.H. *A Mathematician's Apology*. Canto Edition, Cambridge University Press. Cambridge, UK. 1992.

Hardy, G.H. and Ramanujan, S. 'Asymptotic formulæ in combinatory analysis.' *Proceedings of the London Mathematical Society*, 2, XVII, 1918, 75 — 115

Kanigel, Robert. *The Man Who Knew Infinity: A Life of the Genius Ramanujan*. New York; Washington Square Press, 1991.

Ramanujan, Srinivasa. 'Highly Composite Numbers.' *Proceedings of the London Mathematical Society, Series 2 14 (1915)*, 347–400.

Ramanujan, Srinivasa. 'Some Properties of Bernoulli's Numbers.' *Journal of the Indian Mathematical Society*, III, 1911, 219-234.

Ramanujan, Srinivasa. 'Some properties of p(n), the number of partitions of n.' *Proceedings of the Cambridge Philosophical Society*, XIX, 1919, 207 – 210.

du Sautoy, Marcus. *The Music of the Primes: Searching to solve the greatest mystery in mathematics.* HarperCollins Publishers. 2003.

Alvar – Any one of the twelve Vaishnava poet-saints in Tamil Nadu in the 7th to 10th centuries CE.

Annapurni – (fem. of Annapurna), Hindu goddess of food and nourishment.

appam – A pancake made with a fermented batter of coconut and rice flour.

aval – Rice grain pounded into thin flakes then boiled.

Ayurveda – A traditional Indian form of medicine that often employs various herbs and minerals.

Bharata Natyam – A classical dance of South India, with stylized hand gestures and rhythmic foot beats.

bidi – A cigarette made of tobacco flakes wrapped in plant leaf.

Brahmin – Social class, or caste, in India, traditionally priests, teachers, or protectors of sacred learning.

channa dal – Split chickpeas.

chapatti – An unleavened flatbread made with wholewheat flour, cooked on a *tava*.

chaturthi – The fourth day of the waning phase after the full moon.

dal – Different dried pulses (lentils, beans, or peas).

dosa – A flat, fried crepe-like pancake made from a fermented batter of ground *urud dal* and rice, cooked on a *tava*. Usually folded in thirds on a plate and served with a vegetable filling.

Durga – Protector goddess and sister of Vishnu.

Gayatri Mantra – A well-known mantra from the *Rig Veda* dedicated to the sun.

ghee – Clarified butter.

golu – Display of dolls or figurines arranged in tiers to tell a story.

gopuram – A tall, tiered, ornate tower above the gate to a temple complex. The tallest is nearly 240 ft.; the *gopuram* of the Sarangapani Temple in Kumbakonam is 164 ft. tall.

gulab jaman – An Indian sweet. A small deep-fried ball of milk-based dough soaked in a sweet rose-scented syrup.

hijra – Eunuch, transgendered person, or transvestite; they have an ancient role in Indian society and are often included in birth or wedding ceremonies.

idiyappam – steamed rice noodles formed into a nest-like shape.

idli – A steamed, ovoid cake made from a fermented batter of ground *urud dal* and rice.

Iyengar Brahmin – a caste of Brahmins in Tamil Nadu, divided into the Tenkalai and Vadakalai sects.

kadai – A wok-like frying pan.

Kathakali – Classical theater of Kerala with stylized gestures and ornately painted faces.

Karthikai Deepam – Tamil Festival of Lights, celebrated by Shaivites in the month when the moon is in Karthikai (the Pleiades constellation), November/December. Karthikai, Shiva's son, is also known as Murugan.

kathputli – Rajasthani (north Indian) puppet theater.

kolum – A decorative geometric design drawn at the doorstep of houses with rice powder or other colored powders.

Krishna – The eighth incarnation of Lord Vishnu; he is the pastoral deity, god of compassion and love, portrayed as a mischievous child by Periyalvar. Also known as Kannan in Tamil.

kumkum – A decorative powder made from turmeric or other materials. Slaked lime turns the yellow powder red.

laddu – A sweet deep-fried ball made of sugar and flour.

Lakshmi – Wife/consort of Vishnu; Goddess of wealth, prosperity, and fortune.

Mariamman – The South Indian goddess of the rainy season, appeased to avoid disease.

Mitra – Lord of truth and order, guardian of divine law; companion of Varuna.

mridhangam – a long double-headed drum with one head tuned lower than the other.

murukku – A savory, crunchy snack made from a deep-fried spiral of rice flour and *urud dal* dough.

naga – Hindu snake deity, associated with fertility.

Namagiri Amman – The goddess Lakshmi as worshipped at Namagiri Hill (Namakkal, Tamil Nadu).

Narasimha – The fourth incarnation of Lord Vishnu, a lion-man who vanquished the evil demon Hiranya.

Narayana – Another name for Vishnu.

Navaratri – An autumn festival of nine nights for the goddesses Durga, Lakshmi, and Sarasvati.

peepal tree – Sacred fig, *bodhi* tree, *Ficus religiosa*.

Periyalvar – One of the twelve Tamil poet-saints, or Alvars. who lived in the 9th century C.E.

Pillaiyar – Also Ganesha or Vinayakar; a Hindu elephant god revered as the remover of obstacles; the eldest son of Shiva.

pongal – a rice dish made with sweetened milk and spices.

pooja – Hindu prayer ritual; religious observance of offering to a Hindu deity.

poori – an ovoid, deep-fried unleavened wheat bread.

pottu – Also known as *bindi*, a decorative dot on the forehead.

raita – Yogurt seasoned with vegetables (raw or cooked) and/or spices.

Rama – Seventh incarnation of the Lord Vishnu. He ruled the kingdom of Kosala and married Sita. Sita was kidnapped by the evil lord Ravana, and Rama saved her and vanquished Ravana.

rasam – A thin South Indian soup, usually with a tamarind base.

sabzi – A Persian word used in North India for a form of curried vegetables.

sadhu – Hindu religious ascetic or holy person.

Sandhyavandanam – An ancient investiture ritual accompanied by a recitation of the Vedas.

Sarasvati – Hindu goddess of music, art, wisdom, learning, and knowledge.

sati – An antiquated funeral practice in which a wife joins her husband on the funeral pyre or kills herself soon after her husband dies.

Shaivite – Follower of the Lord Shiva.

Shiva – The Supreme Being in Shaivism, one of the three main deities in Hinduism, including Brahma and Vishnu; he is the destroyer of evil and sustainer of the universe.

Smartha Brahmin – A Brahmin who worships five deities equally: Vishnu, Shiva, Ganesha, Surya, and Devi.

sri-khand – A sweetened yogurt dessert.

tabla – A tuned, single-headed drum.

tali – A necklace that indicates a South Indian woman is married.

tava – a flat, lipless frying pan.

Tenkalai - A Tamil sect of Iyengar Brahmins.

tirtha – A pilgrimage spot, from the Sanskrit "place of fording".

Tirumangai Alvar – One of the twelve Tamil poet-saints, or Alvars from the 8th century, C.E.

toor dal – Pigeon pea, tropical green pea.

Upanayanam – A Hindu rite of passage in which a guru accepts a student into religious studies. The student (male) receives a sacred thread meaning he has entered into formal education.

urud dal – A black lentil, also known as black gram, or *Vigna mungo*.

vadai – A deep-fried savory donut made from lentil flour.

Vaishnavite – Follower of the Lord Vishnu.

Varuna – God of sea and rain; companion of Mitra.

Vedas – Ancient Sanskrit texts, scriptures.

veshti – White or solid-colored unstitched wrapped cloth, like a sarong.

Vishnu – The Supreme Being in Vaishnavism, one of the three main deities in Hinduism, including Brahma and Shiva; god of Protection, preserver of good, the savior deity, also called Narayana.

yali – A mythical creature – part lion, part elephant, part horse, or other variations.

ABOUT THE AUTHOR

David Ackley grew up in Fairbanks, Alaska and raised a family in Juneau. His professional career in Alaska included both fisheries biometrics and management positions with the state and federal governments. David is now retired and living in northern Idaho, where he began a small business in lutherie – building guitars, Irish bouzoukis, and ukuleles (www. dastringedinstruments.com). While his wife was conducting research during a recent stint in India, he devoted time to trying to improve his Tamil and writing fiction to escape the heat of mid-day. Finding himself unable to multi-task easily, the lutherie business has flagged somewhat while he gets some stories onto paper. Please visit the Rain and Breeze Books website, www.rainandbreeze.com, for more information about David and his books.

www.ingramcontent.com/pod-product-compliance
Lightning Source LLC
Chambersburg PA
CBHW031617180726
48284CB00005B/1588